UNSOLVED

JAMES PATTERSON
AND DAVID ELLIS

GRAND CENTRAL
PUBLISHING

NEW YORK   BOSTON

Copyright © 2019 by James Patterson

Hachette Book Group supports the right to free expression and the value of copyright. The purpose of copyright is to encourage writers and artists to produce the creative works that enrich our culture.

The scanning, uploading, and distribution of this book without permission is a theft of the author's intellectual property. If you would like permission to use material from the book (other than for review purposes), please contact permissions@hbgusa.com. Thank you for your support of the author's rights.

Grand Central Publishing
Hachette Book Group
1290 Avenue of the Americas, New York, NY 10104
grandcentralpublishing.com
twitter.com/grandcentralpub

Originally published in hardcover and ebook by Little, Brown & Company in June 2019
First trade paperback edition: February 2020

Grand Central Publishing is a division of Hachette Book Group, Inc. The Grand Central Publishing name and logo is a trademark of Hachette Book Group, Inc.

The publisher is not responsible for websites (or their content) that are not owned by the publisher.

The Hachette Speakers Bureau provides a wide range of authors for speaking events. To find out more, go to www.hachettespeakersbureau.com or call (866) 376-6591.

Library of Congress Control Number: 2018463468

ISBNs: 978-1-5387-3163-5 (trade paperback), 978-0-316-41984-0 (ebook)

Printed in the United States of America

LSC-C

10 9 8 7 6 5 4 3 2 1

RAVES FOR JAMES PATTERSON

"THE PROLIFIC PATTERSON SEEMS UNSTOPPABLE."

—*USA Today*

"PATTERSON IS IN A CLASS BY HIMSELF."   —*Vanity Fair*

"PATTERSON KNOWS WHERE OUR DEEPEST FEARS ARE BURIED...THERE'S NO STOPPING HIS IMAGINATION."

—*New York Times Book Review*

"JAMES PATTERSON WRITES HIS THRILLERS AS IF HE WERE BUILDING ROLLER COASTERS."   —Associated Press

"NO ONE GETS THIS BIG WITHOUT NATURAL STORYTELLING TALENT—WHICH IS WHAT JAMES PATTERSON HAS, IN SPADES."   —Lee Child, #1 *New York Times* bestselling author
of the Jack Reacher series

"JAMES PATTERSON KNOWS HOW TO SELL THRILLS AND SUS-PENSE IN CLEAR, UNWAVERING PROSE."   —*People*

"PATTERSON BOILS A SCENE DOWN TO A SINGLE, TELLING DE-TAIL, THE ELEMENT THAT DEFINES A CHARACTER OR MOVES A PLOT ALONG. IT'S WHAT FIRES OFF THE MOVIE PROJECTOR IN THE READER'S MIND."   —Michael Connelly

"JAMES PATTERSON IS THE BOSS. END OF."

—Ian Rankin, *New York Times* bestselling author
of the Inspector Rebus series

"JAMES PATTERSON IS THE GOLD STANDARD BY WHICH ALL OTHERS ARE JUDGED."   —Steve Berry, #1 bestselling author
of the Colton Malone series

For a complete list of books, visit JamesPatterson.com.

1

I AM neither evil nor deranged. I am not uneducated, I am not poor, and I am not the product of an abusive upbringing. I do what I do for one, and only one, reason.

The man in the beige jacket pulls his SUV into the strip-mall parking lot and kills the engine. He steps out of the car, straightens his jacket, and lightly brushes his hand against the bulge at his side, the concealed handgun.

The setting summer sun casts a dim glow over the strip mall, nearly empty. The laundromat at the end is dark; the catering service is shuttered, a metal grate across the window. The convenience store, displaying ads for cigarettes, beer, two-for-a-dollar hot dogs, Powerball tickets, is the only thing open.

There is one other vehicle in the lot, a Dodge Caravan the color of rust that's parked nose in about eight spaces away.

A man in a wheelchair is in the middle of the lot. He bends over at the waist, reaches down to the pavement, and struggles to pick up several items that have spilled out of a plastic grocery bag. He also works the joystick on the arm of his wheelchair, but in vain—the motorized chair fails to respond to the command.

A disabled man in a broken wheelchair.

Only moralists or lemmings think that weakness requires compassion and mercy. Any student of history, of science, knows the opposite is true.

We are supposed to extinguish the weak. It always has been and always will be so.

The man in beige calls out, "How 'bout I give you a hand with that, mister?"

The wheelchair guy straightens up with some difficulty. His face is red and shiny with sweat from the effort of trying to retrieve the toiletries rolling around on the pavement. He is wearing a camouflage hat and an army fatigue jacket. Decent upper-body build, to be expected of someone who's lost the use of his legs. His unshaven face is weathered and dull except for a small, shiny scar in the shape of a crescent moon near his right eye.

"I s'pose I could use a hand," says the wheelchair guy. "I 'preciate that."

"No trouble at all."

Nothing like the gentle facade of manners, of charity, to reel in your prey. Far easier than lying in the weeds and waiting for the wounded animal in the pack to come limping by, unsuspecting.

"Not a problem at all," the man in beige says again. He scoops up a tube of Crest toothpaste, a stick of deodorant, and a green bottle of Pert shampoo, puts all the items into the man's plastic grocery bag, and hands the bag back to the wheelchair guy, who is struggling between gratitude and wounded pride, a feeling of helplessness. The guy pushes on the joystick again, but again the wheelchair fails to respond; the wheelchair guy curses under his breath.

"Having some trouble with your wheelchair?" asks the man in beige. "Need help getting in the van?"

Don't talk to me about cruelty or pity. The thinking man has no affections, no prejudices, only a heart of stone.

I am as I was made. I am a product of the laws of nature, not of laws passed by some inane body of human beings.

The wheelchair guy lets out a sigh. "Well, actually...that would be great."

"Sure, no problem." The man in beige extends his hand. "I'm Joe," he says.

"Charlie," the wheelchair guy says, shaking his hand.

"Nice to meet you, Charlie. Where do you get in the van?"

"The back."

The man in beige, Joe, takes the handles of the wheelchair and wheels Charlie to the back of the van. He reaches for the door, but Charlie hits a button on his key fob, and the door slides open automatically.

"Cool," says Joe. "Never seen that on a back door."

"You probably never been in no wheelchair neither."

Charlie punches another button on his key fob to activate the hydraulic drop-down ramp.

Joe pushes Charlie up the ramp and into the bed of the van. The ramp rises up and folds back into place. The van's interior is customized, of course; there is a front passenger seat and a rear one directly behind it, but the other side is a clear path to the steering wheel, which has manual controls to operate the van.

A nice, open space.

This is where I will kill him. But I will not be cruel—*that word again. I have no desire to inflict more pain than is necessary to eliminate him.*

But first, a little conversation, for distraction and to keep the victim at ease.

Joe looks down at the bed of the van and sees a hardcover book lying there, a tattered bookmark jutting out from the middle of it. The book is titled *The Invisible Killer: The Hunt for Graham, the Most Prolific Serial Killer of Our Time.*

Joe picks up the book and opens it to a random page. "Hey, I know this person," he says. "The FBI analyst who caught Graham. Emmy Dockery."

Charlie works his joystick and rotates in his wheelchair until he's facing Joe. "You know Emmy Dockery?"

"Well, she e-mailed and called me. I'm a cop, see, and I had a case I thought was an accidental death, but Emmy, she asked me to reopen it as a homicide investigation." Joe squats down and gently places the book back where he found it as darkness begins to creep over the van's interior.

The rear door closes with an ominous *thunk.*

"Ah, so it *was* Emmy who made you reopen the Laura Berg case," says Charlie. "I couldn't be sure."

In the process of straightening up, Detective Joseph Halsted registers all this in the time it takes his heart to beat once—*Laura Berg. The controls on Charlie's wheelchair suddenly working. The rear door closing*—before he feels the electrode darts hit him in the stomach.

The detective jerks at the jolt of electricity seizing his body and immediately loses muscle control. He collapses onto the bed of the van hard, unable to break his fall.

"You immediately discounted me as a threat," says Charlie. "Even you, an officer of the law."

One hand still holding the trigger, continuing to deliver the powerful charge to his victim, Charlie reaches down to the bag by his side and removes three pairs of handcuffs, a large plastic bag, a rubber racquetball.

"You feel like a prisoner trapped in your own body," he says. "You feel vulnerable and helpless."

Detective Halsted lies on the floor of the van, his body convulsing, his eyes wide, his mouth hanging open like a dropped drawbridge.

"If it's any consolation, Emmy was right," says Charlie. "Laura Berg's death was not an accident. Yours won't be either."

2

I PULL up the e-mail with the search results. There are 736 hits.

Talk about a needle in a haystack. The haystack has too much hay. The search is too broad.

You've known that for weeks, Emmy. But you're so afraid of making the search too narrow and missing that one needle.

Okay. Exhale. *Let's do it.*

A gas explosion in Gresham, Oregon, claiming the lives of two people, a mother and daughter...a man electrocuted in his backyard in Gering, Nebraska...a teenager found dead in a pool in Brookhaven, Mississippi...

I push up from the desk too fast, get a head rush.

The north wall of this room is papered with more than a hundred letters, all of them copies; the originals are still under forensic analysis.

One day our blood will mix, Miss Emmy. You and I will make a child together and think of the things he will do. But until that day I will not stop killing. I can't. I will wait for you to catch me. Do you think you can?

Dear ms Dockery can i call u Emmy? congradulations on catching graham but i hope u know theres others out there like me even worse than him

EMILY WHERE ARE YOU, YOU USED TO LIVE IN URBANNA BUT NOT ANY MORE, WELL I HOPE ALL IS WELL AND I JUS WANTED TO TELL YA THAT I HAVE KILLED 14 PEOPLE!! AND I DON'T PLAN ON STOPPING TILL YOU FIND ME

The room's east wall has the timeline, the articles cut from newspapers or printed out from websites.

VIENNA, VIRGINIA: ACTIVIST DEAD OF "NATURAL CAUSES"
INDIANAPOLIS: FAMILY, FRIENDS STUNNED BY MOM'S SUICIDE
ATLANTA: AD EXEC DEAD IN APPARENT DROWNING
CHARLESTON: MOTHER'S DEATH RULED OVERDOSE
DALLAS: FAULTY WIRING BLAMED IN SOUTHLAKE MAN'S ELECTROCUTION

Beneath each article are the photos, the autopsy reports, and, where they exist, the police investigators' notes.

A buzzer sounds. My iPhone alarm. A reminder pops up on the screen: *Get some sleep, dummy!*

It's 3:00 a.m., so this is probably good advice. Maybe later.

I walk into the kitchen, make a fresh pot of coffee, pace back and forth while the water passes through the cone of ground beans; the pungent aroma helps wake me up, but not enough. I walk into the living room, lie down on the carpet, and do fifty abdominal crunches. I still have the residual pain in my rib cage after all this time, but I use it, anything to keep me alert.

I pour a blazing-hot cup of coffee and head back to my desk, the computer screen.

A man drowns after falling off an embankment into Lake Michigan...a young couple missing after renting a kayak in Door County, Wisconsin...a father and son killed by a lightning strike...

No. I'm not looking for couples, only single victims. I need to figure out how to narrow this search to exclude multiple victims. But if I narrow it too much, I might miss the one I'm looking for, so I'm left hopelessly combing through tragedy after tragedy: a grandfather dead after striking a power line while digging in the backyard, a woman in New Orleans found dead in a bathtub, a father—

Wait. Back up.

A New Orleans woman found dead in a bathtub. Click on that one.

Nora Connolley, 58, a senior health-care specialist, was found dead in her bathtub Monday morning after an apparent fall in her shower in her home in the St. Roch neighborhood. New Orleans Police Department spokesman Nigel Flowers told the *Times-Picayune* that no foul play is suspected at this

Hmm. Maybe.

I do a quick background check on Nora Connolley. First I do a few things anyone can do, Facebook and Instagram and Google searches. Then I do something only law enforcement can do, searching vital records in Louisiana. Then I go back to things anyone can do, this time looking at Google Earth and residential real estate websites.

When I find what I'm looking for, I slap my hand on the desk, making the coffee spill and the computer monitor shake.

Nora Connolley is one of the victims.

I pull up another website, find the e-mail for the New Orleans PD's public information bureau, and start typing to Nigel Flowers, the department spokesman, beginning with my customary preface:

> My name is Emily Dockery. I am a senior analyst with the FBI. But I must stress that I am <u>not</u> contacting you in my official capacity with the FBI or at the direction of the FBI.

The lawyers came up with that last sentence. I'm not allowed to let my "wild-goose chases" bear the imprimatur of the Federal Bureau of Investigation, not unless the Bureau agrees to open the investigation.

I press the backspace key and hold my finger down, gobbling up word after word like I'm playing Pac-Man, completely erasing that last sentence.

I start typing again. There. That's better.

> My name is Emily Dockery. I am a senior analyst with the FBI. I would be interested in speaking with the detective in charge of investigating the death of Nora Connolley. I have reason to believe that her death was not an accident or due to natural causes. You can contact me at this e-mail or at the number below. Five minutes is all I need.

I hit Send, bounce out of my chair, and experience the vertigo again, as well as pain in my ankle. I really have to stop doing that.

I walk back over to the timeline and scan each article and its accompanying notes, photos, and autopsy findings, especially the various details highlighted: petechial hemorrhages, congestion in the lungs, bloody froth in the pharynx, unexplained puncture wounds...

And the first one, the death of Laura Berg in Vienna, Virginia. I'm still waiting for a return call from Detective Joseph Halsted. He was reluctant initially, but he seems to be coming around now.

"Call me, Joe," I mumble. "Help me find this guy."

Then I head back into the kitchen for more coffee.

3

THE MAN who calls himself Charlie when he's in character finds the PBS video on YouTube. It has gotten over two million hits. He clicks on the red arrow and settles in.

Words appear on the black screen in white block letters—THE REAL EMMY DOCKERY—then dissolve.

Images of front pages of several newspapers fade in and out like whack-a-moles:

FEDS NAB   **MANHUNT FOR "GRAHAM"**
"INVISIBLE KILLER"   **ENDS IN CANNON BEACH**

FORD FIELD BOMBER DEAD   **"IT'S OVER" — GRAHAM**
      CAPTURED AND KILLED

The screen goes black again, then opens to an aerial view of a house, orange flames sweeping out of its second-story windows, then the roof collapsing.

"Fires," says the narrator in a soothing baritone voice. "Homes are engulfed in flames every day due to various accidents—an overturned candle, a cigarette, a frayed wire. Every year, three thousand people die in their homes from fires. A house goes up in flames every ninety seconds in the United States, in neighborhoods big and small, rural and urban. Atlantic Beach, Florida. Monroe, North Carolina. New Britain, Connecticut. Lisle, Illinois."

The screen shifts to the aftermath of another fire, the structure battered and shrunken to gray ash.

"Peoria, Arizona."

A screenshot of a newspaper, a headline from the *Peoria Times:*

HOME FIRE KILLS PEORIA WOMAN

"Marta Dockery was killed in that fire in Peoria. Officials said the fire was an accident. Everyone agreed. Everyone but Marta's twin sister, Emmy."

A photograph of two girls in their teens, tanned and squinting into the camera, one a bit shorter than the other, with darker hair and fuller cheeks. The twin thing, you could see it, but they were anything but identical, these two. The camera zooms in on the taller and ganglier girl.

"Emmy insisted that it wasn't an accidental fire. That it was murder."

The screen goes dark.

Then a shot of the J. Edgar Hoover Building in Washington, DC, headquarters of the FBI.

"Emily Jean Dockery was a data analyst for the Federal Bureau of Investigation," says the narrator. "Her life was numbers and statistics. She wasn't a field agent. She wasn't a fire investigator. So when Emmy Dockery insisted that her sister's death was murder, nobody believed her."

Images of excerpts from another newspaper article, enlarged:

Eight months after her sister's death in a house fire, Emmy Dockery is still on a crusade to convince the Peoria Police Department that Marta Dockery's death was not an accident, but murder.

"All forensic evidence points to death by an accidental fire." A middle-aged woman appears on the screen with the caption *Nancy Parmaggiore, chief of staff to the director of the FBI.* "Emmy was able to convince a very skeptical team of seasoned veteran investigators not only that her sister was murdered but that a serial killer was out there committing some of the most gruesome crimes imaginable."

Now there's an elderly man on the screen; the caption identifies him as *Dennis Sasser, special agent, FBI (ret.).* "Nobody believed Emmy. I didn't. But we never would have caught Graham if it weren't for Emmy. In fact, we never would have even known that crimes were being committed in the first—"

Charlie fast-forwards the video. He knows this part. Everyone does. The manhunt across the country. And then the final showdown, Graham dead and Emmy, well...alive, at least.

He stops about forty-five minutes into the documentary. The screen has faded to black again.

Then the narrator: "And what has become of the FBI analyst who caught and killed Graham?"

An image of paramedics hauling a woman on a gurney down a driveway toward an ambulance, the entire scene filled with police cars and flashing lights and armed law enforcement. This, Charlie knows, was after Emmy's face-to-face encounter with Graham.

"According to reports, Emmy Dockery suffered extensive injuries that day: deep scalp lacerations, burns over a large portion of her body, a punctured lung, a broken ankle."

Dennis Sasser again: "Emmy was horribly injured. She endured terror that is difficult to put into words."

Then the narrator: "It took half a dozen surgeries and three months before Emmy Dockery was released from the hospital. And then..."

The screen goes dark. An ominous sound, a single beat of a soft drum.

And this newspaper headline:

PARAMEDICS CALLED TO GRAHAM-CATCHER HOME IN URBANNA

The screen fades to black again. Then an older woman, her gray hair pulled back, wearing a defiant expression, appears. The caption reads *Dorian Dockery*. "My daughter wasn't trying to kill herself," she says.

Charlie pauses the video and takes a breath. He's read many of the various reports that came out afterward—that Emmy Dockery had suffered a nervous breakdown, that she'd gone into hiding, that she was receiving both death threats and love letters from purported serial killers.

"You broke into pieces, Emmy," he whispers. "But you put yourself back together. You survived. Just like me."

Charlie closes his eyes and does what he always does when he remembers. First he beats back their garbled shrieks, the hot breath of their terror, the smells of scorched flesh and splattering blood and perspiration and pure human fear burning his nostrils even now.

And then he accepts them. Lets their contents settle inside him, mix together, and jell.

His body cools. His pulse slows.

"It is a thinking man's war," he reminds himself. A quiet war, Charles Darwin said, lurking just beneath the serene façade of nature.

His eyes open. On the screen, the video is still paused, having just transitioned from the words of Emmy's mother to a photo of Emmy, her hair in a ponytail, a fierce look on her wounded face. Her eyes on his. His eyes on hers.

Lonely, determined eyes.

"We could do so much together," Charlie says.

4

HARRISON BOOKMAN—known as "Books" to everyone—feels his phone buzz at his hip as he helps a customer choose the right nonfiction selection for her grandfather, a history buff. They decide on a book about LBJ's struggle to get Congress to pass the Civil Rights Act of 1964. He feels a small flicker of satisfaction as he rings up the transaction. He loves everything about books, but this is his favorite part of the business, talking with a customer and finding just the right novel or nonfiction work, like a sommelier helping diners choose the perfect bottle of wine to pair with their meal.

Now if only there were more customers.

At least he has Petty, bald and clean-shaven, sitting in the corner in one of the comfy chairs reading *The Sun Also Rises* by Hemingway; next to him is a cup of the coffee Books always has brewing. It probably isn't the greatest idea to let a homeless man hang out in your store, but Petty keeps to himself and keeps himself reasonably presentable, and, really, how could Books turn away a guy who served two tours in Desert

Storm and gave up so much for his country, not least of which was his sanity?

Petty is a part-time resident of the inventory room in the back of the store. He's slept there a few nights a week every week since Books first met him six months ago, last December, sitting on the sidewalk outside the store. He shaves and washes up in an old shower that Books revived after converting the space from an old apartment.

Books watches his customer leave. His eyes wander over to the front window, where the name of the store—THE BOOK MAN—is stenciled prominently; the newest releases and local favorites are arranged just so to lure in the shoppers and the passersby in downtown Alexandria.

Then he turns the belt pouch holding his phone upward so he can see who just called. He glances at it, then does a double take.

Moriarty.

William Moriarty, the director of the FBI.

Not a social call. Bill never makes social calls.

Books considers returning the call right away. No customers in the store now, after all. And he can't deny that tiny surge of adrenaline. You can take the boy out of the FBI, but you can't take the FBI out of the boy.

The door chimes behind him. A customer. That makes the decision for Books. The FBI will have to wait.

He turns and sees two people enter the store, men in dark suits, each of them removing sunglasses. Jesus, they really have to stop reinforcing that stereotype.

One of them he doesn't know, but the other, the taller one, is familiar. Desmond, part of the director's advance team.

"Hey, Books," Desmond says, glancing around.

"Hey, Dez . . ." Books gives him a confused look.

"The director needs a moment. He called."

Yeah, he called two minutes ago. It's not like he made an appointment last week or anything.

"Somewhere private you could talk for a moment?"

Books lets out a breath. "Sure. The stockroom. There's a service entrance out back where—"

"He's already parked there." Dez nods.

Of course he is. "Okay," says Books. "Let's do it."

5

BOOKS LEADS the advance team into the back room. There are piles of inventory, books ready to be placed on shelves, books ready to be sent back to the publishers, a stand-up display for the children's author who did an appearance last week. Dez arranges two chairs at a table while his partner pushes open the back door.

"There he is, the bookseller." Director William Moriarty has aged, and not so gracefully, in this job. He has been a public servant all his life, first as a special agent, then as a federal prosecutor, later as a congressman, and after that as a federal judge. The stress of all of those, he said, paled in comparison to running the FBI. He has lost most of his hair, and his face and torso have widened, but he still has that same no-nonsense stare.

Bill had made no secret of his profound disappointment in Books when he resigned. He'd tried everything to keep Books in the fold. He offered him a promotion, a raise, a better office. He even threatened to take him into federal custody, though Books was reasonably sure that was a joke.

"Hi, Bill."

"You married yet?"

They take seats across from each other at the table Books uses when he's balancing his ledgers.

"No." That answer, Books thinks to himself, is accurate but tells Bill nothing. *Not yet* would be more informative. So would *No, the wedding's this September. No* could mean a lot of things, including *No, we're not married yet, and I'm not sure we ever will be.*

It's been nearly a year and a half since he proposed to Emmy (for the second time) and she said yes (for the first time). And yet no date has been set, no china patterns picked out.

"But you two are still . . . together?"

It's not like Bill to make small talk. Not like him at all. What does he care about whether Books and Emmy are heading down the aisle or toward separate lives?

"Yeah," Books says. Two loaded questions from the director, two single-word responses from Books. The director's a smart guy. He's read between closer lines than these.

"I need you, Books. An assignment. A special assignment."

"The Bureau is filled with talented and dedicated agents."

"I need someone from outside the Bureau."

"From outside," says Books. "A double-I?"

Internal investigations are typically handled in-house, just like all other investigations. The Bureau rarely wants to admit that it needs outside help. If the director is asking, this is not the typical double-I. This is not about a boss chasing a subordinate around a desk. This is not about an agent using a Bureau computer to sell beauty products or surf porn. It means something far bigger than that.

It means the director doesn't know whom to trust within his own agency.

"You have a mole."

The director nods, some color to his face. "We do. You'd run the investigation. You'd report directly to me. Nobody else."

"I pick my team," says Books, realizing how quickly he jumped so many hurdles in his mind, how easily and almost naturally he said yes. Like there was never a doubt. "Starting with Emmy," Books says, "and not because she's my fiancée. Because she's the best analyst the Bureau's ever had. I know she hasn't been the same since—"

"She *is* the best." The director makes a face. "No question. But I have to say no. You can pick anyone else, Books, but not Emmy. Not this time."

Books stares at the director, reading him, noting the averted eyes, the discomfort. This is also not like him. Not like him to beat around the bush. Not like him to ask about Books's personal life either, especially his relationship with Emmy.

Books feels something sink inside him. "No," he says, as if he can will it away.

"Gives me no pleasure to say it." The director shrugs. "But Emmy is the target of the investigation. We think your girl-friend is the mole."

6

I PUT it all together, everything I've been able to collect on Nora Connolley, on a biography sheet, the same kind I've compiled for each of the victims on my wall. It's missing some pieces, but it's enough for the time being.

Now if only the New Orleans PD would call me back. I e-mailed them yesterday. I usually get a phone call, at least, even if the person's voice is laced with skepticism.

Speaking of which, why hasn't Detective Halsted called me back about Laura Berg?

The clock says 11:45. I should probably eat lunch. No, I should sleep. I did put my head down on a pillow last night for a few hours. I didn't sleep, but I rested. My mother used to say that to me when I was kid, when I tossed and turned, that at least I was resting. I never really understood that. Either you sleep or you don't.

I don't.

My laptop—my main one—pings with an e-mail. An invitation from some prosecutors' association to speak at their annual event. I type a quick no-thank-you.

Another e-mail. A Google search alert, not my normal one that produces hundreds of stories a day, my needle-in-a-haystack search. No, this one is more specific.

When I see the headline, I suck in my breath.

VIENNA PD DETECTIVE FOUND DEAD IN HOME

"No," I whisper. "No!"

Vienna Police Department detective Joseph Halsted, 48, a nineteen-year veteran of the force, was found dead this morning in his condominium. He was unresponsive when paramedics arrived. A spokesman for the department said that the cause of death was a heart attack.

I drop my head into my hands. "Oh no. No, no, *no!*" My phone buzzes on my desk. "I did this...I did this..."

I told him to look into Laura Berg's death. He never would have given a second thought to it if it weren't for me. I led Joe Halsted to the slaughter.

It means something else, I realize, though it's hard to focus on it right now. It means I was right about Laura Berg.

My phone is lighting up, grunting at me. I reach for it. The caller ID shows a New Orleans area code. Oh, right, New Orleans—

"Hello?" I manage.

"Agent Dockery?" A New York accent. "This is Sergeant Crescenzo with the New Orleans PD. You e-mailed us about Nora Connolley?"

"Yes...um...uh...thanks for getting back to me."

"Bad time to talk?"

I have to get a grip. This is my chance. I clear my throat. "No, sorry—I'm fine. Thank you for the call."

"Ms. Connolley fell in her shower, Agent Dockery."

I'm not a special agent, but I don't correct him. He's assuming this is an official investigation of the FBI and that I'm a special agent, even though I never said either of those things. I haven't lied to him.

"And you've been to the scene?"

"I was there, yes. You have some reason to believe—"

"She was selling her house, wasn't she?"

"She—what was that?"

"Her house was for sale."

"Uh…hang on." I hear muffled voices, the sergeant asking someone else about whether Nora Connolley's house was for sale. I already know it was.

"Yeah, guess so," he says, returning to the phone. "You coulda figured that out from any old computer."

That's the point, Sergeant.

"So how does that make a slip-and-fall in the bathroom a murder?" he asks.

"I think it fits into a pattern," I say. "I'm investigating the possibility of a killer who's making the victims' deaths appear accidental or natural."

"Huh. That sounds like that case you all had a couple years ago, that guy who tortured people and torched the crime scenes."

"Something like that. But someone even more skilled."

A pause. "Well, listen, who am I to tell the FBI to stand down? But I gotta say, it sounds like a stretch to me. You wanna take over this investigation, it's all yours."

But that's the thing. I can't. I don't have the authority, and

I won't unless I can make a case to the Bureau. That's the catch-22. I can't open an investigation to prove that an investigation's warranted. I need this guy. I need Sergeant Crescenzo.

"Would you be willing to open the investigation locally?" I ask. "I'd prefer to stay below the radar for now."

"You want me to start an investigation based on the fact that someone put her house up for sale and then slipped and fell in the shower?" Sergeant Crescenzo lets out an amused grunt. "I need more than that to open a homicide investigation."

Sure he does. I can't blame him.

"Graham—the arsonist you mentioned? Graham was good," I say. "But this guy's better. Graham brutally tortured the victims, then covered up the crime scenes by setting fire to them. This guy? His victims show no sign of foul play. He comes and goes without a trace. He's a ghost."

Another pause. I've got him thinking, at least. "I'll come to New Orleans tomorrow," I say. "We'll take a look at the crime scene, nice and quiet, and if you still think I'm full of hot air, I'll leave you alone."

"Tomorrow, huh?"

"And one more thing, Sergeant. Please keep this out of the press. For everyone's sake."

He's apparently mulling this over.

"I'll call you when I land," I say, and I hang up before he can protest.

7

THE FLIGHT into New Orleans is bumpy, but luckily the weather is clear. Rain is the last thing I need. I drive a rental car to St. Roch, a neighborhood still struggling to bounce back from the beating it took from Katrina. There are vacant homes and plenty of potholes in the roads, but there are also planters of fresh flowers in the boulevard medians and some new construction in the commercial areas.

When I pull up to the house on Music Street, a graying African-American man in shirtsleeves, tall and broad, is leaning against a sedan and reviewing a document. When I get out of my air-conditioned car, he nods at me.

"Sergeant Crescenzo," I say, startled by the blazing heat.

"Call me Robert," he says, shaking my hand. "Agent Dockery, you are a master of understatement. You didn't tell me you were the one who caught Graham."

"I worked on the case, yes. And call me Emmy."

"Worked on the case." He chuckles and sizes me up, probably looking for scars. I'm wearing a scarf that covers my neck, so there's nothing to see here.

"You brought the coroner's findings?" I ask.

"There was no autopsy," he says. "No need for one. But we have her initial investigation notes, yes. And I brought the photos too."

That should be good enough. I turn to the house. Nora Connolley lived in a one-story, stucco A-frame with tomato-red and lime trim. The tiny front yard is enclosed by a wrought-iron fence. A red, white, and blue For Sale sign from a real estate company called Jensen Keller is attached to the fence.

"Wanna go inside?" he says, opening the gate and walking toward the front porch.

"I want to go in the back way," I say. "Let's start with the detached garage."

Crescenzo turns to me. "There's a detached garage? How did you know that? That Google Earth thing?"

"The video on the real estate agent's website," I say. "That's how he knew it too."

"*He* being the killer." Not hiding the skepticism in his voice.

I walk around the house, following the wrought-iron fence, which encircles the whole property. The backyard is far larger than the front yard.

"Nothing was taken from the home," Crescenzo says, keeping pace with me. "No sign of sexual assault. No sign of struggle."

I can't blame him for thinking this was exactly what it looked like, a slip-and-fall in a shower. He has no reason to think otherwise.

"Were there unexplained puncture wounds on her torso?" I ask.

"How——" He stops in his tracks. "Now, how in the hell did you know that?"

"Lucky guess." I stop and look over the area. She kept a nice yard. A vegetable garden in one corner, a neat cobblestone walkway leading from the garage to the back patio.

"Needle punctures," he says.

"Two of them."

"Yes, Emmy, two of them. You know a lot."

"How big a woman was she?" I ask.

"The deceased? Oh, she was a tiny woman. Maybe five two, five three. Not thin like you, but not heavy either."

She looked petite from the photos I saw on Facebook, but you can never be sure.

We reach the detached garage, a small, windowed structure with aluminum siding. We walk through the fence into the alley. The garage door is closed and locked. We walk back around to the door that leads into the yard. The door is locked from the outside.

"I didn't ask the real estate agent to open the garage up," says Robert. "Just the house."

I push on the handles of the window and it gives. I lift the window as high as it can go. Then I turn to Robert Crescenzo.

He raises his hands. "Don't look at me." He's well over six feet tall and broad-shouldered. No way he could fit through that opening.

"Okay if I slip in?" I'm tall myself, but I'm skinny as a rail these days.

He thinks about it a moment but probably realizes there isn't any harm.

It's easier than I expect. I slide in headfirst, facing up, and when my torso is through, I reach out, grip the interior frame of the window, and bring my legs in. I grit my teeth and ignore the pain in my ribs. My landing on the garage floor won't qualify me for the Olympic gymnastics team, but I stay on my feet.

I take my first breath inside and I'm hit with the smell of gas and lawn clippings. With the light coming through the window, it isn't hard for me to navigate around the parked car and open the door into the yard. I flip on a light switch too. The garage is small, only enough room for a single car, a bicycle, and assorted lawn equipment.

Robert Crescenzo comes in through the door I opened. He shines a flashlight into the car's interior. He tries the door, and it's open, so he pops the trunk, goes around, and lights that up too.

"Nothing obvious, at least." He looks at me. "Did you think there would be? You think, what, she was ambushed in her garage?"

No, that's not what I think. But I say, "Maybe," and gesture to the car. "You mind if I get in?"

"Suit yourself."

I get in on the driver's side and sink back into the seat. I don't want to touch the steering wheel, but I reach for it, noting that I can barely touch it with my fingertips even though my arms are fully extended. My feet don't reach the brake and gas pedals.

"Could we trade places?" I ask.

"Okay..."

I get out, and Robert gets in, settles in the seat, puts a hand atop the steering wheel.

"Pretty comfortable fit for you," I say.

"Yeah."

"But not for a woman who's a foot shorter than you."

Sergeant Crescenzo blinks twice, thinks about it, then turns and looks at me.

"Someone other than Nora Connolley drove this car last," he says.

8

SERGEANT ROBERT CRESCENZO and I leave the garage and go back to the patio. He walks along the cobblestone path. I walk in the grass next to him.

"At the risk of stating the obvious," he says, "just because someone else drove her car last doesn't mean that that somebody killed her."

"You're absolutely right," I agree.

"Maybe one of her kids drove it. She had two children, I think."

"Three," I say. "Mary lives in Oklahoma, Sarah lives in Baton Rouge—"

"But her boy, Michael, lives here in New Orleans. An officer spoke with him."

"Yeah, but he was in Dallas the week she died."

Sergeant Crescenzo stops walking. I turn to look at him.

"You've been contacting witnesses on my case?" he says.

"I didn't contact him. I saw his trip on Facebook. Besides," I say, "I thought it wasn't a case. Her death was an accident, right?"

He gives me a sidelong glance.

"I just used public information," I say. I turn back to the patio. It is no wider than the sliding glass door but it's large enough to allow for a small table with an umbrella and a gas barbecue grill.

"The patio is immaculate," I say.

Sergeant Crescenzo stands next to me. "A clean patio? If that doesn't say *murder*, I don't know what does."

"It's not just clean, Robert. It's spotless. Like it was scrubbed down."

He takes a look and lets out an equivocal hum, conceding the possibility without conceding the importance.

I step from the grass to the patio, walk to the sliding glass door, and look back down at the path I just made.

"See my shoe prints on the concrete?" I say. "All I did was walk from the garage to the back door on the grass, and the dirt on my shoes made faint marks. And the grass is dry."

The sergeant doesn't seem impressed.

"She was found dead in the morning, right?" I ask. "By the cleaning lady?"

"Right."

"The day before that, did it rain?"

Robert looks up, trying to remember. "I don't recall." He closes his eyes. "But something tells me you already know the answer."

"It rained the day before she was found dead," I say. "It rained just over half an inch. It stopped by four p.m." I point to the concrete. "I made a faint impression on the patio after walking on dry grass. If she came home after four and walked from the garage to the back door on wet grass, she would have marked up the patio. And it hasn't rained since then, so don't tell me a later rainfall washed it off."

"Hey, I'm not telling you *anything*," he says a bit defensively. "You don't know that she went out at all the previous day. And even if she did, you don't know that she took this same walk from the garage to the back patio. And why wouldn't she walk on the cobblestone path, which would keep her shoes drier? Hell, you don't even know that she drove her car that day. Maybe she took the bus. There's a bus stop a block away."

"You're right," I say. "I don't know any of those things. But neither do you, Robert."

He does that double-blink thing again.

"That's why you should open an investigation," I say.

9

SERGEANT CRESCENZO opens the back door to Nora Connolley's house.

"You're not gonna find anything in here," he says. "The
place is immaculate."

"Like her patio."

"She was selling her house, Emmy. She kept it looking
nice."

"One of many reasons she was a good target," I say. "Nobody wonders why it was cleaned up so neatly."

We open the door to the kitchen. It is a simple square
shape. The cabinets are dated. The tile floor is clean but not
just-washed clean. No doubt the responding officers were inside here, and the cleaning lady wouldn't have come again
once she discovered her boss dead. Everything is in order. No
dishes in the sink, no crumbs on the counter. There is a small
silver garbage can by the dishwasher. I put my foot down on
the lever, pop the top, and look inside. Empty.

"What time did the medical examiner give for her death?" I

ask. "I assume, based on lividity and all the stuff they do, they put her death at the night before, not the morning."

I look at Robert Crescenzo, who allows a grudging smile. "That's correct. She slipped in the shower the night before. The shower was running when the cleaning lady found her the next morning."

"So she took a shower at night."

"Some people do that, Emmy."

True enough. I look in the refrigerator. There is a gallon of skim milk, unopened. A full bottle of orange juice, the top still sealed. The fruit drawer below is filled with apples and strawberries, not quite fresh anymore. A pound of ground turkey, still wrapped in plastic, rests next to a six-pack of yogurt.

"Looks like she'd just picked up some groceries," I say. "Never got a chance to eat them. Y'know, Robert, if we did an autopsy, we'd know about her stomach contents. Whether she ate dinner the night she died."

"Right," he says. "If it turns out she didn't eat dinner the night before, we'll know for sure she was murdered!"

"Robert, Robert, Robert." I close the refrigerator. "I'm not saying that. But who comes home and takes a shower before eating dinner?"

"I'm sure some people do."

I raise my eyebrows. Robert leads me out of the kitchen and into the master suite, the bedroom and bathroom. The dresser has a hairbrush on it and several photographs, presumably of Nora's children and grandchildren. On the bed is a pile of clothes—probably the ones she took off before the shower—and a cane.

The master bath is small. A single vanity, a toilet, a bathtub/shower. A terry-cloth robe hangs from a hook on the door.

I step carefully toward the shower. A dark spatter of blood near the top curve of the tub and a drip downward. By all appearances, she was facing the shower fixture, slipped, fell back, and hit her head. As she lay there dying, her body slid farther down into the tub.

We leave; Robert locks the front door behind him.

"There's a visitation tomorrow," he says. "Funeral's the next day."

"You need to do an autopsy," I say. "And open an investigation."

Robert uses his arm to wipe away some sweat on his forehead. "Emmy, listen. You know how this goes. You can throw out plenty of theories that I can't disprove. You could say that a Martian did this, and I couldn't prove that that didn't happen. But I also couldn't prove that it *did* happen. There's an innocent explanation for everything you're saying. And even if you're right about all of this, a defense lawyer would tear our case to shreds."

"I'm not trying to convict him," I say. "I'm trying to catch him."

"Look, I hear you. I've seen some crazy shit myself. But unless you can give me more—"

"Here's what I can give you," I say. "I know of six victims in his current spree. Each victim did charity work of some kind for the poor or homeless or sick. Each of them lived alone. Each of them lived in a single-story house. Each of them had a garage and a private backyard hidden by foliage. Each of them lived very close to a bus stop. Each of them had his or her house for sale and posted photos and videos of the home's interior on the internet. Each of them had tiny, needle-size puncture wounds on the torso that could not be explained."

"And what was injected? What did the tox screens reveal?"

I let out a breath. "I can't get anybody to investigate. Because each of the cases in isolation looks like Nora's case. The easy explanation is the one the police choose. I don't blame them," I say, registering the look on Robert's face. "It makes sense. But you start putting all these together, and there's a pattern."

"Okay, so investigate it yourself," he says. "You're the FBI. You can cross state lines."

I do one of those double-blinks Robert has perfected.

"Oh." He steps back from me. "Your own agency won't green-light this."

"That's correct, Sergeant."

"But *I* should, huh?"

"Yes," I say, trying to control my frustration. "You should. Because it's the right thing to do. Just do a preliminary look, Robert. What's the harm? Check her credit cards. Find out if she went out that day. See if she ate dinner that evening. Do a tox screen and find out what was injected into her body."

The sergeant chews on his lip.

"I think he knew all about her from researching her online," I say. "He knew she had a single-story. He knew the interior. He knew her habits. So he traveled here and followed her during the day. He subdued her. Then he drove her back in her own car and forgot to readjust the car seat. He dragged her through wet grass and had to clean up the patio afterward. He slammed her head against the tub to make her death look like an accident. And then he left and took the bus back to wherever his car was." I nod. "Yes. I think all of that. And he's counting on you saying, 'That's going to an awful lot of trouble,' or 'That's a real stretch, Emmy.' He's *counting* on local cops seeing nothing amiss and moving on."

"And why is he killing these people? And why only owners of single-story homes?"

I shrug. "I don't know. I don't have all the answers."

Sergeant Robert Crescenzo looks at the house, mulling it over. Probably considering his huge backlog of cases and knowing how little time he has for a wild-goose chase.

"Let me think about it," he says.

10

FOLLOWING A late dinner at a place down the street, Books returns to the closed store and spends hours balancing the ledgers, switching out inventory, reviewing catalogs, tallying up the day's receipts. These are the more tedious aspects of owning a business, but he dives into them, hoping to lose himself in the details.

Trying not to focus on what's coming next tonight.

He kills the lights in the front of the store and heads into the inventory room.

In the corner, his homeless friend Petty is curled up on a sofa that Books moved here from his house, a duffel bag holding all his possessions resting next to him. He's reading *The Art of War*.

"I'm out, Sergeant Petty," he says. He doesn't know much about Petty other than that he reached the rank of gunnery sergeant serving two tours of duty in Desert Storm. He doesn't even know his first name. *Name's Petty. Sergeant Petty,* the man said the first time they met, on a cold winter day about six months ago. He'd been sitting outside the store, and Books had bent down to talk with him. Petty's eyes glaze over whenever he gets into any kind of detail about his service overseas, when he talks about the blazing heat or the pressure or the heavy weight of fear, so Books never pushes it.

"Yes, sir, Agent Bookman." Petty looks over his reading glasses—cheap ones, cheaters from Walgreens—and gives a grateful nod. Books told him long ago to stop thanking him for letting him sleep here, that Petty was doing Books a favor by watching over the store a few nights a week. They both pretended to believe that that was true.

"*The Art of War,* eh?" he says to Petty. "'Keep your friends close and your enemies closer'?"

Petty makes a noise, something like a chuckle. He's wearing his army jacket over a blue T-shirt advertising some street festival. He looks down at his book. "'He who is prudent and lies in wait for an enemy who is not will be victorious.' Yeah, this guy Sun Tzu's got some good lines."

But the way Petty says it, with a touch of disdain in his voice, you can tell that for him, they are only lines, just words on paper, that he knows it's different when you're the one in the war, weapon in hand, awaiting an enemy who will kill you without hesitation.

Books feels a pang of sympathy for Petty in moments like this, when he sees a trace of the man's lucidity. He's a smart man who should have been able to make it out in the world, but something must have broken inside him while he was overseas, and it prevented him from rejoining society in any constructive way. Something had been disconnected or had died.

"See you in the morning," Petty says to Books, as if he senses his pity and doesn't want it. "I'm good here."

Good is probably not the right word, but he has a comfortable, warm, safe place to sleep and a clean bathroom. It's all relative.

Books leaves out the back door and starts up his car, wishing he could do more for Petty. He took him to a mental-health clinic a couple of times, but Petty wouldn't stay. He's taken him to job fairs; he even tried to put him to work in the store, not with customers but with inventory in the back room—something, anything to give him a sense of purpose and a few bucks in his pocket—but it just didn't stick. Petty, for some reason that Books will never fully understand and that Petty will never share with him, is destined to live on the street. He has gratefully accepted the offer to sleep inside a few times a week, and, yes, he appreciates the coffee, but he won't take anything else.

Traffic is light this time of night. Alexandria is dark and sleepy and the highway's nearly empty, so the entire trip takes less than twenty minutes. Books pulls his car up to the curb and kills the engine. When he does, four men emerge from the car in front of him, getting out almost in sync.

The guy who came from the back seat on the driver's side is the leader, Special Agent Lee Homer from the FBI's tactical operations unit at Quantico.

"I wasn't sure you'd come," Homer says.

Books hadn't been sure either until he drove here. He is filled with dread; his stomach has been in knots all day, and he's had a throbbing pain in his shoulders since he woke up this morning. When he was an agent, he'd had to make some tough decisions, do some things that felt wrong, but he'd always told himself he was doing it for the greater good. What he's about to do now—he's not so sure there's a greater good behind it.

This may be the worst thing he's ever done. And it may change his life forever.

Special Agent Homer hands Books a Kevlar vest. Books doesn't bother to protest.

"Let's get this over with," Books says.

11

A QUIET residential street in Lincolnia, Virginia, at midnight. The brick three-story condo building fits right in. The perfunctory waist-high metal gate, unlocked, is more for delineating boundaries than for security. The front door of the building, however, is a security door that you can access only if you're buzzed in or have a key.

Books has a key. His stomach churning, he slips the key into the lock. *I can't believe I'm doing this,* he thinks as he pushes the door open.

Agents of the FBI's tactical operations unit file in, one after the other, and take the stairs to the second floor, Books following.

Faintly, from above, there is music, probably on the third floor. Someone is still awake at this hour. Not terribly surprising.

The team members step noiselessly down the hallway. They appear to be walking casually, as if there is nothing unusual about their presence here, but Books knows they are moving on the balls of their feet, minimizing the sound of their foot-falls. Anyone who is sleeping will not be awakened. Anyone who sneaks a glance through a peephole—well, that person might have some questions.

It was a risk they had to take. There had been debate about when to do the op. Daytime made some sense, but two of the people living in this building work from home, so the decision was made to try to sneak in during the wee hours.

These tac-ops guys are pros. He saw them break the win-dow of a corrupt governor's campaign office in the middle of the night, move in, hide electronic surveillance devices, clean up the mess, replace the window, and go without leaving a trace of the operation. He watched them open a supposedly impenetrable safe-deposit box without a key in the span of sixty seconds. The greatest safecrackers and cat burglars in the world work for the Federal Bureau of Investigation. He's always known this, but it's somewhat unsettling now that he thinks about it as a civilian.

But those skills aren't needed to access the condo on the second floor any more than they were needed for the front door because Books has a key for the condo too. He opens the door while one of the tac agents holds the trigger of a repres-sor to freeze the alarm system.

And then they are inside, all of them. The security alarm re-mains quiet.

The door closes. The condo is completely dark; the win-dows are covered by drapes that block any outside light.

They will move to an interior room, away from the front door, before turning on an overhead light. They don't want the glow from the light bleeding into the hallway.

Flashlights go on. The beams illuminate a small kitchen, a

living room. He follows the agents into one of the two bedrooms. There, one of the agents flips on a light.

Books squints for a moment. Then his eyes open fully.

There's a part of him, if he's honest with himself, that is not surprised at what he sees.

"Oh no," he whispers. "Oh no, Emmy."

12

INSIDE THE bedroom that Emmy uses as an office, the tac officers are all business. One agent photographs every single document in the room, wherever it is—on the desk, on the walls, in the file cabinets, on the floor—taking care to leave them just as they were found. Another uses a portable hard drive to download the contents of Emmy's computers. A third installs the first of several eavesdropping devices, this one inside a carbon monoxide detector.

Books can't take his eyes off the walls; a cold shiver runs through him.

One wall is lined with copies of dozens of letters addressed to Emmy, some handwritten, some typed:

Catch me if you can, Emmy. If you do, I'll show you what I do with their internal organs.

I wish the rest of the cops were as smart as you and could STOP ME

IM BETTER THAN GRAM IN EVERY WAY IM SMARTER AND
STRONGER AND YOULL NEVER CATCH ME AND ONE DAY I
WILL COME FOR YOU AND I WONT KILL YOU UNTIL YOU
BEG ME TO

On another wall, there are poster boards filled with notes in Emmy's handwriting. One of them, titled "How to Make It Look Accidental," has bullet points noting ways to subdue victims and stage evidence and plan escape routes. Another one lists victims' characteristics, not just race and gender and age but also sexual preference, marital status, education, political ideology, group affiliations, criminal history, social media posts, voter registration records, driving records, military service, professional background, credit ratings, pets, allergies, hair color, weight, height—

Yet another wall is filled with newspaper articles: Suicides and drownings. Overdoses and electrocutions. Deaths determined to be due to accidental causes. The cases come from around the country, from Atlanta, Charleston, Dallas, New Orleans.

He stops on that last one. New Orleans. Someone named Nora Connolley, who apparently died recently after a fall in the shower.

New Orleans, where Emmy is right now. She told Books she was going to visit some college friends.

Books brings a hand to his face. Emmy has gone rogue again.

Another chase through thousands of cases across the nation. Another exhaustive, and exhausting, daily probe of incidents around the country—the overwhelming majority of which are noncriminal, accidental, just plain old bad luck—in search of that tiny hint that will reveal a pattern of brilliant, diabolical criminality.

He thought she was done with this. That the days of obsessively scouring the web and police databases and breaking-news e-mail blasts were behind her, that she had finally come to understand that she was not the country's supercop, that she didn't have to solve every problem in every jurisdiction in every state in the union. That for once, she was going to think about herself, about getting better, about moving on.

And to think about *them*, Emmy and Books, a couple with a future together.

Books blinks out of his trance and looks around at the agents. They continue their work, rifling through more drawers and taking more photos and planting more eavesdropping devices. They are here to find out if Emmy has been leaking confidential information on a high-profile case. They are trying to determine if she has betrayed the FBI.

Books doesn't believe she has. Never did. The only reason he agreed to work this investigation into Emmy—the only reason—was he was sure that she'd be cleared of any wrongdoing, that the Bureau was wrong. Emmy would never betray the job, the work to which she is so devoted.

But apparently, she's willing to betray everything and everybody to accomplish that work.

His phone buzzes in his pocket. He pulls it out and sees who's calling. Speak of the devil.

"This is Emmy calling me," he says to Agent Homer.

The agent looks up at him with a question on his face. Books nods. Everyone stops moving.

His chest burning, he answers the call with "Hey there."

"Hey, hope I didn't wake you. Whatcha up to?" The connection's not good; Emmy sounds distant.

What am I up to? he thinks. *I'm searching through your apartment, finding out that you've been lying to me.*

"Getting ready for bed," he says. So now he is lying too. "How's N'awlins?" he asks.

"Fun. We're having a good time. Just wanted to say good night and love you."

He could press Emmy for more information. The names of the friends she claims to be visiting. The restaurant or bar or hotel she's calling from. The places they've gone. But he can't bring himself to do it. He can't bear to hear even one more lie from his fiancée.

Instead, with four federal agents watching, feeling as if his insides are being ripped out, he says to the only woman he has ever loved, to the fiancée that he thought he understood so well: "Love you too."

He means those words. He's never meant them more. But saying them under these circumstances... he feels like he is lying again.

"Are we still good for tomorrow?" she asks.

That word again, *good*. For his homeless friend Petty, *good* meant a warm, safe place to sleep. What does *good* mean for Books? A woman he dearly loves but who cannot love him back?

"Yeah, sure, of course," he hears himself say. "We're always good."

13

I SWAT at my smartphone on the nightstand of my hotel room, but the sound of harp strings won't stop. My head feels like it weighs a hundred pounds as I lift it off the pillow and try to bring the clock into focus; strips of sunlight glare at me through the blinds.

I hit Accept. Words come through the receiver. "Hello? Emmy Dockery? Hello?"

I try to speak into the phone, but all that comes out is a gravelly growl. I clear my throat and try again.

"My name is Nadia Jacobius," she says. "I'm a reporter with the *Times-Picayune*."

But...who knows I'm here? I haven't exactly advertised my visit. I don't advertise anything about my whereabouts these days.

I blink, give myself a moment to wake up.

"Would you care to comment on your investigation into Nora Connolley's death? Is this another serial killer you're chasing?"

"I . . . don't talk to reporters," I manage.

"Don't hang up. I know you don't talk to reporters. I get that. But just listen, okay? No harm in listening, is there?"

I can't fault the logic in that.

"I know you're here to investigate her death. I know you think this is the work of a serial killer. Let me help you get it out to the world. Shouldn't the public know that another Graham is on the loose?"

I sit up in bed. Yes, of course, when the time is right, everybody should know about him. When the time is right, I will shout it from the mountaintops. But the time isn't right. I have no profile of this guy. What can I tell people right now? *If you live in a single-story house with easy access from a garage that's close to public transportation, watch out?* It's too vague, too early. All that will do is tip him off that I'm investigating him. All that will do is risk the lives of other cops. I convinced Joe Halsted to open an investigation into Laura Berg's death and suddenly he had a heart attack. I can't let the same thing happen to Robert Crescenzo down here in New Orleans.

"Background only," I say.

"Okay, background."

"Hold your story," I say. "Because there's nothing to report right now."

"I have twenty paragraphs already."

"But no details, I'll bet. You couldn't. Because I don't have any details. You'll endanger lives."

"How's that? How could I possibly be endangering people by telling them there's a serial killer on the loose?"

I can't give her more. Not even on background.

"I'm running the story with or without you," she says. "I'm giving you the chance to control it. Wouldn't it be—"

"Hold it," I say, "and I'll give you an exclusive when there are details to report. When the moment comes, I'll go to you and you only."

A pause. She's considering the hook I've thrown her.

"How long are we talking? Weeks? Months?"

"I wish I knew."

Another pause.

"No chance you'll tell me anything on the record right now?"

"No chance," I say. "So do we have a deal?"

A loud exhale through the phone. "No promises," she says.

14

THE FLIGHT back from New Orleans is nice, if *nice* includes being in the middle seat in the back row of a packed plane between an overweight lawyer who eats spicy peanuts and spreads colorful legal briefs across his tray and onto mine on one side and an elderly woman who is pleasant enough but begins snoring the moment the airplane takes off and who apparently ate a lot of garlic recently on the other.

I have notes and research in my lap, but my eyes glaze over and I think of Books, our short phone call last night. I lied about my reason for going to New Orleans, and then I lied again last night about the fun I was having with my unnamed college friends.

The guilt, I can handle. I can tell myself that I'm protecting Books by keeping him from worrying about me, that once I have enough to get the Bureau to officially investigate, I'll explain what I did and why I chose not to tell him.

But it's not the guilt that swims through my stomach. It's the feeling that I'm screwing things up with Books, that by withholding anything from him for whatever reason, I'm laying the first bricks in a wall between us. I can justify my actions all I want, but the truth is I am keeping a secret from Books, and it doesn't matter why.

Lord knows, he deserves better than this, better than me.

A memory: Walking along F Street after work, the air warm and breezy, the two of us side by side, our arms grazing, our conversation pleasant but stilted (Books is not exactly a smooth talker), and I'm wondering if this makes sense for me, if this by-the-book, no-frills agent is my type of guy. The broad shoulders, the kind eyes; yes, that definitely works, but the whole just-the-facts-ma'am routine, which for him is not a routine, doesn't feel like my speed.

And he's being polite, keeping the conversation on me, asking me about my family, about my twin sister, Marta, when we see it unfold right before our eyes: a young kid comes seemingly out of nowhere, swipes the handbag from an older woman walking toward us, and then starts to rocket off, angling between pedestrians, his snatch-and-grab complete.

Books turns as if to shield me, and I'm still in shock, watching this happen, the whole thing spanning two or three seconds, the woman so stunned and scared that she hasn't made a sound, and then Books tackles the young thief, using some kind of takedown he probably learned at Quantico, his movements so quick and decisive and his voice so commanding that the kid doesn't make a move after Books subdues him. He puts his hand lightly on the kid's chest as he lies flat on the sidewalk, looks him square in the eye, and starts talking to him. *What's your name? Why did you do this? Don't you know you could have hurt somebody?*

They stay like that for a good ten minutes, Books and the boy. The woman recovers her purse, and the other pedestrians give them a wide berth. A street cop finally shows up, but by the time he gets there, the boy is on his feet, still engaged in conversation with Books. It turns out he has a story that isn't all that surprising under the circumstances—no father, a mother in rehab, two younger siblings.

The cop goes without making an arrest. The boy shakes the woman's hand and apologizes. Then he surprises Books with a hug before walking away.

Books turns to me. *Rough start to our first date,* he says.

But all I can think is *I could love this man...*

On the plane, I feel my head loll forward, and I jerk awake. This is when I'm sleepiest, when I can't work, when I don't have access to my research, which is why I have insomnia at home. It's hard to sleep when you know somebody's out there planning his next murder, and your laptop is right next to you, waiting for you to find that tiny morsel, that one detail that will break it all open. But the moment my research is unavailable, the overwhelming sleep deprivation takes hold. I go to a movie for relaxation and I'm asleep in five minutes. I wait in a doctor's office and find myself quickly floating away.

So I don't fight it. I close my eyes and lean back against the headrest, my arms tight to my sides on this small seat with the lawyer's papers spilling around me. I let sleep take me and tell myself that Books will understand when I explain what I've been doing.

15

"SO SHE'S off on another one of her *investigations*." FBI director William Moriarty plays with his gold-framed reading glasses as he sits at the head of the walnut table. He utters the last word like it's dirty.

Books, sitting to Moriarty's left, feels the need to come to Emmy's defense. He isn't happy about what she's doing either, but for a different reason—because these investigations are slowly driving Emmy mad. Moriarty's making it sound like Emmy's doing something innocuous but silly or perhaps harmful. He must have forgotten that Emmy more or less single-handedly stopped a serial killer who would probably still be committing his atrocious acts if Emmy hadn't discovered his crimes and then found him.

But this is not the time to pick a fight.

"So what in sweet Christ are we supposed to do about *that*?" Moriarty asks.

"We don't do anything," Books says. "Is she violating protocol? We told her—the, uh, Bureau told her that she couldn't do her own investigations in the name of the FBI. She can't claim to be speaking on behalf of the Bureau. But as long as she isn't doing that, she's just doing personal stuff on her own time. Some people do yoga. Some climb mountains. Emmy hunts for serial killers."

"I have to disagree with you, Books." This from Assistant Director Dwight Ross, the agent running the operation that includes Emmy, the operation on which Emmy is suspected of leaking secrets. Books has been through doors with Ross, has seen him up close and in action, and his view of Ross is the same as his view of many people he encountered at the Bureau—he overvalues his own importance and takes himself too seriously, but at the end of the day, he is doing the job for the right reasons.

"We told her," says Ross, "that if she was going to reach out to local jurisdictions, she had to emphasize that she wasn't speaking in her official capacity as a Bureau analyst. We even wrote up the words she had to use. But she hasn't been using them. Reading her e-mails, I can see she's leading people to believe that she's doing official Bureau business."

"Sounds like a technical foul to me, at worst," says Books.

Ross says, "You call conducting unauthorized business in the name of the FBI a *technicality?*"

Books looks at Ross, then at Moriarty, his eyebrows raised. "Yes," he says. "What's the harm? If her hunt leads nowhere, no big deal. You don't waste any resources, and the only thing *she* wastes is her own personal time. But if it leads to something real, then she's helped stop a killer. When did that become a bad thing? I thought that was, y'know, kinda what you guys did here."

"Books, I know you're close to this," says the director.

"Maybe, but I'm still right. She's not hurting anything or

anybody." *Except herself*, he does not say. "She discovered Graham's crimes," Books goes on, "and the Bureau took down an evil sociopath."

"*Emmy* took down Graham," says Ross. "Or so the press seems to imply. You'd think the rest of the Bureau had nothing to do with it."

Books turns on Ross, feeling the heat rise within him. "Emmy didn't grant a single media interview. She never said a word in public. Nothing. The victims' families spoke up for her. Local cops she'd contacted for help spoke up for her. Other agents on the team—Lydia and Denny and Sophie and I—spoke up for her. Because she *deserved* it. She never sought credit for it even though the rest of us had our thumbs up our asses while she was uncovering the most brilliant and horrific crime spree I've ever seen."

"Enough," says the director.

"I mean, that's what this is really about, isn't it, Dwight? That a lowly data analyst did the work that the superstar special agents were supposed to be doing—and did it better than them? That you got shown up by some numbers girl?"

"I said that's *enough*." Moriarty raises a hand.

"That's not true at all," says Ross, his eyes cold.

"It's a little true, Dwight," says Moriarty. He looks at Books. "But listen, Books, we can't have her running around claiming that she's doing FBI business when it's *not* FBI business. Dwight's right about that. Your girl's doing that. And she can't." He lets out a sigh and looks up at the ceiling. "But we can't call her out on this without revealing that we've been inside her computer. She can't know we're onto her until we're ready to make a move."

Books feels something stir inside him.

"*If* we make a move," the director says, correcting himself.

Books turns to Ross. "You haven't found any evidence that she's leaking secrets, have you? Forensics hasn't pulled anything incriminating from her computer?"

"Not yet," he says. "It will take us some time."

They won't find anything. Books is sure of it. Emmy's no traitor. "You still haven't told me about the case she's working on," says Books. "The one where she's supposedly leaking secrets."

"Emmy never mentioned it?"

Books shrugs. "It's Bureau business. I'm a private citizen. She keeps that wall up."

Ross seems dubious about that claim. But it's true. Emmy and Books don't discuss her work. He doesn't even bother asking. If the roles were reversed, he wouldn't say anything to her either.

"Tell him, Dwight," says the director. "Tell him about the investigation."

16

"YOU'VE HEARD of Citizen David," Ross says to Books.

Of course he has. Books has read several accounts of his exploits. He'd even discussed it with Emmy one lazy Sunday morning while they were reading the *Washington Post* in bed.

Citizen David is the person who has claimed responsibility for a number of acts of civil disobedience and domestic terrorism over the past six months. His manifesto is, simply stated, *The deck is stacked against the little guy in this country. Businesses have no moral center and will rob, cheat, and steal their way to maximum profits at the expense of the consumers. Higher education is reserved for the elite who can afford the ridiculous tuition. The criminal justice system will give liberal breaks to affluent white people but trample the rights of minorities and the poor and disenfranchised. In every way big and small, the powerful keep their power, and the rich keep the poor down.*

David versus Goliath, only this David, whoever he is, has more than a slingshot. He has money, resources, and sophisticated technology.

One of his talents is hacking. He hacked into the admissions system of an Ivy League university to reveal how little merit went into merit-based selection and how many students were admitted because of the size of their parents' wallets.

He hacked into the computer system of a pharmaceutical company and leaked e-mails showing that the company knew but never publicly admitted that an ingredient in one of its hepatitis vaccines caused renal failure.

He hacked into the computers of a minimum-security prison in Georgia and popped open all the cell doors at once to protest the incarceration of a young African-American man whom an all-white jury had declared guilty of the murder of a white teenage girl in what many critics believed was a wrongful conviction.

But he hasn't limited himself to cybercrime. He was responsible for the bombing of several buildings in the United States. A bank in Seymour, Connecticut, accused of discriminating against minorities in its lending practices. A fast-food restaurant in Pinellas Park, Florida, after reports came out about the franchise's cruelty to the chickens it slaughtered. A city hall in Blount County, Alabama, where officials had refused to grant marriage licenses to same-sex couples.

The bombings always occurred in the middle of the night and always after a bomb threat was called in, ensuring that nobody was around when the explosives detonated.

Citizen David is part Robin Hood, part Edward Snowden, part Bernie Sanders, part Black Lives Matter, and part Unabomber.

Some people call him a hero. Others call him a reckless anarchist. The Bureau calls him a domestic terrorist.

But the FBI agents don't know where he is, and they don't

know who he is. Citizen David uses anonymous networks so his crimes can't be traced to him, effectively shielding himself from view.

That's where Emmy was supposed to come in. They wanted her to try to predict his next move, to discern some pattern in what he did. It was right up her alley.

"You think Emmy's leaking the details of your investigation to the person who calls himself Citizen David?" asks Books. He asks the question with disbelief, even scorn.

But he has a sinking feeling in his stomach.

Because he's remembering that quiet Sunday morning a few weeks back when there was a big front-page profile in the *Washington Post* about the anonymous Citizen David, and Books had read it while making comments on it to Emmy. Saying the kinds of things he always said: *We have laws, we have rules. Protest and dissent are important, commendable, but you can't do it by blowing up private property and invading confidential computer files. If people are breaking the law, report them or sue them, but we can't have a nation of anarchists who take the law into their own hands or who create their own rules and punish anyone who doesn't abide by them.*

He doesn't remember his exact words. But he remembers every word Emmy said in response.

He's scaring the people in power, she said. *Maybe that's the only way to get them to change. Nothing else has worked.*

That was it. It was one of those lazy mornings where conversations started and stopped and shifted. He never followed up. It didn't stick out in his mind at the time. After all, Emmy had always been a protester at heart, ever since she was in high school, the sober, socially conscious girl, nothing like her popular-cheerleader-girl twin sister.

It gnaws at him now. Emmy might not approve of all of Citizen David's tactics, but deep down, all things considered, she might be quietly rooting for him.

And that isn't even the worst part.

"We don't know how yet," says Dwight Ross, leaning back in his chair, "but she's leaking to that reporter."

That was the worst part. Books had forgotten, but now it slams against his chest like a stiff forearm. The reporter who wrote the *Post* piece was Shaindy Eckstein.

Does the Bureau know that Shaindy and Emmy are close? That Shaindy is quite possibly Emmy's only friend these days?

Shaindy, the one who learned about Emmy being rushed to the hospital after taking a combination of painkillers and amphetamines a year ago but who didn't break the story after Books asked her not to, after Books looked her in the eye and said that it would be so painful for her to have it publicized. Some gossip rag got wind of it, probably from some paramedic or nurse on its payroll, and it all came out anyway, but Books never forgot what Shaindy did. Neither did Emmy. A friendship formed. *Trust* formed.

And now Shaindy Eckstein is writing stories on the FBI's hunt for Citizen David, stories rich with details.

"No way," Books says, trying to keep his voice strong, no longer sure what he believes.

17

THE MEETING is adjourned. Books gets to his feet on unsteady legs, a dull, sick feeling in his stomach. His brain tells him that Emmy looks guilty. His heart doesn't want that to be true. His instinct, his gut, believes it *can't* be true.

Dwight Ross leaves the room. Director Moriarty puts a hand on Bookman's shoulder. "Like I said before, I'm sorry as hell about this. And I'm even sorrier to involve you in the investigation. But it has to be done."

"Emmy's not the leaker." But even as Books says the words, he feels a distance forming; the picture of the woman he loves is fading and blurring. After all, she's back to her obsessive hunt for a serial killer, and she didn't tell him a thing about *that*. What else hasn't she told him?

"Maybe not, maybe not," says the director, though it comes out sounding like a lame attempt to placate him.

Books clears his throat and gives the director a curt nod. "Hey, Bill, I need to make a call. A landline. The cell reception in this place..."

"Not a problem." The director gestures to a phone in the corner of the room.

Books wanders toward the phone, lost in thought, taking his time, waiting for the director to leave him alone in this room. He removes his wallet from his pants pocket and fishes out the business card, by now ragged at the edges and smudged with an unidentifiable substance.

His hands are shaking. He misdials the first time. He's grown unaccustomed to landline phones; he has one at the bookstore but almost never uses it to call anyone.

A woman answers. "Dr. Bakalis's office."

Books takes a deep breath before speaking to Emmy's therapist's receptionist.

18

I GO straight from the airport to the Hoover Building. In the lobby, I figure that if the elevators are efficient and not too crowded, I might get to this meeting on time. I'd prefer to park my roller suitcase at my cubicle but there's no time for that, so when I get upstairs, I leave it with Dwight Ross's receptionist, a saintly woman named Roberta.

I pull the relevant files out of my folder, take a moment to compose myself, and stride down the hall to the conference room. I'm the last to arrive, as usual. The rest of the team members are present and alert: Carlton from the National Security Branch, Sloan from the Criminal Investigative Division, Mayfield from Intelligence, Cobbs from the Science and Technology Branch. All dark suits, crisp white shirts, boring ties. The men of the FBI; their motto could be "What We Lack in Imaginative Wardrobe, We Make Up for with Colorless Personalities."

And Dwight Ross himself, the executive assistant director of the Criminal, Cyber, Response, and Services Branch, at the head of the table, running the operation.

"Dockery, you're late," he says, glancing at me and then at the clock.

"Sorry, sir." One and a half minutes late. Ninety seconds.

"This will be the last time you are late," he says.

"Yes, sir," I say, because men like Ross like that kind of sub-missive response from women, even though we both know it's probably not the last time I'll be late.

I'm not really sure why I'm here at all. These days I do most of my work at home, my secure undisclosed location, thanks to all the threats I've received. With multiple computers, secure access to the Bureau databases, a cell phone, and a video feed, I can do pretty much anything from my home office.

It wasn't my choice to work from home—at least, not at first. The doctors wouldn't clear me to return to the office for nearly a year, so working from home had been my idea, a way to "take it easy" and "rest and recuperate" but still contribute. Then I realized how effective I could be if I didn't have to leave my apartment. I could eliminate the commute, the small-talk conversations throughout the day, the unnecessary staff meet-ings, the cake-in-the-conference-room birthday parties.

And yes, I admit it—I have to acknowledge it—staying home lessens the fear. I tell myself it's in the past, but every now and again, it creeps up behind me and wraps its arm around my throat. When I'm in the car, on the elevator, at the grocery store. And it doesn't slowly build up—it steals my breath and squeezes my neck and pummels my chest all at once.

So, yeah, if I'm going to have a panic attack, if I'm going to collapse to the floor and curl up in a fetal position and have to breathe into a paper bag, I'd rather not do it in front of my coworkers.

Ross eyes me with that expressionless, cold stare. I think he wanted more than a "Yes, sir" from me. He wanted more groveling, more remorse, for being ninety seconds late to the meeting.

Before his recent promotion to executive assistant director, Dwight Ross was in Intelligence, where, as far as anyone could tell, he had his head so far up the director's ass that when the director belched, you could smell Dwight's cologne. He likes the people who work under him to follow that model, which is one of the reasons we don't get along so well.

We are here about Citizen David, the domestic terrorist who has given the Bureau fits and become a darling of social media in the process.

Carlton, who has a buzz cut and thick glasses, begins. Nothing new from the National Security Branch. No evidence that David is connected to any active terrorist cell, no chatter or indications of coordination.

Sloan, from the Criminal Investigative Division, doesn't help much either—David isn't leaving any traces behind when he blows up buildings. David seems to know how to avoid the CCTV cameras. He uses local materials for his rudimentary bombs. And it seems that Citizen David is working alone.

Nothing from Science and Technology either, says Cobbs, because David uses an anonymous server to post his messages on Facebook. The Bureau has tried to trace his messages and thus far has pegged him in Ukraine, in Mexico City, in New Zealand, and in Uruguay.

Everyone looks at me. I raise my shoulders. "The sample size of his bombings is too small for any discernible pattern," I say. "He started in the Northeast, with the bank bombing in Connecticut, then he went down to Florida with the chain restaurant, then he headed west to Alabama and blew up the city hall. So that tells us, obviously—"

"That he's heading west," says Ross. "We know that."

I take a breath. Ross didn't interrupt any of the men even once.

"Given the length of time between the bombings," I say, "my guess is he's driving. He drove from Connecticut to Florida, which is about twenty hours if you take the fastest route, but he wouldn't go the fastest way. He'd want to avoid the toll cameras and the ALPRs—automatic license-plate readers—and the speed traps. He'd go by back roads. So I'd say it took him a good four, five days to get to Florida. And then he spent a day or two planning the bombing, buying the supplies, and plotting out exactly how to do it. That's a good week, right there, which is exactly the space of time between the Connecticut and Florida bombings. But the city-hall bombing in Alabama was four days later. He traveled about four hundred miles, which you can do in two days even if you're being careful. And then two days to plan."

Ross opens his hands. "And now it's eleven days since the last attack. He could have driven anywhere in the country."

Sloan, from the Criminal Investigative Division, winces at Ross's interruption. Ross really should just let me talk.

Ross glances at the map of the United States on the wall. "You think, what, California? Las Vegas? A target-rich environment that would take several days by car heading west. The Grand Canyon, maybe?"

Cobbs nods at that, as does Mayfield.

"I was thinking Manhattan," I say.

The room goes quiet as everyone calculates.

"Doubling back," says Carlton.

"Throwing us off," I say. "Knowing that we're trying to discern a pattern. And a target in New York City is a tougher nut to crack than some small town in Alabama. He'd need more time to prepare."

"Interesting," says Sloan.

Yes, interesting. Everyone's wondering whether *interesting* means "accurate."

And they're probably also wondering how long it will be before this *interesting* conversation finds its way into an article by Shaindy Eckstein in the *Washington Post*.

19

I THREAD my way through the crowd and miraculously find a spot at the bar. This place, Deadline, is only a few years old but it has a throwback, old-school feel, with its dark wood and dim lighting. I've been told (I'm not much of a nightlife gal myself) that this has become one of the hangouts for the Washington press corps and the political class.

There is a mix of ages, but it leans to the younger side, congressional staffers and campaign consultants and youthful journalists who publish mostly online. I spot a U.S. senator in a corner booth, an older white man whom I've seen on the news shows, holding court for a throng of admiring staffers, disproportionately female and attractive. Everyone here is ambitious, everyone is hungry, and most of them are ruthless.

Shaindy Eckstein is standing with a group of men and women nursing a colorful drink, but I pretend not to notice her. I finally get the attention of the bartender and order a white wine.

I check my watch. I have about twenty minutes, tops, before I have to leave and go to Books's house for our Friday-night date.

The noise around me is oddly comforting. I spend so much of my time alone with statistics and computers, where I'm safe, so being outside, walking through a grocery store or traveling to work or just running errands, is hard for me sometimes, probably harder than I like to admit, that feeling of being exposed. So you'd think a bar like this would be even worse, but for some reason I feel safer in a crowd of strangers in an enclosed area.

"Hey, you." I turn at these words and see Shaindy standing there, casually dressed in a black blouse and jeans, her eyeglasses perched on her head holding back her long gray hair.

"Hey yourself." I get off the barstool and give her a hug. Shaindy is the only reporter I've ever liked. When I was taken to the hospital a year ago, she just happened to be there. She was in the right place at the right time to break the story if she chose to do so. It fell right into her lap. "Graham Catcher Rushed to Hospital for Overdose," or some attention-grabbing headline like that. She could have thrown in some suggestion of a suicide attempt to make it even juicier. The whole thing with Graham was still pretty hot back then. It would have been the easiest story she'd ever written. But she didn't write it. She let it go when Books and I asked her to leave it alone. She didn't request anything in return either, like most journalists would, like that reporter in New Orleans just did. She just dropped the whole thing.

"You look good," she says now, appraising me. I doubt that, but I've learned how to deal with the scars, how to wear my hair and clothes to conceal most of them.

"Blowing off some steam?" I ask.

She smirks. "This is work. I get more done here than I do in a full day at the office."

That's probably true of the politicians too, all of them cutting deals over glasses of Scotch.

"I've enjoyed reading your stuff on Citizen David," I say.

She has a twinkle in her eye and the hint of a grin that she goes to some lengths to suppress when she asks, "Have you, now?"

"You have an excellent source, it seems."

"I do. I do." She takes a sip from her glass. "The source has been very helpful."

Nice how she put that, not even revealing the gender, no *he* or *she*.

"And if I could say one thing to my source," she says, "I would tell that person this: I will never disclose a source's identity. I'll go to prison first."

I nod.

"My source has nothing to worry about," she adds. "That's a promise. And you know I keep my promises."

"I do know that." I sip my wine, a nice chardonnay with a hint of pear.

Shaindy leans into me. "On an absolutely, completely different topic, having nothing whatsoever to do with what we just discussed"—her expression deadpan—"do you have anything you'd like to tell me, Emmy?"

I can't help but smile. "Are you suggesting that I'm your source?"

She puts a hand over her heart. "I don't know who my source is. I only get text messages from a burner phone. So I have no way of knowing my source's identity."

She says this like I already know this information.

"And I won't try to guess," she says. "But like I said, even if I knew her—or his—name, I would never tell a soul."

"Good to know, Shaindy," I say.

Clearly, Shaindy thinks I'm her source. That's not surprising. She's wondering why I would go to the trouble of texting her anonymously instead of just talking to her face to face. After all, she's already proven that I can trust her.

But she won't ask, and she won't tell.

And neither will I.

She winks at me. "Well," she says, "I'll just keep checking my phone."

20

THE MAN who sometimes calls himself Charlie leans back against the seat of his wheelchair in his custom van, his earbuds in, one hand clutching the cell phone, the other arm hanging lazily over the steering wheel.

He is not, in reality, listening to music or talking on the phone. It is a device to throw off suspicion should someone passing by on the sidewalk happen to glance at the curb and see him inside the vehicle or, God forbid, should a police officer approach. He can simply put a cheerful smile on his face and begin speaking and moving his hands expressively, and he will appear to be talking to someone about something innocuous, not staking out a private residence.

What's interesting is that his speaking on the phone or wearing a smile does not indicate that he is not dangerous or a threat. Why would someone with bad intentions sneer or scowl at people as they pass him, thereby telegraphing those intentions?

But people see what they want to see. They don't want to

see a threat on their quiet little street, and thus they're willing to accept almost any verbal or nonverbal cue—a carefree expression, some forced laughter—that reinforces their preconceived bias.

Harrison Bookman lives on a tree-lined street of brick homes and SUVs; his neighbors are people who walk their dogs and go for early-morning runs and fuck their spouses once a week and worry about retirement and college tuition, not about where their next meal will come from. Bookman's address is unlisted, befitting a former FBI agent, but it wasn't hard to find his town house. It was a simple matter of following him home from his bookstore.

Charlie's senses go on high alert when a car pulls into Bookman's driveway. He does a double take at the woman who gets out of the car. Had he not been anticipating her, hoping for her, he would not have recognized this tall, thin woman who locks her Jeep by remote and heads toward Bookman's front door.

Her hair is longer than it was in the photos they ran a year ago. Different length, different style, different color. He recalls lighter-colored hair pulled back, not ink-black hair running past her shoulders, bangs covering her forehead.

It is a subtle change, and it has a practical value, he recognizes. The bangs, her blouse with the high neckline, almost touching her cheek, blue jeans instead of shorts despite the heat. She is covering the scars.

"You want to hide, but you know you can't," he whispers.

And she's doing a decent job of hiding the limp too, although it's there if you look for it.

"You are scared and bruised and scarred," he says. "But you adapted and overcame. You keep fighting. You keep doing your job."

She primps a bit as she walks, her fingers swiping at her bangs.

"He won't care about the scars, Emmy. If he is half the man he should be, your scars won't matter at all. Your scars...are what make you beautiful."

He sucks in a breath. Feels pressure in his chest. Jealousy and envy are not emotions that find him easily. The jealous man is the man too weak to reach for what he wants, who occupies his time with longing and regret instead of action. A moment of envy is a moment wasted.

The thinking man has no affections. Only a heart of stone.

Hate, anger, love, sadness—all are irrelevant. All are distractions. Happiness is too; at least, how most people define the word. Happiness is not an emotion to be felt every day, a selfish indulgence to be hoarded and constantly relished. Happiness is the ultimate goal, and it comes not from egotistical pleasure but from knowing that one has achieved one's aim.

"I do not love you or hate you," he says to Emmy as she reaches the front door of Bookman's town house. "I do not like you or dislike you. You are an impediment, nothing more."

He says these words so he will believe them.

The door opens, and Emmy enters the town house.

Charlie hits a button on his dashboard. The back door to the customized van slides open, and the hydraulic ramp unfolds and drops down to the pavement.

Charlie removes the earbuds but keeps his cell phone in his hand. He grabs the bag of toiletries off the floor and navigates the wheelchair down the ramp. He could use the remote but chooses to manually move the wheelchair instead. He rolls up a driveway two doors down from Bookman and moves along the sidewalk until he reaches the back of Emmy's Jeep.

He looks at his cell phone as if it were ringing, then raises it to his ear as if he were answering, making sure the bag of toiletries falls from his lap onto the pavement in the process. Oops.

He pretends to speak for a moment while looking with distress at the spilled contents of his bag. He puts the phone in his lap and reaches down for the bottle of shampoo on the sidewalk. He pretends that he can't quite reach it. He cups his right hand under the fender of Emmy's Jeep to pull himself forward.

And to plant the GPS device.

He completes the charade for anyone who might be watching, picking up the toiletries and then continuing to wheel himself down the sidewalk. He will do a lap around the block and return to his van and drive away.

He doesn't have any idea how long it will be before Emmy returns home. She may stay with Bookman, her fiancé, for a few hours or the evening or even the weekend. But eventually, she will return home.

Sooner or later, Charlie will know where Emmy lives.

21

BOOKS OPENS the door for me wearing a button-down shirt pulled loose from his jeans and loafers with no socks. His hair is still wet from a shower, and I catch the scent of soap and musky aftershave.

My heart does gymnastics as he pulls me close and presses his lips against mine with urgency. I feel everything else drift away; serial killers and murdered cops and domestic terrorists and leaks of confidential information recede into fog as we make out like teenagers in the foyer of his town house. Everything safer and happier and ... better. Just better.

We get only as far as his living room, pawing at each other, unbuttoning clothes and yanking off shirts, panting like animals, before he lays me down gently on the carpet. His muscular arms tremble as he hovers over me, his face inches from mine, then enters me with a sharp moan.

Hello, Friday night.

We almost never see each other during the week. Books,

trying to keep his struggling bookstore afloat, has trimmed down staff to the point that he is the only full-time employee, handling the counter and the inventory and the accounting and the marketing, working sixteen-hour days. And I'm my usual obsessive, workaholic self.

He grits his teeth and arches his back and, with one final thrust, lets out a violent grunt, looking down at me with that intense, pained expression, wet hair falling into his face. Then he releases a breath, his expression easing.

"Wow," he says after a few seconds. "I've missed the hell out of you."

My breathing evens out as he lowers himself onto me. I touch his smooth cheek. His smell and his warmth are all I need right now, all I want. I close my eyes and pretend it's going to stay like this.

I pretend that I really am good for him, that we really will get married.

He starts to pull away but I hold him tight. "Just…stay here a minute," I say, opening my eyes.

He smiles that gentle Books smile, kisses me softly.

"I love you, Agent Bookman," I whisper. "You know that, right?"

If he is surprised at the question, he doesn't show it. "You're not just using me for my body?" He slides off of me and props himself up on his elbow. "You okay?" he asks.

"I am now," I say. "I am here."

"You can always be here," he says. I can't see my own expression, of course, but I can see his as he reads mine. It's like the needle screeching off the turntable, and the passion and intimacy disappear as we return to our regularly scheduled program, *My Fiancée Is a Freak,* starring Harrison Bookman as a handsome, brilliant, well-adjusted man drawn to a neurotic woman. "What, I'm not supposed to say that? You *can* be here. I *want* you here. I want us to live together."

I run my fingers gently down his cheek. "I know," I say, which is not much of an answer. "I'm working on it."

The disappointment, frustration, all over his face. We've been through this; I've pushed away the idea of moving in together before, and he's reacted negatively before. But something is different this time—his fuse is a little shorter.

"You have to work on it. I see."

"Books—"

"How was New Orleans?" he snaps, his eyes ablaze, as if that's some kind of comeback, as if that has anything to do with what we're discussing.

"It was...fine." I look away. I do not like lying to Books. It's one thing not to volunteer information about what I'm doing in my spare time. It's another thing altogether to flat-out lie. A relationship is constructed slowly, like a house, and every lie is a stone pulled loose from the foundation.

And it's not the only lie I've told him.

Books abruptly gets to his feet and collects his shirt and jeans. "I'll get us some wine," he says.

"Hey," I call to him, but he's already disappeared into the kitchen.

I have to tell him. I have to tell him that I'm hunting another serial killer. I know everything he's going to say, every objection he's going to raise, the knock-down, drag-out argument we're going to have, but I'm going to tell him anyway. I have to.

This weekend, I promise myself. I'll tell him this weekend.

22

SUNDAY MORNING, *rain is falling...*

Books can't get the song out of his head as he looks out the window dotted with long raindrops at the gray sky. Ordinarily, there are few things Books enjoys more than lazy, damp Sundays curled up in bed with Emmy, reading the paper and sipping coffee and feeling the warmth of Emmy under the covers.

Not so much this Sunday.

He's removed the wet plastic sleeve from the Sunday *Post*, and there are a few thick stains of wetness on the front page but nothing that obscures this headline:

CITIZEN DAVID TARGETING NYC?

Once again written by Shaindy Eckstein.

Books reaches into the back of the kitchen cabinet and removes the burner phone he was given by Director Moriarty. It has been turned off and stashed away all weekend. He couldn't risk Emmy seeing it, much less reading anything that might be on it.

Knowing that he is hiding something from her burns his throat like harsh medicine. He reminds himself that he's trying to protect her, trying to ensure a fair investigation.

No, he thinks, *it's not that.* His own guilt is a diversion, focusing him on his role in all of this. The problem is the why, the reason there's an investigation in the first place. The problem is that the Bureau has turned its considerable resources on Emmy, that she has a target planted on her back.

That he is losing her. That she is losing herself, jumping from the airplane and refusing to pull the cord for the parachute.

He listens for any sound of Emmy moving upstairs but hears nothing. It's only six thirty in the morning. Emmy usually sleeps well past this time. She sleeps hard and long on the weekends. She comes to him on Friday nights beaten and exhausted. It's not hard to imagine why—she works endless hours and gets almost no sleep during the week. Even though she has assured him—lied to him—that this isn't the case anymore, that she has scaled back.

He powers up the burner phone. The screen comes to life. The first new text message is time-stamped Friday at 5:25 p.m.

She just met with SE at Deadline, quick conversation and left.

Books feels a slow burn through his chest. She must have come straight from that meeting with Shaindy Eckstein to his house. He'd thought he'd tasted wine on her mouth when he first kissed her, but he was too busy ripping off her clothes to think much of it.

Friday, happy hour, she meets with Shaindy. Sunday morning, Shaindy is revealing the Bureau's thoughts on Citizen David's plans.

He pictures agents following Emmy, clicking photo after incriminating photo of her whispering to a *Washington Post* reporter in a popular, crowded bar.

His heart asks him, *Why would she do this in plain sight of hundreds of onlookers?* His brain answers, *It's the perfect place, lost in a crowd, a brief stolen moment that could easily be passed off as a quick hello, small talk.*

"Oh, Emmy," he whispers, "please don't let it be true."

The second new text message is from this morning, less than an hour ago:

We're going to have to act on this.

Followed by a link. Books clicks on it. It's an article from the *Times-Picayune*.

FBI LINKS LOCAL DEATH TO SERIAL-KILLER SPREE

The article notes that FBI analyst Emmy Dockery, known for her hunt and capture of the notorious serial killer Graham, was dispatched to New Orleans to investigate the seemingly accidental death of Nora Connolley.

She talked to a reporter when she was down there? Books wonders. If so, he doubts it was by choice. She was probably accosted, a reporter with a camera and recorder following her doggedly.

But it doesn't matter. Her secret—one of them—is out now. Books can't pretend not to know. The Bureau won't be able to feign ignorance. Something will break as a result.

He finds himself constructing a scenario that would solve all of this: Emmy is kicked out of the Bureau over this new serial-killer search of hers, thus depriving her of access to the Citizen David investigation. There are no more leaks. The people at the Bureau will think, *She's gone and the leaks have stopped, but the proof of her leaking isn't conclusive, so maybe we'll just leave it at that and be glad it's over.*

Yeah, sure—and maybe his car will turn into a pumpkin at midnight, and the glass slipper will fit Emmy's foot.

But he goes over it in his mind, his fantasy solution, praying that some scenario like that will play out and make everything better, that Emmy will snap out of this funk and get her head straight.

Something, anything, to make this nightmare go away.

23

HIS INSIDES still burning, Books walks into the bedroom with the Sunday paper under his arm, holding two empty mugs and a pot of coffee. Primed for an argument, loaded for bear, he pauses as he watches Emmy sleeping.

So tranquil, so defenseless. Emmy has had little peace since the attack by Graham, between the pain and the nightmares and the panic attacks and her obsessive need to continue her work and find the next serial-killer-eluding-detection. She has changed. It would be impossible not to. He has tried to hold her hand throughout this process, but she has, for the most part, yanked her hand free and demanded that he let her find her own way. Maybe he has failed her.

But maybe this is beyond his control. During his tenure in law enforcement, first as a cop and then with the Bureau, he saw the toll that violent crime took not just on the victim but on family and friends. He saw how the death of a child could destroy a marriage. He saw how vicious attacks completely changed some people, made them unable to cope with the new reality suddenly forced on them. He saw victims of crime leave their spouses, quit their jobs, completely reverse course on issues like religion or politics, take up or give up various pursuits or, in some cases, give up altogether.

Maybe, due to forces beyond their control, he and Emmy never had a chance after she was attacked. But he refuses to believe it.

Emmy moans and rolls her head from side to side on the pillow, her eyelids fluttering. Is she dreaming? Is it a nightmare? Is she about to start screaming *No, no, no!* before opening her eyes wide, frightened and disoriented?

Her hair is mussed and flattened on one side, and she's wearing nothing but a V-neck T-shirt, so Emmy's scars, the ones she goes to great lengths to obscure, are plain as day. The scars from the sutures along her hairline. The skin grafts on her chest and neck to repair the second-degree burns she received. Asleep, unguarded, she looks so much like the very thing she refuses to see herself as—a victim.

Let me take you away from this, Em, he thinks. *Let's forget about all of this. Everything. You'll get better. I know you will. I'll help you. Let me do that. Take my hand, and let's start running.*

No more lies. No more of you pretending to be strong enough to handle all of this alone. No more hiding all the pain.

Let me back into your life.

24

I OPEN my eyes, turn my head, and feel a pain shoot down my neck. I'm always stiff when I get a lot of sleep.

I blink, try to focus. The smell of coffee, Books's favorite Italian blend. We both savor these slow weekend days, but something immediately feels different about this particular morning.

Books stands in the corner, a coffee mug in his hand, looking out the window at the rainfall. On the bed next to me is the Sunday *Washington Post,* folded, slightly damp from the rain. I see the headline "Citizen David Targeting NYC?" above Shaindy Eckstein's byline.

Well, that didn't take long.

I stir and moan, enough for Books to hear me, but he is lost in thought, still as a statue, looking out the window. He is always up first on the weekends, and he always crawls into bed with me when I wake up.

Not this time.

"Morning," I say.

"Morning," he answers. No movement.

Is he worried about the bookstore? It isn't easy, in these days of digital sales, to run a bookstore, but he has had some success focusing on books that people like to hold in their hands—kids' books, self-help books, some nonfiction—and doing endless promotions with local authors and reading groups to generate interest.

I grab my phone and check my e-mail. It is flooded with Google alerts and breaking-news items about various deaths around the country based on my search terms, data that will take me days to pore through and plug into my algorithms. But one particular article steals my breath away.

It is from a New Orleans paper, the *Times-Picayune*. "FBI Links Local Death to Serial-Killer Spree." It's by that reporter who accosted me by phone. I thought we had a deal, that she would hold the story. Apparently not.

My head drops back on my pillow. I am so screwed. Dwight Ross will have my head for this. And Books...oh, Books.

Books raises the mug to his mouth, takes a sip, lowers it.

"News out of New Orleans this morning," he says. "Don't know if you had a chance to see it yet."

I do a slow burn. He saw it. He's probably read more than a dozen stories online already. He always reads articles involving the Bureau. He may have left the job, but he hasn't lost his interest in all things FBI.

"I was going to tell you," I say.

"Meeting up with college friends, you said. A mini-reunion, you said."

"Books—"

"You left out the part about investigating a slip-and-fall in a shower as part of a serial killer's crime spree."

"Will you please turn around and at least face me?" I say. I get out of bed, feel a stabbing pain in my right ankle; I put too much pressure on it too quickly.

He turns to me, red-faced, his eyes blazing. But it's not anger I see. Anger, I could handle. Anger, I deserve.

The arched eyebrows, the straight line of his mouth. If I had to name it, I'd call it *fear*.

"I was going to tell you this weekend," I say. "Today."

He tries to give me an ironic smile, but he can't manage even that. "We've been together since Friday night. Why the delay?"

I cut the distance between us in half but I don't get too close. I'm still hobbling a bit. "Because I knew it would start a fight."

He nods. "That's quite a standard for honesty you have there. Only tell me things I want to hear."

I drop my head. What can I say? He's right.

He sets his coffee mug on the windowsill. His forehead wrinkles and his shoulders rise. "How—how many times do you have to learn your lesson, Emmy? It wasn't, what, two months after the attack, you could hardly move from your bed, you still had *tubes* sticking out of you, for God's sake, and you were killing yourself trying to solve that rash of deaths of homeless people in Los Angeles. Remember that? I do. I sure do. The doctors had to confiscate your computer."

"I know, I—"

"Oh, and then," he says, circling the room, "*then* you were convinced a bunch of senior citizens in Scottsdale who'd died of natural causes were being murdered. You were barely out of the hospital, your health was precarious at best, and you took pills to stay up at night. Remember how *that* turned out?"

The bad combination of meds that the papers described as an overdose. How could I forget?

"I stand by that work," I say. "Los Angeles? Scottsdale? Those weren't deaths due to natural causes. Those were murders."

"Right, because old people never die naturally," he says. "And homeless people are always so healthy. Of course. They all must have been murdered!" He throws up his hands.

"They *were* murdered," I say. "I just never got the chance to prove it. You may think I'm crazy for doing this work, but I've never heard you say I was *wrong*."

"It doesn't matter if you're right or wrong." He shakes his head. "You swore to me," he says, pounding the nightstand with his fist. "You *swore* to me it was over."

I walk to him and put a hand on his chest. He recoils. I realize he's shaking.

I ask, "If you knew somebody was out there killing people, and the police didn't even know he was doing it, would you do something about it? Or would you do nothing?"

He steps back from me. He opens his mouth as if searching for words. I think it's a legitimate question—the only question. And he seems to think, judging from his reaction, that I am missing the point entirely. That *we* are missing each other entirely.

My phone buzzes, a call. Instinctively, I look at my phone. Then back at Books, who is slowly shaking his head.

"Go on, check it," he says, pushing past me. "I'll be downstairs."

25

THE MAN who calls himself Charlie has time on his hands. He rolls his wheelchair along the red-brick sidewalks of Old Town, enjoying the mild morning air, whiling away the hours until Emmy drives her Jeep from Harrison Bookman's house back to her own. The GPS tracker in his pocket has shown no movement in Emmy's car since it was parked by Bookman's house Friday night, when he planted the device under the fender. He drove by the house once on Saturday just to be sure.

True, he had hoped that, at most, she would spend Friday night at his house and then return home the following morning. He hadn't expected her to spend the entire weekend at his house. But it's not a total loss. Alexandria is quite beautiful, especially Old Town—the scenic waterfront of the Potomac, the historic architecture. The George Washington Masonic National Memorial is his personal favorite.

He hums to himself as he rolls along the empty sidewalk, empty because it is not yet seven in the morning, enjoying the early sparks of dawn as the world stretches and yawns. Down the way, a few places are coming to life—a pastry shop emits delicious aromas of baked goods and fresh coffee, and a waiter is setting up outdoor tables in preparation for brunchers. But Charlie, on the sidewalk near a real estate agent's office, its window filled with photos of *gorgeous* and *charming* and *adorable* properties for sale, is completely alone.

The sidewalk ends in a slope down to pavement, something that most people wouldn't think about. But if you're in a wheelchair, you notice a change in the surface. You are constantly on the alert for anything that might bar your way or force you to rethink your route.

It's an alley, a narrow one between two buildings, wide enough for a single truck to travel through.

Wide enough, as well, for a homeless person sitting against the brick wall, long hair jutting from a maroon baseball cap on backward, wearing a filthy shirt that barely covers his navel, baggy gray trousers, and sandals. An empty McDonald's bag is near him, as are three stray, half-smoked cigarettes.

"Spare change for the train, mister?" he mumbles, straightening up a little.

Charlie uses the remote on his wheelchair to turn toward the homeless man. He would guess that the man is in his mid-thirties, although it isn't possible to discern much of anything given the grunge and foul odor.

"Train fare, mister?" the man says again.

Charlie tilts his head. "That would be an easier sell if you were more presentable, if you really looked like a commuter. From you, I'd expect something more along the lines of spare change for a cup of soup or coffee."

The homeless man blinks, his eyes unfocused, the smell

coming off him horrific. "Please, mister, train fare, mister, please?"

Charlie sighs. "I'll bite. Where are you headed, friend?"

The man looks everywhere but at Charlie. "Met—Metro... station."

"Tell me your destination," says Charlie, "and I'll gladly provide your fare."

A pause. This is bordering on painful.

"Cap—capital," he says.

"Wonderful! Where in the capital, friend?" Charlie looks about. Still nobody nearby. It's been several months for him—in terms of a homeless person, that is. Not since Los Angeles. It was like shooting fish in a barrel out there, but he'd stopped after eleven. A pattern was developing. He couldn't have that. He's checked on the investigation from time to time, and, not to his surprise, the LAPD has lost interest in it, if it ever had any.

The senior citizens in Scottsdale were just as easy, but again he had to abort after nine. He didn't have the patience to wait, and even the elderly didn't die that consistently in one area over one small window of time. Another dreaded pattern.

It's why he branched out. He's thinking bigger now. Spreading out the geography and the time lapse. And his targets now are more meaningful. The homeless and elderly—their life spans weren't that long anyway. What he's doing now is having far more impact.

And now he's perfected his technique. Now he has an ace in the hole.

Now he's ensured he will *never* be caught.

"The...White House, White—" says the homeless man, doing his best. "White House."

Charlie can't suppress a small burst of laughter. "Lunch

with the president?" he asks. "A meeting with the Joint Chiefs?"

Oh, it's tempting.

Charlie prides himself on his discipline. He lives it, day in and day out. It's what makes him different. He has thrived on it. He has never, ever acted impulsively, not once, not even when he was commissioned, *especially* when he was commissioned. Everything always carefully, meticulously planned, every detail considered, every small step executed with precision.

But he can live a little, can't he?

"There is no such thing as unselfish charity," Charlie says. "Pure fiction. Charity is, in fact, quite selfish. People don't give charity to help the recipients. They do it to feel good about themselves. And all the while, we grow weaker and slower as a society. Wouldn't you agree, friend?"

The man seems to shiver. His eyes still won't connect with Charlie's.

"Come closer," Charlie says. "You want money, right?"

The man comes to life again, leans forward and positions his legs to rise as Charlie reaches into the pouch at his waist.

"Th-thanks, yeah, thanks, mister," says the homeless man.

When the man has risen enough to expose his midsection, Charlie fires the darts. They strike the soft flesh of his stomach. He immediately convulses from the electric shock, spit shooting from his mouth, his eyes rolling back, and then falls flat.

Charlie lifts himself from the wheelchair and falls to the ground, still holding the trigger down, still delivering the electric charge to his helpless, convulsing friend. In one fluid, practiced motion, he sets down the Taser, throws the plastic bag over the man's head like a cowboy's lasso, pins one side of the bag down, and wraps it taut over the man's stunned face.

Then he picks up the Taser with his free hand in case he needs to give another jolt.

The man, almost completely immobile, utterly helpless, tries to suck in frantic breaths, drawing the plastic into his mouth and out.

"This is not personal," Charlie says. "I'm doing everyone a favor." He looks away from the man's bulging, desperate eyes. It really *isn't* personal. It's for the best. This man is nothing but a drain on society.

Or he was, at least.

When it's over, quicker than Charlie would have expected—he might have had a heart attack before suffocating, hard to say—Charlie removes the plastic bag, stuffs it back in his pouch, takes the darts from the man's stomach, and climbs back into the wheelchair.

He uses the remote to reverse his wheelchair, ready to shout, *Help, someone, help, this man needs help!*, should anyone happen to be strolling along the sidewalk.

But the street remains empty. He wheels himself forward again, back along the sidewalk, recognizing the recklessness of what he has just done but relishing the minor indulgence, silently congratulating the world on one more step forward. The weekend hasn't been a total waste.

26

I FIND Books in the kitchen, washing the dishes from dinner last night. I'm about to walk over to him but decide against it.

He tilts his head, his back still to me.

"You didn't answer my question," I say. "If you knew somebody was running around killing people and nobody even knew it was happening, would you do nothing, or—"

"I didn't answer the question," he says, putting down the dish in his hand, "because it's beside the point."

"How—*how* could that *ever* be beside the point?"

Books turns to me and peers into my eyes. He's squinting as if he's searching for something, but I don't know what. "You know what's funny?" he says. "You were the one who opened my eyes to the fact that there was more to life than the job. It turns out I've learned that lesson from someone who hasn't learned it herself."

"There can't be room for the job and for us?"

"Oh, forget about *us* for a second." He waves his hands. "What about *you*, Em? You're not even taking care of yourself.

Twice you went back to these maniacal wild-goose chases and almost crashed and burned. Twice you promised you'd stop. And here you are again. You show up on Friday nights looking like you haven't slept all week. You're not doing any of the things you promised to do."

"I'm doing fine."

His face falls and his shoulders slump in disappointment and pain. Books doesn't wear those emotions well. He's the stoic type. It hits me now as it never has before: I have hurt him. I have hurt *us*.

His eyes return to mine. He says slowly, softly, "How's therapy going?"

I bite my lip.

"Don't." A minute shake of his head. "I can't stomach another lie. I know you stopped going months ago. I talked to the receptionist at Dr. Bakalis's office. That's right," he goes on, steel in his voice, seeing my reaction, "I did, I pretended to be your assistant calling for an appointment, and she told me you hadn't been there in months. Months, Emmy." He brings a hand to his forehead, pushes back his hair. "Months."

I step away, lean against the refrigerator for support.

Books lets out a deep sigh, as if preparing for something. I hold my breath.

"You're on a downward spiral, Emily. And I love you, and I'll be there with you every step of the way. I'm all in, if you're willing to let me in. Whatever it takes. But you can't live in denial. You can't do God knows what all week and then show up on the weekend and pretend—to me, to yourself—that everything's okay."

I let out air slowly, a tremble working through me. "I can make adjustments," I say. "I can. I will. But I can't just turn away and let this monster roam the country killing people. I can't just walk away from this job."

He stares at me a long time. "I did," he says.

"I never asked you to leave the Bureau."

"It's not a question of—" He shakes his head and almost laughs, although there is no trace of amusement in his look. "I know you didn't. I did it on my own. Because I realized that the job was swallowing me whole. That I was going to wind up at the end of my life sitting in a rocking chair with nothing to show for myself but a bunch of solves. That if I stayed there, I'd never share my life with anyone, never have kids, never travel, never take time to enjoy the world. I realized that there would always be bad people doing bad things, but I didn't have to solve every problem. I had the right to a life of my own."

"I...I..." I just can't let this go. How can I? I know in my heart that a monster is out there and that I can catch him—that I'm the only one willing to make the *effort* to catch him. How can I let more people die?

Books winces, closes one eye. "I just got it," he says. "Boy, am I slow...I guess it took this"—he draws a finger back and forth between us—"for me to see it."

"See what?"

"This *is* the life you want." He says the words like he's delivering a eulogy, eyes down, face drawn, posture defeated. "Working all hours, day and night, obsessing during the week and taking a breather with me on the weekends. I'm your break in the action. I'm your weekend getaway."

His eyes rise up to meet mine. It lies there before us, a big ugly truth spreading like some horror-show slime, threatening to engulf us both.

I've never loved anyone like I love Books; I've never felt

such an effortless connection. I've never met anyone who could open me up and flip on the switches. I love the way he cuts to the brutal truth. The spark when he touches me. How he's so sure of who he is and what he wants.

"I love you" is all I say, a lump forming in my throat, because I know I'm saying it differently than I usually do. We both know it.

I rush to him, wrap my arms around him. He wraps his arms around me too. His body starts to tremble. I have never seen or heard Harrison Bookman cry.

He turns his head, brings his mouth to my forehead. "Please give it up," he whispers to me. "Please stop the chase."

I have lied to Books, both by omission and flat-out, for too long now. I can't do it anymore. He deserves better—so, so much better. I suddenly realize, like a slap to my face, how selfish I've been to do this to Books.

"I will always love you," I say. I force myself to move away from him, the tears streaming down my face, my body quivering. I remove the engagement ring from my finger and place it on the kitchen counter next to him.

I gather my things and go to the door, crying into my purse, then onto my keys, my hands shaking so hard I can't even put the strap of my pocketbook over my shoulder.

"Emmy." Books, his voice flat, drained of emotion. Altogether different than it usually is. I turn to him.

But he is not looking at me. He squeezes his eyes shut. "I'm not supposed to—but I—I can't not tell you..."

I wipe my face. This is something else entirely.

He lets out a sigh and opens his eyes, but he's still looking far off, not at me.

"The Bureau thinks someone's leaking secrets on the Citizen David investigation."

How would he—why would he—

But it comes to me quickly. Moriarty. The director thinks of Books like a son. Begged him not to leave the Bureau.

"I know," I manage.

"They—they think it's you, Emmy."

I put the strap of my bag over my shoulder. Take one last long look at the man I love.

"I know," I say, and I walk out the door.

27

I SIT at my desk as dusk falls, as the lights begin to go out on another weekend, trying to do my job, trying to push aside everything else and keep banging away at my search for a serial killer nobody else thinks exists, knee-deep in the irony that this hunt, this project, was so important to me that I was willing to lose Books over it but now I can't focus on it because all I can do is think of him.

I stare at data. I stare at theories about serial killers scribbled on sheets papering the walls of my home office. I stare at article after article on my computer screen reporting recent deaths that appear to be accidental or natural or suicides.

I stare but I don't see. The words rush past me like landscape on a highway drive. The only thing that holds my focus, gripping it like a boa constrictor and refusing to let go, is the photo of Books in a simple silver frame on my desk.

He hadn't wanted me to take the picture. He was unshowered, his hair sticking up, wearing a flannel shirt over sweatpants, and holding a cup of coffee. It was a lazy Sunday morning just like this one had been before it went down in flames like the *Hindenburg*.

It isn't fair, I tell myself. *If a child was drowning and he asked you to choose between rescuing the child and marrying him, would you let the child die?*

No, of course not, I answer myself, anger and bitterness gripping me.

But what if there was a child drowning every day? What if all you did, every waking moment of every day, was save drowning children? Would it be fair to expect him to stick around while you're wrapped up in your little world, throwing him crumbs of attention only when you can spare a moment?

No, of course not. Tears blur my vision.

Another e-mail lands in my in-box. Another inquiry from a reporter, greedily latching onto the story in today's New Orleans *Times-Picayune* that there might be another monster out there eluding detection, and do I have any comment, is this another Graham, has the FBI assembled a task force—

My phone beeps. A text from Dwight Ross telling me to be in his office at noon tomorrow. He saw the article out of New Orleans, of course. It rippled across the internet in hours. This is all he needs. If he wants to run me out of the Bureau, this will be more than enough.

I should care about that.

And then my phone starts buzzing. If it's Ross, I'm not picking up. He can yell at me tomorrow.

But it's not. It's my mother. Right. She would be done with her daily happy hour right about now. This is when she usually calls me, when she's nursing a slight buzz, when her emotions are most raw, when she misses me, her only living daughter, the one she was never really able to relate to, the odd duck who was so different than her cheerleader-popular-girl twin sister.

"Hi, Mom."

"Hi, sweetie." A puffing sound. The faint noise of automobile traffic. She never smokes inside her condo, only on the balcony and usually, these days, only after drinks with her other tanned, retired friends. "And how was your weekend?" she sings.

Well, let's review. I lost the only man I've ever loved, and my off-the-record investigation is now known to my superiors at the Bureau. Tomorrow's gonna be even better—that's when they'll fire me! Give me another week or two, and I'll probably be indicted for leaking sensitive information. Other than that, things are great!

"It was fine," I say.

"Are you still at Harrison's?"

I've never understood why she likes to call him by his first name. "No, I'm home."

"I don't know why you don't just marry him. Or at least move in with him. Don't you think it's time you stopped fooling around?"

I touch my face. "You're right." The easiest path with my mother is swift surrender.

But she won't let me surrender. "Listen, kiddo, once you find the person you want to spend the rest of your life with, you want the rest of your life to begin as soon as possible. Take it from me."

Or from Billy Crystal in *When Harry Met Sally.* My mother's advice usually comes from old movies or country songs. Next she's going to tell me that I've got to know when to hold 'em, know when to fold 'em.

I seem to know when to walk away and when to run. Just ask Books.

"I'm serious now, Em. Listen to your mother. It's time to marry that man before he gets tired of waiting."

I grip the phone so tightly that if I had any strength right now, it would burst into pieces. "That's good advice," I manage.

"Take it from me," she says, and I know she's not going to quote some old movie or song. This time, she's going to speak from personal experience.

"You don't want to be alone," she says.

28

BOOKS STRUGGLES to stay alert on the dark, predawn drive to Maryland. He's normally a morning person, but when you haven't slept the previous night, when you tossed and turned and paced back and forth and watched snippets of wretched movies and passed your eyes over the latest must-read novel, getting out of bed in the morning feels like starting a ten-mile run after having just completed a marathon.

He can't focus. He was halfway through his first cup of coffee this morning before he realized he was drinking coffee-flavored hot water, that he had forgotten to put coffee grounds in the coffeemaker.

A cup of coffee without coffee. Books without Emmy.

He parks his vehicle on the curb behind the black SUV with Secret Service agents inside. The kitchen light is on in the imposing brick Victorian. Bill Moriarty is a creature of habit, and apparently nothing has changed since Books left the Bureau. The director still leaves for work at five thirty a.m., and Books would bet his modest pension that right now, Moriarty is having the single cup of coffee he allows himself along with a bowl of cornflakes lightly dusted with a sugar substitute from a blue packet.

Books waves to the agents, including Dez, the director's head of security, and walks up the cobblestone path to the house. The FBI director, showered and scrubbed and dressed in a suit and tie, greets him at the door.

"Good God, Harry, what happened to *you?*"

This takes Books back to his first case with the new FBI director. When he told Moriarty that he went by the name Books, the director seemed amused and stuck with Harry for a time. When Moriarty finally started calling him Books, Books felt like he had passed some test.

"Long night," says Books. "This won't take long. Hi, Betsy."

Books waves to the director's wife, now wheelchair-bound after a stroke five or six years ago that left her brain intact but her legs weakened enough that she cannot reliably walk. Bill built a ground-floor master bedroom and installed an elevator lift on the stairs.

Betsy is up at this ungodly hour because this is probably the only time she sees her husband all day. She waves at Books, then retreats to the kitchen. This is not the first time someone has stopped by at dawn on official business, and she knows enough to withdraw on those occasions.

Bill directs Books to the sitting room, the kind of room that children would not be allowed to play in, with elaborate crown molding on the walls and custom shelving, photos and awards and trophies everywhere. Bill has lived in this house for over thirty years. He has been married to Betsy for over thirty years. He has been in public service for over thirty years. Books feels a twinge of envy for the director's stability, the simplicity with which he has lived his impressive life.

Before they sit, Books says, "Don't fire Emmy."

Moriarty reacts the way he usually reacts to the unexpected, by processing the information with a noncommittal expression. He taught that to Books, once upon a time. *Never let them see your first reaction. Don't let them know what you think until you want them to know what you think.*

"I know she embarrassed the Bureau with her side investigation, the New Orleans story," says Books. "I know she broke protocol. I know it's grounds for dismissal. But think about what she's doing, Bill. She's trying to track down a killer." Books raises his hands as they both sit down. "Whether she's on a wild-goose chase or not, her heart's in the right place."

Moriarty, his right leg crossed over his left, doesn't look well. Running the FBI takes its toll on a person. All the bad things you stop, nobody notices. The one time you miss, the single thing that slips through the elaborate filter created to protect the American people, everyone blames you.

It's not just the hair loss, Books thinks, not just the added layer of wrinkles beneath his puffy eyes, not just the added weight in his midsection. It's his overall look beneath that regal bearing, something that Books might be able to discern better than most—this job is slowly breaking him down.

"Tell me something," he says to Books. "You've seen most of the evidence on the leak investigation. Do you think Emmy's the leaker?"

Books does not want to answer. Yes, he does think Emmy's the leaker. He thinks Emmy is privately rooting for Citizen David, who seems to share Emmy's passion for liberal causes and who has thus far managed to do everything he's done without physically harming another human being.

Add that to the fact that the reporter with the inside scoop is Emmy's good friend Shaindy, not to mention the photos of them together last Friday at that bar—

And then there's the fact that when Books confronted Emmy yesterday, when he told her that she was under suspicion for leaking, she didn't deny it or even act surprised—

Yes, he thinks Emmy's the leaker.

He doesn't say anything, but his nonanswer is an answer.

"You'd rather we indicted her?" asks the director.

Books thinks about it, puts it together. He should have figured it out sooner. "You're saying firing her would be a replacement for a criminal charge," says Books. "She gets her punishment, but it's not based on her leaking information—it's based on this unauthorized side investigation she was doing. A nice, quiet administrative termination. The Bureau avoids the public embarrassment about one of its own leaking to a reporter."

"And your fiancée avoids prison," Moriarty adds. "She gets to marry her wonderful bookseller and have a nice life without a felony record."

Those last words slam into Books like a bus, but now is not the time. He has to sort this out. He hasn't played it out this way. It hadn't occurred to him that being fired by the Bureau might be the best thing that ever happened to Emmy. But would *she* see it like that?

"This...isn't my decision to make," he says. "It's Emmy's."

"No, it's mine," says the director. "We can't lay out this choice for Emmy. She doesn't know that we're targeting her in the leak investigation."

Books nods and breaks eye contact. *She does now.* He shouldn't have told her, but, he rationalizes, she already seemed to know.

"We have to decide," says the director with a heavy sigh, "whether to fire her now, for her own good, or let her stay on, continue to leak information to that *Post* reporter, dig a deeper hole for herself, and go to prison."

Books doesn't know what he would do if he were the director, but he knows what he's hoping for. Emmy would hate to lose her job, but Emmy being in prison is unthinkable. "So... what are you going to do?" he asks.

"I'm going to delegate, that's what I'm going to do," says Moriarty. "I'm leaving it up to Dwight Ross."

29

THE MAN who calls himself Charlie is outside the door of Emmy Dockery's apartment. The infrared scanner confirms that the neighbor across the hall isn't home; there's no sign of life. The hairpins—crude but effective, easy to transport, easy to explain if discovered—are all he needs for Emmy's rudimentary pin-and-tumbler lock.

He opens her door with his gloved right hand, wheels himself in manually with the same hand. Looks to his right and sees the security alarm on the wall, the light flashing red, wanting to blare out a high-pitched whine. But it doesn't, because the Repressor Ultimate in Charlie's left hand, the handheld UHF transmitter, is blinding the master receiver and scrambling the signal, telling the wall unit that everything is fine, nothing to see here, stop trying to talk to the master receiver. It shouldn't take long for the wall unit to agree to stay quiet, ten or fifteen seconds at most.

Once, in Dubai, when his target was a vacationing Kuwaiti sheikh who was becoming too friendly with interests hostile to the United States, it took more than sixty seconds for the alarm to shut itself off. It was, at the time, the longest minute of his life.

This time, after twenty seconds, the wall unit is quiet, the light a solid red again, as if nobody had ever opened that front door.

He closes his eyes and inhales deeply. Everyone has a smell. He wants to know her scent. All that returns is a vaguely musty, sweaty odor overlaid by strong coffee. But that's okay; that's a scent, and a perfect one for Emmy.

"You don't wear perfume," he whispers. "Of course you don't. My lady wouldn't bother with such frivolities."

He opens his eyes and looks around. The place is dark. Drapes are pulled over the window in the main living space. The kitchen looks like the kitchen of someone who favors a microwave over a stove. The living room is carpeted, with a stationary bike and a treadmill for her extensive physical therapy. No artwork on the walls. Simple furniture. Emmy is all business. He wouldn't have her any other way.

He moves down the hall. A bathroom on the left. Two bedrooms, facing each other, on the end. One has a door that's swung open. There is a cheap full-length mirror nailed to it, allowing Charlie to see all of himself, which, he realizes, he rarely gets to do.

He works the remote on the wheelchair, rolls up to the mirror, and takes a hard look at his overall appearance. The unshaven face, the shiny scar shaped like a crescent moon near his right eye, shoulder-length hair pulled back into a ponytail, the camouflage hat and army fatigue jacket. He looks at the wheelchair too. With the American-flag decal on the leather armrest and the bumper sticker reading RANGERS LEAD THE

WAY on the bottom shroud of the wheelchair, he is the quintessential wounded veteran.

He looks past the mirror into the bedroom, obviously the one she sleeps in; there are clothes everywhere, the bed unmade. He turns to the other bedroom, surely the home office where Emmy—

He draws a breath. To call this a home office would not be doing it justice. This is more like command central. Two computers, a desktop and a laptop, on an L-shaped desk. The walls papered with notes and flow charts and articles. He wheels himself inside, thankful that it's hardwood floor and not carpet so no tracks will be left.

He wants to review everything on these walls, but first things first.

He removes his equipment and quickly gets to work, downloading everything from her computers, using his spyware to bypass her password protection, and uploading tracer software.

Soon he will have all her data, and with the software, he will see everything she does on these computers.

He checks his GPS tracker to confirm that Emmy is still in DC. "Now I have some time to get acquainted with you, my dear Emmy," he whispers.

30

I SIT in the conference room like a prisoner awaiting sentencing, my eyes bloodshot and heavy, the beginning of a cold stuffing me up, a dull ringing in my ears.

The turn of the knob startles me, even though I'm expecting him.

Dwight Ross enters without a word and takes a seat across from me at the walnut table. He stares at me, letting the silence ramp up the tension. Maybe he thinks that if he just stares at me, I'll start blurting out apologies, begging for forgiveness, throwing myself on his mercy. If that's what he's waiting for, he's going to wait a long time.

"You know why you're here," he says finally.

I nod.

"You admit you opened an unauthorized investigation?"

"I admit that when I initially reached out to the New Orleans PD, I didn't specify that I was doing so on my own. I gave the impression that I was working in my official capacity. I cleared that up once I got there," I say.

"But you were told that when you were on your little personal crusades, your hunts for leprechauns and fairy princesses and serial killers, you had to make it clear that you weren't acting in an official capacity. You agreed to that."

"I did, yes."

"And when you initially contacted New Orleans, you *didn't* make that clear."

"Not initially, no."

He nods. This is going fine so far. He's making his case against me, step by step.

"In the past, have you contacted other local law enforcement agencies and given them the impression that you were acting on behalf of the Bureau?"

I wonder if he knows the answer to that already. I wonder if he's had a look at my personal e-mail account. But it doesn't matter. I'm too burned out to lie.

"Yes," I say.

"So New Orleans wasn't an isolated incident?"

"I think I just answered that question."

He points at me. "Talking back isn't going to help you here, Dockery. You embarrassed the Bureau. You embarrassed me. You made it look like I'm not in control of my own people."

"Is that what this is about?"

He draws back. Licks his lips, shakes his head, then shows me a nasty grin. "You really are a piece of work, aren't you?"

"I do my job and I do it well," I say. "And on the side, instead of reading books or watching TV or training for marathons, I try to stop serial killers. I don't ask for any help. I do it on my own. Yes, I have misrepresented myself. I admit it. I have occasionally given people the impression that I'm working on a Bureau investigation so they'll cooperate with me. I won't do it again. That's a promise. It'll never happen again. But I won't apologize."

"You *will* apologize," he says. "And do you know why?"

I won't give him the pleasure of a response.

"You'll apologize," he says, "because you need the Bureau's resources to do what you do in your spare time. Without us, you're out of the serial-killer-chasing business."

Maybe it's the sleep deprivation or maybe it's everything that just happened with Books, but I will not grovel for this asshole. He's going to fire me or he isn't.

Ross chuckles. He gets out of his chair and starts moving around the room. "You know what I think?" he says. "I think you got really lucky once with Graham. It made you feel special. It made you feel smart. Everyone admires and pities you because you got all cut up by that creep, but the truth is, getting attacked was the best thing that ever happened to you. Every day, we are all reminded of how brave and smart you are.

"And now? Now it's like a drug. You need it again. You want everyone to think you're special again. But you're not special, Dockery. You're a freak with no people skills who makes herself crazy looking high and low for serial killers who don't exist. You stare at a computer day and night because you know that nobody likes you, and no man would want you."

I look away, holding it all in. He's baiting me. He wants me to blow up. He wants me to explode so he can add *insubordination, erratic behavior,* and anything else he can come up with to the list of my administrative violations.

"Resign," he says, coming up behind me. "Make it easy on yourself."

I put my hands on the table, bracing myself, my skin crawling.

"Never," I say.

"Exactly!" He claps his hands together once. "You can't do it. You can't wean off the drug. This job is all you have. And since I could fire you without thinking twice about it, that means *I'm* all you have."

I close my eyes as he stands behind me. If he touches me, I'm going to deck him.

But he won't. He's torturing me plenty without laying a finger on me.

"This is your last chance. So here are the new rules, Dockery. First off, you come to work every day. None of this crap about how efficient you are at home. No more special treatment for the poor lady who got her face cut up. You show up every day.

"Second, I want a cup of Starbucks on my desk, piping hot, every morning by eight o'clock. You're going to walk it in, you're going to smile, and you're going to say, 'Good morning, Mr. Assistant Director.' I will make a point of saying the coffee's not necessary. And you will make a point of saying that you appreciate how understanding I've been, that it's the least you can do."

My body trembles, but I don't speak. *Focus on the positive—he's not firing you. You're still in the game. That's all that matters. You can deal with Dwight Ross later.*

"I'm sure I'll come up with more as we go along," he says. "Now go back to your cubicle and get to work like a good little numbers girl."

31

THE MAN who calls himself Charlie reads the data and notes on Emmy's wall, his emotions going from admiration to envy to horror. Useless feelings, all of them, but he can't help it as he reads on and on.

The list of homeless people in Los Angeles from a year ago, all of them declared dead of natural causes.

Next, a list of senior citizens in Scottsdale, again all deaths attributed to natural or accidental causes.

He thinks back to the timing of those murders. This would have been while she was still recovering, probably while she was still in the hospital.

What no other law enforcement agency was able to do, Emmy had done from her hospital bed.

He hadn't heard a word of it in the media. He'd had no idea that anyone had connected these deaths in LA and Scottsdale and saw them as murders.

But you did, Emmy. Did no one believe you?

Apparently not. Still, it burns inside him. She has followed everything he's done.

He checks his GPS tracker to confirm that Emmy isn't on her way back home. Then he keeps reading.

The next group of victims is listed on a series of papers descending to the carpet. At the top of the list is the most recent—Nora Connolley in New Orleans. It's been all over the news this weekend, Emmy's visit to New Orleans, her theory that Nora Connolley's death is part of a larger murder spree.

Below her, Laura Berg from Vienna, Virginia, and next to her, Detective Joe Halsted, whom Emmy had coaxed into investigating Laura's death as a homicide and whom Charlie had killed as well. Then heading vertically downward again to victims in Indianapolis, Atlanta, Charleston, Dallas. Every victim accompanied by articles on his or her death, police reports, profiles of the victims, Emmy's handwritten notes.

She missed a couple of victims, but how could she *not* miss one or two? He can't believe she found *these* victims. How many stories of death did she have to sift through on a daily basis to find these people?

And even if she missed the occasional victim, she has seen more than enough. Enough to construct a pattern and a possible profile of the killer.

The victim profile:

- Lives alone
- Single-story home
- House up for sale or recently purchased—video/photos of home online
- Attached garage or detached but private access
- Within two blocks of public transportation

- Nonprofit/volunteer/advocacy work for disabled, homeless, elderly, terminally ill

The offender's methodology:

- Subdues individuals away from home—why?
- Subdues them by injecting something with needle (puncture wounds on torsos)
- Drives victims to their homes (why?) in their cars, not his (why?)
- Takes public transportation back to his car at abduction site

The offender profile, less fact-based and more theoretical:

- Skilled and disciplined
- Medical training? Military special-ops background?
- Doesn't like people in need or the people who care for them
- Doesn't like stairs
- Doesn't like his vehicle being seen
- Either (1) he's frail and infirm and so self-loathing that he lashes out at those like him or their caregivers, or (2) he's taken Darwinism to the extreme and wants to eradicate the weak in our society
- Or both

He feels ripped open, exposed, burned.

He slams his fists down on the arms of the wheelchair over and over like a spoiled child, sweat pouring into his eyes, his body on fire, the useless anger consuming him. *All of this work, all of the care I put into it, all the discipline, the methodology, was foolproof if properly executed, and I did properly execute it, I left behind no trace, I did everything right, but*

*she figured it out anyway, my motives, my design, even a par-
tial profile—*

Then everything goes dark. Utter silence, a complete vac-
uum, no space or time, pure nothingness.

Blackness. Everything seeping out, his body still, the dis-
tracting emotions dissolving into mist.

And then clarity.

Only the worst of fools will fool themselves. There is no
getting around it. Emmy won this battle. No, she didn't pin it
all the way down, and she never, ever would have pinned it
on *him*. But she got close, and *close* is close enough to stop his
work.

"Congratulations, my lady," he whispers. "Round one goes
to you."

He wheels himself over and removes his equipment from
her computers. Everything in them has been downloaded; all
his spyware has been uploaded.

He will need to regroup, assess his failures, come up with a
whole new plan.

He shakes himself, glances at the bulletin board next to the
computers.

Then suddenly focuses.

Nothing on this small corkboard about serial killers. Nothing about the homeless or sick or single-story homes or faking
accidental deaths. No, the notes stuck to this bulletin board
concern another case altogether, one he's read about in the papers.

Citizen David. The crusader who blows up buildings and
hacks the websites of those who do not subscribe to his inane,
politically correct ideology.

"Citizen David," he mumbles.

He closes his eyes and sits completely still, ideas flashing through his brain like lightning, the adrenaline coursing through him. His hands grip the sides of the wheelchair like he's bracing for a hurricane—

He opens his eyes.

"Emmy," he says, "I'm rather looking forward to round two."

32

I OPEN the door to my apartment as the alarm blares out its shrill warning call. I type in the pass code, and the alarm settles down with a couple of beeps, the light a solid green.

I walk in, flip on the overhead light, drop my work bag, and feel a shudder pass through me. I hold my breath, standing still, listening.

A sound? A movement? A different smell?

I don't know. All I know is that something is telling me that there is a stranger inside my apartment.

"H-hello?" I whisper, the sudden jolt of fear weakening my voice.

And then it comes, as it has so many times since my attack: My heart throbbing like a volcano about to erupt. Fire engulfing my chest and cascading down my limbs. My breaths ragged and desperate, as if I'm walled off and can breathe only through a tiny hole.

My legs buckle and I fall to the floor. I plant my hands in the carpet, grip the fibers as if I might slide off the world if I don't hold on. Convinced, absolutely certain to my core, that in my peripheral vision will appear the looming shadow of a stranger coming to hurt me, his feet stopping just short of my face.

If I hold still, I can breathe. *Hold still and you can breathe.*

But nothing is still; the lights are dimming and flashing, my body is scorched and sweating, the furniture is dancing around me, the ground is quaking, and I know he's coming, I know that the stranger will stand before me with a creepy smile, dead eyes, and the glint of a scalpel wet with my blood.

You know what I'm going to do to you, the stranger will say, *and you can't stop me.*

I squeeze my eyes shut and focus on breathing: *Close your eyes and breathe, close your eyes and breathe, close your eyes and…*

When I open my eyes, I am shivering, wet from cold sweat. I suck in delicious oxygen and crawl to the living room, past the exercise equipment, to the couch with the quilt my grandmother knit for me when I was a baby. I wrap myself in it and sit on the floor against the couch.

There is nobody here, I tell myself as I shake like a rattle.

Usually that's enough. It's like coming down from a nightmare, awakening and realizing it was all a trick of your mind, a bad dream.

But…it's different this time.

Nobody is *here,* I think to myself. *But somebody* was *here.*

I get to my feet and walk on unsteady legs through my small apartment, turning on every light as I go, half expecting to find clothes thrown everywhere in my bedroom—more than usual, that is—drawers pulled open, file folders dumped, mattresses overturned, an apartment ransacked.

But nothing looks disturbed. My home office is exactly as it was, the wallpaper of notes, the computers, even the chair left just as I always leave it, tucked all the way in under the desk.

The alarm, I recall, was on when I came home. Nobody knows my pass code. If someone had come in, the alarm would have sounded. And if someone managed to get past it, someone with the technological know-how to do something like that, the alarm would have been disarmed, a solid green, not armed with a solid red as it was when I entered.

Don't be an idiot, Emmy. Nobody was here. Nothing has been taken. It wasn't some sixth sense talking to you. It was just another panic attack.

Shaken, I pour myself a glass of water, sit down at my computer, and begin my nightly ritual of combing through recent deaths deemed accidental or natural.

I work until three in the morning, breaking only for a microwaved meal and a half an hour on the stationary bike. I leave every light on in the apartment and drag my couch against the front door before falling on my bed, exhausted and depleted.

When the alarm on my clock radio goes off, I feel like I haven't slept a wink.

33

"MORNING, ROBERTA," I say as I head toward Dwight Ross's office holding a piping-hot cup of Starbucks.

Roberta, her gray hair pulled back and her eyes staring at me over her glasses, says, "What is that?"

"Just want to show my appreciation for everything the assistant director's done for me," I sing, suppressing my gag reflex.

"Mmm-hmm." Roberta's a saint for working with Dwight Ross. And she's sharp too. She isn't fooled by the ruse. Nobody in the building likes Dwight as much as I'm pretending to.

I walk into his office, and he calls out, "Oh, Emmy, that's not necessary," loud enough for Roberta to hear. But when I set the coffee down on his immaculate desk, he turns his wrist and taps on his watch. "I said *eight,* not eight oh three," he says just above a whisper. "And it better be hot."

One of these days, I promise myself, *I'm going to put hemlock in that cup.*

I go to my cubicle and boot up my computer. Other analysts begin arriving within minutes.

"Hey, lady!" says Bonita Sexton. She has the cubicle next to me and is part of my team on Citizen David; she's grown accustomed to working with me primarily by phone or e-mail, not in person, during my extended absence.

"Hey, Rabbit," I say. Her nickname's due to her vegan diet, I think, or maybe her diminutive size. She was born in the early sixties to radical hippies in Chicago and still has it in her blood. She doesn't wear makeup, leaves her hair long and straight, wears loose-fitting clothes. She even drives an electric car. She raised two boys as a single parent; one of them is an aspiring poet and part-time barista at a Starbucks in New Haven, and the other is a social worker in Tampa.

If you saw Sexton on the street, you'd assume she was a member of a commune, not an FBI employee, but she's held this job for nearly thirty years. She's always said that she stays for the benefits and the health insurance, because her older son has lupus. Yeah, that might be part of it, but her son is twenty-seven now and has his own insurance, and preexisting conditions are—for the moment, anyway—a thing of the past, and yet I don't see her going anywhere. No, for Bonita Sexton, it's about right and wrong, fair and unfair, and there is nothing she'd rather do than chase white-collar rip-off artists through webs of offshore bank accounts or track cargo shipments searching for human traffickers.

"The boss lady's here!" says Eric Pullman. He's the third part of our three-person team on Citizen David, the youngest of the trio. Pully is a computer geek's computer geek. He has the pallor of someone who spends more time in front of electronic devices than outdoors. The hair on his head could best be compared to a mop. He has a long, skinny neck and over-size ears. Put him in a roomful of people, and he'll stand in a corner and stare at the wall or pretend to be on his cell phone. Put him in front of a computer with a load of data, and he will make sense of it before you can say, *By the way, I have a brush if you need it.*

We are the analysts. If the special agents are the movie stars, wearing pancake makeup, moving authoritatively around the stage, and talking about search warrants and high-risk ap-prehensions, then we are the stage crew behind the curtain, quirky and unsightly, a band of talented misfits who use terms like *anomaly detection, logistic regression,* and *inductively gen-erated sequential patterns.*

"We figured you were in hot water after the New Orleans article," says Pully, leaning over the cubicle opposite mine, his chin perched on the divider.

"You think I'm *not?*" I say. "This is what we call a last chance."

"So Dwit spared you, huh?" says Rabbit. She is no fan of Dwight Ross, whom she has dubbed "Dwit the Twit."

"Anyway, I'm back in here full-time," I say, "so you'll have to get used to me again."

"Shit," says Pully, "what cubicle am I gonna use to surf porn now?"

I drop my head. "No sex jokes until I've had my coffee, Pully."

"Who's joking?"

Rabbit, who seems annoyed, says, "Did anyone remind Dwit that the last time you supposedly went rogue, you found a serial killer nobody else even knew existed?"

My crew is protective of me. We are protective of one an-other.

"Anyway," I say, shifting the topic. "Give me a status on our favorite domestic terrorist, cherished team members."

"Ladies first," says Pully, nodding to Rabbit, amusement in his eyes.

"Since when do you have manners?"

"I'm going to start being deferential to my elders."

Rabbit puts a hand over her face. "Eric, honey, never remind a woman of her age." She looks up and addresses my question. "Tollway cameras, so far, are a dead end."

Rabbit has been working the data captured from tollway cameras on the routes taken between the bombing sites, hoping for matches on license plates. If she finds any, she will cross-reference them through criminal history and countless other filters. It's a needle in a haystack. In fact, it's worse than a needle in a haystack, since there probably isn't a needle to find—Citizen David presumably stayed off the highways to avoid this very issue.

But that's what we do. We run down every lead.

Pullman comes around to my cubicle. "Social media hasn't produced anything good," he says. "Overwhelmingly positive. That's the problem. Everybody likes this guy."

That is the problem. Usually, with a terrorist act, the vast majority of social media reaction is negative, and we look primarily for those few responses that are positive or at least vaguely supportive. But Citizen David has been targeting businesses that people love to hate, like banks and fast-food companies that mistreat animals, and he's done it without killing anyone. The ratio of positive to negative reaction on social media is exponentially higher in this case.

"Let me take a look at your algorithms," I say.

"Ooh, I love it when you look at my algorithms," he says.

I glance at Sexton, who forces a smile that seems to say, *This is what I've had to deal with while you've been gone.* But we both know Pullman is a top-notch analyst. He just needs to get laid occasionally.

"Still thinking Manhattan is the next target?" she asks me.

"Don't you think so? I thought you agreed."

"I do," she says. "But just as a hunch. You told the team that's where he was headed next."

I shrug. "I give them my best guess. If I'm wrong, I look dumb."

Her eyebrows rise. "You'll look more than just dumb," she says. "You'll take the blame."

I wave her off, but she's right. If Citizen David strikes somewhere other than Manhattan, people won't have to look very far for the person who made the wrong call.

34

ROBERTA, Dwight Ross's secretary, lights up. "Books!" she says. She removes her glasses, comes around her desk, and wraps Books in a big hug.

"Good to see you, my lady."

"Well, you are a sight for sore eyes. Coming back to us?"

Books shakes his head. "A special assignment. Temporary."

She pulls back from him. "Well, they're waiting for you in there," she says. "You don't want to be late."

"They?" He thought he was meeting only with Dwight.

"They," she says, curling her lips with displeasure.

He knocks on the door and walks in. Dwight Ross is at his desk. Sitting on his desk, a bit more casually than Books would expect, is a blond woman in a sharp gray suit with muted yellow pinstripes.

"Good morning," Books says.

Dwight Ross gestures to the woman, who's now climbing off his desk. "Harrison Bookman, this is Special Assistant Director Elizabeth Ashland."

She crosses the room with her hand out. "Pleased to meet you," she says. She has a strong handshake.

"Call me Books," he says, though she didn't call him anything. "And I should call you..."

She looks him over, blinks. "You can call me Special Assistant Director Ashland."

"Lizzie's running the leak investigation," says Ross, standing up.

Ah, okay. You call her Lizzie. I address her formally. The hierarchy is now established. You're pushing me down the chain, aren't you, Dwight?

"So this is awkward," Ashland says.

"How so?" asks Books.

"Well, with your being engaged to the target of our investigation."

Books pops a quick grin, a reflexive response. It disappears quickly. "Am I supposed to say something to that?"

"If you'd like."

He wouldn't like.

"The obvious concern is your impartiality," she says.

Books looks at Dwight, who seems content to let Ashland continue this attack.

"The director brought me in," Books says, "presumably *because* I was close to Emmy, figuring I might have a better view of things. Do you outrank the director?"

"Obviously not."

"Obviously not," Books agrees. "So what brings you to this case, Elizabeth? I'm sorry—Special Assistant Director Ashland?"

Her eyes light up, but she doesn't smile. "I volunteered," she says.

"You volunteered for what? This is an internal investigation. It's supposed to be secret. How would you even know to volunteer?"

"She's my top deputy now," says Dwight. "I asked her if she'd be a part of this and she was happy to do it."

Ashland nods and eyes Books. "I need to know I can trust you."

"You do?" Books returns her stare. "And what if you feel that you can't? Do you have the power to remove me from this investigation?" He scratches his cheek. "See, there, again, we have that thing about the director outranking you." Books knows he's being difficult, but he doesn't like sharp elbows, and he doesn't like being toyed with. He adds, "If the evidence establishes that Emmy is the leaker, then I will be the first one to say that she needs to be brought to justice. But yes, I'm going to insist that we prove it first."

Ashland takes a step toward him, raises an eyebrow. "You're not happy with the proof we have already? Information funneled to one of her only friends, Shaindy Eckstein? The photo of them at the bar last Friday night chatting, just two days before the *Post* story breaks about Citizen David targeting New York next?"

"It's circumstantial," says Books. "You haven't turned up anything on her computers, have you?"

"She wouldn't be dumb enough to send an e-mail to the reporter from her computer. But don't worry, Books. We'll get her soon. And when we do, you know who's going to put the handcuffs on her?"

Books smiles. "Let me guess. Me?"

She gives a slow nod. "Good guess."

"Or maybe, with Emmy's assistance," says Books, "you'll catch Citizen David even sooner and none of this will matter."

She makes a face. "The leaks don't help. You think David

will go to New York now that we've telegraphed to the whole world that it's where we expect him to go?"

Books feels something move within him, adrenaline quickening his pulse.

She's right. He spent so much time wondering about Emmy, he couldn't see the forest for the trees. The leaks aren't revealing just the progress of the investigation. They're revealing the Bureau's investigative strategy.

They are aiding and abetting the bomber.

Maybe the leaker inside the Bureau isn't merely an informant for the *Washington Post,* irresponsibly disclosing sensitive information.

Maybe whoever's leaking this information is Citizen David's accomplice.

35

COCOONED IN his room, flanked by computers, Charlie has everything he needs. Emmy isn't the only one with a command central.

He's got the clones of Emmy's computers, allowing him to monitor Emmy's internet activity in real time, no different than if he were looking over her shoulder. He watches every click on every link as Emmy pores over data and mines for anomalies in the reported natural or accidental deaths across the country. Amazing. Emmy has managed to distill news and information from around the nation using some algorithm that sorts them by key words, no different than a supercharged version of a Google search.

He watches as she clicks on a story about a drowning outside Minneapolis, an electrocution in Utah, a choking death in upstate New York.

"Sorry, my lady," he whispers, "none of those are mine. But knock yourself out. Chase your own tail. Your endurance is inspiring."

On a laptop, he has the downloaded contents of Emmy's computers, including all her notes on Citizen David. Emmy has described, in great detail, how Citizen David carried out the bombings, choosing low-value targets, using rudimentary materials, gaining access in the simplest of ways.

Charlie devours all the particulars of David's work. He reads about fire exits, metallic tape over door locks, splintered gas lines.

He reads about acetone and hydrogen peroxide and shaped charges and delayed initiation.

He reads about cotton balls and aluminum catering trays and cartoon cats.

Impressive. There are things that Charlie admires about Citizen David, to be sure. His discipline. His methodology. But his good work has gone to waste. The damage he's inflicted is minimal, intentionally so, enough to be disruptive, to make a political statement, but not enough to injure or maim.

Symbolic protest. What pointless drivel.

On his personal laptop, he conducts a search of his own using a string of anonymous proxies so as not to compromise his IP address; this allows him to access whatever information he wants with maximum secrecy. Compared to Emmy Dockery's sophisticated algorithm, his online search is downright prehistoric: *SRO payday uptown 606.*

Not surprisingly, the hits number in the thousands and cover all sorts of topics, most of them completely irrelevant. But not all of them. He pulls up articles that bring back memories. He feels a tightness in his neck, a constriction in his brain as he fights them away. Images, not full scenes.

Images of Fergie, the guy behind the desk of the State Park Hotel, the unshaven face, the cigar stub, the clutter everywhere, reminding Mama about the "visitor fee."

Mama telling him to stay with Fergie, telling him she'd be right back, although he knew it might be hours before she returned, then leaving him in a corner of Fergie's office, sitting on an overturned milk crate with a small pile of comic books that she'd dug out of a dumpster and a Walkman on which he listened to the local radio stations or, when the reception was bad, the cassette tape of *American Fool* by John Cougar. Preferring to hear "Hurts So Good" and "Jack and Diane" over Fergie's comments ("Your ma, she's a popular lady, know what I mean?") and recycled jokes ("Know why they call this the State Park Hotel? Because the state parks all its nutcases here").

Mama, returning, looking different, something gone from her eyes, handing some cash to Fergie, stuffing the rest in her purse, scooping him up, asking him if he was hungry. He was. He was always hungry.

Breathe in, breathe out. Focus on your project.

Three hours pass. A glance at the clone computer shows that Emmy's still up, still searching through her articles. His own search has narrowed. He has found many candidates, but it must be perfect, it must thread the needle.

He keeps going back to Google Earth, checking street-level views, satellite views, angles and alleys and dimensions and escape routes.

It's not exciting or sexy work—it never is—but the feeling of homing in on a target brings a rush better than anything else he's ever felt.

"Yes," he says, touching the computer screen, petting it. "There you are. I've found you."

This counts as sex for him. And the foreplay—the search and execution and thrill of anticipation—is over. It's time for the climax. He'll map out the route tonight and start gathering supplies.

Before the weekend, he'll be in Chicago.

36

MICHELLE FONTAINE sits on the soft waiting-room couch, three minutes early for her first day. The door pops open and a man rushes in, startling her. He's wearing a T-shirt and blue jeans and torn leather moccasins, no socks.

"So you're the newbie," he says. He takes a clipboard off a cluttered desk and reviews something, then puts it down and fixes his eyes on her. "Michelle?" He extends a hand. "I'm Tom Miller, your co-therapist, I guess you'd say. We'll share the same patients."

"Nice to meet you," she says, shaking his hand.

Tom checks his watch, then claps his hands together once. "We have just a few minutes before our first adventure."

"Our first adventure?"

"Every patient's an adventure. You know this is mostly a private-pay facility, right?"

"Yeah."

He raises a shoulder. "Private payers tend to be more demanding. It's their own money, so they feel like they're the boss."

Tom takes her through the first morning at the rehab facility.

There's Mrs. Persoon, the forty-eight-year-old stroke victim who moves with difficulty, using the walker while Tom braces her, gently prodding her and reminding her about her annual Christmas trip to California to see her children—it's a good six months away, but that's her motivation to regain full mobility.

And Mr. Oakley, age seventy-eight, who's bedridden and struggling to do leg lifts. Tom jokes with him about his sex life. All locker-room, politically incorrect humor.

And Mrs. Coxley, age eighty-two, who broke her hip and is in the early stages of dementia. She doesn't respond to humor. Tom keeps her animated by asking about her children. "She'll talk all day about her kids or gardening," Tom tells Michelle afterward.

Michelle scribbles notes on each patient.

"The older women will be the hardest for you," Tom tells her between sessions. "They tend to respond better to older men than young women. It's not fair, but that's the way it is. You just have to be gentle but forceful." He looks her over. "What are you, twenty-five?"

"Twenty-four," she says.

"I'm forty," he says. "I know, it's hard to believe." He does a mock *GQ*-model pose. Tom isn't bad-looking. He has receding hair that he keeps short on the sides and he doesn't have much of a chin, but he's in good physical condition, and his most prominent wrinkles are smile lines at his eyes and mouth—he has a warm, pleasant face.

"Where you from?" he asks.

The question catches her off guard. "The, uh…Mid—Midwest," she says.

"Yeah? Whereabouts?"

How to handle... "Do you mind if I run to the bathroom quick before our next patient?"

"Yeah, that's fine. It's just over there," says Tom.

At lunchtime, they step outside onto a patio surrounded by shrubbery, the warm sun shining down. "Staff eats out here. So do some of the patients," says Tom. "It's kinda nice to interact on a less formal level. Not that any of this is formal."

In the corner, a half a dozen men sit at a long table. Like the patients at A New Day, they range in age from mid-twenties to geriatric.

They are all listening to one man at the end of the table who's holding court, gesturing with his hands and speaking with authority. Michelle can't quite make out what he's saying but she doesn't need to. With his short, crisp sentences, his curt confidence, he oozes authority. Military, she thinks. He talks like her grandfather did.

"I wanted you to meet the lieutenant," Tom says to her quietly, and she instantly knows he's referring to that man. She notes a different tone to Tom's voice, the casual whimsy replaced by a hint of caution. "Everyone calls him Lew. He's fine, but he's sort of a tough nut to crack. You see all his disciples over there."

They slowly move toward the group. She sneaks a look at the lieutenant, wondering why she feels the need to be surreptitious about it. Everything seems different about this patient.

He's in a wheelchair, an expensive model with a dark blue shroud, an American-flag decal on the leather armrest, a bumper sticker on the shroud that says RANGERS LEAD THE WAY.

His hair isn't the standard crew cut, though. It's shoulder-length and gray, pulled back into a ponytail. He is relatively young, probably late forties, his face slightly weathered.

Near his right eye, he has a prominent scar in the shape of a crescent moon.

"He was in some kind of elite Army Ranger unit," whispers Tom. "Hard-core stuff. One of those explosives in Iraq blew up a jeep he was in, sent him a hundred feet in the air. He had all sorts of gear on, so the only wound he got was by his right eye, but the landing paralyzed him. Incomplete SCI. A T nine, I think."

"Incomplete?" she asks. "Can he walk?"

Tom shrugs. "A little. He's made great progress. And he can handle motor functions with his feet."

They move closer and listen to the lieutenant talking.

"...just another way of breaking our spirit. Once we're dependent, we're always dependent," the lieutenant is saying. "Welfare, Social Security—the most deviously unhealthy programs the government could have created. We are puppets awaiting the day—be it old age or unemployment or sickness—that the government will take care of us. The biggest mistake we ever made was promising—"

He notices Tom, stops talking.

Tom gives him a theatrical, overdone salute.

"Always with the jokes, Tommy," says the lieutenant, the side of his mouth upturned. "And who might this young lady be?"

"Lieutenant, this is Michelle, your new physical therapist."

"Call me Lew." He turns in his wheelchair, using his joystick, so he is facing her. Whatever it is coming off him, it's enough to kick her heart rate up a notch. "Let me guess—you're a basketball player," he says.

Michelle tries not to frown at the reference to her height; men always seem to go right to that.

"You're gonna be nice to her, right, Lew?" Tom says.

He fixes his eyes on her. "Tommy, I'm sure Michelle is capable of speaking for herself."

She feels a flutter in her heart and clears her throat. "Nice to meet you, Lew," she says, surprised at the tremor in her voice.

"See?" Not taking his eyes off her but still talking to Tom. "I knew she could speak."

"Lew is here midweek," says Tom. "Most weekends, he's traveling around the country as an activist and speaker."

Michelle nods, but she's wilting under the glare of this man, whose eyes have still not left her. She feels something creep up her spine.

Tom adds, "Yeah, Lew's been to DC, Indianapolis, Atlanta, Charleston, Dallas. I think your last one was…New Orleans, right?"

Lew's eyes don't move from Michelle, but a half smile slightly alters his expression. "That's right, Tom."

"And you're going to…where…Chicago next, you were saying before?"

For a moment, Lew doesn't answer, probing her eyes to the point of discomfort. "Yes," he finally says, "Chicago is next on my schedule."

37

THE SIGN on the large storefront window of Cash 4U Quick announces CASH NOW—NO CREDIT NECESSARY! in large, yellow, rounded letters, the kind one might see painted on the windshield of a used car for sale. The accompanying photograph shows an attractive woman in a revealingly snug shirt handing several twenty-dollar bills, fanned out, to a black man and a white woman, both of whom are smiling widely; this is clearly one of the most pleasant, stress-free business transactions in the history of commerce. *We had no credit, but this lady gave us a bunch of cash! And she's pretty too!*

It's Friday night near six, when the business is set to close. Charlie will need to observe some things but he doesn't want to stay any longer than necessary, for obvious reasons. The spot is a good one, a location that provides a fine view of the store across Broadway Street.

In front of him is a Macy's gift box with no top. Taped to it is a piece of brown cardboard, standing perpendicular to the box so passersby can easily see the words he has scrawled on it with a Sharpie: HOMELESS VET, PLEASE HELP.

He looks the part—a Chicago Bears hat, tattered camouflage shirt, stained sweatpants, thick, dark, square glasses to protect against the rays of the setting sun but also giving the impression of blindness. Glasses that are almost, but not quite, large enough to cover the crescent-moon scar by his right eye.

Broadway Street this far north is commercial and somewhat barren, but there's enough going on—music stores, a car wash, drugstores, plus a Thai restaurant and a dive bar on the corner—to attract people in happy-hour mode and summer attire along with the joggers and dog-walkers and bicyclists.

"You can't be here! You got to go!"

He turns, startled, though he shouldn't be. If there is one thing he's learned about the homeless—and he's learned a lot, especially in LA, where he eliminated so many of them—it's that they all have fiercely proprietary streaks.

The man who approaches is African-American, tall, wearing a green baseball cap turned backward over his dreadlocks and a white long-sleeved shirt, ripped and stained, bearing a faded photo of some rock band in concert. Through the patchy beard on his face, two pale pink spots show on his cheeks—a skin disease or some accident. His eyes are bloodshot and wild with anger.

"Can't nobody be in this spot! This ain't your spot! This is *Mayday*'s spot!" He thumps his hand against his chest, spit flying from his mouth; the putrid combination of body odor and booze and halitosis is so unbearable as to invite vomit.

Under other circumstances, Charlie could neutralize this problem in a heartbeat. But there are people around, and he can't afford to have an altercation.

"Get on, now! This is Mayday's spot!"

Principles of deduction would indicate that this man answers to the name Mayday. "Hold on, my friend." He raises his hand to the man, a peaceful gesture. "Are you...don't tell me...Mayday?"

"You got to go, okay, 'cause this is *Mayday's* spot, always is Mayday's spot—"

"I understand. I'm in your spot. I'm terribly sorry."

The gentle way he speaks seems to disarm Mayday, who presumably is unaccustomed to civil interactions, especially in a turf battle, as this seems to be.

He could point a gun at Mayday, just as a threat, but the last thing he needs is some wild report of a homeless man with a gun. It would bring half of the Chicago Police Department to him.

"Mayday's got Balmoral to Catalpa, okay," says the man. "Balmoral to Catalpa."

"Could I make a deal with you, Mayday? Could I pay you cash for this spot, just for this evening?"

Mayday draws back, wary. He points down at the sidewalk, his hand shaking for emphasis, his finger like a jackhammer busting pavement. "You got to *go*—"

"How much do you want? Name your price."

This encounter is obviously playing out entirely differently than Mayday expected. His anger has subsided. He's realizing that he's going to get paid. His eyes widen at the prospect, but he doesn't know how to respond.

"Sixty dollars, Mayday?"

It doesn't make sense to Mayday that a fellow homeless man would be flush with money, but whether it makes sense to Mayday is not a concern for Charlie at the moment.

It will be later.

"Sixty bucks, okay," says Mayday, embracing his unexpected windfall. "Sixty bucks right now!"

"You drive a hard bargain, sir."

Mayday snatches the money offered. "Only for tonight," he says, his chest puffed out. He walks away to enjoy his surprise bounty, to ply himself with booze or drugs or whatever his self-destructive habit of choice may be.

Don't stray far, Mayday.

"Spare change," Charlie says as people pass him along the sidewalk. He hardly looks at them, his eyes on the store across the street.

At 6:22 p.m., the security guard, tall enough to play professional basketball but with a gut that hangs over his belt like a sack of potatoes, pulls the chain-link security fencing over the storefront window and locks it. Within half an hour, the two remaining employees at the loan company, a man in shirtsleeves and tie and a woman in a jacket and skirt, leave, turning off the outside lights.

At 7:24 p.m., an armored truck pulls into the alley alongside the moneylending store. The security guard opens the side door, and the cash is transferred into the truck.

At 8:04 p.m., the security guard calls it a night. The store is empty.

The passersby are thinning out too, and Charlie's stomach growls at the smell of Thai food down the street. That's okay. He's nearly done.

It's time to pay the moneylending store a visit.

38

THE ALLEY that the armored car occupied earlier, adjacent to the moneylending store, is appropriately disgusting and smells of hot, rancid trash. The alley door to the store is large and wide and presumably thick. On the door, in square red letters, are the words THERE IS NO CASH INSIDE THIS STORE AFTER BUSINESS HOURS.

This is true enough, though there is a functioning gas line.

The door has no knob. The only access to the store from the outside is via the keypad next to the door, which has a lid over it.

From his bag, he removes a small, round, black device, a few centimeters wide, with the logo of a company called Inter-Lock Secure. He wheels himself up to the alley wall, locks the wheelchair, and peels the back off the device to reveal an adhesive surface. He reaches up and sticks the device on the lid covering the alarm pad, careful to center it so it appears to be nothing but a harmless logo.

An hour later, after he has settled himself up the street, no longer across from the moneylending store, the cleaning service arrives. The white truck parks by the curb. Two women get out of the truck and carry their supplies into the alley. He can't see them, but he knows they type in the pass code to enter the store, because a few minutes later, the store's interior lights up.

Shouldn't take them more than an hour. He unwraps a power bar and devours it.

It takes them ninety minutes, actually, but then they are gone, the place locked up and dark again.

He returns to the alley, motors his wheelchair up to the wall, reaches up to the alarm pad, and carefully peels off the InterLock Secure device. He flips it over and pushes the tiny button.

The number 5424 smiles back at him.

The street address for the company. Logical enough. An easy password to remember.

"Until tomorrow," he says.

He returns to his van, parked several blocks away on a residential street that doesn't have zone parking—a rare thing these days in the Windy City, apparently. He enters through the rear, the hydraulic ramp lowering for him, as always.

The van's spacious interior is less so tonight. The items he's purchased are spread out carefully in the back with a tarp thrown over them.

He pulls back the tarp and examines everything: the acetone and sulfuric acid, the bottles of hydrogen peroxide, the bags of salt, the test tubes and glass vials and thermometer, the wristwatch and batteries and wire, and, of course, the aluminum catering pan.

Good enough. Saturday morning will be busy.

Saturday *night* will be fun.

But the remainder of tonight—Friday night—will be for his new friend Mayday.

"Where did you run off to, old sport?" he whispers.

39

AT FIVE o'clock on Saturday night, the Cash 4U Quick moneylending store closes for the rest of the weekend.

At 6:04 p.m., an armored truck pulls into the alley and removes the cash from the store.

At 6:11 p.m., the security guard locks up the store and leaves for the night.

At 9:26 p.m., the cleaning-service people finish their nightly housekeeping and leave through the side door.

Near midnight, a Dodge Caravan pulls into the alley and goes up to the store's side entrance. It leaves less than thirty minutes later.

At 2:59 a.m., the wee hours of Sunday, the 5400 block of North Broadway Street is lazy and quiet. Everything is closed and shuttered and dark. Everyone is asleep.

One minute later, the store bearing the name Cash 4U Quick explodes in a ball of fiery orange, glass shattering forward, the sides bursting outward.

Above the moneylending store, the twelve-story building

buckles and then collapses, its brick-and-mortar walls crumbling, floor after floor succumbing to gravity, crashing down one on top of the other, filling the air with black smoke and dust.

Rescue workers—firefighters, paramedics, police—rush to the scene, the fire blazing, searing heat and toxic dark smoke. The building, what can be seen of it, is reduced to a pile of bricks in a hole in the ground.

The first order of business is extinguishing the fire and rescuing victims.

But the question amid the chaos, through the choking smoke and the blazing furnace that was the building, is this: *Are* there victims? It's the middle of the night in a predominantly commercial area. Was the building empty? A patrol officer assigned to this precinct arrives and supplies the information.

The bottom floor was a business, surely closed at this hour.

Above it, a single-room-occupancy hotel, the Horizon Hotel for Men. A hotel for vagrants, for the homeless, subsidized housing—a single room to sleep in for eight dollars a night.

It will be hours—hours spent extinguishing the fire, combing through the rubble to find bodies burned to ashes or crushed beyond recognition—before the extent of the disaster is known. The hotel's twelve floors had a capacity of sixteen people per floor, and it was at full occupancy last night.

The final body count, which includes the hotel's meager staff, is 197.

40

I RUSH into the office, still foggy, my legs rubbery, my stomach hollow, operating on little sleep and no food, nothing but nervous energy.

The bombing happened at four in the morning eastern daylight time, an hour after I'd gone to bed. I was awakened by the call ninety minutes later, after an agent in our Chicago office arrived at the scene and noted that the commercial establishment on the bottom floor of the building was a payday-loan store, one of the frequent targets of Citizen David's ire.

Bonita Sexton, who's beaten me here, pops up from her cubicle.

"Talk to me, Rabbit," I say, dropping my bag and booting up my computer. "Was this David?"

She looks terrible, but we all will today, having been roused from our beds at dawn. It's more than that, though. She looks pained. And it's not hard to see why. This was different. Up to now, Citizen David has taken great care to avoid casualties, to direct his violence at institutions, not people.

"No way this was David." The answer comes not from Rabbit, who seems stunned into silence, but from Eric Pullman—Pully—who appears above the wall of his cubicle, puffy-eyed, his hair wild. "He wouldn't kill innocent people."

"Not intentionally," says Rabbit. "But this...I don't see how he could've thought the blast wouldn't bring down the entire—" She pushes her hair back from her face. "Oh God."

"Do we even know it was intentional?" I ask. "Buildings blow up. Gas lines break. Come on you, you stupid thing!" I bark at my computer, which is still booting up.

"We don't know anything yet," says Pully.

"Okay, well, until further notice, we're treating this as David. Start with the CCTV cameras, both of you. A ten-block radius. This is Chicago, so they'll have plenty."

"Got it, boss."

I look at my watch. "I have to go see Dwight Ross," I say.

41

SOME OF the team is already there when I arrive at the conference room that serves as our war room for Citizen David; there are people on the phone barking commands, and a few are huddled by the television mounted on the wall. The TV has a live overhead shot of Chicago, where the crime scene looks like a gigantic fireplace, smoke still billowing out, fire trucks and rescue vehicles everywhere, water spewing into the charred remains, although, from what I can gather, the fire itself is extinguished.

Dwight Ross, sleeves rolled up and no tie, looks haggard but as fierce as always. Near him is a woman dressed in a sharp pinstripe suit, her hair pulled back immaculately, looking better than anybody has a right to look after being summoned from bed before sunrise.

Dwight, looking down at some notes, draws a line in the air between the two of us. "Emmy Dockery, Special Assistant Director Elizabeth Ashland."

She gives me a cool stare and a strong handshake. "Manhattan, huh?" she says to me. "Well, you were off by only eight hundred miles."

That didn't take long, and it came from someone I've never met. *Nice to meet you too.* I look at Dwight, our fearless leader, who lifts his eyes from the paper he's reading.

"Arson?" I ask. "Confirmed? Couldn't be, not this quickly."

Dwight removes his reading glasses and rubs his eyes. "Dockery, why are you always asking questions and then answering them yourself? No," he says, "not confirmed. The scene is still hotter than Venus. They're still pulling bodies out of the rubble. Our arson guys tell me it's possible it could be a gas-line break, and then once there was the first explosion, more gas spilled on top of it—a series of explosions, ultimately, fuel on the fire." He stretches. "It could be an accident. But not likely."

"I don't think it was David," I say. "Not his style."

"It's exactly his style," says Elizabeth Ashland. "One of these short-term loan companies. David hates them. He says they prey on the poor, charge outrageous interest—you've seen his rants." She cocks her head. "So, tell me why this *isn't* his style."

"How about the presence of more than a hundred homeless people above the store? Nothing in our profile indicates he wants to kill anyone, much less people who are poor and sick."

She shrugs. "He overestimated the power of his blast. He wanted to blow out a couple of windows and rearrange some furniture inside the payday store, but he used too much charge."

"For the first time ever."

"Well, he's blown up only three buildings previously. The track record's not that long."

"But why *this* payday-loan store? There are hundreds in the Chicago area alone. Why one sitting under a hotel for vagrants?"

"You mean, why not one in *Manhattan,* like you predicted?"

Who the heck is this woman, and is she here for any other reason than to bust my chops? "We don't know anything yet," I say to Dwight. "You want me to hit the CCTV cameras, I take it?"

"Of course."

"We'll pull up everything we can on that building and the payday store."

He nods, his eyes bloodshot and sunken.

"Social media too," I say.

"Yes. We'll have a command meeting soon, this morning."

I leave the room, walk down the hallway, and hit the button for the elevator, all the while thinking through all the different possibilities here, what this could mean—

"Dockery," says Dwight Ross. He's standing not far away. I didn't even hear him follow me.

"Yes, boss."

He steps toward me. "You remember when I told you this was your last chance?"

I don't say anything.

"The bullshit political statements about corporate America oppressing the poor and downtrodden—you can forget all that. Citizen David is no hero. Now he's a mass murderer."

His anger is plain to see, but he is more than mad. He is shaken. Citizen David is his case, in the end, and the stakes just went up considerably. While he was flailing about trying to nab this anonymous crusader, hundreds of people died.

"*If* it was David," I say. "I don't think it was."

"Because if it was, then you were wrong about Manhattan. And we can't have that, right, Dockery?"

I start to respond, but Dwight raises a hand. "It was David," he says. "I don't need distractions. I don't need my lead data analyst spending her time trying to prove she wasn't wrong. I need her full attention focused on catching this asshole." He drills a finger into my chest. "So catch him, and do it fast."

He pivots and walks away.

"I'll catch him, boss," I say. "But I have one request."

42

WHEN I return to my team, Pully and Rabbit are reviewing CCTV footage and calling out to each other over the cubicle dividers.

I look at Rabbit. Behind her, on her desk, are framed photographs of her two boys—Mason, in cap and gown, the social worker in Tampa, and Jordan, who now works at a Starbucks by the Yale campus and writes poetry and who had gone to Yale but dropped out in protest because the school didn't accept enough minority students. Rabbit's a peace-love-and-harmony hippie who raised her two boys to be much the same way.

"I'm flying to Chicago," I say. "I'll stay in touch on the jet."

"Good." She sniffs. Her eyes are red; her face is streaked with tears.

"You okay, Rabbit?"

Bonita nods but doesn't look up. "This feels like Kaczynski all over again," she says. The Unabomber, she means. She worked on that investigation when she was a young data analyst in the nineties.

"We caught Kaczynski," I say. "And we'll catch this guy."

She shakes her head, wipes at her cheek. "We caught the Unabomber after he published that manifesto in the *Times,* and his brother and sister-in-law recognized his rants," she says. "Otherwise, we never would've caught him." She looks up at me. "Nobody likes to admit that. But we never would've caught him."

"Hey," I say. "We have different tools now—"

"This guy killed *homeless* people," she says, her voice breaking. "Poor people who wanted nothing but a safe, warm, dry place to sleep."

This is hard for all of us, but especially Rabbit. She volunteers several times a month at a soup kitchen. She's raised money for homeless shelters. She's on a board that advocates for the rights of the mentally ill, many of whom are homeless. This is about the worst possible crime she can imagine.

I walk around to her cubicle and put my hand on her shoulder. "Bonita, we are going to catch this person. I promise you. Okay? I promise that. And I need your help. I can't do it without you."

"I know." She breathes in, nods. "I'm here. I'm okay."

I look into Pully's cubicle. "No word online from David?"

"Nope. Nothing." He throws up his hand. "Nothing. I don't get it. If someone copycatted him and killed a bunch of people while doing it, you'd think David would rush to distance himself from it, right? Deny it. Condemn it. *Something.*"

He's right. It doesn't make sense. If Citizen David wasn't the one who did this, where is the outrage from him?

"I'm off," I say. "Keep in close touch with updates. Anything at all. Both of you."

I head outside to the car that's waiting to take me to the jet. As I get into the back seat, I see a pair of crossed legs.

"You're late," says Elizabeth Ashland, her carry-on bag at her feet. "And don't look so excited to see me."

43

AN FBI town car drives Elizabeth Ashland and me from O'Hare to the scene of the bombing on Chicago's northwest side. A two-block perimeter has been set up. The air is black, and even inside the town car, we can smell a sickening chemical odor, a toxic barbecue. I close my eyes at the thought of what was barbecued.

"Confirmed it was TATP," says Ashland, putting down her phone. She looks at me with eyebrows raised.

Triacetone triperoxide—TATP—is the explosive of choice of ISIS in Europe, because it doesn't contain nitrogen and can pass through explosive-detection scanners. But nobody thinks this was the work of ISIS.

She's saying this was Citizen David, who has also used TATP.

"Doesn't make it David," I say. "All you need is access to a Home Depot and a beauty salon."

"David's use of TATP was never leaked to the press," she

responds. "We've kept a lid on those details. So it's just a co-incidence?"

For someone who wasn't working on Citizen David until this morning, she sure is a quick study. Or was she on the case earlier, and I didn't know?

"It wouldn't be hard to guess," I say. "And it wouldn't be hard to copy."

We get out of the car, and I find myself holding my breath. I can see the bomb site under plumes of smoke. It's still smoldering. Rescue trucks line the street, leaving a path down the center for rescue workers to haul away bodies and then return and search for more. The FBI has taken over the investigation, but it looks like a multijurisdictional effort, Chicago PD and Cook County Sheriff, firefighters and Illinois State Police.

Storm clouds darken the sky. That's not a good development. Rain might cool off the bomb site, but it will hamper investigatory efforts.

"Assistant Director Ashland?" A man approaches; he's wearing a heavy fire coat, goggles, and a white mask that covers all of his face save his eyes. "I'm George Wilson, assistant special agent in charge. We met once at Quantico."

"Sure, Agent." She shakes his hand and introduces me. He nods like he recognizes my name.

"Put these on," he says, handing the two of us coats, masks, goggles, and booties. We do.

"I want you to come see something," he says. We follow him through the barricades. He talks as we walk, shouting so we can hear him through the mask and over the din of the workers. "I don't know what you know or don't know. It's been pretty chaotic."

"Start at the beginning," shouts Ashland.

There is a sense of urgency among those searching through

the rubble for bodies and for anyone who might somehow have survived. Workers in heavy fire coats and boots and gas masks scurry over scorched brick like ants on a picnic basket, calling out to one another, furiously pulling away debris.

It's a mass grave in which dozens if not a hundred bodies are still buried.

"Gas line was busted in a room on the south side of the payday-loan store," he says.

"Sabotage?" asks Ashland.

"Can't be sure, but presumably, yeah. Otherwise it's a helluva coincidence."

"Okay, what else?" she shouts.

"He had a tray of TATP on a timer. It went off at three sharp this morning."

"A tray?" Ashland asks. Something sinks inside me.

"Some kind of tray, like you'd serve food on, put a burner under to keep warm."

An aluminum catering tray. The same thing Citizen David used. Ashland turns in my direction to be sure I heard it.

TATP—Citizen David. An aluminum tray—Citizen David. The explosives, like I told Ashland, could have been a guess. The aluminum tray? That detail was never released to the public.

"How'd he get in?" I ask.

"Side door, we think. Front of the place was caged up, best we can tell. And he would've tripped the burglar alarm if he went through the front of the store."

"No alarm on the side door?" Ashland asks.

"Side door opens with a code only, and the business had been closed for hours. So he got past the code somehow. Inside, there's no motion sensor until you get into the main offices. He didn't go that far. He stopped at the utility room near the side door. That's where he put down the explosives. He knew not to trip the alarm."

So he dropped the explosives next to a busted gas line?

That doesn't sound like an accident.

We walk down Broadway Street on the east side, across from the bomb site. It's like passing an open oven—the heat is still radiating off it over nine hours later. It is now entirely black, like burned wood in a fireplace, a twelve-story building nothing but a pile of ash and rubble.

I feel helpless. Through a blur of tears, I watch the heroic but presumably fruitless efforts of the rescue workers, who must know how unlikely it is that anyone sleeping in that building last night is still alive.

The sidewalk across the street is a bed of shattered glass and debris. We crunch over the glass, step carefully around pipes, an air-conditioning unit, a wooden frame that probably once held a mirror. Decay and death fill my nostrils and mouth despite the mask.

"You said it was on a timer?" Ashland asks the agent, then she looks at me. And, yes, I know, David did the same thing.

"That's what I wanted to show you," says Agent Wilson.

We walk in silence through the debris on the sidewalk, passing a rescue worker who's sitting on the curb and pouring a bottle of water over his hair, streaking the dirt and ash on his face.

Agent Wilson stops. "Here," he says. "I wanted you to see this."

He steps into the street and we follow, my head swimming, my mind trying to focus on the facts amid the horror and chaos.

David used TATP. David used an aluminum tray. David used a timer.

None of that was disclosed to the public. But none of that is particularly novel. There is only one thing about David that is so unique as to be his unequivocal signature.

"We found the timer," calls out Agent Wilson.

He stops about thirty yards from the blast. A small metal barrier frames a spot on the street, a heavy top over it, an evidence flag waving there.

He removes the top, reaches down, and holds up a wristwatch with a portion of a wire hanging out of it.

It's a child's wristwatch with a red band, its face bearing the image of Garfield the comic-strip cat.

"That mean anything to you guys?" Wilson asks.

It certainly does. It's the same timer Citizen David always uses.

44

ONE BLOCK northwest of the bomb site, the FBI has taken over the vacant ground floor of a commercial three-flat to use as its command center. Better than driving downtown to the Bureau's Chicago field office. We have to stay close to the crime scene.

Elizabeth Ashland and I have removed our protective gear and we're walking with our heads down as we pass an endless gaggle of reporters, local and national, all shouting out to us for comment. One of them recognizes me and calls me by name, which doesn't seem to sit well with Ashland, my superior.

We cross the press barricade and walk into our makeshift headquarters, brown brick with a purple awning and a dingy storefront window, formerly a bakery. Ashland lets out an audible sigh, takes down her hair, and runs her fingers through it. It's blond, although it doesn't look it anymore, not today. Most of her face, like mine, was protected by the mask and goggles, but her hair and the exposed parts of her face—her forehead, the tops of her cheeks—are covered in greasy soot. She looks like some variety of raccoon, and I'm sure I do too.

Inside the vacant store, electrical cords are everywhere; computers have been set up on card tables and on every other available flat surface. A map of Chicago is taped on the lavender wall, and there are thumbtacks on the bomb site and on the perimeter of interest. I glance at a clock on the wall, which features a painted birthday cake in the middle of it. Could it really be six o'clock at night? It doesn't seem possible.

In one corner, some chairs have been set up, and a number of people are gathered there, most of them law enforcement but some civilians too. Wilson, the assistant special agent in charge for Chicago, locks eyes with us and waves us over.

"Okay, let's start," says Wilson. He has the same raccoon face from the soot that everyone else does. Nobody who got within a city block of that crime scene came away unscathed.

"I'm going to introduce some folks," he says, looking at a clipboard. He gestures to a number of people and gives their names. The payday-store owner. The store manager. The security guard. The cleaning-service crew. The armored-truck employees. The manager of the Horizon Hotel for Men.

Everyone, to a person, looks exhausted and traumatized but also energized at being a part of something this big.

Each employee of Cash 4U Quick tells us that nobody set off alarm bells in terms of suspicious behavior over the past week. It's possible the bomber actually entered the store at some point during his reconnaissance, so we have to ask, but I doubt he did. He only needed to access the side door to get in and plant his bomb in the utility room, and the online architectural drawings of the building would have told him where that was. If he's any good, he would never have set foot in that store.

"We did the cash transfer at six, like always on Saturday," says the security guard, Ron Sims. "I locked up a few minutes later. Didn't notice anything funny."

"The door to the utility room was always locked?" asks Wilson.

"Yeah, lock and key. I have a key. But I never went in there."

"You passed by that utility room, though, on your way out?"

"Yeah, I left through the side door to the alley. The utility room was right there."

"You didn't look inside the utility room Saturday night, I assume?" asks Wilson.

He shakes his head. "No, wouldn't have done that. But I didn't smell gas. And if the door had been broken open, I sure would've noticed *that*."

We haven't had much access to the bomb site because of the heat and because it remains a rescue situation. But what we believe was the door to the utility closet was found across the street from the payday store and half a block down, and from what can be discerned from it, it appears the lock was busted, not picked. The handle was missing altogether. Had it stayed in the wreckage, we might have thought it had just melted, but it blew clean from the site. So we're assuming the bomber, alone in the store, busted it off to access the utility room.

The older of the two cleaning-service people, Alice Jagoda, who has gray hair pulled into a bun, confirms in halting English that they didn't enter the utility room either because they didn't clean inside that room and they bring their own cleaning supplies. But like the security guard, she came and went through the side door to the alley and passed right by the utility room. "The door...not broken," she says. "I notice if broken." She looks at her partner, a young Latina named Acevedo, who concurs.

When a timer is involved, as it was here, you always consider the possibility that the bomb was planted days, even weeks, in advance. But because a gas line was cut, it wouldn't have been weeks—somebody would have smelled the gas and called the gas company—and it likely wouldn't have been days either.

But the fact that nobody saw a busted-open utility-room door closes the window even further. The cleaning-service women were the last ones to leave, at approximately 9:30 p.m. Saturday, and the bomb detonated at 3:00 a.m. Sunday. A five-and-a-half-hour window of opportunity for the bomber to plant the device.

"CPD Officers...McBride, Howse, Ciomek, and Gordon," Wilson says, reading off a clipboard. "Patrol officers assigned to this precinct on Saturday."

"There's a fair amount of foot traffic up here," says McBride, one of the two female officers. "And the car traffic—y'know, it's Broadway, it's a busy street. Pretty steady volume of cars all the time. But in terms of pedestrians, someone walking up and down the street, casing the place, wouldn't stand out. And this weekend is hot. Joggers, bikers, that sort of thing. People want to be out."

"What about any kind of vehicle parked in that alley?" asks Elizabeth Ashland.

Another officer, Howse, a tall African-American man with an amiable face, shrugs. "People park in alleys. We tell them to move, or we tow them, but it happens all the time. But a vehicle parked next to the payday store at night, after hours? Ten o'clock, midnight, two in the morning? It would have stuck out. We would've inquired." He shrugs again. "We have a big area, and Saturday night, we get a good number of calls and incidents. However long he was parked in that alley, we probably didn't pass by the store during that time."

Officer Ciomek, the other female officer, says, "We'll look at the surveillance-camera footage in the area. The car wash has cameras. The laundromat. The supermarket. The liquor store. I think the dollar store does too. It must. But there are limits to what the cameras capture."

"And who knows which day it would've been," says McBride. "He could've cased the area a week earlier."

Officer Ciomek snaps her fingers. "You know who would notice? You know who's out there all day, every day?"

"Oh, right," says Howse. "Our eyes and ears."

"Mayday," say Officers Ciomek and McBride together.

45

ON A computer in the opposite corner of our temporary headquarters, a Skype conference is about to begin. Ashland and I go over there, and Rabbit's worried face pops up on the screen.

"Bonita Sexton," I say, using Rabbit's formal name, "this is Special Assistant Director Elizabeth Ashland."

After an exchange of pleasantries, Rabbit says, "CCTV coverage on the northwest side of Chicago is sporadic. They devote most of their resources, apparently, to the south and west sides."

Where all the shootings have been taking place. Makes sense.

"But we have over a thousand hits on license plates. We're already cross-referencing," she tells us.

I say, "We have reason to believe the bomb was planted between nine thirty on Saturday night and three in the morning Sunday, local time."

"Okay. So we'll look at nine p.m. to four a.m., just to capture the whole window."

"What about people on the ground?" Ashland asks.

"We're using whatever we have, facial recognition where possible, but the quality of the images isn't good."

Ashland nods. "He would've staked it out. Easier to do that on foot."

"But he'd have to deliver the bomb materials by vehicle," I say. "TATP is far too volatile to carry around. Unless you're a suicide bomber with a backpack."

"And David is definitely not that," says Ashland.

No, he's not. The working theory is that Citizen David is a man of considerable means and intelligence. He has hacked with the best of them, from the Georgia prison to the Ivy League university to the pharmaceutical company's e-mail system, all without a trace, meaning he's as adept at cyberwarfare as—well, as adept as the best people the Bureau has to counter it. And he's managed to move about the country in his bombing attacks without leaving a trace, which is nearly impossible to do with the CCTV cameras we have today and our ability to track people and discern patterns from any number of decisions a citizen of this country makes daily.

"David? This wasn't David," says Rabbit.

Ashland smirks and looks over at me. "You two seem to have a crush on the lad."

"We have a profile on him," Rabbit says. "And this doesn't fit."

Rabbit and I have been in touch repeatedly throughout the day. She knows that the bomber used the same Garfield the Cat watch that Citizen David used. She's as baffled as I am. Everything about this says it's not David—yet everything about it says it is.

"But I agree that there would be foot surveillance," I say.

"Whoever it is, David or not, he would've had to spend some amount of time scoping out the place on the ground. That would be easier to do on foot."

On the somewhat fuzzy screen, Rabbit seems to recoil at my words, presumably the "David or not" part, as if I've committed an act of treason by allowing for the possibility that the bomber might, in fact, be David. I still believe in my heart that this couldn't have been his work. But apparently I'm going to have to deal with Elizabeth Ashland from now on, and I'm going to need unfettered access to her, so there's no point in going out of my way to alienate her.

Ashland looks at her phone. "Assistant Director Ross is calling me. I have to take this." She walks away, leaving me alone in front of the computer.

"Confirmation bias, Rabbit," I say to her. "A good reminder for me too." It's a problem in our line of work. When you have preconceived notions about an outcome, you fit the data in line with that outcome and ignore alternative possibilities. An open mind is critical in data analysis. Rabbit has been doing this a lot longer than I have, so she knows this. But it's not always easy to remember.

Rabbit rubs her face.

"Hey, girl," I say, "go home and get some rest. You've plugged in all the data to the algorithms. Let it work. You've been at this for sixteen hours. You and Pully need to rotate. Go get a few hours' sleep. Then Pully can sleep."

"Pully's been at this as long as I have," she says.

"Yeah, but Pully's, like, fifteen years old." I'm exaggerating by ten years, but Pully is thirty years younger than Rabbit. "And you look like you're about to fall over, kiddo. So for the first time since we've known each other, I'm going to issue an order. Go home and sleep."

I sign off with Rabbit and find Ashland, who's typing on her phone. The ASAC, Wilson, reaches her at the same time I do.

"Apparently," says Wilson, "they can't find this guy Mayday."

46

ELIZABETH ASHLAND and I, exhausted to the bone, trudge through the doors of a chain hotel a few blocks away. I don't care how long you're in the business or what you've witnessed, seeing what we saw today takes its toll.

"Mayday could've been one of the homeless in the Horizon Hotel," Ashland says as the clerk passes her a room key.

"But the cops said he didn't stay there. So we can hope." I hand my information over to the hotel clerk. "I'm going to review the surveillance footage tonight."

"Make sure you sleep a little," she says, waving her room key. "One thing I've learned, you can't do the job without sleep."

Same thing I told Rabbit a few hours ago; I hope she took my advice.

Ashland lingers for a moment, looking at me like she's about to say something else. Our relationship has been going on all of one very long day thus far. It didn't begin well, and it hasn't improved much. But we've worked intensely alongside a mass grave. We've witnessed unspeakable horror. We've smelled death. We've breathed the oily fire's remnants, tasted it in our mouths. We share something now.

"Anyway," she finally says, "see you in a few hours."

I go to my hotel room and drop my bag. I want to do nothing more than sleep, but I head to the bathroom. It's the first time I've seen myself in a mirror all day, and I'm not a pretty sight; I've got soot and grime on my face and caked in my hair. I turn on the shower and scrub my face until it hurts. I shampoo my hair three times, my fingers digging into my scalp. I brush my teeth over and over again and scour my tongue to remove the taste of chemicals and smoke. It takes soap and a towel at the sink before I can finally rid my face of all traces of the oily grunge. At last, I'm back to myself—a road map of scars on my body, red streaks across my face, but myself.

Then I sit down on the toilet and burst into tears, deep, heaving sobs, as if I'm suffering all of the tragedy and horror that those poor victims must have experienced. They were people who needed help, mentally ill or addicted to drugs, people who struggled for basic things that I take for granted. All they wanted was a place to sleep in peace. And for that, they were incinerated and crushed like human garbage.

I wrap my arms around myself, shivering but not from the cold, realizing how desperately I want someone else's arms around me. I ache, I yearn to hear his voice, to see his eyes squint when he smiles. I want to be there in his bed, tucked inside his arm, with the musky smell of his deodorant, the sound of his ragged breathing, beams from the rising sun striping through the blinds. I want that right now. I want that forever. I need to feel that way again. I need to be human again.

I find my phone and start to dial, then scold myself for thinking of myself at a moment like this, when so many have suffered so cruel a fate. But maybe that's when the importance of these things is the clearest. Maybe it takes something like this for me to see it.

But it wouldn't be fair to him. I've pushed him away. He deserves to move on with his life; he doesn't need to hear the cries and regrets of an ex. He deserves better. He always did.

As I wage war with myself, phone in hand, that very phone buzzes, a text message. It's from Pully.

David finally posted.

I snap back into focus, click on the link and read the Facebook post from Citizen David:

Chicago was not me. I would never kill people. I condemn that bombing! #protestwithoutcasualties

I forward the link to Elizabeth Ashland, then text Pully back and tell him to try to trace the source of the Facebook posting. He already knows to do that, of course, and we both already know that he will fail. We got a court order forcing Facebook to help us trace the source, but David was too adept. Tracing his IP address was like trying to grab hold of sunlight. He used remote servers and anonymous proxies that took us around the globe. He could be in the hotel room next door or in Antarctica.

David has never denied anything he's done. Just a scroll down his Facebook page shows he's proud of the hacking and bombings he's committed in the name of the little guy, the wrongly convicted, the cheated and downtrodden, all of it to rail against corporate fraud and abuse and an unfair criminal justice system.

"You wouldn't kill two hundred people," I say to my phone. "It wasn't you."

You two seem to have a crush on the lad, Ashland said to Rabbit and me. I can't deny that Rabbit and I share the same concerns as David. Our justice system *is* unfair to minorities. Our lenders *do* take advantage of the poor. Most corporations *will* do whatever it takes to make a buck, and only protests or regulations can stop them.

My phone rings in my hand. Rabbit.

"Did you see the posting?" she asks.

"You're supposed to be sleeping," I say.

"I got some sleep. I'm fine. Really. Did you see it? He's never denied his involvement in anything."

"But he never killed two hundred people, even if accidentally," I say, playing devil's advocate.

A heavy sigh from her end. "I'm going in, gonna relieve Pully," she says.

I sign off with Rabbit and drop onto the bed, feeling my eyelids close as soon as I hit the mattress. When my phone rings in my hand, I don't know if two minutes or five hours have passed.

"They found Mayday," says Elizabeth Ashland.

47

I SHAKE off the cobwebs and clear my throat. "They found Mayday?" I say. "Great. Should we meet somewhere?"

"Not unless you want to visit the morgue," Ashland says. "He's dead."

I moan. The police officers made him sound like a plausible lead. "Shit. So he died in the hotel after all."

"Actually, no. They found him dead in an alley a mile away."

I sit up in bed. "Cause of death?"

"They're thinking heart attack. Looks like he's been dead a day or two. But no foul play, they say. Natural causes."

My blood goes cold.

A homeless man.

Natural causes.

Sure, it happens every day, but...

"Where is he now?" I ask.

"Still at the morgue. One of the cops, Ciomek, confirmed the identification."

"Is Ciomek still there?"

"I—I suppose so. I don't know. Why?"

My heart's pounding so hard, I can barely speak. "Never mind. I'll see you in a few hours."

"At this point, just ninety minutes."

"Right."

I check my phone for Officer Ciomek's number. We exchanged contact information with all the officers. She answers on the second ring.

"Officer Ciomek, this is Emmy Dockery."

"Sure, Emmy. You heard about Mayday?"

"I did."

"That's a tough break. Mayday knew everything on that block. We even used him as a CI from time to time."

"Right, you mentioned. Listen, are you still at the morgue?"

"Just leaving. Why?"

"Could you do me a favor? Could you check something for me?"

I explain it to her, and Officer Ciomek seems annoyed, probably because she's as sleep-deprived as the rest of us, as weary and disheartened and drained as everyone else. She never actually says yes, but I can tell she's walking and talking, calling out to people in the morgue, and then the voices are muffled as she presumably drops the phone to her side.

I pace the carpet of this tiny hotel room, my hand shaking so hard I can hardly hold the phone. Then I hear her voice, not muffled at all but clear and loud.

"How in God's name," she says, "did you know there would be tiny puncture wounds on his torso?"

The phone falls from my hand. I grab the dresser to keep myself from falling too.

How, I keep asking myself. *How?*

How could it be the same person?

Killing the homeless is his specialty. The puncture wounds, a death seemingly without foul play. And now he's managed to kill a couple hundred of them, all at once.

But how did he know to use David's explosive, TATP? And the aluminum tray?

And the Garfield the Cat watch?

Nobody knew that stuff. It was never made public. Nobody knew but—

I turn, rush to the bathroom, and make it just in time to vomit into the toilet, gagging on an empty stomach. I turn on the shower, let near-scalding water cascade over my body, and scrub myself with the soap until it's reduced to a useless nub.

So someone *was* in my apartment that day. It was him. He hacked into my computers. He knows everything I know about Citizen David.

He knows everything I know about him. And he knows where I live.

48

I MEET Ashland ninety minutes later in the hotel lobby. She looks immaculate again, hair done just right, pressed suit, her only allowance for the fieldwork today being flats instead of heels. We walk to the bomb site and our makeshift headquarters. We talk about the Citizen David posting on Facebook and the bad luck with Mayday. I don't take it any further. Something tells me that this might not be the perfect time to offer up my new theory.

Officer Ciomek is there when I arrive. I'd been under the impression she was off duty today, but maybe this is a day where no Chicago cop is off duty.

ASAC Wilson confers with Ashland as Ciomek pulls me aside. "Help me out here," she says. "You've never met this guy in your life, but you know he has puncture wounds on his torso?"

I glance over at Ashland to make sure we have some privacy. "Officer Ciomek, you ever run into operational resistance up the chain of command?" I ask.

"I work for the Chicago Police Department, honey," she says. "It's a daily occurrence. And call me Natalie."

"Well, Natalie, I'm experiencing that now. The upper brass and I, we have a disagreement on who's responsible for what happened here."

"Citizen David or not."

"Right. I've never really thought this was David. But now I think the bomber is someone I've been tracking for a long time. Someone who preys on the homeless, elderly, disabled, frail, but hides it by making the deaths look natural or accidental. Not like homicides."

She wrinkles her nose. "You think he was trying to make this bombing look like an accident? Because if so, he didn't do a very good job."

"No, the bombing's different, I realize that," I say, and here I have a preview of how my superiors will react when I lay out my theory. "He must have switched tactics, probably because he knows we're tracking him. This bombing—I think he was trying to hide under the umbrella of Citizen David. But his typical MO has been killing people the way he killed Mayday. The puncture wounds—he's probably injecting something that incapacitates the victims. Then he kills them without a struggle."

"These other victims in the past," she says, "what do the tox screens from the autopsies show?"

I give a grim smile. "I can't get anyone to perform an autopsy."

"You? The girl who caught Graham? You should be running that place by now."

I continue to be surprised at how many strangers know who I am. I will probably never get used to it. "It's a long, bureaucratic story," I say.

She smirks. "Let me guess. The big boys with badges don't like the data girl showing them up."

I haven't done much smiling in the past forty-eight hours—shit, in the past several months—so it feels good on my face. I shouldn't be surprised that a woman cop would put her finger on it right away.

"Well, listen," she says, "I'll get us an autopsy on Mayday. Would that work?"

"That would be ... so great." I almost collapse with relief.

"Hey," Ciomek says, "can you break free?"

I look back at Ashland, huddling with ASAC Wilson. "I think so. Why?"

"Got some things you'll want to see," she says.

49

IT TURNS out that it isn't hard to break free. I tell Ashland I'm running off with Officer Ciomek to interview homeless people who might have been in the neighborhood while the bomber was milling around, which is basically the truth. She's deep in conversation with Wilson, so she waves me off absentmindedly.

We get inside Ciomek's squad car, and she hands me a laptop. "Pull up this surveillance footage," she says, pushing a button. "It's from the car wash a half a block north up the street."

Like a lot of surveillance cameras, this one has its limits. It was intended to cover the lobby of its store, but you can see through the glass walls onto the street a bit, looking south and east. Unfortunately, it doesn't go far enough south to capture the bomb site—the payday-loan store and Horizon Hotel. But there's a decent shot of the east side of Broadway from several days ago. It looks quite different from the Broadway Street I saw yesterday.

On the east side of the street, south of the car wash, the grainy footage shows a tall, thin man in dreadlocks with what looks like a microphone in his hand, gesturing and apparently singing as people pass by.

"That's Mayday," says Ciomek as she drives. "Marlon Mayberry. He had one of those old Mr. Microphones and sang all the time. Made some decent money doing it too. Part of that was his talent and charm. He'd make folks laugh, sing silly songs or tell jokes, and people would reward him. The guy was a fixture on that block. He put in full days. He'd stay until it was long past dark."

I watch him for a while, fast-forwarding through some of the video. I can't make out anything specific about Mayday save for his dreadlocks, but it's easy to see that he's good at engaging passersby. I count at least a dozen people who dropped some money in his collection box, and he always gestured ceremoniously and seemed to serenade them in response.

And Ciomek's right. According to the time stamp on the video, he's still there at nine o'clock at night.

"The other reason for his success was that he was fiercely protective of his turf," she says. "Nobody else got to work Broadway from Balmoral to Catalpa. Nobody."

"Okay. This video is from last Thursday," I say.

"Right. And if you look at video from Wednesday or Tuesday—and that's as far back as they went—you'll see Mayday there all the time, at least until eight or nine o'clock."

"Okay. So?"

"So look at Friday," she says. We stop at a light, and she reaches over and works the computer to pull up the video from Friday.

I fast-forward through it. Mayday is there at eleven in the morning. And at one in the afternoon . . . and three . . . and five . . .

And then he's gone.

I rewind to where he left the camera's field. Just after six o'clock. At 6:02 p.m., he turns and starts walking—briskly, as if agitated—south, going down the street and out of the camera's view. He returns thirteen minutes later, at a quarter past six, walking calmly, even a skip in his stride. He picks up his collection box and walks north until he's out of range of the camera.

"He called it a night early on Friday," I say.

"And that's the last we see of him." Ciomek pulls the squad car over to the curb. "Alive, at least."

I ask, "So what made Mayday leave his spot so early on Friday?"

Ciomek puts the car in park and reaches for her door. "Let's go find out," she says.

50

WE ARE parked outside a bagel shop, the smell of warm bread and pungent coffee unexpectedly making me hungry. I haven't eaten much since we arrived in Chicago. People brought in bagels—from this place, I think—and then, later in the day, sub sandwiches, but I could hardly bring myself to look in the direction of food, much less put any in my mouth.

We get out of the car. Ciomek goes to the trunk and emerges with a couple of granola bars and a plastic storage bag of items. "Care package," she tells me, and inside of it I see some antibacterial hand wipes, one of those pre-toothpasted toothbrushes, travel-size bottles of soap and shampoo, a water bottle.

What's sustained me over the past twenty-four hours, even more than my determination to catch the bomber, are the acts of goodness I've seen, big as well as small—people risking their lives rushing into blasting-hot wreckage to save people they've never met, cops hugging and crying with the victims' friends and loved ones, neighbors in the area bringing cases of bottled water or food for the rescue teams and even us.

"You hand these out?" I ask of the care package in her hand.

"My kids put them together at Sunday school. I see more homeless people than your average person, so..."

At first I don't even notice the homeless man seated against the brick wall of the bagel shop. He is African-American and young, though his eyes are droopy and unfocused. He lights up with a smile of bad teeth when he sees Officer Ciomek.

"Sperry!" Ciomek says in her upbeat way. She squats down and hands him the granola bars and the care package. He takes them without comment and stuffs them into a grocery bag resting next to the ratty plaid coat that serves as his blanket. "How you doin', kiddo?" she asks.

"Girl, know'm sayin', it's bad, girl, bad," he says, his head lolling. He can't be more than twenty-five. The sides of his head are shaved and the hair on top has a scarecrow look to it. His face is marked by acne, and his skin is weathered well beyond what his years on this earth should have done. He's wearing a T-shirt with no sleeves and a filthy pair of beige slacks that don't reach his ankles.

"When's the last time you scored?" Ciomek asks.

My eyes instinctively go to his skinny arms, which are tattooed up and down but have track marks too.

He bursts into laughter and then starts coughing. He settles down and shakes his head, a smile flitting across his face.

She nudges him gently. "When? I need your help, Sperry."

"Brother gots to get his amp on, know'm sayin'?"

She isn't getting anywhere, so she nods and keeps going. "You heard about Mayday?"

"Fuuuuuuck." He turns his head away from her, not that he was focusing on her to begin with. He looks up at me, standing next to the squatting officer, his eyes large and bloodshot, but there's a small trace of youthful innocence in his hardened, drugged-out gaze.

"Who the biddy?" he says.

"This is my friend Emmy."

I squat down alongside Ciomek. He looks at me and nods.

"Mayday," Ciomek repeats. "You heard about him?"

"Yeah, man, everybody heard 'bout Mayday." Sperry's eyes fill; his mouth turns downward. He crosses his outstretched legs and bows his head. I can only imagine what a kid like this sees and how he's learned to process it. But the death of Mayday has affected him. Ciomek chose this guy for a reason.

"Do you know what happened to him, Sperry? Any idea?"

"Last I saw." He flips a hand, sniffs. "He got his gwop, girl. He's all into cranberry and all like, 'I got me a rental, I got me a rental.'"

He's imitating Mayday's voice, I suppose, deep and husky. He raises his head again, tears on his face, but he licks his lips and gestures with his hands. "He all 'bout this whiteboy astro-naut, know'm sayin'? Says he got his sorry-ass self a rental. I say let a muthafucka eat his beans and rice in peace, know'm sayin', but he all about his rental."

"He showed up at Cranston with some money," says Ciomek, translating for me, then she turns back to Sperry. "What's this about a rental?"

"That's what the brother said, know'm sayin'? Says this is how the *rich* folk do it. Ain't gotta hustle if you the muthafuckin' landlord, see. You be gettin that gwop for nothin'."

I think it through—the video, Sperry's words. "Are you saying he was renting the space where he worked on Broadway?"

"Broadway Cat," he says.

"Broadway and Catalpa," says Ciomek. "Mayday was renting his block to another person?"

He points at her.

"When was this?" I ask.

"Woman." He tilts his head up to me. "I look like a damn calendar? Last time I saw'm." He gives a conclusive nod.

"It was Friday night," Ciomek says. "You said you were eating beans and rice, right, Sperry? That's Friday-night dinner at Cranston." She looks at me. That was the night we saw Mayday leave his post on Broadway early. The last time anyone saw him.

What the camera missed during those thirteen minutes when Mayday walked south out of its view and then returned and packed up his gear to leave was someone renting the city block from Mayday.

It's him. The man I've been tracking. I can feel it like I've never felt anything.

"You said the man who rented from Mayday was...a white-boy astronaut?" I ask.

Sperry waves a hand. "Tha's just us playin', girl, know'm sayin'."

"You were joking?" Ciomek asks. "But—I don't get the joke. Why an astronaut?"

"'Cause of what he said," says Sperry. "Says he got his self a rental. Says the man got a moon on his face."

51

BONITA SEXTON, looking slightly like a cartoon character through our Skype transmission, tilts her head as she takes in what I've just told her.

"What does that mean, a moon on his face?"

"We don't know any more than that," says Elizabeth Ashland, who's standing next to me and Officer Ciomek inside the old bakery that's our command center. "It could be a tattoo of a moon. It could be a skin discoloration or a scar." She shrugs. "It could be a circle, a half-circle, even a crescent shape. Any of those could describe a moon."

"Run through everything, Rabbit," I tell Bonita. "Every driver's-license photo from every license plate we tag from CCTV and tollway cameras. Every image at the airports. Every image captured by local CCTV. Every bit of facial-rec we can get."

"I'm on it." Rabbit kills the transmission.

Ashland blows out a sigh. "What are the odds this is a real lead? This is hearsay, from one homeless person to another." She turns to Officer Ciomek for the answer.

"The part about the moon on his face—I don't know," says Ciomek. "But I do know that Mayday owned that part of Broadway. It was his block. He didn't let anyone else work it. And that surveillance footage tells us that the day before the bombing, he left his spot much earlier than usual. That's real."

"And now he's dead," I add. "Not from the bomb. That's also real. And a pretty big coincidence."

"We can't confirm that he took cash from someone to rent the spot," says Ciomek. "But it would have taken *something* to make Mayday leave his post. He wouldn't have just surrendered it. And I can't imagine why Sperry would lie to me about what Mayday told him."

Ashland peers over our heads, thinking it over. "Why would anyone pay him for that spot?" Ashland asks rhetorically. She looks at me. "It's our man, isn't it? Has to be. Surveilling the payday-loan store before he plants the bomb."

"He paid Mayday for the spot," I say. "He staked out the place, made his plan, planted the bomb. And he killed Mayday so he couldn't identify him later."

I don't continue. Ashland needs to reach the conclusion herself. It needs to be her idea. If I jump in with my theory that this bombing wasn't the work of Citizen David, that it was the Darwinian killer I've been tracking on my own, I'll lose all the momentum I've gained with her. If I so much as mention my side work, it's over.

"We can't confirm his death was a murder," Ashland says.

You're getting warm, Elizabeth…

"Not yet, no," I say.

"I'll go to the morgue and get Mayday's belongings, whatever was on him when he died," says Ciomek.

Ashland nods.

C'mon, Elizabeth, get there.

"We'll need an autopsy of Mayday," she says.

Boom.

Finally. At long last, we'll be able to probe one of his victims, see how he's killing them, find out what he's injecting in them.

"That's a great idea," I say.

Ashland glances at me, her lips slightly upturned. I may have oversold it with the compliment. She seems to recognize she was being steered. She didn't get where she is at the Bureau by being dim. I'll have to keep reminding myself of that.

But for right now, it doesn't matter. She's just been roped and tied. I've got my autopsy. I've got the Bureau officially investigating my killer.

Whether the Bureau knows it or not.

52

ON THE flight back to DC on Wednesday morning, Elizabeth Ashland and I are quiet. We are decompressing, in our own ways, from the carnage we just witnessed. Neither one of us would say it, but there is a certain relief in getting some distance from the mass graveyard, the stench of human death, the anguish on the faces of the rescue workers and the families. There is also guilt at feeling relieved.

But we have done what we needed to do at the crime scene. It's time for me to get back to doing what I do best. With Rabbit and Pully at the office, and with an autopsy on the way, I am closer than ever to—

"...getting married, aren't you?"

I snap out of my thoughts and turn to Elizabeth, who is looking out the window. "You're getting married, isn't that right?" she says again. "I'd heard that."

"I was engaged, yes," I say, feeling the ache in my chest when I use the past tense. "Not anymore."

She turns to me. "No?"

"Didn't work out. Married to my job, I guess," I add, not that she asked and not that I owe her any explanation. I begin calculating how long it will take the flight attendant to scoot that alcohol-laden beverage cart down the aisle.

"Sorry to hear that," she says, resuming her view out the window.

I doubt that she's sorry. But she's making an effort, at least, which is a first for her. It's natural that there would be a bit of de-thawing in our relationship after this trip, though we are far away from sharing our most intimate secrets with each other.

"Men can be married to their work, and it's fine, it's normal," she says. "Nobody criticizes or second-guesses them."

And I had one of the good ones, a man who was willing to take his foot off the pedal to have a life, a real relationship. And I sent him packing. But there are only so many times I can have this what-is-wrong-with-me conversation with myself, and I'm sure as hell not having it with her, so I turn the tables.

"Are you in a relationship?" I ask.

She lets out a noise, a small rush of air indicating disdain. "You could call it that, yes. I suppose the answer is yes."

I haven't given much thought to Elizabeth Ashland's personal life, and finding out about it is not high on my list of priorities, but her response all but begs for a follow-up question. And I won't deny that she's piqued my interest; this is the first dent I've seen in her armor. Her appearance is always immaculate, her confidence unyielding, and her Ivy League résumé is second to none, but maybe human blood runs through her body after all.

So I say, "Not going so well?"

"It's…not going, period," she says. "Not anywhere meaningful. We both know it. I think we both know it."

"Do you want it to?"

"I…" Her voice trails off. She brings a fist up to her chin as she gazes out at the clouds. Our relationship got off to a terrible start, with her hard-charging criticism and mistrust before we'd so much as shaken hands. It was easy for me to throw up my defenses, write her off as a queen bitch, and leave it at that. But of course, it's never that simple.

Every time a woman advances in the macho culture of the Bureau, you hear the same shit from the men, buzzwords like *quotas, affirmative action, optics, office politics*. Or it gets more personal, with vague references to how "friendly" she is with the upper brass, if not outright suggestions that she drops to her knees in her boss's office. Anything to imply that the reason for a woman's advancement has nothing to do with merit.

I assume that, if I got to know her, there'd be a lot more to Elizabeth Ashland than meets the eye.

"Most of the time," she says, "I'm happy to have this career. Most of the time, I don't think I need a husband and kids. Or want that. But then…"

I glance at her. Her eyes have closed; her expression is tight.

"But then you see two hundred people murdered," I say, "and you see all their families and friends rush to the scene, and you see their heartbreak and sorrow. And as bad as you feel for everyone, as committed as you are to bringing the killer to justice, there is a small part of you that wonders if anyone's going to grieve for you when it's your time. And you hope someone will. And you wonder whether you've made the right decisions in your life, whether you've prioritized things correctly. And whether it's too late to change course."

Somewhere during my speech, she opened her eyes and turned to me, and she's watching me as if I'm someone she's never met.

"Yeah," she says. "Exactly. Exactly."

"Oh, there's nothing like a brutal crime scene to make you reevaluate your life," I say. "When my sister was murdered, half of me wanted to solve the crime, even though it was clear across the country, and the other half thought it was a wake-up call for me to get on with my life."

"And?" she asks.

"And?" I shrug. "This *is* my life. I can't let it go. I track serial killers. Knowing they're out there and that I'm capable of stopping them if I work hard enough, if I look at one more data set, if I plug a few more statistics into my algorithm—I can't stop."

"So you made your choice," she says.

"It feels more like it chose me," I say. "But it's time that I face reality. I'd love to have a relationship, but this has to come first. It just does."

I confidently deliver this speech as if I have all the answers, as if I have taken all the jagged pieces of my life and turned them into a neatly completed puzzle, but I feel a catch in my throat, and heat rises to my face.

I've just delivered a eulogy at a funeral. It's real—Books and I are finished.

53

I WHEEL MY SUITCASE into my cubicle, and my two partners, Bonita Sexton and Eric Pullman—Rabbit and Pully—pop their heads up. I huddle with both of them in Rabbit's pod.

"This is for your ears only," I say.

Rabbit draws back. That's the code we've always lived by, always keeping one another's confidences, our team against the world. So the fact that I'm making a point of reminding them has the intended effect.

"The bombing in Chicago wasn't Citizen David," I whisper. I give them a brief rundown of my side venture tracking my killer; how the murderer of the homeless man, Mayday, tracked those murders; how he must have hacked into my personal computers to learn the specifics of Citizen David's work so he could imitate David.

"So—what?" Pully asks, looking like a teenage boy who just rolled out of bed, clumps of his hair sticking up. "He knows you're onto him, so he's trying to hide behind Citizen David?"

"And kill the same kind of people—the frail, the weak—but by a factor of a hundred," I say.

Rabbit brushes a strand of gray hair from her face, her eyes intent. "So we have a body of work," she says.

"Yes. Scottsdale. Los Angeles. Vienna, Virginia. Indianapolis. Atlanta. Charleston. Dallas. New Orleans. And now Chicago. But I'm not sure about the *we* part."

"Why not?" she asks. "We're a team."

I put a hand on her forearm. "If I so much as suggest that Chicago wasn't the work of Citizen David, I'll catch hell. They'll redirect me. I have to do this under the radar."

"But we'll help you," Pully insists.

"No. I'm not taking you down with me. If this blows back, I can't let it blow back on you."

"I hereby volunteer," Rabbit says, raising her hand.

"Me too," Pully chimes in.

"No, guys. No."

Rabbit grabs my hand. "Now, you listen to me, Emmy Dockery. This man just killed two hundred homeless people. I'm working this whether you like it or not."

Pully starts in. "And so will I—"

"Uh-uh-uh," Rabbit clucks, her finger wagging back and forth like a metronome. "No, boy. You have a long career ahead of you. You don't need to get crosswise with the brass. Me? I'm closer to sixty than you are to thirty. I have my time in. I'm fully vested. What can they do to me?"

I thought I was supposed to be the boss.

Pully sits back, brooding.

"Focus on Chicago, Eric," Rabbit says. "There's plenty to do there. Emmy and I will cross-reference with those other crime sites."

My phone buzzes. I pull it out and check the message. "Shit," I mumble.

54

WHILE ERIC PULLMAN mines the data from the Chicago bomb site, I hole up in my cubicle with Bonita Sexton and bring her up to speed on the killer I've been tracking.

"Senior citizens in Scottsdale," she says to me, summarizing what she's learned. "Homeless people in LA. Then a series of one-off murders spread around the country."

"Let's start with the one-offs," I say, showing her a chart I printed out from my laptop. "Each of them was an activist or an advocate for the poor, sick, or elderly. Each was found dead at home. Each lived alone in a one-story house within a block or two of mass transit. Each either had the house up for sale or had recently bought it—"

"So there was a real estate agent's video or at least some photos of the house online," she says. "Something Darwin could use to stake out the place from a distance."

"Darwin?"

"Darwin," she says. "Appropriate name for our offender, don't you think?"

Okay, fine—that's as good a name as any. Darwin it is.

"Why does he pick people living in single-story homes?" she asks.

"I don't know."

"Why near public transit? Oh." She remembers. "You think he subdues them away from home and drives them back in their own car."

"I definitely think that's what happened in New Orleans," I say. "The seat of the car was pushed much farther back than the victim, Nora Connolley, would have had it. Someone else drove it."

"Okay. So you think he subdued her, drove her back to her house, killed her, then took a bus or train back to his car?" Bonita chews on her lip, eyes narrowed, thinking this over.

"I know, I know—he went to an awful lot of trouble, right?" I say, reading her thoughts. "That's what Detective Crescenzo in New Orleans said. But that's why nobody suspects foul play, Rabbit. There's no sign of forced entry because he has the keys; no sign of struggle at the house because he subdued the victim, probably by injecting something, away from the house. Everything points to an accident or death by natural causes. It's a lot easier to believe that a woman slipped in her shower than that a killer subdued her somewhere else, transported her home, then concocted some elaborate scheme to kill her and make it look like an accident."

"It's why you can't get the police to investigate," says Rabbit.

"And the one cop I did persuade to investigate, Detective Halsted in Vienna, Virginia, ended up dead in his home. A forty-eight-year-old man supposedly dead of a heart attack. Stranger things have happened, but it's getting pretty coincidental."

As open-minded as Bonita is, especially to my opinions,

even she seems to think it's a stretch. "What does the timing tell us?" she asks.

I look at the chart, though I have all the details committed to memory. "Well, most of them were killed on a Monday or very late on Sunday night," I say. "Not the first one, Laura Berg. She was a Tuesday. And the cop who was investigating her death, Detective Halsted, was on a Wednesday."

"But the rest of them were Monday."

"Yeah." I look at her. "What are you thinking?"

She gets out of her chair with a moan. Tired, weary bones. If Bonita Sexton has slept in the past forty-eight hours, I sure can't tell.

She starts to pace, but that's impossible to do in my cubicle, so we move into the hallway.

"Darwin picks them from a distance, right?" she asks.

I nod. "I think so. It's not hard to identify people who are activists; they tend to make themselves noticed online. And he finds videos of their houses online or he can use Google Earth to see if they have the right kind of house."

"So why a Monday?"

"Laura Berg wasn't a Monday."

"Forget Laura Berg." Rabbit waves me off. "And forget the cop who was investigating Laura Berg's death. The rest of them—why Monday?"

I breathe in, think it over. "Mondays are workdays. You have your routine, built around your work schedule. Weekends? Much less of a routine. You travel. You go out at night. But Mondays are predictable. He could anticipate their movements."

"That's right," she says in a tone suggesting I'm only halfway there.

"But Mondays, in that sense, are no different than Tuesdays, Wednesdays, Thurs—"

"Right, so why are most of the murders on Mondays?"

I deflate. "Just tell me."

She wags a finger at me. "Darwin travels on the weekends, he attacks late Sunday or early Monday, and he returns home Monday night or Tuesday morning."

That makes sense. "He probably has a job."

"Sure. A job with flexible hours."

"Or fixed hours, but those hours are fixed in the middle of the week. He works Tuesday through Friday, or maybe just Tuesday, Wednesday, Thursday."

"Which means," says Rabbit, "that he wouldn't kill on Tuesdays or Wednesdays."

I look back at my chart. Laura Berg—Tuesday. Detective Halsted—Wednesday.

"And yet he did," I say as it slowly dawns on me. "And what do Laura Berg and Detective Joe Halsted have in common?" I ask.

"Vienna, Virginia," we say in unison.

"He's local," I say. "He didn't need to build in travel time to Virginia because he's already here."

55

MICHELLE FONTAINE pulls into the parking lot of A New Day, now into her second week at the rehab facility in Fairfax, Virginia. Forever worried about being late, she arrives nearly half an hour early—9:30 a.m.—not relishing her first assignment of the day.

She walks into the staff room and sees a TV in the corner, a couple of people sipping coffee and watching the banner across the bottom of the screen: STILL NO SUSPECTS IN CHICAGO BOMBING. Two hundred are dead—two hundred homeless people.

Her mother must be popping Rolaids one after the other right now.

Just before ten, she enters the fitness room and finds her first Wednesday appointment—the lieutenant—seated in his wheelchair, curling thirty-pound dumbbells. She feels the anxiety swim through her.

"Hello, Lieutenant," she says. That's the way her partner, Tom, told her to address him.

"Ah." He leans forward and sets the dumbbells down on the mat. "The new girl. Your name escapes me."

Girl? She bristles but lets it slide. Any physical therapist has her share of older, and old-fashioned, men. Her job is to improve their physical condition, not their political correctness.

He uses the wheelchair's joystick to turn and face her. Sweat has darkened the neckline of his gray T-shirt. His upper body is pumped from the weight lifting, his biceps popping from the short sleeves like small melons.

"It's Michelle," she says, trying to keep her voice strong.

"Yes, Michelle, the new girl." Repeating that phrase. Testing her. He stares through her, as he did the last time she met him, every inch the military man except for the long gray hair pulled back into a ponytail. That makes him look more like the wounded vet he is.

"Lieutenant!" Tom Miller rushes in, wearing a red Nationals T-shirt and jeans. Tom has been great so far, showing Michelle the ropes, easing her transition, and his entry cuts the tension that seems ever present around the lieutenant. Tom claps his hands. "Ready to get loco?"

The lieutenant keeps his stare on Michelle, slowly moving toward Tom. "The Lokomat, yes, Tommy."

"Let me see you on your feet first," says Michelle. She can't hide behind Tom forever; she has to have some authority in here or she can't do her job.

The lieutenant turns to her again. "I'm sorry?"

"I've read your file," she says. "The incomplete SCI. I understand you can stand and walk with assistance. I want to see your progress." She catches Tom's eye. His smile has vanished.

"And am I here for what *you* want or what I want?" asks the lieutenant.

She draws in a breath, steels herself. "I'd like to see how

you're progressing, Lieutenant, rather than reading about it in a file."

"C'mon, Lew," says Tom, "she's new and wants to see what you can do. Show off for her." Michelle can hear the thread of fear in Tom's voice.

The lieutenant blinks and holds his stare on Michelle. "Some mettle," he says. "I like that. Get me a walker." He puts out his hand. Tom grabs a walker and rolls it over to him.

The lieutenant, making a production of it, locks the wheels of the wheelchair, grips the arms, and pushes himself to his feet, trying not to show the strain on his face. His arms are powerful, but his legs, covered by black sweatpants, are not.

"Let's use the belt," says Tom.

"No." Patients resist their therapists all the time, but the way Lew says it and the way Tom immediately complies tells Michelle that this particular patient is different.

The lieutenant, keeping his eyes on Michelle, grabs the walker. He staggers forward, one difficult step after another, Tom hovering nearby but not getting too close. *Heel and toe,* Michelle thinks instinctively. *Heel and toe...*

Six plodding, painful steps later, the lieutenant reaches Michelle, his piercing eyes on her. It's all she can do to stand her ground.

"Did I pass your test?" he whispers, his face a shade of crimson from his exertion, highlighting the gray crescent-moon-shaped scar by his eye.

"Here you go, Lew." Tom brings the wheelchair over to him. "Sit right down. Great job. Hey, how was Chicago last weekend?"

Lew settles himself back in the wheelchair.

"I guess not so good," Tom says, answering his own question.

The lieutenant spins around and heads toward the Lokomat—the walking harness suspended over a treadmill. Michelle goes over and starts to adjust the straps.

"Why would you guess that Chicago was not so good?" asks Lew.

"Well, I mean—with the tragedy there, the bombing."

"Two hundred people off the welfare rolls? I wouldn't call that a tragedy. I'd call it a good start."

Michelle's head snaps around at those words. "*What* did you say?"

"Oh, the lieutenant was just kidding. Weren't you, Lew?" says Tom, ever the peacekeeper. "We're running a little late here. We need to get started on the gait training." He catches Michelle's eye and waves her off. "His bark is worse than his bite," he whispers to her as she passes him.

"Well, I don't think that was funny," says Michelle, not willing to let it go, anger replacing her sense of intimidation. "I think it was an asinine thing to say."

Tom shows her an apologetic face, searching for some way to break the impasse, to keep the peace. The lieutenant cocks his head, eyes narrowed, as he stares at Michelle. As withering as that stare is, Michelle finds herself unwilling to break eye contact, to be the one to blink first.

What kind of a monster would say such a thing?

56

"THE BEST thing about this book, about this entire series? The teenage girl is tough as nails and as brave as any fictional heroine—but she listens to her parents."

"Oh my gosh—imagine that! You know what, you've sold me."

"And I don't even work here!"

Tired after a long day, near closing time at six p.m., Books watches from the register as his homeless friend Petty charms a woman looking for a young-adult book for her daughter, a birthday present. By the time Petty's finished talking, he's sold her all five books in the series. *Probably better than I would've done,* Books admits to himself. *I wish he'd been here this morning when I couldn't close a sale to save my life.*

That's Petty, smart enough, occasionally personable enough, to work in any number of jobs. What is it about his broken mind that prevents him from doing it, from making a decent living, from living a somewhat normal life?

"You should put that man on commission," the woman says as she takes her credit card back from Books.

"Yeah, I know." Books hands the bag to the customer and watches her leave. Meanwhile, Petty is reshelving the other books that the woman pulled out. "Say, Petty," he says. "I was thinking. Instead of staying here a few nights during the week, what if you stayed here every night?"

Petty slides the last book back onto the shelf and turns to Books.

"I was thinking I could put you to work," says Books. "I could use some part-time help. You'd be perfect. You've read just about every book in the store. And you seem to enjoy sales. So...you work for me here and there—we'll make up a schedule—and in exchange, you can live in the back room. It's not much, but it's a place to stay, and—and I'll throw in lunch every day."

Petty doesn't answer immediately. Books has tried to find Petty work, but every time, he turns away from it, unable or unwilling to commit. Even something like this, which he clearly enjoys, he won't commit to.

Where does Petty sleep the nights he's not here? Books wonders. Outside? On the train? Books has inquired, but Petty either doesn't answer or deflects the question with some vague assurance that he manages fine. Books and Petty have become friends, but Petty has opened the door on his life only so far, and Books respects the boundaries.

"Well, now, I dunno," Petty says. "I dunno. You been so good to me already."

"It would be good for me too."

For a moment, Petty seems lost, pushed out of his comfort zone—if drifting from shelter to shelter, never having a job, never knowing where your next meal will come from can be considered "comfort." Books suddenly regrets his offer. "Something to think about," Books says. "No big deal." He will probably never understand the damage inside Petty's mind, the ways that the war twisted and warped him.

The familiar *ding* of the door opening—not as familiar as Books would like—and Petty says, "But I'll be happy to help with this customer."

They both turn to the door. Books feels something light up inside him.

"Hi, Petty," says Emmy. She turns to Books. "I got your text."

57

"WATCH THE FRONT, would ya, Petty?"

"Yes, sir, Agent Bookman."

Books walks back into the inventory room while Emmy finishes her small talk with Petty. It's the first time he's seen her since they ended things at his town house. The mix of emotions swirling through him is enough to make his legs weak.

Emmy walks into the inventory room, and his heart skips a beat, as it always does. *As it always will,* he thinks.

She is dressed in a long-sleeved blouse with a scarf around her neck. Before the attack, Emmy wasn't a scarf kind of woman, but since then, she is never in public without her neck and chest and legs covered. Even in the midst of a tropical summer like this one, no off-the-shoulder tops or plunging necklines, no shorts or skirts. She is covered neck to toe, hiding all of Graham's damage. She even has bangs covering the scar at her hairline where the serial killer had tried to perform surgery on her scalp.

She doesn't want your pity or your help, he reminds himself. *She doesn't want you.* "How are you?" he asks.

She looks at him, holds his gaze. Not answering. Not because she has nothing to say, Books assumes, but because there's so much to say.

"Look, Emmy—"

"I take it, from our last conversation," she begins—*The one where you walked out on me? You mean that one?* he thinks—"that you're assisting the Bureau on the leak investigation. I mean, how else would you know I was the target of the investigation?"

Books nods.

"Director Moriarty pulled you back in?"

He nods again.

"And you figured—what—you could use our relationship against me?"

"It's not like that."

"Record our conversations? Memorize my incriminating statements?"

"It wasn't like—I didn't do that."

"No? Then what *was* it like, Books? What did you do?"

"You were already a target," Books tells her. "Moriarty presented it to me that way. I thought if I could be a part of it, I could at least make sure that things were done fairly. Make sure you weren't railroaded."

She raises her chin, but her eyes narrow. "So you were *protecting* me."

"In a sense, yes, absolutely."

"I should be *thanking* you, then. Thanking you for working undercover to spy on me while I shared a bed with you, while I wore your engagement ring on my finger."

"Well, that's not an obstacle anymore, is it?" says Books. "You took care of *that* problem."

"Did *I* take care of that, or did you? You're the one who made me make a choice—a choice that a man would never have to make."

"Well, *this* man made it." Books jams his thumb into his chest harder than he intended. "I would drop everything for you. I'd walk away from anything if it meant I'd have you. Can you say the same thing?"

Emmy looks away, tears welling in her eyes.

"You think I don't miss the Bureau every single day?" Books goes on. "But I scaled down my life, my eighteen-hour days, so I could have more of a life to share with you. Not you, though—no compromise on *your* part. No, sir. Never." He waves his arms and bangs his knuckles against the metal shelving behind him. "Damn it," he mumbles, rubbing his hand.

When he looks back at Emmy, she has fixed her stare on him again. "Why am I here, Books? To relitigate this?"

Maybe. Maybe also because I was looking for any excuse to lay eyes on you again. Hell, maybe a small part of me was hoping that you'd reconsidered, that you were going to tell me that you were leaving the job with the Bureau and would fly off with me to some island or something.

Who am I kidding? Every single part of me was hoping that.

Instead, Books says, "No. Emmy, I just spoke with Moriarty. I think we've been looking at this leak the wrong way. The things that have been leaked have been tactical, right? Things like where we expect David to go next, the profile we've drawn up. The leaked information helps Citizen David, doesn't it?"

She nods her head. "That sounds right."

"I don't think this person is just a leaker. I think he, or she, is an accomplice."

Emmy's expression tells him that she hadn't considered the possibility. "You think he's working with David?"

"I do. And no matter how much you may admire David from afar, I know you'd never actually help him blow things up."

She lets out a mock laugh. "Thank you for that. So I'm crossed off the list?"

"I'm being serious, Em. Yes, you're off my list. But that means someone in the Bureau is Citizen David's accomplice. And maybe you can help me find out who."

She closes her eyes, shakes her head. "Well, the list of people is fairly long. Carlton and his agents from National Security, Sloan from CID—"

"Cobbs from Science and Tech, and Mayfield. And their agents. I have the list."

"And the analysts are me, Bonita Sexton, and Eric Pullman."

"And don't forget Elizabeth Ashland and Dwight Ross."

"And you're going to do—what?" she asks.

Books shrugs. "We assume Citizen David is a man with resources, right? To understand bombing techniques and move about the country and escape detection all the while, he'd have to know a lot and have a lot. He's wealthy."

Emmy nods. "Follow the money," she says.

"Follow the money. Whoever's helping him isn't doing it out of the kindness of his heart. He's getting paid."

"And communicating with him by leaking to Shaindy Eckstein."

"Sure. What better way to hide what you're doing than by leaking information through a reporter who'd go to prison before she disclosed the source? Our rogue agent never has to make direct contact with David. The reporter is the perfect intermediary."

"Makes sense," Emmy allows. "Well, then, follow the money. I don't see Rabbit or Pully buying Cartier diamonds or Lamborghinis or dining at the finest restaurants."

"Me neither."

"The rest of the people, I couldn't form an opinion. I don't know them well enough."

"But they know you," says Books.

Emmy looks at him.

"There are hundreds of reporters in this town alone," he says. "Whoever this is didn't pick Shaindy Eckstein out of a hat."

Emmy nods. "They picked her because she's a close friend of mine."

"Exactly."

"They're setting me up."

Books nods. "I'll keep working on this and keep you updated," he says. "But in the meantime, you might want to grow some eyes in the back of your head. Someone has it in for you."

58

MY CONVERSATION with Books ends with my nodding in agreement and saying a quiet thanks for his information. Instinctively, I take a step forward as I say goodbye, being in the habit of giving him a kiss and an embrace of some kind, but then I realize that we don't do that sort of thing anymore. We are exes now.

I see the same start-and-stop movements from him, as if we're in a game of Mother, May I. A long, silent pause follows.

I wonder if his stomach's in knots, if his chest feels like it's on fire, if he hurts so bad that it defies words. If he wants to kiss me right now as much as I want to kiss him.

"Emmy," he says. "No matter what, we'll always——"

"I'll see you soon." With that, I rush out, unable to bear hearing him call me *friend,* understanding why people shouldn't stay in touch with their exes. And yet there I was with the "I'll see you soon," holding the promise of another encounter, unable to decisively cut the cord myself.

I walk past Petty, who is shelving books like an employee.

From what I know of him, he's a sweet man who was chewed up and spit out in the war, left with a brain that operates like a flickering light bulb. The light seems to be on right now, as he gauges my mood, focuses on a paperback novel, and mumbles a "Good to see ya, Emmy," keeping it detached and unemotional.

There is a mist in the air and in my eyes as I leave the store. I text Eric that I'll be there in twenty, which might be optimistic with traffic and an oncoming storm.

When I reach the stoop of my apartment building, I find myself glancing around. I jump when a car door opens on a parked car down the street, but it's only Eric Pullman getting out.

"Sorry if I kept you waiting," I say as he approaches.

"No problem, I was just texting back and forth with this supermodel who has a thing for me. I'd rather not say her name."

Pully always makes me smile. Pully is like a kid in big boy clothes, with that unkempt hair, the long neck and goofy expression, his self-deprecating comments and ill-fitting clothes. You'd almost forget that between those ears that protrude from his head like antennae is a mind that can sort out complex mathematical problems and breezily navigate computer code. He sees computers the way Beethoven saw pianos.

But his joke aside, it would be nice for him to have a girlfriend. Or at least get laid every now and then.

I punch in the code, and we enter my building and take the elevator up. I'm too drained for stairs. I feel a sense of dread as I approach my apartment, knowing that Darwin—Bonita's nickname has stuck—has walked this hallway, has entered my apartment, has rooted around in my things. Pully isn't exactly bodyguard material, but still, I am profoundly relieved to have someone with me.

I unlock the door and turn off the alarm. Pully leans into the alarm pad and declares, "This wouldn't be hard to bypass."

Well, that's what Darwin must have done. When my alarm is armed or disarmed—whenever its status changes—an e-mail is sent to me. Darwin somehow managed to enter my apartment without the alarm so much as blinking.

I make some decaf coffee and let Pully do his thing in my office. I sit in the living room, feeling like a stranger in my own apartment. This was my refuge, where I lived and where I worked. It was my comfort zone. Now it's been invaded.

Nice week I've had—I've lost the man I love and the sanctity of my home. I'm alternating between heartbreak and fear.

Thirty minutes later, Pully walks in and sits down next to me. "Well, you've definitely been hacked," he says. "I can't tell who or when, but definitely a hack job. Your desktop and your laptop. He cloned them and downloaded everything." He keeps his voice down, as if he thinks he might be overheard.

"So he has everything I've done on my computers, and he can see everything I do?"

"In real time. Yeah. You do a Google search for *single white female seeking Ukrainian-midget porn star* and he'll see it. You click on a link for sex-starved thirty-somethings and he'll know you clicked on it and he'll see what you see."

"So if I'm searching for his latest victim, he'll know it."

"Yeah."

"Will he see what I type on a word-processing document?"

"Sure. Everything, girl. If you type *I secretly yearn for Pully and his sexual charisma,* he'll be reading right along."

So he's basically taken away my personal computers. They've become useless.

I push back my hair and look up at the ceiling. Then a

spark of an idea, and I turn to him. "Can you trace it back to him? Is there some signal he's sending that we could trace—"

"No, no, sorry." He waves his hand, fanning out the flames. "He's fully encrypted."

"Are you sure? Isn't it even worth a shot?"

"Emmy, if we tried, he'd know we were trying. It wouldn't work, and you'd show your hand." He pats my knee in a friendly, nonsuggestive way. "You need a new computer, Miss E. One he hasn't compromised."

But even if I start using another computer going forward, Darwin knows I'm hunting him. He knows everything I know about him. "Thanks, Pully," I say as he starts to go. I suppress the urge to ask him to stay, but I dread being here alone. "And, hey—Ukrainian-midget porn stars?"

"Don't be judgmental. They're people too." He points at the door. "We'll need to update your home security too."

But . . . I feel like I'm missing something somehow. The hacking of my computers, however creepy and however much it has set us back . . . maybe it can provide some kind of opportunity too.

"Hey, Pully," I say as he reaches for the doorknob. "Hold on a sec. I have an idea."

59

EVEN SEVERAL days after Chicago, he is still glowing from the triumph.

He's not given to self-congratulation, but he must admit, it was a work of art—the toppled building, the fiery, smoky graveyard. And he took out more of those worthless drains on society in one weekend than he could have in one year under his old method.

All thanks to Citizen David providing him the perfect cover.

And the next one's going to be even bigger and better.

The café has few customers as darkness falls, as closing time nears. He sits protected against a wall, his laptop screen visible only to him, looking for all the world like a harmless army vet in a wheelchair enjoying a cup of coffee and a scone while he catches up with the latest news.

He should be spending time on his next project—*projects, plural*—but he can't help pulling up news accounts of Chicago. Profiles of some of the dead homeless people. Citizen David, publicly denying involvement on social media.

The FBI, tight-lipped but seemingly with no leads. And nary a mention of yet another homeless man, dead not from the bomb but from natural causes a few blocks away, a man known as Mayday.

He opens his clone laptop to monitor Emmy's nightly work. It's only just past nine, and Emmy typically works until the wee hours of the morning, but what she's already begun tonight catches his attention. It's a Word document entitled "Personal Notes—CD," her personal observations on Citizen David, that she created months ago and updates regularly.

She's been quiet since the bombing. He's been dying to know her reaction, but she hasn't updated this document, and he admits to himself that a small sliver of worry had begun to creep into his thoughts.

But she's back at it tonight, and he reads as she types:

The use of the Garfield the Cat watch as the timer in the Chicago explosion points to only one suspect—Citizen David. That detail has never been made public. Only David would know.

Exactly. Precisely how he planned it. He exhales with a mix of pride and relief.

Oh, how he enjoys playing with them, batting these FBI idiots back and forth with his massive paws, sprinkling a few false clues here, some red herrings there, watching them chase their tails. Is he really so much smarter than everyone else?

Yes. But it's more than that. It's his discipline that sets him apart, his planning and execution. Most people are lazy.

Emmy Dockery isn't, which is why she's presented such a challenge. He admits he was beginning to worry about her, but look how easy she was to fool!

As he basks in the glow of his success, words fly past him

on the screen. He blinks out of his moment and focuses on them.

> That's what he wants me to think, anyway. I know it's not true.

> Citizen David is too expert at explosives to use that much blast by accident. And he never would have risked the very people he champions—the poor, the mentally ill, the homeless—by bombing a payday-loan store right beneath a homeless shelter.

As if he's been shoved in the chest, he draws back, catching his breath. It—it didn't work? That can't be. Everything he did was perfect—

"Are you finished, sir?"

His head snaps toward the barista in the long green apron and hat, who jumps back at his reaction. "What?" he snarls at him.

"Sir, are you finished with your—"

"Does it look like I'm finished? Why are restaurants always in such a goddamn hurry to take your plate?"

"Hey, easy, guy, it's all good, no worries." The boy raises his hands in surrender.

He watches the kid retreat, scolding himself for the outburst. *You always,* always *stay in character. You don't let the anger show. Not in public. Not while you're playing the role.*

Besides, he consoles himself, taking a breath, *what Emmy's saying is just a theory. The FBI can't know anything for certain. Yes,* he decides, *it's just a theory she's kicking around. Emmy hasn't been able to get anyone in the FBI to listen to her ideas about me so far. Why should now be any different?*

His attention returns to the screen of his clone, which is mirroring every word Emmy writes:

Everything changed when I found Mayday.

He gasps, grips the sides of the laptop like he's about to shake it. His eyes dart about the room, panic overtaking him, everything upside down, spinning out of control—

He reads it and rereads it, confirming that he's really seeing those words, that his eyes aren't fooling him, that this isn't some momentary nightmare. His thoughts zigzag and his eyes bore into the words until the letters start to move and dance about, growing and shrinking, mocking him, laughing at him—

I f o u n d M a y d a y
I f o u n d M a y d a y

"Sir, are you okay? Sir? *Sir.*"

He looks up at the man addressing him, older than the first one, probably the store manager in his white shirt and green hat and name tag. The man takes a step back. "Is something wrong, sir?"

He closes the laptop gently and drops it into his bag, suddenly aware of his trembling hands, the heat on his face.

"I'll leave," he whispers. "I'll leave right now."

60

Everything...changed...when I...found...Mayday.

I finish typing and scoot back my chair, assessing the words.

Pully, sitting next to me, chews on his lower lip and stares at the computer screen with the expression of a fascinated child. I've always wondered if he was cut out for the FBI. He's a computer genius, no doubt, and we've put his skills to tremendous use. But this job requires a strong stomach, even for the analysts who stay behind their desks. Financial crimes are one thing. But the brutal stuff—human traffickers, sex offenders, murderers who cross state lines and trigger our jurisdiction—is not for Pully.

I told him—actually, Rabbit told him, but I agreed—that he couldn't be part of our hunt for Darwin, and yet here I am, involving him. But only because of his skill with computers; I needed him to see if Darwin had hacked into my laptop and desktop. Rabbit is good with computer-tech stuff, but Pully is a magician.

"Penny for your thoughts," I say, instantly dating myself to this millennial.

"What? Oh." He shrugs. "Well, mentioning Mayday will definitely get his attention. But you're tipping him off. You're telling him that we're onto him."

"Yeah, I am."

"Wouldn't it be better to make him think he's getting away with it? To let him feel warm and comfortable while we close in on him?"

He has a point there. If my only goal were catching Darwin, then the last thing I should do is tell him that we know he was responsible for the Chicago bombing. But catching him isn't my only goal.

I close the document on my computer, satisfied. "Eric, before I wrote this, what do you think Darwin was doing?"

Pully shrugs. "Planning his next crime."

"Right. Blowing up another building with a bunch of innocent people. Why not? His first bombing worked to perfection. Why not keep going? His confidence is at an all-time high."

Pully nods toward the computer. "So this was your way of shattering his confidence."

I pat him on the cheek. "Exactly. Now he's scared. His methodology didn't work. He'll be looking over his shoulder now. He knows we know about Mayday. He's probably wondering if we got surveillance footage of him at Mayday's spot across from the payday-loan store."

"We didn't. But he doesn't know that," Pully concedes.

"Right—he doesn't know *what* we know. So what's his most likely move? What would you do if you were him?"

"Me? Shit, I'd go into hiding." Pully grabs his bag and hikes it over his shoulder. "I'd stop, at least for a while."

"And that, my friend, is what I'm shooting for. I want to catch this guy as much as anybody, but more than anything else, I don't want a repeat of Chicago."

"So you're slowing him down. Making him reevaluate."

"Slowing him down is the best I can do right now," I say. "And while he's sweating a little, looking over his shoulder, lying low—I'll use that time to catch him."

Pully still seems unsettled, like there's more he wants to say, more on his mind, something he can't quite put together.

I walk him to my front door, ready for another long night of analysis. I briefly consider what Pully does in his free time. He's single and young enough that he should be going out tonight, but my guess is that he'll be sitting in front of a screen playing some video game or engaging in an online chat about Dungeons and Dragons or whatever the rage is nowadays.

Pully turns to me. "I'd make a terrible agent," he says. "I can't think like these people. I'm a numbers-and-algorithms kid."

"A damn good one," I say, but I can see that he wasn't fishing for a compliment. He was warming up to something else.

"What you wrote," he says. "'*I* know' Chicago wasn't Citizen David. '*I* found Mayday.'"

"Yeah?"

"You used the first person," he says. "Not 'the Bureau knows.' Not 'we found Mayday.' You wrote *I*."

Maybe there's more to Pully than computer code and algorithms after all.

"His problem is you," he says. "It has been all along. You tracked him all this time by yourself, right here in your apartment. Not the Bureau. Shit, the Bureau doesn't even approve of what you're doing. It's all you, Emmy. Even now. *You* know he did the Chicago bombing. *You* found Mayday."

"Eric, what I wrote will give him pause. He doesn't know what the Bureau thinks or knows. If he has brains and a sense of self-preservation—which he does—he will suspend his plans for a while and wait for the dust to settle. He'll check the news and read whatever I write on my computer. He'll lie low and give me time to catch him."

Eric's cherubic face pales, and he grimaces.

"You could have accomplished the same thing without using the first person," he says. "You're putting a target on your back, Emmy. You want him to come after you."

61

HE STARTS at the bottom and moves up.

That's what makes the most sense to Books. If you're looking for the mole in the organization, the one leaking information for money, and you have no obvious suspects, you start with the people who make the least money.

So while Petty, his homeless friend who is quickly blossoming into a master salesman, plugs a new novel set during the Revolutionary War to a mother and daughter ("Have you seen the musical *Hamilton*? Then you'll love this book!"), Books pores over the documents obtained from multiple subpoenas issued for him by the Justice Department. He starts with the field agents from the various branches of the Bureau—National Security, Intelligence, CID, and Science and Technology— who've been assigned to the Citizen David task force.

So far, nothing.

No irregularities in bank accounts. No large deposits. No series of small deposits meant to disguise a large bribe. No evidence of wire transactions. No Swiss bank accounts.

Credit card transactions reveal nothing of interest. There are no ridiculous expenditures that would stand out for an agent on a government salary—no major home remodels or expensive cars, the kinds of things that can be paid for in cash to launder the bribe money.

And nothing, thus far, revealed in online activity. No suspicious e-mails. Websites are all over the place—including a fair amount of porn for a few of the agents, even some of the married ones—but nothing that sounds an alarm for Books, no secret message boards or additional e-mail accounts where the agent might surreptitiously rendezvous with Citizen David.

But whoever he is, he wouldn't be that stupid. He probably doesn't have any interaction with David at all. The leaks to Shaindy Eckstein at the *Post* are likely his sole means of communication at this point.

He raises his eyes and looks at Petty, who is asking the customer's young daughter what kinds of TV shows she likes so he can analogize it to books. That's the right technique for people who walk into a bookstore with no real idea what they want. It took Books, a cop by trade, quite a while to figure out that that's how you sell books. He's always loved everything about books, the way they transport you to another place, stimulate your mind, widen your horizons, but he doesn't enjoy the sales or business side of it. Petty, however, has proven to be a natural at finding out what people want and then closing the deal.

Too bad, Books thinks, that a talented guy like Petty can't have a more normal, stable life. But then, what the hell is normal? Petty has never seemed particularly unhappy, never showed the slightest hint of self-pity. He drifts along, sure. His future doesn't look so bright. But he's apparently fine with living in the present.

And what does Books really know about this guy other than that he was messed up in the war, loves to read, and sleeps in the bookstore's back room during the week?

You're one to judge, Books thinks. *Your bookstore's on the verge of failing, yet you're more concerned with your temporary Bureau job. And you can't find a way to make things work with Emmy, the only woman you've ever loved, the best person you know. And you think you can decide what Petty needs to be happy?*

He returns to his investigative work, stopping only to answer the phone and ring up customer purchases. There aren't many. It's been a rough couple of months for his store. Okay, it's been a difficult year.

But how easily he dives back into *this* work, the Bureau stuff. How quickly it revs his motor. He loves hunting for clues. Discerning patterns. A game of chess. A game made all the more enticing because the people he's investigating are trained agents who've done the very thing he's doing right now and who know how not to leave bread crumbs.

I'm going to find you, he vows to himself, the bravado of an agent returning to him. *You're in here, in these papers somewhere, and I'm taking you down.*

62

I SMILE at Dwight Ross's secretary, who shakes her head dismissively as I pass her with the grande cup of Starbucks. When I enter his office, Dwight is standing by a table in the corner that is stacked with folders. Elizabeth Ashland has her nose in a file. She looks up at me, then at the coffee, a question on her face.

Dwight, reading something on his phone, notices me and mumbles, "That's not necessary, Emmy," part of his standard routine, then he glances at his watch to see if I've made it by eight a.m. I'm supposed to reply with a *Just wanna show my appreciation,* but I don't bother. Elizabeth nods at me with a slight pursing of her lips that is supposed to convey something short of outright hostility, then she looks again at the coffee. I put it down on his desk and go back to my cubicle.

Rabbit and Pully have beat me to work. Rabbit's gray hair is pulled back in a bun, which is about as fashionable as she gets, though it's meant to be practical rather than stylish. I'm just about to call for a quick morning update when my phone rings. The caller ID says Sgt. Crescenzo NOPD.

"Robert Crescenzo!" I say into the phone, hoping that my trip to New Orleans paid off, that our visit to Nora Connolley's house bore fruit. At this point, I'd settle for a tiny shred of hope. Or is he going to tell me that he's done some looking and I'm completely wrong?

"Good morning, Emmy."

"You got the results from the tox screen?" It was the one concession I dragged out of him; because of the unexplained puncture wounds on Nora Connolley's body, he agreed to have the ME test her blood.

"I do," he says. "It's negative. Negative for illegal drugs, paralyzing agents, anything that would have subdued her."

I close my eyes. If I didn't have bad luck, I wouldn't have any luck at all.

"But you put a bee in my bonnet," he says. "Are you near a computer?"

"Uh—yeah, give me one minute." I turn on my computer and wait for it to boot up, wondering what Sergeant Robert Crescenzo has for me.

"So you piqued my curiosity about Nora Connolley, and I followed up on a few things," he says.

"Thank you," I say. "I appreciate that."

"You don't have to thank me for doing my job. Anyway, I checked her credit card activity. The night before she was found dead"—*Sunday night,* I think—"she went to the grocery store. I've seen the interior video and she's on it, she's in there, but there's nothing unusual about it. I can send it to you just in case."

"Please do." With my free hand, I type in my computer password.

236 · JAMES PATTERSON

"The store has exterior surveillance too. Cameras that look over the parking lot. I saw something interesting there. Something that—well, it's interesting. I just e-mailed you the clip. You remember her car?"

"Yeah. It was a pretty standard car. A Honda, I think."

"Honda Accord."

"I remember getting inside it in her garage. And the driver's seat was way too far back for her to have been driving it last."

My computer comes to life, and I open the e-mail from Robert Crescenzo. "The attachment here is the video of the grocery-store parking lot?"

"Yup," he says.

I click on it. The video is gray, colorless, showing a large parking lot, probably eight rows wide and twenty deep. The store wasn't getting a great deal of traffic that night, so there are only about fifteen cars parked near the front of the store.

"You see Nora Connolley's car pulling into the sixth slot, one of the middle rows?"

I do. At the time stamp of 17:33:04—just after 5:30 p.m.—the Honda Accord angles into a slot, and Nora Connolley emerges from the car, her purse hiked over her shoulder. She is petite, as described, walking with the cane that I found in her house, and looking rather athletic at the age of fifty-eight (her details are coming back to me) as she approaches the store.

I get the creeps and shake them off. I'm watching a woman who has no idea she has only hours to live.

"Nothing happens for about four minutes. Fast-forward to five thirty-seven."

At 5:37, the parking lot still looks like a normal grocery-store lot: people carrying bags or pushing shopping carts to their cars, some of the carts with children sitting in the front compartment. Two women stop near their cars and chat; a man grabs his little boy's hand before they cross the lot into the store, pausing for a vehicle moving past; a man in a wheelchair rolls past them toward his car.

"What am I looking for?" I ask.

"You're looking for the wheelchair guy," says Robert Crescenzo.

"Seriously, Robert."

"I'm as serious as a heart attack," he says. "Watch the guy in the wheelchair."

63

ON THE fuzzy gray screen, the man in the wheelchair has his back to the camera. He keeps his eyes forward, his face turned away. He's wearing a baseball cap and a light jacket of some kind with the collar turned up, further obscuring him. Also wraparound sunglasses, even though shade has covered this parking lot.

He's motoring his wheelchair down a row of cars. But not just any row. The row where Nora Connolley parked her Honda Accord.

He stops right by her car. He leans forward and then to his side, as if checking something on his wheelchair, the wheel or the brake.

I lean forward too, toward the fuzzy images on the screen.

He's not looking at something on his wheelchair, I realize. He's pretending to while he glances around, making sure nobody's watching him.

In one smooth maneuver, the man in the wheelchair reaches out with his left hand, tucks it under the rear bumper of the Accord, and leans forward. Not much to see here—it looks like he's checking something by his feet, using the car bumper as a brace so he won't fall out of his wheelchair.

But that's not what he's doing. His hand isn't gripping the fender. His arm isn't tensed. It looks like he's . . .

"Is he putting something under the bumper?" I ask.

"Seems like it," says Robert Crescenzo. "I can think of only two things it could be. One is some kind of explosive. But he didn't blow up her car, did he?"

The wheelchair man motors on, continuing in the same direction he was headed, maddeningly away from the camera. When he turns his wheelchair to the right, giving us the first chance to see his profile, he's much too far away for these rudimentary cameras to pick up any details. Eventually, he disappears out of range.

"He didn't have a car parked in the lot," I say.

"And he never entered the store either. I checked the video for the entire day and never saw him. He must have come up to the store from the side and angled his way toward the row of cars where she was parked. He knew where the cameras were, Emmy. He kept his face out of sight. He ran a little half-loop through that parking lot and disappeared."

I rewind to the point where we first see the wheelchair guy. Robert is right; as he comes into focus near the front of the store, he has already turned mostly away from the camera, and his head is tucked low enough that all you can really see are the sunglasses and baseball cap.

"That guy had no reason whatsoever to take a detour through that parking lot. He had no reason to be there at all."

"Except to stop at Nora Connolley's car," I say.

"Right. Nora Connolley left that store a little after six o'clock. She drove to her bank to make a deposit at the ATM.

Then she stopped and bought a few things at a hardware store. I've got video footage of her at that parking lot too. But no sign of the wheelchair guy. He didn't follow her."

"He didn't need to," I say. "Because he knew where she lived. And he planted a GPS device under her bumper so he would know exactly when she was arriving home."

"Right."

"My guess?" I say. "He couldn't lie in wait and ambush her, not in a wheelchair. He set up near her house, probably in the alley, and put himself in a position that she'd stop and help a guy in a wheelchair. Then he attacked her and managed to get her and her car home. His legs must work well enough to drive a car a short distance, at least."

"And once he got her in that garage and private backyard," says Crescenzo, "he could set up things at her home however he wanted and stage it as an accident."

"Sounds like a good working theory, Detective."

"It's hard to believe and even harder to prove, Agent Dockery. But my gut tells me that's what happened."

"Call me Emmy. I'm not an agent."

"Well, maybe you should be," he says. "Because I believe you now. I'm opening a homicide investigation into Nora Connolley's death."

"That's great, Robert. But remember what we talked about."

"I do, I do. I'll keep it under the radar. No public statements. No press."

"Good," I say.

The last detective I convinced to open a homicide case had made it public, and that got him killed.

64

"A WHEELCHAIR," says Bonita Sexton. "Darwin's in a wheel-chair?"

"It was right there for me to see," I say. "I don't know how I missed it."

She looks back at the computer screen, which is paused on the video from the parking lot. "His victims all have single-story homes...yeah. Holy shit."

"I mean, for God's sake, Rabbit, I even had in my notes that the subject doesn't seem to like stairs. And my amateur profile on him was that he might be self-loathing."

"He's killing people just like himself," she says. "Or the people who help them."

"He lures them in somehow. It wouldn't be hard. If you're an advocate for the homeless or the sick, and a guy in a wheel-chair approaches you, you're not going to see him as a threat."

"And then he injects them with something and subdues them."

I nod. "Once subdued, they're at his mercy, even if he's

wheelchair-bound." I click on the video again and watch the man move his wheelchair farther and farther from the camera's view. "It's motorized. So he can move pretty well. I'm not sure how he does it, but once he subdues the victims, he gets them back in the house. And he stages a scene that makes it look like they died in an accident or of natural causes."

"That's why he does it at night," she says. "He uses the cover of darkness. He—so he transported Nora Connolley from her garage, through her backyard—"

"Her *secluded* backyard."

"—her *secluded* backyard, into her house, and up to the shower. Then what?"

"I don't know," I say. "Either she was already dead and he posed her, or he put her in the shower and banged her head against the base of the tub to kill her."

Bonita muses on that, looking upward. "Whatever he injected her with must have knocked her out or paralyzed her. It would show up in her blood."

I shake my head, recalling my conversation with Robert Crescenzo. "The New Orleans medical examiner found nothing in Nora's blood. No roofies or paralyzing agents or illegal narcotics."

"They'll have to dig deeper."

I wave my hand. "Which is why I've been begging someone to do an autopsy."

At that moment, my phone buzzes—a call, not a text.

Speak of the devil.

65

WE DON'T bother with a conference room, choosing instead to communicate by Skype.

"Well, this is déjà vu, isn't it?" says Dr. Janus, gesturing around the room she's in.

Dr. Olympia Janus—Lia—is a special agent and a forensic pathologist. When the FBI does its own autopsies, she's usually the one with the scalpel.

She helped me catch Graham. When I finally convinced the FBI to look into the deaths of Graham's victims, it was Lia who peeled back the layers (no pun intended) of forensic evidence that would suggest accidental death and uncovered the truth locked deep inside the victims' bodies—torture, mutilation, agonizing deaths. Homicides.

I'll never forget sitting in a conference room at the Cook County morgue in Chicago while Dr. Janus walked us through detail after painstaking detail of the most sadistic yet meticulous example of torture-homicide she'd ever seen. I almost passed out. When it was over, the other agents looked like they'd just been through a turbulent flight on a small plane.

And though I'm in the Hoover Building in DC, I'm looking at Lia Janus in that same Cook County morgue, this time after she's performed the autopsy on Mayday, the homeless man in Chicago who might help us catch Darwin and solve the Chicago bombing. Hence her déjà vu comment.

"You look exactly the same, Lia," I tell her, a routine compliment but nonetheless true. She is wearing a doctor's white coat, unlike last time, but otherwise she is unchanged—a strong, confident woman with short dark hair and simple jewelry, her glasses on a beaded chain around her neck.

"And how are you coming along, Emmy?" No similar compliment in return, but nobody who knew me before Graham would even pretend that I look the same. I've heard what people say, that I look like I'm hiding, wearing bangs to conceal my forehead, growing my hair longer to obscure my neck, covering everything below my chin in clothing. And I know it's more than my physical appearance that's changed.

Officer Natalie Ciomek, the Chicago cop who put me onto Mayday in the first place, is with Lia at the morgue.

I introduce them to Bonita Sexton, who's sitting with me, and when we are finished with pleasantries, Lia clears her throat. "We'll have our full briefing later," she says as a reminder, as if I needed one. I asked Lia to give me a sneak preview before the entire team heard her report. "Call this an informal chat."

"Sure, great," I say.

"Mayday was the name you used for the decedent?"

"Mayday, yes."

"All right." She folds her hands in front of her. "I should

start by telling you that I'm not prepared to give conclusions within a reasonable degree of medical certainty."

"Okay," I say, as if I expected that. In a way, I did, because Darwin's been so careful. But forensic pathology is based on the idea that the body doesn't lie and that some things can't be covered up. Graham, by Lia's own admission, was as skilled as anyone she'd ever seen, and yet she uncovered the details of those murders.

"I can't state, to a reasonable degree of medical certainty, the manner of death. The cause of death, certainly. The cause of death was asphyxiation. Those signs are evident. Bloodshot eyes, mucus in the back of the mouth, frothy fluid in the air passages, high levels of carbon dioxide in the blood, slight but acute edema of the lungs, hemorrhages and congestion in the internal organs."

"You're saying he suffocated?"

"He suffocated, no doubt. The cause of death is asphyxiation. But the manner of death? That, Emmy, I cannot conclusively say."

"Okay, but we aren't in court," I say. "What do you think?"

She nods. "Best guess? Your Mayday died of natural causes."

66

NO. THAT can't be.

I stare at Lia's face through the grainy Skype transmission and see a hint of apology in her expression.

It's like the oxygen has been sucked out of this cubicle where Rabbit and I are sitting. I look at Rabbit as if somehow she can help.

Just when we were getting some momentum...

"Why, Lia?" I manage weakly. "Why natural causes?"

"The decedent had chronic obstructive pulmonary disease. Lung disease."

"COPD," I say.

"Yes, COPD. Undiagnosed, I gather. Certainly untreated. We've been unable to track down any medical history on the man." She looks at Officer Ciomek, seated next to her at the morgue.

"I doubt that Mayday had seen a doctor in the past decade," Ciomek says. "He did have a pretty bad cough. I once told him he should see somebody about it. He just said he had a cold."

"So...COPD."

"I can't rule out that he asphyxiated due to untreated COPD. But I have to say, Emmy, that the reason I can't rule this out is due, more than anything, to the lack of evidence of any other manner of death."

"Nothing that suggests murder."

"Nothing that suggests homicidal smothering. I'm sure you can understand that, while asphyxiation itself is easy to detect, evidence of foul play often is not. Your decedent unquestionably died of asphyxiation, but I can't call it homicide."

"Can you *rule out* homicide?" I ask, a drowning woman reaching for a life preserver.

"No, I certainly can't rule it out. But I found almost no signs of antemortem injury suggesting a struggle."

Antemortem—before he died, she means. No signs that Mayday struggled with an attacker.

"Nothing under his fingernails indicating he scratched at an assailant. Little in the way of external antemortem injuries. There was a contusion on his left ear and skull just above the ear, but the contusion doesn't suggest a blow to the head as much as it does a fall. There was minor bleeding at the wound site, and mixed in with the blood were some chemicals common to asphalt as well as some grease. He was in an alley, after all. That's a hard, dirty street surface."

"He fell and banged the left side of his head on the street."

"Yes. Which could happen for any number of reasons. If he struggled to breathe, he could have collapsed. From the fall, I can't rule out homicide, accident, or natural causes."

"Okay..."

"There was no neck compression, and thus little in the way of petechial hemorrhaging. No tiny blood vessels bursting," she explains, probably for Rabbit's benefit, not knowing how much she knows about forensic pathology. She knows that I have more experience with it than I care to admit. "If he strangled him, we'd likely see burst blood vessels in the neck region. We don't have that.

"Hand compression—smothering with one's hand—that didn't appear to happen here either," she continues. "The violence done to the nose and mouth would be evident in many ways that are not present here. Lacerations to the nose, lips, gums, tongue. We don't have that."

He didn't strangle him. He didn't close Mayday's mouth and nose by hand. What did he do?

"Any possibilities, Lia?"

"One," she says. "The decedent presented with minor petechial hemorrhages in his eyelids and pericardium, and his head and face were pale—more difficult to detect in an African-American man but nonetheless present."

I don't know what a pericardium is, but I guess I don't care. I just want the punch line.

"And I did find very slight trace evidence of polyethylene on his tongue and in his lungs."

"What does all this mean, Lia? How did he die?"

"If this was a homicidal suffocation, and that's a big *if*," says Dr. Janus, "my guess is that the offender wrapped a plastic bag over Mayday's head."

67

RABBIT AND I look at each other, trying to incorporate what Lia Janus just said into what we've learned about Darwin. Could a man in a wheelchair suffocate another man with a plastic bag?

Yes. If he got him to the ground and subdued him. That could work. But it wouldn't be easy.

"The decedent was a good-size man," Lia says as if reading my mind. "At presentation, he was over six foot two and weighed two hundred and twenty-one pounds."

"And yet no signs of struggle," I say. "He didn't put up a fight."

"The unexplained puncture wounds," Rabbit chimes in.

"Yes," Dr. Janus agrees. "That's where the relevance of the puncture wounds on his torso become critical."

"He injected Mayday with something," I say.

"He didn't inject chemicals," Lia says. "The tox screen was clean. No illicit drugs, no paralyzing agents. Nothing that would have rendered the decedent powerless."

Just like the tox screen for Nora Connolley in New Orleans.

"I can think of only one possibility," says Dr. Janus.

"What's that?"

"A Taser," she says. "The two puncture wounds are the approximate relative distance apart of two Taser darts."

"But—we ruled that out," I say. "That was the first thing I thought of, long ago. But every cop in every case has said this doesn't look anything like a Taser wound."

Lia draws back, looks over at Officer Ciomek, then at me. "I wasn't aware of other cases. You think this is another... another serial—"

"Let's—let's just focus on this case, Lia. Why did you think of a Taser?"

"Well." She still seems disturbed by my revelation. I'm not ready to go public with my theory tying the Chicago bomber to Darwin and his other crimes. I can't risk the Bureau shutting down my work.

Shit, I just screwed up.

"Well, I'd have to agree—this doesn't look anything like a Taser wound. For one thing, a Taser dart has a barb on one side, so it can latch on—hook into the skin, so to speak, not terribly different than hooking a fish. And when you remove the barb, the hook, you can't help but reinjure the skin, even when it's done in a clinical setting. I see none of that here. These are pinhole punctures, Emmy. These are punctures made by a needle.

"And Tasers conduct electricity. Bruising aside, we typically see burn marks on the periphery of the external wound. The punctures on our decedent's torso are not the size of a traditional Taser dart and do not share the same characteristics of a wound caused by a traditional Taser dart."

I sit back in my chair and look at Rabbit, who shrugs.

"But a Taser is the only thing that would make sense," she continues. "If this was a homicide—*if*—then the offender wrapped a plastic bag over the decedent's head or forced plastic wrap over his face while the decedent held perfectly still."

"Perfectly still," I mumble.

"Perfectly still, or at least not resisting. That's nearly impossible to imagine unless he was subdued in some way. And if he was subdued by a chemical, I'd have found it. He must have been temporarily paralyzed by a Taser. The offender probably had to stun him more than once."

"So he built his own custom-made Taser," I say.

"Yes. A taser with darts like needles, no hooks. And something that prevents electrical burning around the wound. My guess—I don't know, Emmy, I'd be going far out on a limb here with my speculation."

But that's Darwin's brilliance. Nobody would believe it. Nobody would go that far out on a limb, not even to speculate.

"Please," I beg her. "Speculate. I'll take your best guess."

She nods. "My guess is that the end of the dart is a needle, but then it has some kind of stopper that holds the needle in place. And it's made of some nonconductive material, so it prevents the electrical burn from penetrating the outer skin."

"So it won't look like a Taser-dart injury."

Lia waves her hand. "Well, it certainly doesn't look like a Taser-dart injury. So, yes, in this hypothetical—that would be the offender's plan."

Rabbit puts her face in her hands. I know the feeling.

"I wouldn't have the slightest idea how to design something like that," Lia says, "so I couldn't tell you if it's even possible. Like I said, I'm well over my skis on this."

"But when you're briefing the FBI later, your best guess is natural causes. COPD."

"That's correct." She gives me a faint smile. "Why do I have the feeling I'm disappointing you?"

"No, not at all." I assure her that the facts are all that matter.

"Look, if you have information on other deaths, I'd be happy to compare results."

"Can we just strike that part from our unofficial record, Lia? I'm not ready to put that out there yet."

"Sure, of course. Well, okay." She claps her hands. "I don't think this was murder, Emmy—but if it was, this offender is more meticulous and careful than any I've ever seen."

"Including Graham?" I ask.

"Graham couldn't fool a forensic pathologist," she says. "This guy can. Even if you catch him, you'll never convict him."

68

I STARE at the grainy image frozen on my screen, at the man in the wheelchair. A wheelchair!

Nobody would ever suspect a man in a wheelchair of being a serial murderer.

Even if you catch him, you'll never convict him. Dr. Lia Janus could be right about that. But I'll worry about a conviction later.

The parking-lot video is stopped at the moment when the wheelchair man—Darwin—first enters the picture. He was smart, avoiding the camera until he had no choice, and even at that point he was already turned so that he was captured only briefly in profile before he turned his back and moved down toward Nora Connolley's car. But the brief profile glimpse isn't much.

"Nothing," Rabbit says, looking over my shoulder at the computer screen. "Between the baseball cap, the wraparound sunglasses, his jacket collar pulled up—"

"And his face turned away," I add.

"Facial recognition won't have anything to play with. We can't see his face."

And certainly there's no moon on his face, whatever that might mean.

I sit back in my chair. "COPD," I say. "Of all the luck. Mayday has a lung disease that could've caused his death."

"*Is* it luck?" Rabbit asks. "Or is it deliberate? Is he picking out victims that way? So the autopsies won't be conclusive? So there will be an alternative possible cause of death?"

The thought occurred to me too—that Darwin was choosing people with medical problems that could disguise their murders, even after an autopsy. But I just don't see it. "Darwin couldn't have known Mayday had COPD. It doesn't even seem like *Mayday* knew it. It hadn't been treated. He wasn't receiving medical care. No," I say, shaking my head, "Mayday wasn't someone Darwin chose after lengthy research. He didn't choose him at all. He needed Mayday's spot across from the payday-loan store to do surveillance before the bombing. And he had to kill Mayday because Mayday had seen Darwin's face."

Rabbit moans in agreement.

"There's gotta be something on this video," I say, trying to recapture the momentum. "What about the wheelchair itself? Anything distinctive?"

Rabbit hums as she leans forward.

"We know it's automated," I say. "He wasn't rolling it by hand. The little control thing—the joystick?—must be on the right side, because I can't see it on the left. Is that unusual?"

"A right-handed remote? Wouldn't think so. Actually, I have no idea."

Me either. "We can't tell the color from a black-and-white

image. You see anything that looks like a brand-name label on there?"

She doesn't. I don't either. The picture is too grainy.

"Seems like a nice one," she says. "It has front and rear wheels. When I had knee-replacement surgery, they put me in a simple two-wheeler that I had to roll myself, and the wheels were skinny. And the seat sure as heck wasn't leather. This is a four-wheeler, and those back wheels are thick enough to be bicycle tires."

"Okay." I nod. "So we have a four-wheel, leather, remote-powered wheelchair. And we think he's local, so—Virginia? Maryland? Everyone in a wheelchair who lives in Virginia or Maryland or the District of Columbia. Who has a moon on his face."

Rabbit is silent, unmoving.

"Am I missing something?" I ask.

"Hang on." She leans closer. "What is . . . that? On the . . . left arm of the chair."

"His *arm* is on the left arm of the chair. His forearm and elbow—"

"No, underneath. The arm of the chair. It's leather."

"Yeah, that seems right." I look closer. I see something too. Something on the leather arm . . . like . . .

"Like a sticker," Rabbit says. "A bumper sticker. A decal. Zoom in."

I do as she asks, but when the camera zooms forward, the image only gets blurrier.

"Let's send it to the lab," I say.

"Lab, schmab."

Rabbit and I both turn around. Eric Pullman looks like a Howdy Doody puppet, his chin perched on the top of his cubicle divider as he peers down at us.

"Pully," says Rabbit, "aren't you supposed to be minding your own business and solving the Citizen David case?"

His grin is so wide, his eyes practically disappear. "Give me the rest of the day with that image," he says, "and I'll tell you what it is."

69

IN ONE of the Bureau's myriad conference rooms, Dwight Ross, Elizabeth Ashland, and I sit, turned toward the screen on the wall, where Dr. Olympia Janus has just completed her summary.

Dwight lets out a sigh of disgust. "So, Agent Janus, best guess is natural causes."

"Best guess," Lia says, no longer at the morgue. She's now at the FBI field office in Chicago, and the image is much better than it was over our Skype call earlier today, but her message is no better, and it's even more depressing to hear it the second time.

"But I couldn't say to a reasonable degree—"

"Of medical certainty. Yes, I understand."

"It's certainly within the realm of possibility that his death was wrongfully—"

"Right, there's always some possibility of homicide," he says, interrupting her again. "But that's not what happened here." Dwight nods at Elizabeth, who's sitting next to him. "Okay, Agent, thank you for the good work."

The screen goes dark, and Dwight pushes himself up from his chair. "It's a dead end," he says.

"It was worth a look," says Elizabeth. "This man was the only—"

"It was worth a look," says Dwight, "and now it's a dead end."

"Just because she can't prove it in court doesn't mean it isn't worth investigating," I say. "Not every lead is provable in court. It's still a lead."

Dwight removes his glasses and rubs his eyes. "'Not every lead is provable in court.' Thank you, Dockery, for that insightful wisdom."

"He could have smothered Mayday without leaving signs of struggle. If he Tasered him—"

"If he *Tasered* him! Yes! Leaving marks that don't look anything *like* a Taser's! So Citizen David isn't just some crusader for the poor and downtrodden—he's also a diabolical serial killer who can fool the Bureau's top forensic pathologist!"

"Sir—"

"Look, Dockery, we all know you helped catch Graham." He waves his hands theatrically. "We all know—believe me, we know; *God,* do we know—that you helped bring down a brilliant serial killer. Okay? But quit looking for lightning to strike twice. Quit making this about you. You had your moment in the sun, and it's over now."

With blood rushing to my face and anger welling up inside me, I struggle to find words to answer him. *Keep it together,* I tell myself. *Don't be the "hysterical woman" he wants you to be.*

"This wasn't the work of some evil, sociopathic genius, Dockery. Citizen David is a crusader. He goes after corporations and government entities when he thinks they're unfair to the poor. He doesn't sit at home and build custom-made Tasers and devise diabolical schemes to murder the very people he's trying to protect."

I clear my throat and place my hands in front of me, forcing them not to ball into fists. "Sir, I'm only saying—"

"This man had a lung disease, for Christ's sake. A homeless man who—I'm going to take a wild guess—didn't lead the healthiest of lives on his best day, who had a chronic pulmonary disease that he didn't get treatment for, probably didn't even know about, but we should focus on his 'murder'"—he puts air quotes around the word—"because he had traces of plastic on his tongue, which even Agent Janus said could come from simply unwrapping a sandwich and eating it. Yes, let's drop everything else we're doing and spend all our resources on *that* lottery ticket."

"I'm not suggesting that we drop—"

"Or," Dwight says, yet again cutting off a woman, this time raising his index finger as if a thought had suddenly occurred to him, "we could leave the work of agents to agents. You wanna be one, go to Quantico. Until then, stick to your patterns and algorithms."

"Mr. Director," says Elizabeth.

"No." He slices a hand through the air as he turns to Elizabeth. "She got her follow-up. She got her autopsy. I didn't stop it, did I? And it came back inconclusive, at best—at best. Nobody thinks this homeless man was murdered. However," he says, turning back to me, "if memory serves, a few blocks away from where that man died, *two hundred* homeless people absolutely, unquestionably *were* murdered in the bombing of a building."

"That's what I'm—"

"Focus. On. That." He punches a finger at me with each

word. "No more about this—May-whatever. Mayday? Enough of him. Enough!"

I drop my head but don't say anything.

"I warned you that this was your last chance," he says. "I catch you one more time going on some self-promoting witch hunt instead of following the real clues, and you're done, Dockery. You get me? *Done*."

I close my eyes as I hear the door to the conference room open and then slam shut.

70

I RETURN to my cubicle, suddenly feeling the weight of sleepless nights, the roller-coaster ride of momentum and set-back, in my neck and shoulders, in my rubbery legs.

I'm on my own, as usual. No support from the Bureau. Just me and my gang of analysts.

Well, so be it, I tell myself. *We've done it before. We'll do it again.*

"How did it go?" Rabbit asks me.

"Great, wonderful, peachy." I throw down a file on my desk. "Dwight said that he admired my tenacity, that I've earned his respect and trust, and that no matter what Dr. Janus says, I should continue to follow any leads that I deem worth pursu-ing. He's also giving us all bonuses for our good work."

Pully's head pops up above his cubicle. "You need cheering up?"

I snap out of my funk, remembering what Pully promised— that by day's end, he'd get a clear visual of that decal on the arm of Darwin's wheelchair.

"I definitely need cheering up," I say.

"Then let me e-mail you something."

I sit down at my desk and wait for the e-mail. "You got a clear image of that sticker for me, Pully?"

"Pretty clear. Not in color, of course," he says. "But you won't need color."

The e-mail pops into my in-box.

The subject line: Pully is a genius (but we already knew that)

I open it. It's a screenshot from the video after Pully used whatever image-enhancement tools he had at his disposal.

A close-up of the arm of the wheelchair, mostly obscured by Darwin's forearm, which makes it hard to see too much of the sticker. But the good news is that the sticker wraps around the side of the armrest, clear enough to see.

In the left-hand corner of the sticker are stars. Beneath them, horizontal lines, uniformly spaced.

Stripes.

Unmistakable, even in black-and-white rather than red, white, and blue.

"You *are* a genius, Pully."

"But the bigger point is, we already knew that."

I pop up to my feet. "Team meeting!" I call out, which means we all stand and look at one another over our cubicle dividers. "We have another data point. Let's review what we know."

"Number one, he has some kind of a moon-like tattoo or scar on his face," says Rabbit.

"If we can believe a homeless person's account of what another homeless person said to him," I say. Rabbit makes a face, but I shrug. "I'm thinking like an agent. Like a prosecutor who's going to have to ask a judge for a warrant."

"Okay, I get it." Rabbit nods. "We have a wheelchair," she says, ticking off point number two. "And now, thanks to our resident genius Pully, we have a wheelchair with a sticker of the American flag on the armrest."

"If," I reply, "we can believe that the man who put something under Nora Connolley's car in that parking lot is our killer. Which we don't know. Or we can't confirm, anyway."

Rabbit deflates. "I don't like it when you think like an agent."

"But they'll shut us down if we don't have more. The key is the wheelchair," I say. "That's a huge lead. He has a car, a van, a vehicle of some kind, right? He must."

"So we start with disability license plates," Pully chimes in. "What's our range?"

"We think he's local to Vienna, Virginia, right?" I say. "A day's trip away, no more?"

"Right," says Rabbit.

"So let's do a multistate search. An eight-, maybe ten-hour radius. That's gotta be—what—DC, Virginia, Maryland, West Virginia, North Carolina, Pennsylvania…let's add Tennessee and Kentucky. Start there."

"Got it."

"I want DMVs," I say. "All disability license plates in those states. The driver's-license photos too. Then cross-reference with CCTV tollway footage in Chicago near the time of the bombing. And in New Orleans around the dates of Nora Connolley's murder."

"Men only?" asks Pully. "A certain age?"

"Everyone," I say. I'm not putting anything past Darwin. He's almost certainly on the younger side—somewhere between twenty and fifty-something—but who knows? And he's almost certainly a man, but can we completely dismiss the possibility that Darwin is a woman posing as a man? I'm not dismissing anything with Darwin.

"Okay," says Rabbit. "It will take some time."

I know. But this is Rabbit's specialty. Nobody is better at taking raw data and collating it into a usable format. It's the backbone of our operation. Books once used a basketball analogy to describe Rabbit: she doesn't get the score, but she gets the assist.

"Do your magic, Rabbit," I say. "And do it fast."

71

CLOSING TIME. Only one customer is lingering in the store along with Books. Books hardly pays any attention to the customer, telling himself that he's giving the man some space—some customers don't want to be followed around and hassled; they want to browse in peace—but the truth is that Books is so captivated by his work searching for Citizen David's accomplice within the Bureau that he hasn't paid much attention to any of the goings-on in his store today.

He finished looking at the financial records of the field agents assigned to the Citizen David task force earlier this afternoon, flagging a couple of items for follow-up but not seeing anything that set off an internal alarm, nothing suggesting the receipt of large amounts of cash, no suspicious website traffic.

Next, the analysts Bonita Sexton and Eric Pullman. Nothing there, unsurprisingly. Pully spends almost no cash, using his debit or credit cards for everything, though "everything" in his case is the innocuous stuff of today's mid-twenties computer geek—video games, computer software, techno-savvy items. Rabbit continues to live her bohemian existence, spending more than Pully but nothing extravagant, most of it going to health-food stores and charities and yoga classes.

The field agents—done. The analysts—done. And he has almost nothing to show for it. The only people left are at the top of the food chain—the heads of the divisions. And the people above them.

That's what has occupied him for the past ninety minutes. He started with the basics—bank statements, a list of expenditures and receipts.

And something is wrong.

He checks and rechecks them. He goes back six months. Nine months. Maybe he's misreading them. So he pulls some records from one of the field agents who uses the same bank. No, he's not reading these statements incorrectly. The account holder's ATM transactions are located in a particular spot at the top of each month's statement.

He's reading them correctly. And there's something wrong.

There's something missing.

"Do it again," he tells himself. "Be sure."

He flips through the statements again, going back a full year. Checking the spot on the statements for ATM transactions. Looking at the few checks she's written. Scouring her credit card transactions.

"Wow," he says.

Rewind to a year ago. Then she was transacting in a normal way. Took out cash at an ATM every few weeks, usually two hundred dollars a pop, sometimes more, sometimes less. Used her credit card at Starbucks in the morning, at someplace near the office for lunch, at the supermarket for groceries, at Target for clothes or other items. She bought gas for her car.

Purchased clothes and shoes at standard places like Neiman Marcus and Nordstrom and at some local boutiques—she does dress quite nicely, he's noticed.

But nine months ago, that changed. She still used her credit card, on autopay, for some bigger-ticket items like car and insurance payments, her mortgage, a club membership. Multiple expensive dinners and several hotel stays are on there too. But groceries? Coffee? Lunch? Gas? Dry-cleaning? Even clothes? Nope. Not a single debit or credit card transaction.

She's been buying all those things with cash.

Yet she hasn't made a single cash withdrawal from an ATM or bank branch in the past nine months.

So where is Elizabeth Ashland getting all that cash?

"Didn't find what I was looking for," says the customer, giving Books a perfunctory wave.

Books looks up at him, nods, and smiles, and the customer leaves the store. "I think I just did," he whispers to himself.

72

THE NEXT morning, weary from staying at the office past midnight, I enter the Hoover Building holding Dwight's cup of coffee. We are so close now. This is no time to piss him off.

I smirk at Roberta and knock on Dwight's office door as I enter. He's on his landline and raises a hand to me. Then he covers the phone and says, "Emmy, that's not necessary."

I sigh and play my part, keeping my voice up. "I just wanted to show my appreciation—"

"No. Hang on. Let me put you on hold," he says into the receiver and he hits a button. Then he directs a stare at me. "For real. Stop bringing me coffee. Just don't do it anymore. Stop."

He hits the button again and resumes his phone call, leaving me wondering what in the heck just happened. I walk out of the office, shrugging at the question on Roberta's face, and go down the hallway.

I pass Elizabeth Ashland's office and then stop. Normally, I speed up as I go by her office, wanting to limit contact as much as possible. But she did stick up for me yesterday—a little bit, at least—when I was pressing my theory about May-day's death.

And she was in Dwight's office yesterday morning when I delivered his coffee, and she'd looked quite puzzled by what I was doing.

She is at her desk, reading something on her computer screen and glancing down at something on her notepad. As usual, she's immaculate—sharp navy suit, hair pulled back in a perfect chignon, beautifully manicured nails with pale pink polish. That must be tiring, I imagine, always getting every-thing just so. And how many gorgeous suits does one person need?

When I knock on the open door, she looks up. "Dock-ery," she says. "I was just reading the social media sum-maries on Citizen David. Looks like he's no longer the golden child."

It's true. David has taken a big fall since Chicago. He's repeatedly denied any involvement in the bombing, via his middle-of-the-night, untraceable posts on Twitter and Face-book, but the public has largely turned against him. Social media comments about him are mostly negative now. Edito-rial boards that once gently scolded him for his victimless crimes now denounce him for killing two hundred people in Chicago or for spawning a copycat who did.

She sizes me up, her eyes focusing on the coffee in my hand.

"That's not for Assistant Director Ross, I hope," she says.

"Well, it *was* . . ."

"No, no, you're not doing that anymore. That's ridiculous. You're not his errand girl."

So she *is* the reason the morning coffee delivery is coming to an end. She said something to Dwight. He outranks her, but somehow, she made him stop.

"Thanks," I say, not sure how else to respond.

She waves me off. "Just keep doing your work, Emmy. You're doing a good job. More than good. And he knows that. That's the problem, actually. Sometimes, the men around here—well." She thinks a moment, then shakes her head. "Anyway, keep doing good work. You'll be fine."

I wish that were true, that good work was all it took around here.

"You still think Mayday was murdered," she says.

I'm about to speak, but a big caution flag is waving in front of me. Once I start, there's no stopping. The only way I can explain why I think Mayday was murdered is to point out the similarities between his murder and all of Darwin's other victims. Which means I would have to tell her about Darwin too.

And though she's scoring points with me now, I can't trust her to be a full-fledged ally. She could run right to Dwight Ross with it, and I'd be shut down.

Not now, I think. *Identify Darwin first. Find him. Then you can tell her.*

"I can't argue with a forensic pathologist," I say. "Dr. Janus doesn't think he was murdered. Who am I to say otherwise?"

Her eyebrows move, a brief wrinkle in her forehead. "That doesn't sound like you," she says. "Giving up so easily." Her eyes narrow, like she's trying to read between the lines. Like she's trying to read *me.*

"You don't want to tell me," she says. "You don't trust me."

"No, that's not—"

"No, it's all right." She sits back in her chair, throws her pen onto the desk. "If I were you, I probably wouldn't trust me either. We haven't exactly made it easy on you, have we?"

There's no point in my responding to that.

"You still don't think Citizen David is responsible for the bombing in Chicago, do you?"

I shrug, trying to be noncommittal.

"Off the record," she says. "I hereby grant you immunity for any answer you give." She waves an imaginary wand.

"Immunity from whom?" I ask. "From Assistant Director Ross?"

She leans forward, puts her hands together. "Emmy, I want a result here. I want a solve. Your track record earns you the benefit of the doubt. And I think there's a reason you don't think Citizen David did Chicago. There's a reason you think Mayday was murdered. You won't tell us why. You won't tell us because you're afraid you'll be accused of going off on some wild—well, basically, what Dwight accused you of yesterday. You're afraid Dwight will fire you."

She couldn't have said it better. I didn't give Elizabeth enough credit.

"Tell me," she says. "Me. Not Dwight. If it doesn't make any sense, I'll tell you. You know I will." She chuckles. "And if that happens, it will stay between us."

I'm still not sure how to respond to this sudden thaw in our relationship. Can I believe Elizabeth Ashland?

"If what you're thinking sounds credible, like something we should be pursuing," she says, "then let's pursue it." She opens her hands. "So let's hear it."

I take a breath.

"Trust me," she says.

73

SO I tell her everything. With a flutter in my stomach, and against my better judgment, I tell Elizabeth Ashland everything I know, everything I suspect, about Darwin's crimes and the Chicago bombing. There is something cathartic about it, about laying out everything and making my case, though it's tempered by the unknown—whether she will believe me and, more important, whether I can trust her.

She could run right to Dwight Ross and tell him that I'm off on some harebrained quest again. I'd be packing my bags by the end of the day. I'd lose all of my resources. Darwin would get away scot-free.

But if she believes me...we could devote the full resources of the Bureau to catching Darwin.

As always, Elizabeth remains blank-faced and noncommittal as I go through everything. She doesn't take notes. She sits with her chin perched on her fists, still as a statue.

When I'm done, she pinches the bridge of her nose. "So, this guy you're calling Darwin," she says. "Every one of his victims were homeless or sick or poor or some kind of advocate for the homeless or sick or poor. All died seemingly of accidental or natural causes, but you couldn't convince the local authorities to do autopsies."

"Right."

"And all of them had puncture wounds on their torsos."

"Two wounds. Spread the approximate distance of Taser darts."

"But nobody thought they were from a Taser."

"They didn't look like Taser wounds, Elizab—um, Assistant Dir—"

"Elizabeth is fine," she says. "They didn't look like Taser wounds because they were too narrow and clean."

"Right. There was no barb, no hook. And no electrical burn surrounding the wound."

"Mmm-hmm." Her eyes drift upward. "So then he switches up. He decides to piggyback on Citizen David's work. No more one-off killings. Now he can kill the same kind of people but get a few hundred of them at a time. And blame it on David."

"Yes."

"To do that, he had to know the details of David's work. Stuff that hasn't been made public. Like the Garfield the Cat watch."

"Yes."

"And to do *that*, he hacked into your home computers."

"Yes. So my first thought was to trace it back and find him."

She shakes her head. "No. If he's any good—and he seems to be—it wouldn't be directly traceable. He'd run it over a series of anonymous servers. We'd end up kicking in a door in Buenos Aires or Melbourne, Australia. But here's the bigger problem: He'd know. If he's proficient, he booby-trapped it with alarms. Once he knows we're looking for him, he'll disappear and start over with a new identity."

That, more or less, is exactly what Pully told me. I didn't expect Elizabeth Ashland to have the same level of cybersecurity knowledge as my computer-geek friend.

The look on my face must betray my thoughts. She puts her hand on her chest. "I came from Financial Crimes. We deal with this stuff all the time."

"Sure."

She drums her perfectly manicured nails on her desk, working this over in her mind. "And you think he's in a wheelchair, and he's local, and he has some kind of moon tattoo or scar on his face."

"I do. We're trying to narrow it down right now."

"Mmm-hmm." Still drumming her nails. "Okay, Emmy," she says. "Follow the lead and let me know what I can do to help."

I release the breath I've been holding. Just like that? I'm good? "And Assistant Director Ross..."

"Don't worry about Dwight. I'm giving you the green light. I want constant updates."

"Absolutely. Of course."

She gets out of her chair. "I don't know if this is a real lead," she says. "If it is, you've done great work. If it isn't—well, I can hear Dwight now: 'Emmy's wasted our time with some inane theory that a guy in a *wheelchair* is a serial killer.'"

"Understood." But it's the break we've needed. It narrows down our field immensely.

"You're out on a limb," Elizabeth says. "But I guess now I am too. Go find your wheelchair killer."

74

RABBIT, PULLY, and I spend the day poring over the data that Rabbit spent most of the night compiling and converting into a usable format. There are over twenty thousand drivers with disability licenses in the multistate region we've targeted. The process of reviewing and cross-referencing isn't as easy as it looks on TV, when some geek-chic computer diva types in a couple of words, hits a few buttons, and announces the name of the villain. This could take some time.

We call out progress reports, crack jokes in the heat of the adrenaline. But by five o'clock, the jokes have disappeared, and the comments have become weak, almost robotic updates.

By seven o'clock, the air seems to have completely gone out of my overworked, sleep-deprived team.

"Emmy."

I spin around in my chair to see Elizabeth Ashland standing there with that same implacable professional expression she always displays, the one that seems to put a barrier between her and everyone else. But maybe Elizabeth and I have reached a détente. We may even be developing a friendship, or at least a kinship as women in this male-dominated place. Yes, she initially came at me with her claws out, but since then, she's stood up for me more than once. Who knows, maybe someday—

Well, I'll settle for a détente.

"Sorry to startle you," she says.

"No, no." I wave a hand. "We're working the data. Give us the rest of the night and we'll have it. If it's in there, we'll have it."

"You guys should go home, get some sleep," she says to the three of us. "You're more effective with rest."

"We're close, though," I say. "I think we have the winning formula here. But then going through it all..."

"Going through it all will take time too. And you'll want to be alert. You don't want to miss something."

Like Pavlov's dog responding to the bell, I suddenly feel the weight of sleep deprivation overtake me. I stretch my arms. I look over at my team. Rabbit's eyes are heavy and bloodshot. Pully looks like a cranky little boy who needs a nap.

"Emmy, walk with me to the elevator, would you?" Elizabeth says.

As we get some distance from the cubicles, she says to me, "I spoke with Assistant Director Ross about this. I briefed the task force."

"And?"

"And I told them that I directed you to continue investigating this lead. Dwight didn't like it, and some of the others were skeptical, but they backed me up. So now it's my problem, not yours. You're covered. You can say you were following orders."

We stop at the elevator. She punches a button.

"Wow," I say. "Thank you."

She steps into the elevator. "Thank me by finding him," she says. "See you in the morning."

75

ELIZABETH ASHLAND leaves the Hoover Building just after seven o'clock. He knew she'd work late. She always does; Brooks has seen her attendance records from the card swipes entering and exiting the building. It's consistent with everything he knows about her—her discipline, her adherence to routine. She arrives at 7:00 a.m. and leaves at 7:00 p.m. every day, Monday through Friday.

He raises his camera and gets her in focus. She is walking north, as he expected she would. He is set up at the corner, well north of her, which gives him plenty of time to snap photos of her as she walks toward him, unaware.

She walks briskly with an efficient, confident stride. She removes a phone from her purse and looks at it as she walks. He zooms in on the phone itself. She is texting something, slowing down as she does so. He doesn't have the authority to tap that phone. He wishes he did. He may have to get that authority.

From the decisive movement of her thumb and the fact that

she stopped typing, he takes it that she just sent a text. Then she drops that phone into her purse and pulls out another phone.

So she has at least two phones. That's not unusual for an agent. There's the government-issued phone and a personal phone. No big deal. Maybe.

She puts this second phone to her ear, her expression serious, her head nodding as she walks. Books lowers his camera and jogs north to stay ahead of her; he reaches the next corner and turns to shoot her again.

She ends the call, puts the second phone into her purse, and pulls out the first phone again. She does a thumb-swipe and reads something—presumably a response to that message she sent.

Then she crosses the street. There was a chance she would turn and head toward her condominium a few blocks away. But she doesn't turn. Books didn't really expect her to. He's seen her credit card receipts, after all.

Elizabeth Ashland isn't going home just yet.

76

NEAR MIDNIGHT, he's in the comfort of his van, seated in his wheelchair. The vehicle idles at the curb, air-conditioning blowing hard on his face, some classical music playing low. The man who sometimes calls himself Charlie checks his GPS monitor for the movements of Emmy's vehicle.

In his hands, a piece of paper, the corner bending slightly from the blast of cool air: a printout of an e-mail sent to Emmy's work e-mail address but also copied to her personal e-mail account. Pully is a genius (but we already knew that) reads the subject line. Pully is presumably the sender, Eric Pullman, one of the analysts who works with Emmy at the FBI. A genius, maybe, but Pully shouldn't have copied Emmy's personal account on the e-mail, allowing Charlie to read it. Old habit, he presumes, from the time when Emmy was working from home so often; probably an automatic prompt on his computer. Bad luck for Emmy, good for Charlie.

The black-and-white photo, digitally enhanced, of the arm of a wheelchair, zoomed in to show the American-flag decal on the left armrest. The very wheelchair in which he currently sits.

He crumples the paper into a ball in his hands and squeezes it as if to pulverize it, his whole body quaking with anger.

"I should take you violently," he hisses through gritted teeth. "I should hold you down by the throat, use my knife to slice you open, and make you watch me all the while, knowing you've been defeated, knowing that *I* defeated you. I should watch your pain, hear your cries and pleas."

He nods. Yes.

"And only after it's over would I decapitate you. I would place your head on a spike and drive it into the frontage of the Hoover Building, displaying the slain warrior for all to see, for all to salute."

He smiles.

"I should violate you first," he says. "Violate you, let you feel me inside you, doing whatever I please, before I rip your body open. Let you know that I've defeated you in every conceivable way."

He checks the GPS. Emmy's vehicle is close, only a few blocks from here; she's on her way home. She's been spending long nights at the Hoover Building, a change for her recently. She used to stay home to the point of reclusiveness, but now it's day and night at the office. Why? Did something happen at the office? Did someone tell her she could no longer work from home?

It doesn't matter anymore.

A car comes toward him down the street, make and model uncertain from the front, the headlights on. The GPS tells him who it is. The vehicle turns into the parking lot next to the apartment building. Emmy is getting home just before midnight, a modern-day Cinderella.

He watches her rush from her car to the front of her apartment building, compensating for the slight hitch in her stride from her injuries, looking about nervously.

She has struggled physically and emotionally. That much was chronicled in that PBS documentary they did on Emmy and the serial killer Graham. Also her recovery from the horrific injuries. The pain meds. The rush to the emergency room—and the corresponding question, asked only a year ago: Did Emmy Dockery try to kill herself?

After tonight, in the days and weeks to come, that documentary will receive thousands, if not millions, of hits online as people ask that question again.

"It's not fair to either of us," he says. "You deserve a grander, violent death. And with all you've put me through, I deserve to inflict it on you." He sighs. "But no, Emmy, that won't do. You'll have to go out with a whimper. With an overdose, deemed accidental or suicidal. Fading away instead of standing and fighting."

He reaches down from his wheelchair, picks up the bag, unzips it.

Taser. Plastic bag. Hairpins. The Repressor Ultimate, the handheld UHF transmitter to suppress her security alarm.

"It doesn't mean we can't have some fun first," he says.

77

I REACH into my bag and remove the Glock, a firearm I once swore I would never carry. I drop my work bag quietly on the hallway floor outside my apartment. Put my ear against my apartment door and listen. I hear nothing save for the thumping of my pulse in my temples.

I unlock the door and push it open, stepping back, gun trained inside. The alarm lets out its shrill call. I flip on the nearby lights, then rush over to the kitchen and switch on those lights too, bathing the entire front of my apartment in full-wattage illumination—my heart pounds, but I'm seeing nothing, hearing nothing but that alarm's cry. Then I flip on the lights in the hallway, poke my head into my bedroom, turn on those lights, rush to my office, flip that switch too, then do the same for the bathroom—

I return to the alarm pad by the door and disable it just before the thirty seconds have expired, just before it would have turned into a full-blaring siren and led to a call from the security company.

I bend over and take a breath. This is my life now—I'm scared to enter my own apartment, and I leave the alarm on until I've turned on every light in the place. My own apartment, once my sanctuary, the principal place I did my work, the only place I felt safe, has been stolen from me, first by Dwight Ross, who insisted I show up at the office every day, and later by Darwin, who entered this apartment and discovered everything about me.

I grab my bag from the hallway and bring it inside, then I close the door, lock it, and turn the dead bolt. Push the couch up against the door. Place the large jar of marbles near the edge of the couch's cushion.

I don't want to be here. I wanted to stay at the office, all night if necessary, and finish the job. But Elizabeth Ashland was right. My team, me included, is dog-tired. We need sleep. Even I need a *few* hours.

The couch wouldn't stop Darwin from entering if he managed to get past the locks. But it would slow him down, hopefully long enough to prevent him from reaching the alarm before it turned to a full blare and alerted the police. And he'd knock the jar of marbles to the floor, which should wake me up if the shrill alarm did not.

Who am I kidding? He got past the alarm before, somehow, with some technology you could probably buy online. He wouldn't care about the alarm. And he's in a *wheelchair*. He's not going to break into my apartment in the middle of the night.

He'll come here when I'm gone and wait for me.

My head whips toward the hallway. All the lights are on. But I didn't have time to check everywhere—I had only thirty seconds. He could be here. He could be here.

And I've just blocked the only exit with a couch.

I grip the weapon in both hands. I did some light training with it, but I don't really know how to use it. That adage that a gun can make you *less* safe if you don't know how to use it—that was never truer than with me.

I take a step toward the hallway. Then a second step, lumbering, painful, heavier. My legs start to quiver, then buckle, and I struggle to stay upright, taking one hand off the gun to reach the wall for balance.

My chest about to explode, scorching lava filling me, sucking for air but finding none, my hand missing the wall—

—my shoulder, my head hitting the carpet with a loud, crackling *boom*—

He's coming. He's coming out of my bedroom, he's going to come, any second now, I can feel it—

Buzz-buzz-buzz...buzz-buzz-buzz...

Can't...breathe...

BOOM-BOOM-BOOM.

He's coming...any second now...I can't stop him...

Behind me, the turn of the lock. The *click* of the dead bolt.

The scraping of the couch's leg on the tile entryway.

The crashing of glass falling off the couch, marbles bouncing everywhere.

Trying to raise up the gun, but my arm won't move, my body on fire, trembling—

Behind me. I can't see him, my head and body turned toward the interior hallway.

But he's here. I hear him approaching.

His hand touching my face, his body over me, blocking the light, his tone calm but his words unintelligible through the white noise playing a morbid symphony in my head.

The gun taken from my hand without any resistance. The bag over my face.

A rushing sound...no...

"Shh...shh."

No...

"Shhh..."

And then, as blackness takes my vision, as every thought leaves me, these words power through the haze:

"It'll be over soon, Emmy."

78

I OPEN my eyes with a start and lunge forward, a brown paper bag clutched in my hand.

"You're okay," Books says. He's sitting on his knees next to me, his hand gently rubbing my arm. "Everything's fine." He looks at the blinking alarm pad on the wall. "You want to give me the pass code for that?"

I give it to him, and he puts it in, then returns and moves the couch from the door of my apartment back to its rightful place in the living room, or close enough.

"You had a panic attack," he says, helping me onto the couch. "You hyperventilated and passed out for a few seconds. Everything's fine now." He holds up a bottle of water. "Drink."

He hands me the bottle. I take delicious, greedy sips. I wipe away my bangs, stuck to my sweaty forehead, and breathe out. "Thank you."

"You can't do this to yourself," he says. "I know how much your work means to you, but if you don't take care of yourself, you won't be any good at it."

"I know, but—"

"There's no *but*, Em. What are you going to say? That you're *so close* now? That you have to stop him before he kills again?"

That, actually, is exactly what I was going to say. This man knows me.

"You have to go back to therapy," he says. "And take the medicine she prescribed."

"The meds make me drowsy. The therapist hasn't helped."

"You have to find a tiny bit of room in your life for yourself. That's all I'm saying. I'm not going to lecture you. I know...I know you don't want to hear it." He breathes out, the exasperated sigh of someone who knows he's repeating himself, who knows that his words will go unheeded.

I put out my hand, and he takes it, closes his other hand over it.

"The best thing you can do for yourself," I tell him, "is turn and run as far away from me as possible."

"Don't I know it." He chuckles.

He *does* know it, of course. I'm poison for him. I can't give him what he wants. I can give him nothing but heartache. And yet here he is again—here for me. Here when I need him. Actually...

I look at him. "Why *are* you here?"

"I knew you'd be up. I just got done with work and drove over. I called, but you didn't answer. Your lights were on, so I called again. You didn't answer again."

"Ah. So you used your key."

"Yeah. I knocked on your door, though. I was a good boy. I know the boundaries. I know I can't just waltz in anymore."

I watch him, see the pain in his expression, but I don't say anything. I don't know what to say. I know what I'd like to say—*You can still waltz in. Anytime.* But the best thing I can do for Harrison Bookman is *not* let him know how much he means to me, how much I want to wrap my arms around his waist and feel his breath on my neck and hold him so close that our hearts beat together. The greatest gift I can give him is to let him go.

"So tell me about your case," he says, changing the subject. I tell him. I tell him everything about Darwin—the serial murders around the country, the bombing in Chicago, the wheelchair. As reluctant as I was to share it with Elizabeth Ashland, it's the opposite with Books; it comes gushing out in vivid color.

"A wheelchair," he says, pursing his lips. "The perfect cover. He'd be immediately discounted as a suspect because of that disability. Drink more water."

I finish the bottle. I'm feeling better, much better, and not because of the water.

"You're not safe," Books says. "He's hacked your computers."

"My computers at home," I say. "I'm not using them for any meaningful research anymore. I don't want to stop using them altogether in case that makes him suspicious, but anything of any value, I'm doing on the office computer now."

"But you did type in that message about him killing the homeless man in Chicago. You knew he'd read it. You were letting him know that you're onto him."

"So he'd stop. Or at least suspend operations. I wanted to scare him before he blew up something else."

"I'm sure it worked, Em. But what's a scared killer going to do? He's going to go after the one person who figured him out."

I start to protest, but Books raises a hand.

"You know it and I know it. You've made yourself a target." He shakes his head. "I'm staying here with you until it's over. Or you come to my house."

"Books, that's not a good—"

"It's not about that," he says. "I'll sleep on the couch."

"I slide that couch against the door every night, as I'm sure you noticed," I say.

"Fine, then I'll sleep against the door." Before I can respond, he says, "I'll park my car outside your building and stay in it all night, every night, if you say no. Would you rather have me sitting in a car or sleeping on your couch? Because those are your only two choices."

I drop my head into my hands. I'm tired—exhausted, actually, utterly depleted. It's nearly two a.m., and my team and I agreed to meet early in the morning back at work. I can't deny the relief I'd feel having Books here with me.

I look at him. He has that no-give expression, his eyebrows up, mouth tight. I couldn't win this argument even if I wanted to.

"You never told me why you came over," I say. "What kept you working until midnight?"

He seems satisfied that he's getting his way. He relaxes, then gives me a wry smile that I haven't seen since he left the Bureau and opened up the bookstore.

"I was following Elizabeth Ashland," he says.

79

"SERIOUSLY?" I ask. "You think Elizabeth Ashland's working with Citizen David?"

He keeps that agent's noncommittal expression, but his smirk gives him away. "For about a year, Elizabeth hasn't taken a single dollar out of an ATM or even directly from her bank. That's hard to do. Even in today's world."

"Maybe she's just one of those people who likes the convenience of credit and debit cards."

"But she *isn't* one of those people. She hasn't used a credit or debit card to pay for clothes or shoes or groceries or dry-cleaning or—I don't know, take your pick. Taxis, makeup, shampoo, perfume, nail polish."

"She has great clothes."

"Right, I know. She hasn't bought anything like that with a credit or debit card for nearly a year. Her mortgage is on autopay. So is her car. Her insurance. Her cellular carrier. And her club membership. Those I can track by looking at her accounts. Otherwise," he says with a shrug, "you'd think Elizabeth Ashland never bought so much as a frozen pizza or a tube of toothpaste, much less designer clothes and shoes."

"You think someone's giving her money."

"I *know* someone's giving her money."

"You think it's Citizen David."

"Here, let me show you something." He reaches down to the gym bag at his feet and takes out his camera, a fancy job with a zoom lens and plenty of bells and whistles. He pulls up previous photos and clicks through them. "See that?"

I move in, getting too close to him for comfort, having to stop myself from putting my head against his shoulder as I've done thousands of times. Feeling the heat radiate off him. Feeling drawn to him like a magnet.

The photo he's showing me is a close-up of a cell phone and a manicured, polished fingernail that belongs to Elizabeth Ashland.

"That's a burner phone," says Books. "It's a prepaid job. She didn't buy it with a credit or debit card. It's not her personal cell phone, and it's not a Bureau phone. It's her third phone, Emmy. And it's untraceable."

I think it over. "Shaindy Eckstein's communicating with her source through a burner phone. But lots of people use them nowadays, not just drug dealers and mobsters."

"That's true. People who want to experiment with a service plan before committing to one. Or people who want to rein in their teenagers' phone usage. Sure. But not single people with money who already have their own personal cell phones. Why does Elizabeth Ashland need a second personal phone?"

"And why pick a cheap, untraceable one?" I add.

"Exactly."

Wow.

"I followed Elizabeth tonight to the Payton Club," he says.

"That club over on Third Street Northwest? Fancy," I say. "Exclusive."

"You can't even get through the door of that place unless you're a member or a member's guest. She's been a member for about a year. You know who else belongs?"

I shrug.

"A certain reporter for the *Washington Post*."

"Shaindy Eckstein belongs to that club too?"

Books smiles the smile of someone who loves working on the puzzle—and loves even more when he fits in a big piece. "Can you think of a better place for them to meet than a private club?"

"She contacts Shaindy with a burner phone," I say. "And if necessary, she meets her in person at the Payton Club."

"Right. I've been there as a guest. It's a big place. They have all kinds of rooms. Or, who knows, maybe she drops a handwritten note in Shaindy's locker in the women's locker room," he says. "So Shaindy wouldn't even have to be there at the same time as Elizabeth. They'd never be seen together. It would be so easy."

It would. He's right. I see the animation in his eyes, the thrill of a breakthrough.

"How does David get the money to her?" I ask. "Not through wire transfers."

"No, no, of course not. She's a financial-crimes whiz. She knows that would be easy to trace. No, my guess is he paid her in cash up front. Or he's meeting with her and handing her cash."

I put my hand on my forehead. "Elizabeth Ashland," I mumble. "And I just told her everything."

Books looks at me. "You told her all about Darwin?"

"Yep."

"You told her you suspect him, not Citizen David, in the Chicago bombing?"

"I sure did."

Books falls back against the cushion. "Then she needs to get word to David that he's in the clear. We'll be reading about it soon in the *Washington Post*."

80

AN HOUR and a half, a precious ninety minutes, is all the sleep I get before my phone blares out the sound of harp strings. I leave behind the whispers of a dream, not about serial killers or fires or tragedy, but about a strong, gentle, decent, handsome man who always seems to find me, who always makes things right, who makes my heart pound like a drum, who makes me melt when he touches me.

When I crawl out of bed and walk down the hallway, I find him still sleeping, curled up on the couch in his polo shirt and khakis, lightly snoring, oblivious to the stripes of sunlight peeping through the blinds. I feel everything else drain away. I want nothing more than to curl up with him, to give myself to him and let everything else go...

I could. I could walk away from all of this and be with him.

So what are you waiting for?

But I know the answer. I'm waiting until I catch Darwin. And there'll be another one after him.

Later, dressed and showered, I crouch down next to Books,

still in peaceful slumber. "Hey, sleepyhead," I whisper. His eyes pop open, then he blinks himself awake and sits up, moaning. "I made coffee," I tell him.

"Morning." He rubs his eyes. He didn't get much more sleep than I did, plus he was sleeping on the couch.

I search my refrigerator and freezer. Frozen veggies and some hummus, eggs that should probably be thrown out. "I know I have bread and peanut butter," I say.

"Hey."

I turn to him. He's holding up his phone, his reading glasses perched on his nose.

"The *Washington Post*," he says. "Shaindy Eckstein has the headline. 'Citizen David Not a Suspect in Chicago Bombing.'" He looks at me over his glasses. "That didn't take long."

"Does it give up Darwin?" I ask, rushing over to him. "Please tell me—"

"No, doesn't look like it," he says, scrolling through the article. "'Sources close to the investigation say that the bombing was the work of a copycat.' The rest is just filler from old stories about the bombing."

"Okay. Nothing about a wheelchair or—"

"Nothing like that at all. Here."

I sit down next to him and read Shaindy Eckstein's article. He's right. The only news is that Citizen David has been ruled out as a suspect.

"Our Elizabeth works fast," says Books. "It must have happened last night, when I followed her."

"But we don't know that," I say. "She briefed the entire task force about Darwin yesterday. It could have been any of them."

"*Of course* she briefed the entire task force," he says. "She made sure everyone within the Bureau knew first, *then* she leaked. So the suspicion wouldn't automatically fall on her. So someone like you or I would say, 'It could have been any of them.'"

He's right. Books is in command here, back in his old role as the straitlaced guy who wouldn't dream of breaking the law himself but who, when on the job, resides comfortably inside the minds of the criminals he chases.

He'll have his hands full trying to catch Elizabeth, though. Proving she's the leak. She's no dummy either. But I have someone different to catch. "I have to go," I say.

He turns to me, only inches away, and loses his smirk. A moment passes in which I'm certain his face inches ever closer to mine...and mine to his...

"So, anyway." I clap my hands on my knees and rise from the couch.

"Yeah, right," he says, like he's agreeing with the decision I just made, or at least resigned to it.

When I reach the door, he says, "I'll be back tonight. Let me know when you're getting home from work. I'll be here. Don't thank me."

Which is what I was about to do. He gets inside my head just like he gets in the heads of those criminals.

"If you find him today," he says, "let me know. I'm going to be there when we catch him."

"You're a bookseller," I remind him, "on a special, deputized assignment to identify a leak in the Bureau."

"Let me worry about that."

"You're not my protector, Books," I say, though I can hardly say it with a straight face, given that he's playing precisely that role at the moment.

"You need someone you can trust," he says. "And it's not Elizabeth Ashland."

81

BOOKS MAKES it back to his town house, the feeling of emptiness already blossoming, but it's tempered by the knowledge that he'll see Emmy again tonight. He's staying with her temporarily for all the right reasons—she truly is at risk, both at home from Darwin and at work from a diabolical superior—even if plenty of wrong reasons have slipped in there too.

He sends text messages to the two people who worked part-time at his bookstore until recently, when things started getting so tight that he couldn't afford to pay for additional help. It's still too early to call, so the text messages will suffice. Something came up, wondering if you can cover the store the next few days, he cuts and pastes into his texts. For good measure, he also reaches out to the woman who sold him the store a few years ago. She still lives in Virginia in the summer and stops in occasionally, and she's offered to lend a hand.

Petty could help too—he's probably the best salesman Books has ever had in the store—but he doesn't yet trust the homeless man with the cash register, with the money. And he has no way of reaching him.

He showers and towels off, and he's formulating his plan for the day when his cell phone buzzes. He's hoping it's one of the people he texted offering to cover him for the rest of the week at the store. But it's not.

"Did you see it?" Elizabeth Ashland says to him when he answers. *Good morning to you too, Elizabeth.*

"I saw it."

"The FBI no longer suspects Citizen David in the Chicago bombing. What the fuck?"

The cussing seems out of character for Elizabeth. Is she really pissed off, or is she overcompensating?

"I was just beginning to like her."

"Who?"

"Emmy," she snaps. "Your girlfriend. Ex-girlfriend. What-ever."

Whatever is probably the best description. "I'm on it," he says.

"Are you? Director Moriarty says this is in your hands. You're still up for this, Books? You're not getting cold feet about nailing your ex?"

"I'm on it," he says, and that's all he'll say.

"I'll stay close to her. We're working on an angle for the Chicago bombing right now that might be promising. I'll keep an eye on her and see if there's anything to report."

Books sees his opening. "Elizabeth," he says, "let me in on that angle. Let me in on the Chicago bombing."

"Now, why would I do something like that?"

"You want me close to Emmy, right? The best way to do that is track her at work. That's where she is all the time anyway."

"You're assigned to the leak investigation."

"That's what I'll be doing."

"It won't seem a tad suspicious to Emmy if all of a sudden her ex-fiancé shows up to work on her case?"

"I'll say the director brought me in. That he wanted a fresh look from an ex-agent he trusts."

A pause while she lets that thought marinate. "Well, the director does seem to have a soft spot for you," she concedes, though her tone implies she doesn't understand why.

"You want me to find the leaker," he says, "let me in on Chicago."

More dead air, then a suspicious hum from her end of the line. "What happened to your bookstore? I thought you had a day job."

"Don't worry about the bookstore."

Finally, an exasperated sigh. "Bookman, you're not working both sides of this, are you? You're not here to protect Emmy, you know. You're here to catch the leaker."

"I know my role," he says. "If Emmy is the leaker, I'm going to put the handcuffs on her myself, remember?"

"If you're screwing around on this," she says, "I'll put the handcuffs on you. Understand? Director's favorite or not, I'll lock you up."

Books feels a smile on his face. Her threats aside, he got what he wanted. He's in.

"We understand each other," he says.

82

I MAKE it to the office by 6:15 a.m. Pully, looking worse than he did last night, walks in at the same time. Rabbit has beaten us there. She doesn't look any better than Pully.

"What happened to you?" she asks me.

"To me? Nothing."

"You look terrific."

"I do?"

"What am I, a piece of garbage?" Pully asks.

"Eric, you look like a tired version of Eric. But our Emmy here." She nods at me, then smirks. "I think our Emmy got some last night."

"That's ridiculous." She's wrong about the sex, but in some ways she's correct. I feel it too. Something about seeing him, sharing with him, just spending time with him again...my batteries are recharged.

I put my bag on my desk. "The *Post* dropped a story this morning that Citizen David isn't a suspect in Chicago."

Howls of protest from Rabbit and Pully in their cubicles.

"Did it mention Darwin?" asks Rabbit. I hear the sound of her fingers peppering the keyboard as she pulls up the article.

"No—no state secrets given up. Just ruling out David as a suspect."

"Who the hell's leaking?" Pully asks. "Could've been any of them, right? The whole task force knew as of last night."

"It doesn't matter," I say. "I just wanted you to know. We have one focus today, team, and that's catching our Darwin."

Our area goes quiet save for the sounds of our fingers on our keyboards, the efficient hum of team members fully in sync, jumping right in where we left off yesterday. We call out updates as we review the data from the different states, crossing people off our lists, separating out promising possibilities for further review.

Two hours pass like that, and then the first wave of employees enter. My cell rings. I look at the screen and answer so quickly, I nearly drop the phone in the process.

"Robert," I say to Detective Crescenzo, New Orleans PD, the man investigating Nora Connolley's murder.

"I just got some additional video," he says. "You remember we saw the wheelchair guy put the GPS device under the fender of Nora Connolley's car and wheel out of the parking lot? We lost sight of him. Never saw his vehicle."

"Right..."

"I got it. A pawnshop, three blocks away. You want good security cameras, visit a pawnshop."

"He parked at a pawnshop?"

"No, he parked on the street, but their camera got it. Black-and-white, but we got it. I'm sending it to you."

My pulse is hammering. "Cut to the chase, Robert."

"We got no better look at his face. This guy is careful. Head down, jacket collar up, the sunglasses on, baseball cap pulled low. We never got a look at his face the whole time he came down the rear ramp and wheeled himself onto the sidewalk. We couldn't get his license plates either. It was a profile shot of the vehicle."

I take a deep breath.

"But you got the make and model of the vehicle," I say.

"I sure did," he says.

83

MY TEAM is buzzing on the final sprint.

A Dodge Caravan, Robert Crescenzo said. A Dodge Caravan converted for wheelchair mobility, not to be confused with the Dodge vans originally manufactured for wheelchair use.

We're looking for a Dodge Caravan registered with disability license plates.

With that additional characteristic thrown in, the data set for the state I'm working on—Virginia—is narrowed considerably. I shoot through each data point, cross-referencing with tollway cameras in and around the time of Nora Connolley's death in New Orleans. Nothing.

I try the highways surrounding Chicago on the relevant dates. No hits.

Okay—so when he traveled to New Orleans and Chicago, he didn't use the toll roads. Disappointing but not surprising.

But with the small data set, I can afford to run through each one of the individuals. I scroll through the alphabetical list of Virginia residents, looking at each of the driver's-license photos.

Beamon, Jacob. Cray, Cristina. Davis, Bettina. DiLallo, Janice.

No...no...no...

Espinoza, Jorge. Fredricks, Lyle. Halas, Marcia.

No, no, and no.

I feel the onset of disappointment but I'm buoyed by the notion that if he's not registered in Virginia, he's in one of the other states.

No...no...no...

No...no...no...

The last one alphabetically: Wagner, Martin Charleston. Residing in Annandale, Virginia, not thirty minutes from where I'm sitting. Only ten minutes from my apartment.

I almost bounce out of my chair. A driver's-license photo of a white male with hair pulled back into a ponytail. No smile.

By his right eye, a small, curved scar. The shape of a crescent moon.

"Everybody, stop!" I shout, my voice trembling.

My hands shaking, my vision swimming, the gong of my pulse drowning out everything but that face looking back at me.

I've been hunting you for a year. It cost me the man I love. It almost cost me my job. I've lost weeks' worth, maybe months' worth, of sleep.

But now I've found you, Mr. Martin Charleston Wagner of Annandale, Virginia.

84

MICHELLE FONTAINE braces herself, as she always does before a morning session with Lieutenant Wagner. She's handled all sorts of personalities as a physical therapist—compliant, good-natured, stubborn, flustered, bitter, despondent; it's part of the job. Especially difficult are the older patients, the ones from a different generation. The men call her honey or sweetie, ask her why she doesn't have a husband. Some of the older women don't want to take orders from her *because* she's a woman. But she lets it all slide. Takes nothing personally.

But something about Lew. That horrific comment he made in their last session about the homeless people murdered in the Chicago bombing—*Two hundred people off the welfare rolls? I wouldn't call that a tragedy. I'd call it a good start*—and just the way he carries himself, the way he looks at her, the whole...creepy vibe he gives off.

Yeah, creepy.

She takes the last sips of her morning coffee in the staff room and then heads to the therapy room. Inside, Tom Miller is already setting up. The lieutenant, in the wheelchair, turns and sees her.

Let's get this hour over with, she tells herself. *You're a professional.*

"Hey, Michelle!" Tom Miller sings. At least Tom brings some levity and merriment to the hour. She'll have to rely on him for a buffer, as usual.

The first half an hour passes without incident. They walk with him using the walker and brace, they build his leg strength using weights, and soon it's time for the Lokomat. *Not so bad,* she thinks, pep-talking herself through it like it's a dental exam.

"Michelle is upset with me, Tommy," says Lew, wiping his face with a towel.

"No, Lew, that's not true." Tom adjusts the straps in the Lokomat.

You're a professional, she reminds herself. *You're a professional...*

"She thought my comment about the homeless people dying in Chicago was...insensitive, I suppose."

"I'm right here in the room," Michelle snaps. "And I didn't *think* anything. I know it. It was an asinine thing to say. Now, can we leave it alone?"

Lew claps his hands and chuckles. "That's the spirit, woman. Speak up for yourself." He holds out his hands. "Michelle, do you know how much taxpayer money was spent on those homeless people in Chicago? Did you know that most homeless people are homeless by choice?"

"By *choice*? Are you *kidding* me?" She marches over to him, her face burning. "Most homeless people are either mentally ill or destitute. You have no idea what you're talking about!"

"She's right, Lew," says Tommy, his tone different, asserting himself for the first time. "You're out of line."

Lew seems as surprised as Michelle. "*Et tu*, Tommy? Well, isn't that nice. And I suppose it's our job to care for these people. To pony up cash for them."

"We don't—we should *want* to help them," Michelle says. "It's called compassion."

"Fine." The lieutenant waves. "You want to hand over part of your salary to people who don't want to take care of themselves, go right ahead. Nobody will stop you. But the government shouldn't force us to do it. That's not compassion. That's compulsion."

Michelle, her stomach full of acid, her hands balled into fists, looks over at Tom, who seems to be searching for words to make this all go away.

It's the first time in her life that she's wanted to punch someone in a wheelchair. But she relaxes her hands. She's not going to give him this much power over her.

"You know what?" she says to Tom. "I'm done here. I'm done."

"Michelle, wait," Tom says. He walks up to her, whispers, "Let's just get through the next twenty minutes and then we can—"

"No, I'm sorry." She puts up her hands. "I'm done listening to this idiot."

"So she walks away," says Lew. "The first sign that she's losing the argument."

She stops on that and turns, her blood boiling. "You know what, Lieutenant? Maybe someone should check *your* alibi for the Chicago bombing." She walks out. Returns to the staff room, the pot of burned coffee, the torn couches, the bulletin boards with notices and reminders haphazardly displayed on pink and yellow slips. She drops down on the couch and puts her head in her hands.

Wondering, on the one hand, *How can people think that way?*, while on the other hand scolding herself for not turning the other cheek. *He's a broken man,* she tells herself. *He was horribly injured and he's angry at the world. A professional would have finished the session and not engaged him, just let the whole thing slide…*

Tom Miller opens the door. "Hey." She glances at the clock over his head. It's a bit past ten in the morning. She realizes that, while she's been lost in her thoughts, almost thirty minutes have passed; the session with Lew has ended.

"Tom, I'm sorry—I shouldn't have walked out." But one look at Tom's face, and she can see that he's not upset with her. He looks…spooked.

"What's going on, Tom?" she asks. "Did Lew do something else?"

Tom rubs his head, his hand grinding over his buzz cut, a nervous habit. "He wasn't happy about your last comment, about whether he had an alibi for the Chicago bombing," he says.

Michelle sighs. "Okay, fine, I admit I shouldn't have suggested that he would kill hundreds of people." She chuckles. "Yeah, it crossed the line. But screw him. He can be as pissed off as he wants. I'm done working with him."

Tom starts to speak but then closes his mouth, nods, looks away.

"What, Tom?"

Tom clears his throat, chews on his lip. "It's probably nothing."

"Spit it out," she says, growing concerned.

"The thing is, he wasn't pissed off," Tom says. "He seemed… worried."

A cold wave goes through her chest. Worried? Why would Lew be *worried* about that? Unless...

"Tell me what he said, Tom." A sudden tremble in her voice. "Word for word." The fear on Tom's face matches her own.

"He said to me, and this is a quote, 'You don't think she'd *really* go to the FBI with this, do you?'"

85

LATE AFTERNOON, and Books is sitting behind the desk in his bookstore. The store is dead, empty this time of day, though he had a good morning—a children's author did a lunchtime appearance, an event Books had completely forgotten about, despite advertising it like crazy for weeks, despite having signs all over the store. He'd had to scramble when he got in this morning and realized today was the day, unwrapping the books, arranging the chairs and the display. In the end, it was fine. The author, with her full-wattage smile and her singsongy voice, charmed the crowd. He sold thirty-two books. Not bad at all.

Nobody knew that Books almost blew the whole thing, his attention diverted by his Bureau work.

His laptop is open to the website for Lieutenant Martin Charleston Wagner, motivational speaker and political activist. "Congratulations," he says into his earpiece to Emmy. "This validates everything you've been saying. You did it, Em. You found him."

"Congratulate me when I convince the lawyers from Justice to ask a judge for a warrant. It won't be easy."

"No, it won't," Books agrees. "When do you meet with them?"

"Seven o'clock tonight. Between now and then, I have to come up with everything I can possibly find."

"I'll be there," says Books, "now that I'm on the team."

The door chimes. In walks his homeless friend Petty, bald and clean-shaven, wearing a T-shirt and shorts, his camouflage duffel bag slung over his shoulder. He sees that Books is on the phone and gives a curt wave before heading into the back room, which is set up for him to wash up and sleep.

"Maybe someday you'll explain that to me," Emmy says to him. "How you managed to convince Elizabeth Ashland to let you in on the Chicago bombing investigation."

"Simple. I'm investigating you for the leak. This allows me to stay close to you." Books comes around the counter, folds up the chairs from the author's appearance, stacks them against a bookcase.

"You do realize you're putting yourself at considerable risk, Agent Bookman. You're on a high wire."

"Says the woman who practically dared a serial killer to come after her. Besides," he adds, "I like the high wire."

"Says the man who operates a bookstore."

"It's...thrilling in its own way. Trying to figure out how I'm going to pay the monthly lease, for example—that's a real heart-stopper." Books feels a smile on his face, realizes how much he's enjoying the banter. It feels like old times, when he and Emmy first met, when there wasn't the pressure of *marriage* or *the future*—just the two of them together.

"Speaking of which—any luck finding someone to mind the store?"

Petty comes out from the back room, wiping his hands on his shorts, looking around the store. His gaze settles on the open laptop on the counter, and his eyes narrow.

"So far, nobody can do it," Books says into his earpiece. He turns away and says, quietly, "Maybe...Petty?"

"Oh, Books, I love the guy, but—you can't leave the store in his hands."

He turns back. Petty is still looking at Books's laptop, open to the website of Lieutenant Wagner, his lips moving slightly as he reads.

Books slinks farther away, folding up more chairs, keeps his voice low. "He's a helluva salesman. He's rough around the edges, but he...I don't know, he gets people. He has a real way with them."

"Sure, I know, he's great. But...what do you know about him? You don't even know his first name; he's just Sergeant Petty. He comes and goes at random. Who knows what else he does?"

Books turns back. Petty has moved in closer to read the laptop.

"He's actually pretty regular," Books says. "Monday through Thursday, he comes in like clockwork in the afternoon, stays the night, and he's gone before I arrive in the morning. He keeps that back room spick-and-span. He's had plenty of opportunities to steal something, but he hasn't. All I have to do is teach him the credit card reader and the cash register."

"And what does he do the rest of the week?"

"None of my business."

"It's your business if you're going to hand over the keys to your store to him. And today's Wednesday. Can you count on him for Friday and the weekend?"

Emmy has to run—she's scrambling to compile information for the warrant application—so they sign off. Petty comes over and helps carry the chairs to the storage room.

Books sighs. Emmy's right. He's known Sergeant Petty for, what, six months? He met him during the depths of winter, sleeping outside his store, and invited him in. He's come to enjoy the guy's company, and he trusts him not to steal or mess up anything in the store—but running it? He can't place *that* kind of trust in him. Hell, Petty wouldn't even take a job as a salesman; he sure as hell wouldn't agree to run the whole store, even for a few days, even if Books asked.

"Sergeant Petty," he says, "I'm going to be closing up the store for a few days."

Petty emerges from the storage room. "Going on vacation?"

"No, just some outside work I'm doing. Helping out Emmy on a case."

Petty nods, breaks eye contact, as he usually does. His eyes drift back to the laptop. "Another serial killer, I s'pose?"

"Yeah. She thinks she found her man."

"Where this time? California? Texas?"

"Right here in Annan—well." Books catches himself. "Not far from here, anyway." He has to be more careful about revealing information. He probably shouldn't have left the laptop open to Lieutenant Wagner's website either. But it's only Petty.

"Listen, you gonna be okay while the store's closed? You can still sleep here. Like always. I can give you a key."

"I don't wanna put you out, Agent Bookman."

"It's not a problem." It's no different than he's been doing, letting Petty sleep here at night. He tosses a spare key to Petty, who catches it in one hand.

"Actually," says Books, "I'm probably going to close the shop right now. I have to be at the Hoover Building tonight."

"Things are moving that fast, huh?"

"Yeah, meeting with prosecutors tonight. We could be executing a warrant this evening, although tomorrow is more likely."

Petty nods, looks down at the key in his hand, showing Books the crown of his shiny bald head. "It's . . . really good of you," he says. "Trusting me with a key like that."

Seeing this homeless veteran with all his worldly possessions shoved into a single bag, it hits Books again, as it does so often, how unfair life is. Why isn't there some big red button you could push that would give everybody a slice of comfort and success—just enough so that no one has to sleep in an alley or eat out of a garbage can.

Or whatever it is that Petty does when he's not here.

"Of course I trust you, Sergeant," he says.

86

AT 6:45 P.M., he sits in his wheelchair before his bank of electronics: The computer monitoring Emmy's home PC, however inactive it may be these days. The GPS keeping tabs on her vehicle. The tablet displaying Emmy's e-mails. His own laptop, full of research on his next bombing site. Dinner—rice and chicken in lemon sauce—on a plate to the side, untouched.

He tries to still his hands, which are quaking as he forces them down on the desk.

"Well, there's no doubt now, is there?" he whispers. "You are most definitely out of time, soldier."

He slams his laptop closed. He hurls the GPS monitor against the wall. He sweeps the plate of food off his desk, and the plate clangs to the floor; sauce and sticky rice stain the wall. He closes his eyes, his chest heaving.

He missed his chance last night with Emmy, when Agent Bookman showed up at her apartment just after she did. True, he could've taken them both out, but there would be no passing *that* off as an overdose or suicide. It would have been a brutal, messy double murder. The spotlight on him would only have grown hotter.

It's unraveling too quickly. They could be here any time now. Suspicion has grown far too heavy on a cantankerous wheelchair-bound war veteran from Annandale, Virginia.

He pops up from the wheelchair, kicks it backward with his foot.

I can walk! It's a miracle! Hallelujah!

He's silently cracked that joke to himself so many times. Oh, how often he's wanted to do that, to bounce up in the middle of the sidewalk or in some public place, just to see the look on everyone's face.

But he is finding no humor right now.

He does some stretches, releasing nervous energy, bounces in place like an athlete gearing up for a game. He walks over to the wheelchair that's halfway across the room, the RANGERS LEAD THE WAY sticker on the shroud, the American-flag decal on the armrest, and pats it lovingly.

What a superb tactical advantage it's provided. How many people he has been able to subdue and kill simply because they never imagined that he could be a threat. *A man in a wheelchair? Harmless. What could* he *do to me?*

True, it's been a real pain in the ass, having to pretend his legs don't work, keeping them perfectly still whenever he's in character. Lucky for him, nobody ever suspected the ruse. But why *would* anyone suspect him? Who, after all, would *pretend* to be confined to a wheelchair?

Well, he would.

"You've been a good friend," he says to the motorized chair. "But I won't be needing you tonight."

Tonight will not be subtle. Tonight will be hands-on. Tonight will be violent.

He's rather looking forward to it.

If the FBI doesn't get here first.

87

"LIEUTENANT MARTIN CHARLESTON WAGNER," I say to the room. "Age forty-four. Honorably discharged from the U.S. Army three years ago after an injury in Iraq, an IED explosion that left him partially paralyzed. Relocated to Annandale, Virginia, eighteen months ago, where he lives on his army pension and is self-employed as a motivational speaker and political activist."

After discovering Martin Wagner this morning, we spent the day gathering whatever information we could to present to the task force, a group joined today by lawyers from the Department of Justice, who will need to seek a warrant from a federal magistrate.

I press a button on the remote in my hand, and the video display (thank you, Pully) on the projection screen changes to a screenshot of the home page of his website, Lieutenant Wags.com. There he is in all his glory, his gray hair pulled back in a ponytail, the crescent-moon-shaped scar on the side of his face.

"He gives motivational speeches, mostly to others with disabilities," I say. "He preaches self-reliance. 'Don't ask the government for anything. Don't accept handouts. Do it on your own.' He wants to abolish welfare and Medicaid and Social Security and Medicare. He's written a number of essays on the subject. He self-published a book. And he speaks all over the country."

I punch the remote as I talk, displaying various articles and a copy of the book he wrote. I punch it again, and up pops Wagner's tour schedule.

"Look at the cities and the dates," I say. "Indianapolis. Atlanta. Charleston. Dallas. New Orleans. And Chicago. Against each of those dates, we can match the murder of some activist for the poor or the sick or the homeless. And, of course, Chicago was the bombing of the hotel for the homeless."

"Let's start there, Chicago. That's why we're here, right—the bombing?" This from the top prosecutor in the room, a woman named Amee Czernak. She's dressed in a charcoal suit, has sand-colored hair pulled back neatly at her neck, and is looking at me over the glasses perched on her nose. "Did you confirm that he attended that speaking engagement in Chicago?"

"Yes," I say. "There's some video of it on his website and on YouTube. He spoke at three p.m. on Saturday. The bomb detonated twelve hours later, in the early hours of Sunday morning. He would've had plenty of opportunity to stake out the payday-loan store and the hotel above it that weekend and plant that bomb."

"How do you know that?" she asks. "Do you know when he arrived in Chicago that weekend?"

"No. He didn't fly, and he didn't take any bus or train that we could find, so we assume he drove. And avoided the toll roads."

"So you don't know when he arrived in Chicago. Do you know when he left?"

"Not yet," I concede.

"Can you account for his whereabouts at any other time that weekend in Chicago?"

"No, I can't. Not yet. We think he began his stakeout across from the payday-loan store at six fifteen on that Friday evening. That's when he paid off the homeless man, Mayday."

"And you think he murdered that homeless man."

She's done her homework; she had this information for only an hour before we met.

"So he couldn't be a witness later, yes. Mayday's death is consistent with the other murders we've chronicled around the country on dates that Wagner was in those cities."

"Murders that haven't been called murders by anyone else but you."

"New Orleans PD has opened a murder investigation into Nora Connolley," I say. "But otherwise, you're correct."

"Our top forensic pathologist doesn't think this Mayday individual was murdered," she says. "And his death is similar to other deaths across the country that, to date, have not been called murders either."

"Well, that may be true, but—"

"You can't prove any of these were murders, Ms. Dockery. And you have no proof whatsoever that remotely ties Lieutenant Wagner to the Chicago bombing other than the fact that he was one of three or four *million* people in Chicago that weekend. And, oh yes, that he had...what was it? A moon on his face, which is a description we received from one homeless man's account of what another homeless man said. It's..." She sits back in her chair. "How am I supposed to take this to a judge?"

"You can take *this* to a judge," I say. I punch the remote to display the close-up image Pully got of Wagner's wheelchair. "A man with an American-flag decal on the arm of his wheelchair placed something under Nora Connolley's car only hours before she died." I punch the remote again. "And here—from Wagner's website—here he is, Martin Charleston Wagner, posing for a photo with a group of wounded war veterans. With the same American-flag decal on his wheelchair."

I wait for a reaction but get only a blank stare from the prosecutor.

"While in New Orleans," I summarize, "ostensibly to give one of his motivational speeches, Wagner went out of his way to park his vehicle a good three blocks down the street from a grocery store, by a pawnshop, and then wheeled himself all that way—nearly half a mile—to the parking lot of the grocery store, for no apparent reason other than to place something under the fender of a car owned by Nora Connolley. Then he went straight back to his vehicle and drove away. He could've easily parked his vehicle in that grocery-store parking lot, but he didn't. He had one and only one goal—to put something under the fender of a car owned by a woman who died a few hours later and do it without detection. Does that seem the least bit odd to you?"

The prosecutor allows that it does, then plays with her pen, tapping it against a notepad. "Books, I understand you were just assigned to the case. What's your take?"

Books hadn't planned on speaking tonight, being new to the case and given our relationship. He straightens. "Yes, I was just assigned. There hadn't been an agent assigned so far; it was just analytics. I've had only a bit longer than you with this information, but I'm convinced by what I've seen."

Amee Czernak's eyes drift to the ceiling. "How fast could you serve this warrant?"

"Tonight," he says. "I'll walk the application over to the emergency judge if you green-light it. If the judge signs off, I can have a team in Annandale by two, three a.m."

"You think this would satisfy a judge?" she asks him. The ultimate compliment, a lawyer asking an agent for his legal opinion.

"I do," he says. "Get us that warrant, Amee, and we'll prove it. We'll have this guy in custody before dawn."

88

QUARTER TO ELEVEN. His mind is ready, his body is ready, but he must wait. He's going to wait until the target is asleep. And the target is a night owl.

A target, yes. Not a person.

If it's someone you know, he was taught, *forget that. It isn't a mother or a father, a daughter or a son, a wife or a husband. It's not someone you know. It's a target. An obstacle to your goals. Eliminate the obstacle.*

And that's exactly what the target is—an obstacle. If the FBI finds this person, it's all over for him.

He moves the wheelchair into a closet. He grabs the plastic bag of clothes that he's never worn inside the apartment, that have never touched a surface in here, never collected a single fiber. Long-sleeved shirt, long pants. Rubber gloves. Flat shoes, no treads. A skin cap for his head.

In his garage, he walks over to the side wall, where various gardening items hang from pegs—extension cords, a hose, a shovel, a water sprinkler.

And a small loop-knot of nylon cord. A vestige from his time in the service. It's a bit frayed on the ends, showing some wear. But it's still the most effective garrote he knows.

Quieter than a gun. No blood. Strong enough to withstand any resistance. Easy to grip. Victims are immediately silenced.

Seven different people on three different continents have felt this cord close around their throats, crush their tracheas, cut off their oxygen. But that was then, during his time in the service. He hasn't used it as a civilian. Tonight will be a first.

Now he just has to wait until two a.m.

89

I LEAVE my car at the Hoover Building and go with Books in his, rolling down the passenger-side window as we drive, letting the wind hit my face. I check my watch. It's 1:45 a.m.

"You're quiet," says Books.

"I'm pissed. *Frustrated* is a better word."

We need more, Amee Czernak, the prosecutor, told us. *You're close, but not close enough for search warrants.* She shut us down.

"I don't know what else to do," I say. "We've spent the last five hours, since she sent us packing, trying to dig up everything we can."

"You called your contact in Chicago, that cop," he says.

"Yeah." I asked Officer Ciomek to look at footage from POD cameras around the bombing site in Chicago, now that we have a specific vehicle—a Dodge Caravan—and a specific license plate. "But that could take days. And she said those POD cameras are pretty grainy."

Books doesn't respond, which means he's thinking. I put my

head against the cushion and close my eyes, my eyelids heavy
as wet doormats...

"Let's go there," says Books. "Let's go to Morningside Lane."

I shake myself out of the steady drift toward slumber. "Go
to—go visit Darwin?"

"Wagner." Books smiles. "He has a name now."

"Go visit Wagner?"

"Maybe," he says. "We don't need a warrant to do that. We
can ask him to voluntarily consent to questioning. We can ask
him to consent to a search of his house. He can say no, but we
can ask."

"So...we just drive over to Morningside Lane, knock on
the door, and say, 'Hi, Lieutenant Wagner, got some time to
talk? Mind if we look around your town house?' Just like
that?"

"Pretty much," he says.

"Just...drive over there right now and knock on his door?"

"Well, not right now." He glances at the clock on his dashboard. "It's nearly two in the morning. If he woke up at all,
he'd likely refuse to consent. And then we'd alert him, and
we'd give him the rest of the night to dispose of anything incriminating."

"But he might say yes."

"Yeah, he might, but a judge would likely throw out the
search. You don't shake someone awake in the dead of night
and ask for their permission to search. It's too heavy-handed.
Too coercive. If the search is invalid, we can't use anything we
find. It's too big a risk, Em. First thing in the morning. Dawn."

Books takes the exit for Alexandria.

"We're not going to my apartment?" I ask.

"We are, but I want to stop by the bookstore first. My
Maglite's there. I'm not doing a search without my Maglite."

Fifteen minutes later, Books pulls around to the alley behind his bookstore, where he gets his deliveries.

"The back entrance?"

"Back's easier, just a key. The front, I have to unlock the chains. Come on."

"I'll stay here."

"No," he says.

"You're just popping in to get your flashlight."

"I'm not leaving you alone out here, Em."

"For five minutes? What, you think Darwin's going to come wheeling into the alley and kill me in the next five minutes?"

Books gives me a hard look, the kind, I imagine, he used to train on suspects or reluctant witnesses. "I think that *Wagner* has proven himself to be quite effective," he says. "And I think you, my dear, have a target painted on your back. So, yes, you're coming with me."

So I get out with him, the security camera trained on us. Books pops the lock and pulls open the thick, heavy door.

"Be quiet," he whispers. "Petty's probably asleep."

We tiptoe through the large storage room, piled high with books and posters and displays and a bunch of chairs, along with a large safe for the days that Books doesn't run the cash to the bank. The room is black as pitch, no windows, no outside light whatsoever.

"It's behind the counter, I think," he whispers.

He heads into the main room. I hear him rummaging around. My phone buzzes. It's a text message from Natalie Ciomek, the Chicago cop: No luck so far. Somebody better be paying me overtime for this. Followed by an emoji of a smirk and a wink.

It's 2:07 a.m. in Virginia, so it's an hour earlier in Chicago. Still an ungodly hour. God bless her, pulling out all the stops to search through the POD camera footage in Chicago. I type, I O U huge, and send it.

Then I turn to my right and look toward the corner where the bed is set up for Petty. I listen. I don't hear any breathing, no sleeping sounds at all. I turn my phone, still lit, toward the corner.

I take a step closer, holding the phone out in front of me.

A noise from the front room. Books joins me again. "Got it," he whispers. "What are you doing?"

I take another step toward the corner.

"Emmy—"

"Shine your light, Books," I whisper.

"Huh?"

"Do it."

He clicks the Maglite on and off real quick, like a compliance signal from a ship, so as not to disturb Petty.

But the bed is made and empty. Petty isn't here.

He flips on the overhead switch, bathing the room in light. Petty isn't here, and neither is that big duffel bag he always lugs around.

Just a perfectly made bed and, next to it, two stacked crates serving as some kind of nightstand. On top of that is a glass vase full of fake flowers that Books had put in the storage room.

"Huh. That's weird," he says. "I guess Sergeant Petty got a better offer. Anyway, let's go. We won't get back to your apartment until two thirty. That gives us maybe three hours of sleep before we have to get up and visit our serial killer in Annandale."

I take one last look in the corner, then turn to Books. "You're right," I say. "Let's go."

90

NOT SOMEONE you know. It's a target. An obstacle to your goals.

Eliminate the obstacle.

He stands outside the back door of the apartment, his pulse even, a cool breeze on his face. He doesn't have his phone with him, but he knows it's well past two in the morning. From what he can see of the interior, all lights appear to be out. Good. Even night owls have to sleep.

He goes to work on the lock with the hairpins. With a final, satisfying *click* of the lock, the knob turns. He opens the door with one gloved hand; with the other, he holds the Repressor Ultimate to scramble the alarm pad.

But there isn't an alarm. Good. Surprising, but good.

He hears the faint sound of snoring to his right, in the bedroom. He softly closes the door and listens again—the same whispery sounds of sleep from the bedroom.

He removes the nylon cord from his bag and walks on the balls of his feet, slowly transferring weight, nimbly onward.

When he reaches the bedroom, he lets his eyes adjust to the room's darkness, illuminated slightly by a clock radio, the rhythmic breathing of a body asleep. He tugs at the sides of the cord to widen the noose, allowing it to fit over a human head.

His pulse drums through him; heat rises to his face. Something primitive is awakening inside him.

He draws a breath and focuses on his training.

Once in the room, move quickly toward your target.

Done. He's by the bedside in three long strides.

Lasso the noose around the target's head while he's still sleeping.

Done. He hits the pillow with the rope and slides it down over the head in one fluid swoop before the target awakens.

Yank it tight, while he's still disoriented, waking from sleep.

Roger that. His fingers grip the small knots on each end. He pulls with all his might, snapping the noose taut, and there's one loud, wet squelch—a horrifically desperate gagging sound coming from the target, the target, not a human being, not someone you know—

If you are quick enough, he will never gain consciousness sufficient to offer resistance. It will be over before it starts.

But just in case—knees on the arms, if possible.

Check. Knees pinning down the arms, now unable to flail.

A target will do anything—arching his back, kicking out his legs—but as long as you pull that noose tight, immobilize the arms, and don't get too close to the face, he can't stop you. He's helpless.

He keeps his chin up, pulls on each end of the cord so hard that his shoulders tremble, his biceps burn, sweat drips into his eyes. His jaw clenched, he remembers to exhale through his nose.

The target's desperate body beneath him, torso heaving upward, but to no avail, only bucking his own body forward so his weight presses down harder still on the helpless arms, his grip on the nylon cord never wavering, his shoulders screaming out in pain, sweat blinding him, arms trembling from the strain.

"Fight," he whispers. "That's right...fight." The knots of the nylon rope dig into the flesh of his hand, but the pain disappears, replaced by a consuming feeling of euphoria, of power, coursing through him more rapidly than blood, pumping through him like fresh oxygen. No, it doesn't matter if the target is a mother of three or a father of four or even if it's someone you know—someone he knows—*someone I know*...no, that makes it more satisfying still. *I have conversed with you, I have argued with you, I have watched you, and you have never known who I am or what I can do, but now you do, now I am showing you, now you are watching me take your life, now you see that I am more powerful than you and I have conquered you—*

He opens both hands and the nylon cord drops to each side. He takes a huge breath. He got carried away. That was sloppy. There could have been blood, even a partial decapitation. That would have ruined everything.

He steps off the bed and onto the carpet, wipes away sweat with his sleeve.

The bedside clock says 2:32 a.m.

So much more to do before he's done tonight.

91

NOW IT'S time for a hasty exit, time to leave the past behind.

He throws open drawers, grabs underwear and socks and T-shirts, whatever he can cram into two medium-size moving boxes. He pulls shirts and pants out of the closet and places them in a heap on the floor. From large plastic boxes in the back of the closet, he pulls out some military records, some medical records.

Underneath the bed, there's a long box filled with memorabilia and some personal items—birth certificate, stray photos from childhood and from the time in the service, an insurance policy, a high-school yearbook. Bringing that whole box.

Everything on the walls will stay except for a framed photograph of a former president of the United States with an inscription in black marker: TO LT. WAGNER—I HONOR YOUR SERVICE. That will come along with him.

He stops and listens. Slinks over to the window and carefully parts the blinds to look out. Nobody there. Not yet. So far, so good. He checks his watch, monitoring the time closely.

Now, time to haul this stuff away. Three trips to the garage carrying boxes, clothes, documents. He dumps them in the rear of the Dodge Caravan.

There's plenty of room in the van's rear compartment, even with the corpse, zipped up good and tight in a body bag he stole from an Arizona morgue a year ago.

He goes back inside the apartment, stops, and listens to the ringing sound of silence. Looks through the blinds again. Checks his watch again.

He takes one last glance around the bedroom, at the drawers pulled open, the stray hangers everywhere. No time or reason to clean up.

He pats his pocket and remembers what's inside. He almost forgot.

In the kitchen, he lifts the lid on the garbage can, a white plastic job, and pulls out the small trash bag half full of food and dirty paper towels and rubbish, the scent of orange peels, of soy sauce, of old yogurt.

He reaches into his left pocket—no small feat while wearing rubber gloves—and removes a Garfield the Cat watch, the same kind he used for the timer on the bomb in Chicago. He drops it into the trash and then lifts the bag and shakes it gently, allowing the red watch to settle deep inside.

He pulls the bag's drawstrings tight and ties them. He stops and listens for any sound. He gently opens the rear door, peeks out into the darkness to ensure he has no company. Then he walks down the ramp and over to the garbage can by the door, which is beige with the house's street number, 407, scrawled on the side in black Magic Marker. He opens the lid and drops the trash bag in on top of two other bags, a tight fit.

Garbage pickup is today. They usually come early to mid-morning.

He goes to the garage and gets in the disability van; the wheelchair's already in place, secured, in front of the steering column. He turns the rearview mirror toward him and takes one last look at himself: long gray hair pulled back, his eyes dull, the crescent-moon scar by his eye a bit shinier by contrast. He moves the mirror back and places his thumb against the garage-door opener affixed to the visor.

He imagines what he will see when the garage door lifts up—unmarked cars blocking the driveway, bubble lights on their dashboards, a SWAT team with weapons aimed at him. *FBI! Freeze, Lieutenant! Show us your hands!*

He takes a decisive breath, presses the garage-door opener, and winces as the door grinds upward in the middle of the still night.

Nothing but a dark, empty driveway and a dark, empty street.

92

NEVER HAS it been more important to keep his wits about him. Never has it been more critical to drive normally—to keep the van straight, obey traffic signals, and not speed, of course, but not drive precisely at the speed limit either.

He knows the route by heart. It was part of the preparation. Avoid the highways, stick to local roads.

Two stops. The first one, thirty-five minutes away. The second, just ten minutes farther.

He rolls along through the local roads, hilly and curvy, dark and quiet. He makes it to the county road without incident—long stretches of pastures and farms, occasional gas stations. Some areas are more residential, and he passes mailboxes and sidewalks.

He turns down a broken road and heads toward the fossil-fuel generating plant closed some thirty years ago, now abandoned, looking like a massive piece of gothic lore in its loneliness and decrepitude. He drives until the road dead-ends into the plant, then continues along the remnants of the parking lot, going slowly over the battered, uneven pavement. He passes the enormous first building and drives over wild grass toward his destination behind the building.

He dug the ditch when he first arrived in Virginia, months ago; it was always part of the plan.

He stops the van and doesn't bother with the charade of putting down the rear-door ramp; he just climbs out of the driver's side. He shines his flashlight over the earth and is not surprised to find the ditch precisely as he left it, heaps of dirt to one side of a large piece of plywood resting on the ground.

He gets his hands under the plywood. It takes some effort with this heavy wood, but he pulls it toward himself and shuffles backward, revealing a gaping hole in the earth—a long, deep grave.

He opens the back of the van and clears space down the middle. He grabs hold of the body bag and pulls it toward him, gets the corpse in his arms. He carries it over to the grave, steadies himself so he doesn't fall in with it, and drops the body in. It lands with a delicious *whump*.

He retrieves a shovel from the van and starts throwing the dirt back into the grave, on top of the body. Lucky for him, it hasn't rained here for over a week, so the dirt is relatively workable. Still, it takes him the better part of an hour, until nearly four in the morning, to fill the grave. He pats the earth with the shovel, tamping it down as best he can. Then he moves the large piece of plywood back over the grave and returns to his car.

He has accomplished one of the two most important tasks of the night. Because this body must never be found.

Now for the second task.

Feeling considerably relieved with the body disposed of, he

drives back to the county road for the next stop. It's just a few miles up ahead.

He follows the curves of the road. He doesn't have GPS because he doesn't have his phone—or, rather, he does, but it's turned off, with the SIM card removed, to avoid tracking— and, if memory serves, it's easy to miss this turnoff if you're not careful. It should be only about two more miles...

As he comes around a blind curve obscured by trees, he sees color in the sky. Flashing color. He hits the brakes, but he's already around the curve before the van comes to a stop. His headlights are already shining forward. He's already announced himself.

Less than a quarter of a mile away, squad cars spread across the road—three of them, their bar lights spraying obnoxious flashes of blue light through the darkness.

A roadblock. And it's too late to turn back.

93

HIS PULSE hammering in his chest and throat, he eases the van forward, toward the roadblock. Not a formal one, he quickly realizes. They aren't here for him. Not a DUI checkpoint either. A car accident. A sedan in a ditch to the right. An ambulance drives up and joins the three police cars. There's a second vehicle spun sideways along the road, the front passenger side gashed open.

A state trooper, standing amid flares set up to block the road, notices the van and puts his hand up. The trooper sizes up the van and then slowly approaches with one hand on his holstered weapon. It doesn't seem to be a threatening posture, more likely just part of the law enforcement swagger, but it's hard to say.

He rolls down the window and leans out but stays quiet, letting the trooper take the lead. Hoping the officer won't ask him for his driver's license, though he's ready to produce it. Hoping he won't ask for registration, though he will hand it over. Hoping the officer won't ask him what he's doing on the road at this hour, though he's ready with a cover story about early babysitting duty for nieces and nephews.

The trooper, in his gray uniform with his badge and arm patches, his wide-brimmed hat, is stone-faced. "Morning. Where you headed?"

He tells him where he's headed and doesn't mention the cover story, not wanting to seem too eager to provide details.

The trooper gives him an appraising stare.

Let me go, Officer. Live to see another day. His pulse is vibrating in his throat, his temples.

"Well, I don't think you can pass." The trooper looks back. "The drop-off on that shoulder's too steep." He nods. "What you wanna do—that turnoff you just passed about a half a mile back—"

"Yes, sir."

"You wanna take that about a mile or so north. You'll hit a downtown. You follow the signs there and you can hop on the interstate."

But he doesn't know that town. And he can't just "hop on the interstate." His turnoff is less than a mile away.

So close, and yet so far. *Of all the fucking luck.* "All right, Officer. Thanks much."

There's no other way to access his next stop except for this county road. And if he parks his car here and waits instead of taking the trooper's advice, he will look suspicious. To say nothing of the fact that *he needs to make this next stop as soon as possible.*

This wasn't part of the plan, wasn't part of the plan—

Stop. Deal with it. Do what the trooper said.

Take a route you haven't scouted, haven't scouted, haven't scouted—

His jaw clenched, he executes a three-point turn and heads

back in the direction he came from. Per the trooper's instructions, he takes the first turnoff, follows it a mile into the downtown of the small town.

Maybe we'll meet again someday, Officer, and I can show you what I think of your advice.

He keeps his breathing even and scans the area as he travels through the small downtown—real estate agent, clothing store, tailor, ice cream parlor. He sees signs for the interstate that he will not, *cannot,* take, then finds another road, a road he doesn't know and never scouted but that will at least allow him to get back to the county road he'd been on when he hit the police barricade.

It's now 4:45 a.m. He's lost thirty minutes. He passes a restaurant topped with a glowing neon hot dog. Then a Walmart. Then some kind of boat-repair shop.

He reaches the intersection with the county road again. He looks to his left. No sign of the police barricade. He figures he's about two miles west of it. Maybe three? He's not sure if he overshot his next stop or not, so he doesn't know whether he should turn left, east, or right, west.

He doesn't have his bearings because *this was never part of the*—

He turns left, making an educated guess, seething with frustration.

Yes. He guessed correctly. There it is, on his left, the second stop.

"Let's get this over with," he whispers.

He turns the van onto the gravel road and heads toward a large rectangular sign reading XTRA STORAGE, a row of sheds below it.

He pulls up to the third shed from the end. He climbs out of the van from the passenger side, again not bothering with the wheelchair exit from the back—no cameras out here—puts the key into the lock, and turns it.

The door lifts upward with a smooth hum. The shed is empty, or almost empty. He gets back in the van, pulls it into the shed, and shuts the door behind him.

And releases a breath. Out of sight now, finally.

He gets out of the van and takes a moment to appraise the situation. He looks inside the van, at the wheelchair behind the steering column. At some point soon—maybe five minutes from now, maybe five days from now—the FBI will come to Annandale, Virginia, looking for a man who cannot walk, who sits in this very wheelchair. They will go to 407 Morningside Lane and execute a search. They will quickly learn that the man they are seeking has left town, and rather hurriedly. They will issue an APB on this very Dodge Caravan. They will scour the roads and highways for this van.

But this van isn't going to be on the roads. It will stay here, tucked away in this anonymous shed, for the immediate future.

It would never occur to the Feds hunting for a paralyzed, retired army lieutenant to search the highways and byways for a motorcycle.

In a corner of the shed, a cloth draped over it, is his Kawasaki Ninja sport bike, metallic blue, 650 cc engine, used but in pristine condition. He removes the cloth.

"Annandale? Lieutenant Martin Wagner bids you adieu." He throws on his helmet, presses the button to lift the shed's door, and starts up the motorcycle.

94

BOOKS RINGS the doorbell a fourth time.

"It could take a while for him to get out of bed," I say. "The wheelchair and all."

Books pounds on the door, his knuckles hitting it just below a plaque with the number 407 in gold.

Morningside Lane is a quiet street off the main artery of Lathrop Avenue in Annandale, Virginia. Lieutenant Wagner lives in a row of apartments at the intersection; his unit is the end one.

We get no answer and step off the front porch. Books, keeping his body slightly turned toward the front door—not knowing what to expect—walks over to his car, parked in the driveway. The garage door has a small window. Books raises up on his tiptoes and looks through it. "Van's not here," he says. "Garage is empty."

"Where would he be at six forty-five in the morning?"

"Don't know. Come on." All business, firmly in command, Books walks around to the side of the building, bordering

Lathrop, where there are some shrubs and a small lawn. We can see a window with the shades pulled. No lights on inside.

We keep walking to the rear of the house, which serves as a small walkway behind all the units. A wheelchair ramp leads up to the back door. There's a beige garbage can with the number 407 scrawled on it in black.

A noise from down the street. We both turn to see a garbage truck using a hydraulic lift to dump the contents of a garbage can into its rear compactor.

"Wait here," says Books, and he heads around the building again.

There is a window by Wagner's back door, but it's up too high for me to see in. The lights are off, though. I knock on the back door hard, urgently. Maybe this door's closer to the bedroom, and he'll hear it.

I put my ear to the door and listen. Nothing. No movement.

"What are you doing?" Books asks when he returns, fitting his hands into a pair of yellow rubber gloves.

"I might ask you the same thing," I say.

"Here." He tosses me a pair of rubber gloves too.

"What are we doing, Books?"

"We're going to take a look at his garbage," he says.

"We don't have a warrant."

"Don't need one. Not for garbage. It's considered abandoned. Supreme Court said so."

He lifts the lid off the beige garbage can. A garbage bag—kitchen, not lawn—nearly topples out. He catches it and sets it on the ground. "The most recent stuff he tossed out," he says. "Let's start here. There's two other bags inside. A treasure trove."

"I've never thought of garbage as treasure."

"You would if you were an investigator. You'd be amazed what it reveals."

He tries to untie the drawstring, but it's too tight, so he just rips the whole thing open.

"You're ruining his garbage bag."

"I know. I feel awful." He winks at me, then sucks in his breath and dives his hands in. He tosses out crumpled paper towels, soda cans, trays for microwavable meals, an empty yogurt cup. A flattened box, empty soup cans, junk mail, an empty bag of microwave rice, a cardboard paper-towel cylinder—

And then he freezes. His hand slowly rises out of the bag, holding something. He shows it to me.

It's wet from some liquid inside the trash. He wipes off a couple of grains of rice.

A Garfield the Cat watch. The red band. The cartoon cat on the face.

"Holy shit," I whisper. "That's it. The same watch we found in Chicago."

I knew Wagner was our guy. I knew it in my bones. But seeing this kind of proof sends a jolt of electricity through me.

"Take a photo of it with your phone," Books says. "And text it to Elizabeth Ashland."

"This is good," I say, scrambling for my phone.

"This," he says, "is probable cause."

95

BOOKS PATS the steering wheel, practically buzzing. It's now just past nine. We are down the street from 407 Morningside Lane, within sight of it but keeping our distance. Three other cars of local FBI agents have joined us, but they are keeping their distance as well and are spread out on all sides, trying not to stand out too much. There is still a chance that Lieutenant Martin Wagner will return home from wherever he is, and if he does, we don't want to scare him off.

Once we get the search warrant, we'll swoop back on that apartment like bees to honey. Until then, we wait.

We wait for a call from Elizabeth Ashland, who amended the application for a search warrant, grabbed a lawyer from Justice, and rushed it in front of a federal magistrate.

"Elizabeth did it herself?" I ask. "She wouldn't delegate that part to someone lower down on the chain?"

Books makes a face. "Well, in fairness to her, there really isn't a chain on this one. This case was never staffed with agents." He shakes his head. "Because nobody believed you."

"They do now."

"But mostly," he says, "I think Elizabeth wants in on this. Trying to steal some glory."

"Well, she *did* go to bat for me. She convinced Dwight Ross to let me pursue this. If it weren't for her, we wouldn't be here."

Books turns to me. "People have more than one face." It's a saying he often used to describe the criminals he chased. The duality of man, so to speak. How good and evil can coexist inside a person. The example he frequently cited was a local city bureaucrat he once busted who was taking thousand-dollar bribes to fix liquor licenses and who also devoted his free time to starting up a battered-women's shelter. "Elizabeth does the right thing on this case. But on the flip side, she tips off Citizen David in exchange for gigantic cash payments."

"You don't know she's David's mole. You suspect it."

"All that cash?" he says. "I'll prove it. I just have to figure out how."

I look at the Garfield the Cat watch, which is resting on the console between us in an evidence bag. "You think Lieutenant Wagner's in the wind?"

He shrugs. "It's odd for someone not to be home at dawn. But who knows? Maybe he has a lady friend and he stays at her place. Or maybe he has some morning routine. We don't know much about him." He looks at me. "But, yeah, if I'm putting money down—I think he's gone."

"Shit," I mumble. I suppose I spooked him. It's always one step forward, two steps back with this guy. "But you have alerts out for his van?"

"Everywhere," he says. "Local cops, state troopers. Every county road, every highway. If he took off, we'll catch him."

His phone rings. He punches the button for the speakerphone.

"We got the warrant," Elizabeth Ashland says. "I'm on my way."

96

ALL FIVE vehicles converge at once on 407 Morningside Lane. Five male and three female agents, all wearing blue windbreakers with FBI on the back, plus Books and me.

And Elizabeth Ashland and Dwight Ross, who arrived with the search warrant. Everyone wants in now that my search has borne fruit, now that it's no longer a wild-goose chase.

One of the local agents picks the locks on the front door in less than a minute, and we enter. Books calls out, "Lieutenant Martin Wagner! FBI! We have a warrant to search these premises!"

It doesn't take long to confirm he's not here. The place isn't that big. A living room in front connected to a kitchen in the rear. To the left, a door to the garage, a small powder room, and the one and only bedroom.

I watch my step and don't touch anything. I follow Books. Elizabeth and Dwight, I note, waited until the place was confirmed empty before they walked in.

In the bedroom, the bed is unmade. A small bedside lamp

is on the floor. There's a low dresser with the drawers pulled out to varying degrees. The top drawers are empty. The others are mostly empty. Hangers are spilled across the carpet.

The closet, which has a low bar for a disabled owner, is nearly empty, just a couple of shirts and a pair of pants in a bundle on the hardwood floor. In one corner of the closet are two large dust outlines, one a square, the other a rectangle. Boxes or containers that rested there for a long time, now gone.

One picture missing from the wall, the nail there naked.

"Packed up and gone," says Books. "He was in a hurry too."

On a desk in the bedroom is a neat pile of bills. I find one from AT&T and get his cell phone number. I dial Rabbit and read the number to her. "Do your work," I say. "Do it fast."

The bathroom attached to the bedroom is empty of toiletries; some of the drawers beneath the vanity are open. The shower curtain is pulled back; the ledge above the disabled-accessibility bar, where presumably he'd keep soap and shampoo, is empty.

"He's going to have a hard time on the run," I say. "He can't just stop at any old hotel or stay in any old place. He needs disability access."

Books hums his doubt. "If he's as good as you say, he probably already thought of that."

We are almost bumping into each other in here. It feels like overkill, twelve people searching an apartment that can't be a thousand square feet. I go to the living room and look at the books in a small bookcase—*The Art of War, The Book of Five Rings, The Prince, Intelligence in War, Deep Undercover.* I could spend all day in this apartment, getting inside his head. I've spent so long chasing him. Chasing him, to be sure, for the purpose of arresting him, but still—it's hard for me not to feel a strange sort of bond with this monster.

From the bedroom, Elizabeth Ashland calls out, "Books!"

We both return to the bedroom. One of the female agents is on her hands and knees. Next to her is a weapon, black and yellow, that looks like an elongated handgun, like something out of the Star Wars movies or a comic book.

"It was under the bed," says Elizabeth. "I think this is the Taser."

"You were right about this whole thing, Lizzie," says Dwight Ross, his hand on Elizabeth's shoulder. "Sorry I doubted you."

"Yeah, this was Elizabeth's hard work," Books whispers to me. "What would we do without her?"

I squeeze his arm, my way of telling him to let it go.

Books and I crouch down by the Taser. "He customized it," says Books.

"How'd he keep the darts from burning the victims' skin?" I ask.

"I don't know. I'm not an expert on Tasers. Maybe he insulated the darts somehow. With rubber, probably. We'd have to fire it to find out." He rises to his feet. "This guy is not screwing around."

"But it's odd," I say. "He left it behind."

"He doesn't need it anymore. Now he blows things up."

"Whoa!" We hear this from the kitchen, which is only a few steps away, connected to the bedroom. With so many agents and so little space to cover, the revelations are coming at us one after the other.

"*Whoa* is right," says Books when he enters the kitchen. At the base of the stove is a small pull-out drawer. I have one of those. I shove frying pans in there. Lieutenant Wagner, apparently, uses it for something else.

He's filled his with cash, enclosed in brown paper bags. The agent sitting on the floor pulls out one brown bag after the other from the neatly stacked rows. Another agent has one of the bags on the counter and is counting the money inside. "There's . . . five grand in this one bag," he says. "Fifty bills. A hundred dollars each."

The agent on the floor counts the bags in the pulled-out tray. "So that's . . . twenty-two bags, total."

"A hundred and ten thousand, if every bag has the same amount," says Elizabeth.

Cash. Over a hundred thousand in cash. "It doesn't make sense," I say.

"Sure it does," says Elizabeth. "He wants to avoid detection when he's traveling around the country committing his crimes. Credit cards pin you down. He pays for everything in cash."

Yes, Elizabeth, I know why criminals use cash. That's not what I meant. That's not what I meant at all.

"Count up the money, guys," Elizabeth says. She turns to me. "Emmy, the people he's killed. Are they all in the ground?"

Still thinking, I shake my head, confused. "Are they . . ."

"Buried," she says. "Are all the victims buried?"

I close my eyes. "Nora Connolley isn't. The New Orleans victim. Sergeant Crescenzo convinced the family not to bury her until he's finished his investigation."

"Good. Let's try to tie that Taser to the wounds on her body."

"I'm on it," I say. But at the moment, my thoughts aren't on the Taser or Nora Connolley's wounds.

I'm still thinking about all that cash.

97

WE DON'T want to be obvious about it. We stay in the apartment, continuing the search, until Books and I get a moment to ourselves in the living room.

"All that cash?" I whisper to Books.

"I know," he says, stone-faced. He walks out the front door. He wants to talk privately. Once outside, he stops and turns so quickly that I almost run into him. Some neighbors are gathered a few driveways down, wondering about all the law enforcement vehicles. Books notices and keeps his voice low.

"Is it possible that the person funneling money to Elizabeth is...Wagner?" he says.

"*Citizen David* has been funneling cash to Elizabeth. That's what we think, right?"

Books nods. "Why can't Wagner be Citizen David?"

"I...Wagner? So Darwin and Citizen David are the same person?"

"Why not?" says Books. "They're both smart. Highly disciplined."

"They're polar opposites. David is a crusader against corporate greed and oppression and all that kind of stuff," I say. "He's for the little guy. Wagner wants to kill the poorest and the weakest. He's the anti–Citizen David."

"Which is why it's the perfect cover," he says. "Think about it, Em. He sets himself up as this righteous, modern-day Robin Hood. He sees how the FBI responds. He gets better. It's all a setup to do what he really wants to do, which is use his bombs to kill the poor, the sick, the homeless."

I pace the front yard. The heat is already blossoming from warm to oppressive. Some neighbor is recording us with a smartphone.

"You really believe that?" I ask Books.

"I'm not sure, no. But it's a thought. I mean, why—" He catches himself, lowers his head, draws closer to me. "Why is Elizabeth Ashland so goddamned interested in this case all of a sudden?"

"To steal credit for catching the Chicago bomber. Just like Dwight. But—Elizabeth is the one who gave me the green light. If it weren't for her, I'd still be sitting in front of a computer begging someone to listen to me. We wouldn't have a dozen agents and search warrants."

"True." Books stuffs his hands in his pockets. "But maybe she realized how strong a case you were building. She wanted to get on the train before it ran her over."

Maybe. The pieces haven't fallen into place yet. But at least we *have* some pieces now.

My phone buzzes. Rabbit. I almost drop the phone, I'm trying to answer it so quickly. "You have something good?" I ask. I put her on speaker so Books can hear too.

"Negative on current CSLI." Cell-site location information, she means. Cell phones are always scanning the environment for the best signal—the closest cell site—even if the phones aren't being used, and sometimes even when the phones are turned off. Every connection with a new cell site generates a time-stamped record of cell-site location information—CSLI. Once I gave Wagner's cell phone number to Rabbit, she was able to go to work on the CSLI.

But there's no current CSLI, meaning Wagner's phone isn't sending out any signals right now. He either destroyed his phone or removed the SIM card. We were hoping he'd make a rookie mistake.

"Last CSLI for Wagner's cell phone was in Annandale at two thirty-eight a.m. So that's when he killed it or pulled the SIM card."

"That's when he left Annandale, in other words."

"Well, that's when he wanted us to stop tracking his movements, anyway," says Books. He looks at me, shaking his head. "Two freakin' thirty-eight. If we'd gotten that warrant last night…"

I know. We'd have caught him.

"You guys didn't think I'd call you with only bad news, did you?"

"Let's hear it."

"We got two hits on ALPRs last night."

Books almost jumps in the air. "Where? When?" An ALPR—for "automatic license-plate reader"—is a device mounted on a squad car or some stationary object that reads every license plate that comes within its field of vision and logs it.

"A Fairfax County Police patrol car caught the plate on a county road about a half an hour from you guys, due west," says Rabbit. "Time of four thirty-one a.m. There was a two-car accident on the road and they were blocking it off."

"And the other?"

"The second was caught farther west, but he was heading southbound, back toward the county road. Time of four forty-six a.m."

"He went off the county road and got back on?"

"I'll send you the map. Looks like he had to backtrack and take a different route to go around the car accident and get back on the county road."

"He had to call an audible," Books says.

"So he kills his phone at two thirty-eight a.m. in order to conceal his movements from us," I say. "Then we catch his license plate at four thirty-one a.m. on the county road. And it took him only about thirty minutes, you said, to reach that spot."

"Approximately, yes," Rabbit says.

"So that's a two-hour window, with only thirty minutes built in for travel. What did he do in those other ninety minutes?"

As if Rabbit knows.

We'll deal with that later. This is huge. Wagner finally made a mistake. Looks like he was forced into it, but we'll take a mistake however we can get it.

"Let's go," says Books.

98

WE USE the data points that Rabbit sent to our phones. It takes us less than thirty minutes to reach the spot on the county road where Wagner's license plate was tagged first. We are out of town, a rural area full of cornfields.

"There," says Books, pointing off the road toward the sloping shoulder at a car's fender, bent and battered, part of the carnage from the car accident. Some shattered glass is sprinkled along the side of the road.

"So Wagner gets to this spot and he hits a police blockade, he can't go any farther," says Books. "He has to backtrack. We know he ends up taking Bell Road to get back on the county road about two miles up ahead."

Books does a three-point turn and drives east to the next turnoff. "He'd have taken this road," he says. We go left and follow the road until we reach a strip mall. There's a tailor shop, a real estate agent, an ice cream parlor. Signs for the interstate point left.

"We know he didn't take the interstate," says Books. "But this will get us to Bell, right?"

"That's what the map says."

So we turn left, heading west again, until we reach Bell Road. He takes another left, and we travel north, back toward the county road. On top of the sign for the approaching intersection with the county road is a mounted reader, the one that tagged Wagner's license plate the second time.

Books moves the vehicle up to the T-intersection and pulls over to the side.

"So what does Wagner do at this point?" he asks. "Does he go right—west?"

"Probably," I say. "That's the direction he'd been headed when he hit the police barricade."

Books looks at me. He reaches for his phone and dials up Bonita Sexton. "Rabbit," he says, "we're at the intersection of Bell and the county road. If I turn right and go west, when's the next ALPR?"

"It's…three miles up ahead. There's a speed camera and an ALPR."

"But he didn't hit that one," I say.

"No, he didn't. That ALPR didn't register Wagner's license plate last night."

Books asks, "Are there any turnoffs between where I am right now and that ALPR?"

"Not according to this map," I say, looking at my phone.

"No," says Rabbit. "No turnoffs."

"So he didn't turn right at this intersection," says Books. "He must have turned left."

"He headed back east?" I ask. "Back toward the police barricade?"

Books's eyebrows lift. "Maybe there's something between

here and that police barricade." He turns left and heads east on the county road.

Nothing but foliage and green fields for the first mile. Then we see the sign, XTRA STORAGE, standing tall and wide, far off the road.

A storage facility. An acre of concrete. A series of large sheds with wide white doors. Large enough to park a tractor or a boat in.

Or hide a person in.

Books pulls the car over again, this time along the side of the county road. He picks up the phone and dials it. "Elizabeth," he says, "I need agents right now."

99

WITHIN THE hour, federal agents have swarmed the storage facility and are searching around the perimeter. They're wearing flak jackets, their weapons drawn. For all we know, Wagner is inside one of those locked storage sheds. It would be odd, but everything about this case is odd, and nobody's taking any chances.

The storage site is not manned by any employees. That would have helped. Apparently, this is the kind of place that lies dormant most of the time and doesn't require much daily upkeep.

Back at the Hoover Building, agents are trying to contact the owner of the facility to find out who rented these sheds and how to get them open. Arguably, we need a search warrant for this, so Books is working with a lawyer at Justice on yet another warrant application.

Books kills his phone and looks out over the sea of agents. "If he's here, he's done," he says. "He's not getting away. It's just a matter of time."

"He's not here," I say. "I don't see him pinning himself down that way."

Books shrugs. We just don't know yet. We can't even be sure that Wagner came here.

"This will take a while," I say. "Let's make our next stop. We can come back."

We get in his car and head to our next destination. I drive so Books can keep in touch by phone with Justice and check on the attempt to get inside those storage sheds.

While he talks, I try to sort through everything we've learned today. It all adds up to...weird. All that cash. The Taser under his bed. The Garfield the Cat watch in his trash...

I see the sign up on my right, a polished slab of granite that reads A NEW DAY: REHABILITATIVE AND PHYSICAL THERAPY.

Which matches the name on a business card we found in Wagner's home this morning.

Books shows his badge at the front desk to an elderly man, bald with a ruddy complexion. It's always something to see the look on a person's face when he hears an agent say, "FBI."

"Lieutenant Wagner," says the man in answer to Books's question. "I haven't seen him today." The man starts leafing through the daily sign-in sheets. "He's usually here early on Thursday mornings."

"You know him?" Books asks. "You'd recognize him?"

"Oh, sure, everyone knows Lew. He's quite a character."

"He's usually here on Thursdays?"

The man hums to himself. "I wanna say Monday, Wednesday, and Thursday? He's outpatient. He comes for PT. No," he says, looking up from the pages, "he's not here today."

It's what we figured. It wouldn't be much of an escape from the authorities if he'd stopped in for his physical-therapy session first.

"You said Wednesday was one of his days," I say. "So was he here yesterday?"

"Well, now, I think I saw him yesterday. Let me see." He flips back and sorts through some pages. "Yes, he was. Signed in at eight forty-seven a.m."

"Is his physical therapist here?" Books asks.

"That I don't know. I don't know who works with who."

Books nods and smiles. "Would you do me a favor and call your administrator or whoever runs this place?"

"Yes, sir." He picks up his landline phone and punches a button.

Just then, my phone rings. Officer Ciomek from Chicago. "Natalie," I say into the phone.

I hear her saying something, but it's garbled. And then the connection fails.

I call her back, or try to, but the call won't go through.

"I can't get a signal in here," I tell Books. I walk outside into the climbing heat, the sun high overhead, and call her again.

"Sorry," I say. "Call dropped. You got something for me?"

"Got some vid for you, girl. From the Friday before the bombing."

"Tell me."

"I have POD footage capturing a Dodge Caravan—the same Dodge Caravan—driving past the payday-loan store three different times between three twelve p.m. and three twenty-eight p.m. that Friday. That would be three hours before Mayday disappeared from his spot."

Right. In the store video from the car wash north of the bombing site, we saw the homeless guy, Mayday, leave his spot across the street from the payday-loan store at 6:15 p.m. the Friday before the bombing. That, we think, is when

Darwin—Wagner—paid him off for that spot. Now we have Wagner in Chicago three hours earlier.

"He drove by the store three times in, what, sixteen minutes?"

"He was casing it."

"And it was Wagner's plates?"

"Can't get a license plate. Our POD cameras aren't that focused."

"Did you get a shot of him driving?"

"Nope. You know how our PODs work, right? The cameras rotate every few seconds. We just get a little video clip, then the camera turns away and picks up a different angle. It gives you a freakin' headache going through them."

Inside the clinic, Books is talking to some woman, probably the one who runs this place.

"Natalie," I say, "are you sure it's the same Dodge Caravan?"

"They all look like the same van to me. And what are the odds that three different Dodge Caravans were cruising around that spot at that time?"

I don't know. I don't know enough about cars. I thank her and end the call just as the phone beeps with the arrival of the video clips.

I pull them up one at a time. Each one, grainy, black-and-white, shows a four- or five-second clip of a Dodge Caravan proceeding southbound on Broadway in Chicago; the time stamp in the corner of the screen shows the various times between 3:12 p.m. and 3:28 p.m. that Friday, as Natalie said. The angle is different than the one we saw in the side-profile, ground-level surveillance footage from the pawnshop in New Orleans. This one is from a police observation device mounted on a traffic light on Broadway and aimed downward; it shows the rear, passenger side, and roof of the van. Looks like the same van all three times to me too.

I head back inside to where Books and the facility's head administrator are talking. "Emmy Dockery, this is Louise Hall," Books says. We shake hands.

"Oh, here he is," the administrator says, looking down the hallway. A middle-aged man with a buzz cut approaches us; he's wearing a white T-shirt, sweatpants, and running shoes.

"This is Tom Miller, his physical therapist," she says.

Tom nods to his boss. "You need me, Louise?"

"Tom, these people are from the FBI."

"The F—" Tom Miller looks at Books and me with an expression that's a combination of startled and curious, a typical reaction. "Michelle *called* you?"

Books says, "Michelle who?"

"Michelle Fontaine," he says. "One of the other PTs."

"Why would Michelle Fontaine have called us?"

Miller draws back. "I'm confused. Is this about...Lieutenant Wagner?"

Books and I look at each other. "As a matter of fact, it is," says Books.

"Wow." Tom Miller puts his hands on his head. "This is real."

"We're going to need to talk to you right now," says Books. "Somewhere private?"

"Sure, yeah, of course."

"Is this Michelle person here?"

"No, she didn't come to work today," Louise says. "She sent an e-mail last night saying she quit."

100

TOM MILLER leads us down a long hallway. We pass patients of various ages and shapes and sizes moving with the assistance of wheelchairs, canes, crutches, or walkers. Every one of them says hello to Tom, and Tom's ready with a cheery response: *Hey, Claire, you got some sun! You see those Nationals last night, Mr. Hoyt? Shelvin, you look like a movie star today!*

I couldn't be a physical therapist. I don't have the patience or the rah-rah disposition.

At the end of the hallway is a stairwell that goes down to the basement—the exercise rooms, Miller tells us—and up to the second floor, where we head. "Second floor's being remodeled," he says as we climb the stairs. "But they're finishing one room for us to use as our conference room. You can't get reception on the main floor or in the basement. Cell phones are totally useless. Second floor, they work. Here." We turn from the stairwell into another long hallway, the walls unpainted, the floor partially carpeted, some ladders and drop cloths and construction equipment lying around. The first door on the left has a white sign taped to it that says CONFERENCE.

In the center of the room, there's a nice oak table surrounded by assorted chairs, and in one corner, there's a television and a DVD player. But the rest of the room is a work in progress. Half of one wall is painted a light purple, the rest unpainted with tape along the edges; cans of paint and drop cloths and roller pans are everywhere, and there's a twenty-four-pack of bottled water on the floor with the plastic sheath ripped open. The windows have no blinds, and the afternoon sun is blasting through. I start sweating the moment I enter the room.

"No AC yet, sorry," he says.

"That's no problem, Mr. Miller," says Books.

I nod toward the pack of water bottles in the corner. "You think anyone would mind if I stole one?"

"I'm sure it's fine." Miller lifts a bottle through the ripped sheath of plastic and puts it on the table in front of me.

Books says, "So what can you tell us about Lieutenant Wagner?"

He gives us what background he can—Army Ranger, injured in Iraq, came to the clinic less than a year ago—but I already know most of it. "He has an incomplete SCI at T nine," he says, which he translates for us as a spinal-cord injury that allows some movement in the legs. "He can walk a little with a walker. He's made good progress."

"Tell me about him personally," says Books.

Miller says, "Oh, he's kinda what you'd expect of a war veteran. He's a crusty old guy. Very opinionated. He goes around the country and talks about how people are too dependent on government. He preaches to a lot of the folks around here. A lot of them look up to him."

"Do you?" Books asks.

"Oh, well—you get all sorts in PT. If you're my patient, chances are something bad happened to you. Or you're old and losing functions. Some people handle that better than others. But Lew's okay."

"So tell me about Michelle...Fontaine?"

"Michelle started just a few weeks ago," says Miller. "She's great. But she didn't get along with Lew. He'd say things that were pretty, uh, insensitive. They clashed a lot."

Books nods, stays silent.

"So," says Tom, heaving a sigh. "He goes to Chicago one weekend, y'know, to do one of those speeches. And that's the same weekend as that bombing there. So Lew makes a comment like 'A bunch of dead homeless people is a good start.' And Michelle, she kinda flips out. They argued about it, more than once. She asked him yesterday if *he* had an alibi for the Chicago bombing." He looks at us for a reaction. "Which I'm thinking...must be why you guys are here?"

Books says, "What did Wagner say when she asked him about the alibi?"

"Well, she didn't really wait for an answer. She just stormed out. She wasn't serious. But Lew—*Lew* took it pretty seriously. He asked me if I thought she might turn him in."

"He felt threatened by Michelle."

"Sure seemed like it. He definitely wasn't happy."

Books mulls that over for a moment. So do I.

"And then Michelle quit yesterday?" I ask. "Just a few weeks after she started?"

"Yeah. She sent an e-mail last night, apparently," says Miller. "Louise showed it to me. She said it wasn't a good fit for her and she was sorry, but she was leaving, effective immediately. She was leaving Virginia, actually. Moving back home or something."

"Where's home?" I ask.

"I don't know. Never got to know her all that well. Nice lady, though."

"She said in her e-mail it wasn't a good fit," Books says. "You think she quit because of Lieutenant Wagner?"

Miller shrugs. "I mean, probably. But you'd have to ask her."

I'd love to ask her. But she isn't here. She seems to have vamoosed.

At exactly the same time as Lieutenant Martin Wagner.

101

BOOKS AND I look at each other, each with questions about Michelle Fontaine, but Books's phone buzzes before he can speak.

"Excuse me," Books says. He gets up and leaves the room.

A break in the action. Miller drums his fingers on the desk. "So how real is this?" he asks. "Are you sure about Lew? I mean, he's rough around the edges, but..."

"Tell me more about Michelle," I say, avoiding the question.

"Not much to tell," says Miller. "I know she'd worked as a therapist before. She said that. But she didn't say where. She was kind of private."

"Describe her to me."

"Describe her? Well, she's tall, maybe a little shorter than me, but tall for a woman. She's—I wouldn't call her heavyset but...not petite. Lew asked her if she played basketball. I think she was insulted."

I nod, thinking all this through. Trying to put together so

many things that don't make sense. The cash...the Taser...
the Garfield watch...

"Why do you ask?" Tom asks. "Michelle's a great person."

"Tell me something," I say, avoiding another one of his
questions. "Did Wagner ever talk about money?"

"Money?" He shrugs. "Not really."

"About banks, maybe? Do you know why he would have
kept large sums of money at his house?"

"Like under his mattress or something?" A humorless
smirk plays on his lips. "Kind of a paranoid, antigovernment
thing to do, I guess. But no, I don't know about that."

Books pops back in. "Emmy, can I grab you a second?"

I join him in the hallway. "What's going on?"

He's holding his phone. "I totally forgot. I have a shipment
coming today at two."

"A shipment of books?"

"Yeah, for that other job I have, where I own a bookstore?
The one I suck at, apparently."

You don't suck at running a bookstore, I want to tell him. *You
just don't love it like you love being an agent.* "Is Petty there?" I
ask. "It's Thursday afternoon."

Monday through Thursday, Books said, *he comes in like clockwork in the afternoon, stays the night.*

Then again, Sergeant Petty wasn't there last night—
Wednesday night—so who knows how reliable his schedule
really is?

"If he's there," says Books, "he's not answering the door
while they pound on it from the alley. He probably doesn't
think he should, with the store being closed."

"And you can't call him?"

"It's not like he has a cell phone, Em. He's a homeless guy."

Right. I guess that makes sense. "So go, Books," I say. "Go

take care of it. You can be there in half an hour, accept the shipment, and come back. Barely more than an hour. It might take them that long just to open the storage sheds. It's not like Wagner's here anymore. You can spare an hour."

He looks up at the ceiling and groans.

"I suppose you're right. Okay," says Books, "be right back. Call me if anything—*anything*—comes up."

He leans in and gives me a quick kiss, then draws back and realizes what he did. "Oh, I—I wasn't thinking—"

"It's okay, just—go," I say, turning so he won't see me blush. But he's already bounding down the stairs.

And then my phone buzzes. It's Elizabeth Ashland.

"The owner of Xtra Storage is here," she says. "He has a list of the people who rent the storage sheds. Wagner's not on the list."

"He probably used a fake name. He's careful about everything else."

"So let me read you the list, Emmy. Maybe you'll recognize somebody."

She goes through the list of people who've rented out these storage sheds. Cunningham, Morris. Cole, Nathan. McDaniel, Steven. Spielman, Ellen—

"Wait," I say. *McDaniel, Steven. McDaniel*—"Steven Mc-Daniel!" I shout. "Let me check something, Elizabeth. Hang on a second." I scroll through the notes folder on my phone.

There. There it is!

"Steven McDaniel," I tell Elizabeth, "was one of the Scotts-dale victims. One of the senior citizens he killed there."

"Okay, hang on a minute," she says. I hear her asking some-one, "Why is there an asterisk by his name?"

A man responds but I can't make out the words. Then Eliz-abeth is talking to me again. "Steven McDaniel rented out this locker last December," she says. "He paid in advance for three years. He used a credit card over the phone."

"That's it!" I say. "Wagner must have purchased it with McDaniel's credit card after he killed him in Arizona."

"Okay, Emmy, great work. We're going to open that shed now."

I'm about to say, *Hold on, give me a few minutes and I can be there*. But then I realize two things. First, I'm not an agent, so I probably don't have the right to insist. And second, and more important, with Books off to his store in Alexandria to receive a shipment of new novels, I'm stranded here at the clinic.

"You want me to patch you in?" Elizabeth asks me.

"I—can you—yes, yes!"

"I'll put you on FaceTime," she says. "I'll call you back in ten."

I hang up and walk back into the conference room, where Tom Miller has remained in his seat. "Everything okay?" he says. "I heard some shouting."

"Yeah, everything's fine. Look, I'm going to need this room. Alone. Is that okay?"

"Sure. Actually, I have a patient in a few minutes, so I'll be in the basement."

"Great."

He stops on his way out and turns to me. "Agent Dockery?" he says.

"It's Emmy. And I'm not an agent."

"Okay, Emmy," he says. "Should I be worried about Michelle?"

102

MICHELLE FONTAINE parks her car in her designated spot. Walks up the back stairs to her apartment. Passes by her two suitcases, sitting by the back door, ready to be thrown into the car.

In the kitchen, she picks up her landline phone and checks her voice mail. One new message.

"Michelle, this is Louise at the clinic. I got your e-mail and I understand you're leaving us. I won't pretend I'm not disappointed that you didn't give us some notice, but—there's actually another reason I'm calling. The...the FBI is here, Michelle. They're asking about Martin Wagner. Lieutenant Wagner? He's gone missing, apparently, and he's wanted for questioning. They said they'd like to—"

Michelle drops the phone and rushes to the back door. She grabs her two suitcases and carries them with some difficulty down the steps, nearly tumbling forward in the process. She loads them into the trunk, starts up the car, and drives away.

103

"HERE WE go," says Elizabeth Ashland. We're on FaceTime. She turns her phone outward, capturing the scene for me.

Multiple agents surround the storage shed, their weapons drawn, riot shields up, helmets on. Through a bullhorn, one of the agents calls out: "Martin Wagner, this is the FBI. We are entering the shed. If you have a weapon, drop it or we will shoot. Get down on your knees and put your hands on your head."

An agent approaches the shed from the side, turns the key in the lock, then steps away. The garage door slowly grinds open.

Will Wagner be inside? I doubt it.

What about Michelle Fontaine? More likely. My heart hammers in my chest.

The only thing inside the garage, right in the middle, dominating the space, is a Dodge Caravan. The agents shuffle in, weapons trained on the vehicle, peer inside, then shout out after the inspection, "Vehicle is clear."

"It's his van," says Elizabeth, going closer now that the threat of gunfire is over, moving the camera in on the license plate.

Yes. It's his plate. The one the ALPRs caught last night.

What about inside the van?

As if someone is reading my thoughts, the image on the screen jumps back and the rear of the van lifts open. A hydraulic ramp rises, unfolds, and drops to the ground.

"You see inside the van, Emmy?"

I do. In the rear of the van are several open boxes filled with underwear and socks and T-shirts, a pile of shirts and pants, and what appears to be two storage crates, the ones whose dust outlines we saw in Wagner's apartment this morning.

This keeps getting stranger and stranger...

The phone turns so that Elizabeth is looking at me. "He had a getaway planned all along," she says. "He must have been in a hurry. Wait." The screen is suddenly pointing downward, and agents are calling to Elizabeth. The jerkiness of the video would be nauseating if I weren't so transfixed.

I reach for the water bottle that Tom Miller gave me but then stop short.

"Does this look familiar?" The screen shows the driver's seat of the vehicle, which is Wagner's wheelchair, complete with the American flag on the armrest.

His van and his wheelchair, both left behind.

"Elizabeth," I say, "can you run the camera around the van? So I can see all sides of it?"

"Sure." She lowers the phone again; I'm staring at the side of her pants, then the floor, then the sky. I look away to avoid motion sickness. When the image stabilizes, I see that Elizabeth has backed up to give me an overall view of the van's driver's side. An agent is holding a mirror on an extension pole under the vehicle, searching for explosives. Another is doing the same thing over the top of the vehicle.

"Wait," I say, catching something in the top mirror's reflection. "The roof of the van. I saw something. Some color. Something yellow."

Elizabeth calls out to the agent. She walks toward him—more queasiness-inducing movement of the phone—and fixes the camera right on the mirror hovering over the roof of the van.

I see a yellow star on a black background, the words U.S. ARMY below it.

A U.S. Army seal painted on the center of the roof of the Caravan.

"Elizabeth, let me call you back in two minutes," I say. I end the connection and pull up some of the videos that Officer Ciomek sent me from the Chicago POD cameras. The ones from the mounted camera with a downward angle.

Each one, to varying degrees, shows the roof of the van. The video clips are grainy, and they're in black-and-white, but they're enough for me to see what's on the van's roof—and, more important, what is not.

No yellow star. No U.S. Army seal.

I call Elizabeth back. "It's not the same van," I tell her. I explain about the video clips I have from the POD cameras in Chicago.

"Well, he might have a second van," says Elizabeth Ashland. "In fact, that's probably how he made his escape last night. He kept a second van here in the garage. He dropped off the one registered to him and drove off in the second one. I bet he has a second wheelchair too."

Maybe. It's possible. But I don't know what to think about anything Elizabeth says anymore.

The cash. The Taser. The Garfield watch. And now the clothes. Four things that don't make sense.

Books. I need Books. It's been about half an hour since he left; he's probably just getting to the store to receive the load of new releases.

I dial his number and wait. He doesn't answer. It goes to voice mail. I don't leave a message. He's probably busy dealing with the new shipment.

Maybe Petty's there to help him.

Petty.

I breathe in and out.

Maybe the cash, the Taser, the cartoon-cat watch, the clothes—maybe they make sense after all.

I hang up and dial Rabbit. "Hey, kiddo."

"What's the latest?" she asks.

I give her my best one-minute update. With my free hand, I reach for the bottle of water Tom gave me, lift it by its blue top, and drop it into my bag. I need to eat and drink soon or I'm going to pass out.

"I need some quick background, as fast as you can," I say.

"Hit me with it," she says. "I'll get Pully on it too."

I finish with Rabbit, hang up the phone, leave the conference room, and run down to the basement to find Tom Miller.

He's with an elderly patient, working on some kind of squatting exercise. He sees me and nods, gently helps the man into an upright position, and excuses himself. "Everything okay?" he asks me.

"The patients here," I say. "The people who Lieutenant Wagner preached to about politics."

"His disciples, sure," Tom says.

"Right," I say. "Were any of them named Petty?"

104

"SORRY AGAIN that I kept you waiting," Books says to the delivery guy as he's leaving. He watches the man drive the truck out of the alley, then closes the heavy back door and stands in the back room of his bookstore looking at the gigantic crate of new releases.

The thought of unloading them and switching out inventory makes him feel more exhausted than he already is. "Am I fighting an uphill battle?" he whispers to himself. The store's basically a one-man operation now, his finances squeezed so tight he can scarcely afford even part-time employees.

Well, there's Petty, whom he doesn't even have to pay, although he compensates him by letting him stay here. But even Petty doesn't come every day. Books just doesn't have enough help.

He checks his phone. He felt a vibration a few minutes ago but he had his hands full. It's Emmy, as he suspected. He calls her back.

"Oh, good, you're okay," she says.

"Why wouldn't I be okay? What's wrong?"

"Are you alone?"

"Yeah, I am. Where are—"

"Petty's not there?"

"Sergeant Petty? No, he's not here. Why?"

"I—I think Petty might be our guy."

"Petty might be...what guy?"

"Our guy, Books," she says. "I think Petty might be Darwin."

"What?" Books chuckles. "Not Wagner?"

"Not Wagner. Listen, they just opened the storage shed," she says. She tells him about finding Wagner's van inside, about the U.S. Army seal painted on its roof, and about how that doesn't match the roof of the van they saw on the Chicago POD cameras.

"Okay, so Wagner had two vans," he says. "One was registered in his name, the other wasn't. That's the one he used for his crimes, and now he's using it as his getaway vehicle. He probably kept the getaway van in the storage shed. He dumped the one registered to him, because he knew we'd be hunting for it, and drove off in the one we aren't looking for."

"That's what Elizabeth said. That's exactly what she said."

"But you don't think so?"

He hears Emmy heave one of her patented sighs. "He left all his clothes inside," she says. "What kind of getaway is that?"

"A rushed one, I guess."

"He leaves behind over a hundred thousand dollars in cash in his apartment. Cash, Books. This guy's on the run. He's a fugitive. He can't use credit cards. Cash is his lifeblood. He took the time to empty out his drawers so he could bring along socks and underwear. He pulled clothes out of his closet and dragged out storage files—but he leaves behind all that cash?"

"He left behind the Taser too. And the Garfield watch."

"Right, and that's weird too. He sticks the Taser under his bed. Like we won't find that? Like we won't look under his bed?"

"And the watch in his garbage outside..."

"Yeah, it looks like he's trying to hide it. But didn't you say trash is one of the first things you search? It's a treasure trove, you said."

Right, he did say that. "What's your point, Emmy?"

"My point is our supposed criminal mastermind, our evil genius, forgot to take a boatload of cash that could have kept him afloat for years on the run. His socks and underwear and shirts and pants were apparently more important than a hundred grand in cash, but then he left the clothes behind in the storage shed too. Oh, and what else does he leave at his apartment? Highly incriminating evidence—the Taser, the watch—that he made only the feeblest of attempts to hide."

"You're saying..." Books pushes his hair off his forehead, letting this wash over him.

"Wagner is a patsy," she says. "He was set up to take the fall."

"Wagner...isn't Darwin," Books says. "So where's Wagner?"

"Dead, I assume. Darwin made it look like Wagner escaped. He killed Wagner and took away his clothes, toiletries, whatever, so it would seem like Wagner fled."

"And he didn't take the hundred grand in cash..."

"Because he didn't know it was there, Books. It wasn't his apartment. It wasn't his money. He didn't know Wagner was using the bottom drawer of his stove as a piggy bank. He just grabbed the obvious stuff—clothes, toiletries, some boxes full of personal information—to make it look like the guy was on the run. Then he drove away in Wagner's van with Wagner's wheelchair. And Wagner's body, which he must have dumped somewhere."

"Okay, Emmy, slow down." Books starts pacing, a habit when his mind is racing. He walks into the main room. Nothing disturbed. The front door still locked, storefront window still secured.

"What about the storage shed?" he says. "The clothes, like you said. It's a clue that he didn't really go. If he's so smart—if Darwin is so clever—why would he leave those clothes there for us to find?"

But he answers that question in his head before Emmy does.

"He didn't *want* us to find them," she says. "We were never supposed to find that storage shed. He mapped out an entire route to that storage shed where there were no cameras, no license-plate readers. Right? He can look up the information about cameras and ALPRs online. He can do scouting runs and see for himself. He mapped out a perfect route. We never would've known."

"But then he caught some bad luck," says Books. "That police barricade."

"Exactly. The squad car at the scene picked up his license plate with its reader. And then he had to alter his route, and an ALPR on Bell Road caught him too."

"So this whole thing..."

"This whole thing was set up so Lieutenant Wagner would take the fall. It wouldn't have been hard. Wagner publicizes where he goes, right? He has a damn tour schedule on his website. Wagner goes to Indianapolis, Darwin goes to Indianapolis—to kill some homeless advocate. Wagner goes to Charleston, Darwin goes too—and commits another murder."

382 · JAMES PATTERSON

"Wagner goes to Chicago," says Books, "and Darwin does too. And blows up a homeless shelter."

"Right. I'll bet Darwin got a van just like Wagner's. He customized it, I'm sure, exactly the same way. Only he didn't know that Wagner had a U.S. Army seal painted on top of his van. You can't see it unless you have an extension mirror."

"Wow," says Books. "Wow." He shakes his head. "And what about the moon thing on his face? The long gray hair?"

"Makeup and a wig," she says. "On close inspection, sure, no one would think he was Martin Wagner. But generally? In passing? A guy in a wheelchair with long gray hair and a prominent crescent-moon-shaped scar on his face? That wouldn't be so hard, would it?"

"So this guy may not even be in a wheelchair."

"He probably isn't."

"He did everything like he was in a wheelchair. Picking victims who lived in single-story homes, using the same customized Dodge Caravan, the same wheelchair with the same American-flag decal—he just mimicked Wagner in every way. But it was all fake."

"I'm sure he hoped we'd never catch on at all," says Emmy. "But if we did, all trails would lead to Lieutenant Wagner."

105

"OKAY, OKAY," says Books. "What you're saying is plausible. Maybe it isn't Wagner. But Petty? Petty is . . . Darwin?"

"Just listen to me, Books. And don't say anything. Just hear me out."

"I thought I was already doing that."

She lays out her reasons. How little they actually know about Petty. And what they do know about Petty—his weekly comings-and-goings, when he arrived in Virginia the first time. "Petty's bald," she adds. "A wig would be easy to wear."

"I suppose so."

"And Books, think about it—of all the places he could have chosen to sleep, he picks a spot right outside a store owned by the fiancé of the woman who's tracking him, hunting him? That's just a coincidence?"

Books shakes his head, frustration mounting. "He was keeping an eye on you through me," he says. He slams his fist on the counter. "And I fell for it."

His thoughts are interrupted by a noise from the inventory room.

The unmistakable sound of the solid rear door opening from the alley.

Only one person other than Books has a key to that door. Books gave it to him yesterday.

"Hello?" Books calls out, his heart racing, adrenaline seizing him.

"Is that Petty?" Emmy asks in his ear.

Books walks into the back room, brushing the palm of his hand against the grip of his sidearm, secured in a slant holster at his right hip. Lucky, at least, that he took off his suit coat when he arrived to unload the new releases.

"Agent Bookman," says Petty. He's dressed in his army jacket and jeans, the overloaded duffel bag slung over his shoulder. "Didn't think you'd be here."

"Do you have your weapon on you?" Emmy asks in a harsh whisper.

He does. And Petty sees it.

"Hey, Sergeant Petty," he says. *If that's your real name. If you really were a sergeant.* "Emmy says hi," he adds.

"Oh, okay." Petty nods. "How's your big case? You catch your guy?"

"Tell him he got away," Emmy whispers. "Put him at ease."

"Not yet," Books tells Petty.

"Do you want me to send agents to the store?" Emmy asks.

"No," says Books.

"No what?" Petty looks at him with a question on his face.

"I'll call you back, Emmy."

"Books, wait—"

Books ends the call. Drops the phone in his left pocket. Keeps his right hand down, close to the holster. Petty watches him without comment. Sees Books's right hand poised by the weapon.

"We didn't get our guy," says Books. "But he couldn't have gotten far. He's in a wheelchair, so his options are limited."

"Your killer's in a wheelchair?" Petty asks. "That's kinda... unusual, isn't it?" Petty looks Books in the eye, something he rarely does.

"He's an unusual guy," says Books.

Petty blinks, glances away. Looks at Books's right hand again, the gun.

"I stopped by last night," says Books. "Thought you'd be here."

"Yeah, well..."

Busy killing Lieutenant Wagner last night? After I basically told you we were about to raid his house?

"Is everything... okay?" Petty asks.

He can imagine how he looks to Petty. Not in a casual polo shirt and jeans but wearing a suit and tie and carrying a sidearm. Not a bookseller but an FBI agent. An FBI agent who is clearly on edge, no matter how Books tries to hide it; his heart is drumming in his chest, adrenaline pumping through him.

"Everything's fine, Sergeant. Why wouldn't it be?" He recognizes how strange his own voice sounds—unnatural, forced.

Petty remains still, apparently uncertain of what to do. He doesn't have a visible weapon. If he reached for one, Books could outdraw him, his right hand still dangling by his weapon.

"Well, so—I just stopped by to grab something," says Petty, hitching the duffel-bag strap higher on his shoulder.

"You're not staying? You usually stick around on Thursdays."

And then disappear Friday through Sunday. Just like Lieutenant Wagner.

"No, I can't stay," says Petty. "Just need to grab something." He looks at the gun in Books's holster again, then up at Books, as if seeking permission.

"Sure, no problem," says Books.

Petty walks over to his corner of the room, looks at his neatly made bed, the two stacked crates he uses as a nightstand, the glass vase full of fake flowers that Books had taken out of the main room and put back here in storage.

Petty reaches under his pillow.

Books takes a step back and gets ready to draw his weapon. He's out of practice, hasn't been to a range in months—

Petty turns, holds up a Bible, then shoves it into his already overstuffed duffel bag, which gives Books time to move his hand away from his holster.

"Don't know how I forgot this yesterday," Petty says. "So...guess I'll be on my way. Hope you find your bad guy, Agent Bookman."

He looks in Books's direction but avoids eye contact.

"Me too," says Books.

Petty goes out the back door, which closes with a thud. Books exhales, shaky from adrenaline. He looks up at the live video of the closed-circuit camera trained on the alley outside and watches Petty hobble along with that heavy bag.

He calls Emmy. "He just left," he says. "I'm going to follow him."

"Please be careful. You want backup?"

"Definitely not. He's careful. I'll be lucky if he doesn't make me. Add in other agents, and it could be a disaster."

Petty disappears from the screen, and Books calculates how much longer it will take Petty to clear the alley. He gives it that much time and a bit more, for good measure. Then he pulls open the door and closes it as quietly as he can manage.

Books reaches the end of the alley and slowly looks out. He spots Petty easily enough, crossing the street. Holding up a key remote. Opening the door of a navy-blue sedan and climbing inside.

His homeless friend has a car.

106

"SORRY TO rush you," I say to Louise Hall, the rehab facility's administrator. "But I need to stay in contact with one of the agents, and I can't get reception in here."

"Right, you can only get it on the second floor," she says, opening the door to the staff room. "This won't take long. Michelle's locker is the last one on the left."

I walk down the row of employee lockers and stop at hers. I use my shirt to lift the latch. I'm not sure what to expect, but all I find is a hand mirror, a hairbrush, and a tube of lip balm.

Any of them could work. Michelle would have held these in her hand, leaving some nice fingerprints.

I lift up each item with a tissue and drop it into a brown evidence bag, one of many that Books brought along today.

"You have some reason to suspect... *Michelle?*" Louise asks.

"Oh, it's probably nothing. Now, if you don't mind, I have to get outside and back on the phone. An agent's picking me up."

We walk quickly toward the reception area. She says, "I'm sorry that we don't have a patient named Petty, but you think he might have used a different name?"

"Possibly," I say. "Or he might be one of those veterans who hung out in the courtyard when Lew gave his political speeches."

"I wouldn't know about that," says Louise. "I'm usually back in the administrative offices. But Tom said he saw those people. If you could get him a photo?"

"Working on it," I say. At the reception area, I stop and shake her hand. "You and Tom both have my cell phone number. Call me if anything comes up."

I head outside and dial Books just as my ride—one of the agents from the search of Wagner's home—pulls up in a Crown Vic.

Books picks up. "Hey," he says. "I'm driving, so you're on speakerphone."

"What's going on?" I ask.

"Turns out Petty has a car."

"He does? And you're following him?"

"Yeah, but he's way ahead of me. He got through a light I missed. I'm rusty at surveillance, apparently. But I see him up ahead."

"You get a license plate?"

"No. But I will. I'll start breaking traffic laws if I have to."

"You want me to pull up a map?"

"Only if I lose him. I won't lose him."

"Okay. What's your plan?"

"I want to see where he goes. If he has a home, he assumes nobody knows about it. Talk about a treasure trove."

"Don't do anything stupid," I say.

"What would I do without your advice?"

"I mean don't confront him. Not by yourself."

"I got it, Em. How did you do?"

"They don't know Petty by description, and he's not listed as a patient. I need a photo. But I did get some fingerprint samples that should work."

"Great. Remember, when you get back to Wagner's apartment, talk to Agent Rudney. Best fingerprint guy in the Bureau."

"Okay. Try to get a photo of Petty, would you?"

"I will. I have to go now. It's too hard to talk and drive and watch him."

"Okay, go. And be careful."

"Yep."

"Books, wait," I say quickly, suddenly full of worry, suddenly realizing how much danger I've placed him in, suddenly overwhelmed by missed opportunities and lost second chances and... tears brim in my eyes. I can't say anything; my throat's too choked with emotion.

"Me too, Emily Jean. Me too. I'll be fine," he says. And the phone goes dead.

We reach Morningside Lane a few minutes later. As Books suggested, I find the lead agent on the forensics team, Rich Rudney, a friendly-looking guy with gray curly hair. I gave him a quick summary of our progress.

"So this might be a murder scene now," he says. "Well, there isn't any blood, I can tell you that. But we're doing a full work-up."

"And there's some prints I need you to pull," I say to Rich, reaching into my pocketbook for the brown evidence bag. "A rush job. It's probably nothing, but..."

"Probably nothing," he says, "is sometimes something."

107

BOOKS HITS the brakes, managing not to rear-end the car in front of him, which has stopped for a red light. Up ahead, Petty's navy-blue sedan is driving on. Books keeps his eyes trained on it.

His phone is in his left hand — he's hoping that, if nothing else, he can get a photo of the license plate of Petty's vehicle.

Petty's car eases into a left-turn lane at the next intersection, a red light. The light controlling Books turns green. He's stuck behind a car moving much slower than he'd like. At the next intersection, Petty executes the left turn and disappears from Books's view, heading north. The left-turn signal changes to a solid green.

Even if Books can reach that intersection before the light turns red, he'll have to wait through a glut of traffic before he can turn. It will be too late.

Books makes a quick left turn into the parking lot of a hardware store, drawing objecting horns from oncoming cars but not caring. If his attempt at a shortcut doesn't work, Petty will be gone.

He drives through the parking lot to the back of the store and takes an alley toward the road onto which Petty turned left. He looks ahead and spots Petty's sedan. Good.

Books noses his car out onto the street against traffic, drawing more horns, but the cars he's obstructing, however annoyed their drivers may be, stop and let him pass. He completes the left turn, speeds up, and finds Petty's sedan in the right lane. Then Petty's right-turn signal starts blinking. His sedan turns into the drive of some building.

Books slows his vehicle as he nears the spot where Petty turned. It's a high-rise apartment building, faded yellow brick, something like twelve stories. Books takes the turn, which probably leads to a parking lot in the back. This must be where Petty lives.

He can't believe he's thinking those words—*where Petty lives.* Where Petty lives. Where Petty parks his car. What, does he have a wife and three kids too?

He stops halfway along the side of the apartment building. If he comes roaring into that parking area in the rear, Petty will almost surely see him. But if he doesn't, he'll lose Petty, who will presumably walk into the building and disappear.

Well, not disappear. He'll be in a building. Books won't know which apartment, but one step at a time.

Books kills the engine. Gets out of the car. There's a door right by him and a sign on the wall saying ABSOLUTELY NO PARKING. He stays close to the wall as he approaches the rear of the building.

He listens. All he can hear is a humming noise, the low buzz of an outdoor air-conditioning condenser unit. He peeks around the corner and retreats. Peeks out again.

He sees the blue sedan Petty was driving, parked down the way. No brake lights. Nothing coming from the exhaust pipe. Seems like the car's turned off. Petty must have hustled into the building through the back door.

The lot is filled with vehicles, all parked nose in. Petty's is more than halfway down, not far from the back entry to the building, covered by a blue awning.

He walks slowly toward the car, looking to his right and seeing the rear door to the apartment building and the AC condenser that's making all that noise while it transports cool air into the high-rise. The residents will need that AC; it's growing more suffocatingly hot by the minute.

Well, at least he'll get a make and model and license plate. The car probably won't be registered to Petty, at least not in that name. But the circle is closing. With any luck—

Over the din of the condenser unit, he hears footfalls, urgent, close—

Books is shoved from behind, hit low so his upper body bends back and his arms flail out. He stumbles forward and his face smacks the asphalt, sending stars and bright colors through his eyelids. Stunned, the wind knocked out of him, lying on his stomach, he reaches for his side holster. A foot is planted on the weapon and his hand.

He looks up to see Petty, the searing sunlight behind him.

"How many more are coming?" Petty snarls.

He turns his head back to the pavement. "Petty—"

"*How many more?*" he demands.

"It's . . . over, Petty. You can't . . . get away—"

"It's not over. It'll *never* be over."

Books turns toward Petty again and lifts his head a little, just in time to see something dark come crashing down on his skull.

108

"THANKS, RICH," I say to Agent Rudney, the fingerprint guy, at Wagner's house. "You'll let me know as soon as you can?"

"No problem, You and Bonita Sexton," he says, holding up the card I gave him—one of mine, but I wrote in Rabbit's name and number too.

I dial Books. The call goes to voice mail. He's concentrating on the tail, I assume, trying to stay far enough away that he won't be noticed while also staying close enough to keep tabs. I send him a text: Check in when u can.

With all the people here, it almost feels like a party inside Wagner's small apartment; there are about a dozen FBI agents and techies working it over, bumping into each other, calling out to one another. Someone even made a pot of coffee. I'm too jittery for coffee right now. *Call me, Books.*

Outside, a crowd has gathered. We've taken over Morningside Lane for the better part of a day now. Neighbors are gathering, then losing interest, then returning, then losing interest again. Agents are going door to door asking questions about Lieutenant Martin Wagner. Traffic along Lathrop has backed up due to rubberneckers. Some reporters are out talking to someone from our office. I imagine their questions are getting a whole lot of variations on *No comment at this time.*

An SUV pulls up around the barricade. Elizabeth Ashland and Dwight Ross emerge from the vehicle.

Elizabeth. Elizabeth, who insists that I'm Citizen David's mole. Who seems to have an inordinate amount of cash on hand all the time. But who green-lighted my investigation when nobody else would. *People have more than one face.*

Is Books's suspicion correct—are Darwin and Citizen David one and the same? It's possible, I concede. I can't put it all together, but I may lack some of the pieces of that puzzle. And is Elizabeth connected?

"Nothing else of note from the storage shed," Elizabeth says to me. "We're processing it. But Wagner's gone. That much is clear."

That much *isn't* clear. But I will keep that opinion to myself for the time being. If I don't trust her, I don't trust her.

"The question is how," says Dwight, always the master of the obvious. "In what vehicle. We can't send out an alert if we don't know the vehicle."

"Can one of you drive me to my apartment?" I ask. "I'm not far from here. I need my car. I'm going to go back to our offices and start pulling data from the tollway cameras and the license-plate readers in the area and cross-match them against Dodge Caravans and other disabled-plate vehicles. If we work backward, we might be able to identify the vehicle."

It's not a lie. I'll do that. I don't think it will produce any helpful information. I don't think Wagner's our guy. But I'm not sure. I'm not sure of anything.

"Where's Books?" asks Elizabeth.

"Personal business," I say. "The bookstore in Alexandria."

That statement was true half an hour ago. Books is no longer on personal business. But I'm keeping Elizabeth on a short leash for the time being.

Dwight makes a face. "Why would an agent at the top of his game throw it all away to run a bookstore?"

He did it to have a better lifestyle. He did it so he could spend less time on the road and more time with his fiancée, yours truly, who then proceeded to break up with him.

"We can drive you," says Elizabeth. "We're going back to Hoover too. Just let me check in with the agents inside."

While Elizabeth and Dwight head into the house, I call Books again. Voice mail again. Damn. I text him again: Just send me a quick note that ur okay.

A few minutes later, Elizabeth and Dwight walk out. "Let's go. Nothing left for us to do here. The techies are on it."

"Okay," I say, walking with them to their SUV.

Call me, Books, I silently pray. *Please call me.*

I jump in the back of their SUV, and we drive off.

109

"SIR? *SIR*. Are you okay?"

Books hears himself moan as he opens his eyes and squints up at an older woman and a child, harsh sunlight behind them.

"Would you like me to call an ambulance?"

He quickly pats his side holster. He still has his weapon, thank God. The woman steps back as she sees it.

"I'm an FBI agent," he says reassuringly. Though these days, it seems, people don't always find that reassuring.

He sits up and regrets it immediately; his head feels like a bowling ball, and laser shots of pain fire back and forth inside his skull. He scans the asphalt around him for his phone. He finds it, thank God again. "I'm all right, ma'am."

"Your face is...red." She touches her left cheek. He touches his own and feels the abrasion he got when his face smacked the asphalt.

"Did you...see where he went, ma'am?"

"I just saw him leave in that blue car," she says. "I saw him hit you too. My granddaughter and I just got back from the grocery store. He hit you with...something, a club or something, and then he saw us pull into the lot. He jumped into a blue car and drove away. I'm sorry I didn't see more."

"No need to apologize," says Books. *You probably saved my life.*

Books tries to get to his feet, using a nearby SUV to brace himself, but an alarm goes off inside his head, and he sits back down. He landed on the left side of his face, and Petty struck him with the baton, or whatever it was, on the right side of the skull, cracking his head against the pavement a second time in the process. He touches the knot on his head, and his hand comes away from his hair sticky with blood.

"You should go to the ER," says the woman.

"I'm okay." The physical pain is nothing compared to the stupidity he feels. Petty jumped him. He puts it together now. Somehow, Petty made him; he knew Books was following him. He parked his car, doubled back, and hid behind something until Books passed him on his way to the blue sedan.

That stupid AC condenser, still chugging along with its loud hum, helping Petty sneak up behind him. But that's no excuse. *I screwed up.* "Did you recognize him, ma'am?"

"I don't think so, no. He was bald and wearing a camouflage shirt. I didn't get a good look at his face, but it wasn't someone I recognized."

"What about the name *Petty?*" Books asks. "Recognize that name? Maybe Sergeant Petty? Someone who might live in this apartment building?"

It's doubtful, he realizes. If Petty was suckering Books into an ambush, he wouldn't have driven him to the place where he lives.

"It doesn't sound familiar," she says. "And I think I know everyone in this building. Sir, you really should see a doctor."

"I will, I will. Thank you again, ma'am."

"I wish I could be more help."

"You interrupted him," he says. "Who knows what he might have done if you hadn't come by when you did?"

That seems to make her feel a little bit better. "I could try to help you up," she says.

"No, I think I'll sit right here for a few minutes, let my head clear a bit."

They say their goodbyes. The woman and her granddaughter retrieve their groceries and head into the building. Books calls Emmy.

"You want the good news first," he says, "or the bad news?"

110

I PULL my car into the lot of the apartment house in Huntington. I had been halfway to the Hoover Building when Books called me from here.

Petty jumped him, Books told me, but when I see him coming out of the rear door of the building, it looks more like Petty ran over him with a truck. The left side of his face is bruised and scraped. The right side's okay, but above his ear the hair is caked with blood and the area's swollen, as if he'd grown a tumor since I last saw him.

"You shoulda seen the other guy," he says when he gets in my car. "I feel like such an idiot."

I put my hand up to his face, though it's hard to touch it.

"I'm okay," he says.

And suddenly I burst into tears. He brings me close while I release the nervous energy, the worry, the feelings I've suppressed.

"I didn't...know...what happened to you," I say after a few minutes, catching my breath, the sobbing finally passing. "I hadn't heard from you..."

I look at him. He's trying to smile. It's not easy with all the bruising.

"I can't lose you, Books. I don't know what that means. I really don't. But I can't." I take a deep breath. Where did all that emotion and confession come from?

"Okay, first of all, I'm fine," he says. "Second of all, I suggest we tackle the task of finding our serial killer before we address the far more difficult and complex mystery of Emmy and Books."

I wipe my face, laughing. He always makes me laugh. "Deal," I say. "But how about before we do either of those things, we take you to the emergency room?"

"No, I'm okay. My pride is wounded, I have a massive headache, and I'm going to look like the Elephant Man for a few days, but otherwise I'm ready to dance a jig."

No, he's not. "Can you drive?"

"Yeah, I'm okay to drive."

"Then follow me to the nearest ER. I'm not taking no for an answer."

He sighs. "My head hurts too much to argue with you."

"And then you'll go home and rest."

"No, I'm not going home to rest. I'm following Elizabeth tonight."

"Elizabeth? Still?"

"What?" he says. "Nothing's changed. I know someone's funneling cash to her. I still think it's Citizen David. But why can't Petty be Citizen David? If he can be Darwin, he can be David too."

"I don't know . . ."

"If I'm wrong, I'm wrong," he says. "But there's only one way to find out. She'll leave tonight the same time she always does, I bet. And I bet she goes to the Payton Club again for one of her little meetings."

"Even tonight, after the day we've had?"

"*Especially* tonight, Em. I don't know who she's been meeting with or what she's been saying, but I know this much—she has a lot of new information to share after today."

"Take backup, then," I say. "Take me."

"No and definitely no," he says, "in that order. Nobody else at the Bureau knows I'm looking at Elizabeth Ashland. I can't drag other agents into this and tell them we need to investigate someone who could ruin their careers if she ever found out. And even if I could, it's too much of a risk that she'd sniff it out. And you? I'm not letting you anywhere near that place. Besides, you have plenty to keep you busy, don't you?"

"Yes, sir, I do."

"I'm going alone," he says. "And I promise you this—that's the last time anybody jumps me."

111

BOOKS AND I drive our separate cars to the ER in Hunting-ton, where they clean the wound on his head, stitch him up, and give him some pain meds. He doesn't like it, but even he concedes it was the right decision.

Afterward, we split up, Books heading out for his evening of surveillance, me heading for my evening of research. I return to Hoover to find Rabbit and Pully looking like two kids cramming for an exam, moving from their telephones to their computers, papers all over their cubicles.

They are doing so many things at once. Monitoring hits on license-plate readers and cameras in every direction from Annandale, Virginia. Doing background checks on our various suspects. Searching for Dodge Caravan registrations and trying to tie them, in any way, to Petty or Lieutenant Wagner.

And I'm going to add at least one new assignment—searching for registrations for Chevy Impalas, which Books thinks is the car Petty was driving.

But at least I can help now too.

"Have you guys eaten today?" I ask.

"No" and "No time" are the answers I get, nearly in unison, from Rabbit and Pully.

"You need to. This may take days, guys. You barely slept last night. You have to eat and you have to sleep or you'll fall apart."

Rabbit throws off her headset and sits back in her chair. She blinks her bloodshot eyes as if it's the first time today she's looked at anything but a screen. Pully stands and moans, his palms on his back, stretching like an old man even though he's barely old enough to drink.

"Listen, guys," I say. "It's almost seven now. You've been at this all day. You've exhausted nearly everything you can find in terms of data. And any human intelligence—those people aren't getting back to you tonight, so there's no point in waiting for them. Let me take it from here."

"No way," says Rabbit. "The guy who blew up a homeless shelter is mine. I'll stay up for a year if that's what it takes."

"She's serious," Pully says. "Remember, you're talking to someone whose idea of fun is organizing protest rallies and volunteering at soup kitchens."

"A little volunteering would do you good, Pully," she shoots back. "Get out in the real world instead of sitting home playing Dungeons and Dragons."

"Dungeons and Dragons?" He laughs. "I think I was *born* the year that went out of style."

"Okay, people, listen," I say, reclaiming their attention. "Last I checked, I'm your boss. And you're supposed to listen to your boss. I know I read that somewhere."

"I think it's in the manual," says Pully.

"Right, so go home. Have a meal, get a decent night's sleep. Return in the morning and all those people will begin calling you back, and the pieces will start fitting together." I clap my hands. "Really, guys. What was your plan? Pull an all-nighter? You'd be hallucinating by dawn."

"And what about our fearless leader?" asks Rabbit, who is warming up to the idea of food and a bed despite herself.

"I haven't spent all day cooped up like you two," I say. "And anyway, I have a few things to take care of, then I'll go home too."

They drag their feet a bit, but it helps when your boss is pushing you out.

When they're gone, I sit down in front of the computer. When Citizen David started his bombing spree, Rabbit began collecting raw data from around the bombing sites—CCTV-camera footage, license-plate readers, tollway cameras. Then she took the raw data and put it into a useful format so we could play with it—perform cross-references, run pattern analyses, dump it into algorithms, isolate various characteristics.

Are Darwin and Citizen David the same person? Books could be right. I admit, it never would have occurred to me.

We know this much from the bulk data around the sites that Citizen David bombed: No single vehicle with the same license plate was captured at all of the locations—Connecticut, Florida, and Alabama—during the relevant times. We would've picked *that* up immediately. But maybe Petty drove his Chevy Impala to *one* of the bombing sites. We never had a reason to focus on this particular make and model of vehicle before.

So it's a long shot, but it could be a home run. If, that is, Petty is Darwin. And *if* Darwin is Citizen David. And *if* Petty was driving a Chevy Impala, as Books believes but isn't sure. A long shot, yes. But that's what data girls like me look for.

I glance at the time. It's now exactly seven o'clock. If Books is right about her regimented, seven-to-seven schedule, Elizabeth Ashland will be leaving for the day right now.

I go onto the data drive on my computer, the W drive. The bulk data—all the information assembled from all the sources from all three of Citizen David's bombing sites—is in, appropriately, the bulk-data folder. The folder is pass-code protected.

I type in the pass code and pull up the bulk-data file.

"Wait a second," I say aloud, though I'm alone.

This isn't the bulk-data file. Not the raw data, anyway.

This has been edited.

Edited by whom?

I think it through. The members of our data team—Pully, Rabbit, and I—have access to the raw data. We have the pass code. Who else does?

Supervisors in our chain of command. The director, of course, as well as the assistant directors and . . .

Does Elizabeth Ashland, a special assistant director, qualify for clearance?

I pull up the clearance manual. Yep. She sure does.

Elizabeth has access to our raw data.

112

HE RUNS through his house removing everything that could incriminate him. In his upstairs bedroom, the materials he used for the scar: the makeup pencil he used to draw the outline of the scar, the rigid collodion scarring liquid, the powder, the lip gloss to give the scar a bit of a shine. The gray wig, of course. He puts it all in a grocery bag.

He looks in the mirror and forces himself to take a deep breath. Things didn't go well today. But it could have been worse.

You have to trust your plan, he reminds himself. *They can't tie anything to you. Even if they suspect you. Even if they're sure it's you.*

It all leads to Lieutenant Wagner. Everything. Every murder was committed in a city that Wagner was visiting. The Taser, the watch, both found at Wagner's house. And of course, Wagner has now fled! Only a guilty man would flee!

They'll never find Wagner's body, buried at that deserted power plant. Sure, the drive to the storage shed was compromised, thanks to that damn police barricade, but the trip to the abandoned power plant was pristine. Nobody could possibly know that he buried Wagner there. Nobody was going to be looking at the power plant.

They won't find the duplicate Dodge Caravan either, the one he used for all his travel, all the murders, the one he customized just like Wagner's. It's several towns away, in a private rented garage paid for in cash. And even if they did find it, it's just a vehicle. It may be souped up exactly like Wagner's, but so what? They can't tie it to him. It's been wiped clean. It's not registered to him. The license plates have been removed. There's no connection to him.

The duplicate wheelchair he used? Now, *that* could be a problem. It's one thing for the FBI to find a dime-a-dozen Dodge Caravan in some private garage. It's quite another for them to find a wheelchair that's not only the same make and model as Wagner's but has the same American-flag decal and RANGERS LEAD THE WAY sticker on the shroud.

No, it's time to retire, once and for all, the duplicate wheelchair. He pulls it out of his downstairs closet and wheels it into the garage.

First, he puts on gloves and wipes down everything. He vacuums the leather seat. No reason to leave a stray print or fibers.

Next, disassembly. It will be much easier to dispose of this chair in parts instead of tossing the whole thing in a river or somewhere. The armrests, the shroud, the wheels, the footholds, the joystick, the motor—everything is unscrewed and separated.

Now it's simply a matter of taking the parts to various different spots—garbage dumps, recycling centers, storm drains, municipal garbage cans, ponds and rivers, alley dumpsters.

He looks at the time. It's 7:00 p.m.

Lose the wheelchair, he thinks, *lose the makeup and wig, and there's nothing tying any of this to you.*

And then he can finalize his plans for the next target, which will make the bombing in Chicago look like amateur fireworks.

113

BOOKS PARKS his car on the street not far from the Payton Club. He doesn't bother tracking Elizabeth from headquarters. He's that sure she'll come here tonight.

He waits across the street, a busy avenue with plenty of vehicle and pedestrian traffic, so he's not worried about sticking out. His heart races as he sees Elizabeth, buttoned up as always, with the same self-assured stride as always, taking the steps up to the main door, ornately decorated in gold and framed by the flags of the nation, the District, and the club. The door opens as she approaches. Books sees a warm exchange between Elizabeth and the doorman before it closes.

Now it's waiting time. He could badge his way in there, but he doesn't know the layout of the multistoried club or where Elizabeth could be. He could lose the element of surprise. All he knows is that she tends to spend a few hours there. His best guess is that she has a cover for being there. She works out there or she eats dinner there or both, and then she somehow meets with her source. She might meet with the source first, right away; doubtful but possible. Or they might meet at the end of her time there.

No way to know, so he has to keep his eyes glued to the front door. It's the only means of entry and departure in the evenings; he's checked on that and confirmed it. Maybe the person Elizabeth is meeting has yet to arrive. Maybe that person beat her, and Books, here. But that mystery man or woman's going to have to leave at some point. Books is prepared to wait until ten, when the place closes, if necessary.

He touches his face. The abrasions on his left cheek from where he hit the asphalt hurt more than the bump on the right side of his skull, where Petty struck him with the baton. The pain meds he got from the ER are helping, at least.

As stupid as he feels about letting someone like Petty get the better of him, he knows he's lucky too. Petty could have killed him. If that woman and her granddaughter hadn't arrived when they did . . .

A group of men in suits enter the Payton Club. Books snaps photos of each of them, zoomed in. It's a Thursday night, a prime night for socializing. His camera will get a lot of use.

You're in there somewhere, he thinks. *And you're going to have to show yourself sooner or later.*

114

NINE O'CLOCK. It's taken me two hours to reassemble the raw data that was sent to us by the various agencies and that Rabbit organized and collated for us so we could run our searches. It's not the first time I've done this sort of thing, but it's been a while, and I have a newfound appreciation for the work Rabbit does.

Somebody tampered with the raw data after it was put into an organized, usable format. But whoever it was couldn't tamper with the original data delivered to us. That would be impossible.

"You didn't think we'd re-input the original data, did you, Elizabeth?" I whisper.

Finally, it's ready to run. I start with the basics, the first thing any analyst would run. A simple compatibility search to see if the same license plate was captured around all three of the bombing sites—Seymour, Connecticut; Pinellas Park, Florida; and Blount County, Alabama—during the relevant time periods. I run the search and press Enter.

And I get a hit. One hit. One license plate that was tagged at each bombing location.

I nearly jump out of my seat. I pull up the license plate and do a search for the vehicle registration.

When I get the results, I really do jump out of my seat. Then I back away from the computer like it's suddenly radioactive.

"My God," I say.

I've had this wrong. I've had this wrong all along.

115

ELIZABETH ASHLAND leaves the Payton Club at a quarter past nine. She walks out the door and down the steps with the same confident stride, the same put-together presentation, as she had when she entered.

Books waits. The place will close at ten. At most, he'll have to wait another forty-five minutes for Elizabeth's contact to leave too.

Will it be Shaindy Eckstein, the *Post* reporter?

Or Petty, who, up until yesterday, Books would not have thought capable of walking into an exclusive social club like the Payton?

Michelle Fontaine? He doesn't know much about her, only that she happened to quit her job at the same time Lieutenant Wagner either left town or was murdered.

Maybe Lieutenant Wagner? Whatever Emmy thinks, there's no way to be certain that Wagner was framed—set up as the patsy and murdered. Nothing is certain right now.

Wait—what if it *is* Wagner? Wagner's in a wheelchair. He wouldn't be walking up the steps.

"Shit." Books breaks from his spot and jogs over to the intersection. There it is—the wheelchair-accessible entrance, on the east side of the building. He'd forgotten about that. So now Books has to cover both the front entrance and the side entrance? He's standing right on the corner, not exactly hidden.

Did he already miss Wagner, or someone else, leaving from the wheelchair-accessible exit?

"Damn it," he whispers. Did he make another mistake? First being jumped, then failing to cover what, in hindsight, should have been obvious—

Books freezes as the front door of the Payton Club opens and a man comes out and goes bounding down the stairs. Into a waiting town car.

No. No way.

Books remembers to breathe, his mind buzzing now. As the town car pulls away, Books hustles to his own car, jumps in, and follows.

He learned today, a lesson from Petty, that he's rusty when it comes to vehicular surveillance. But it doesn't matter. Not this time.

"You've gotta be kidding me," he whispers.

After the two vehicles break free of the traffic and head out onto an open road toward the interstate, Books draws his car up behind the town car. No use in pretending. Nobody's pretending anymore.

The town car pulls over to the side of the road. Books does the same.

One of the back doors of the town car opens. An invitation. Books kills the engine and gets out of the car. Walks over to the town car and gets in the back seat. There are two men in the front seat, only one in the back.

"Life can be complicated, Books, wouldn't you agree?" says FBI director William Moriarty.

116

"COMPLICATED?" BOOKS ASKS. "It doesn't have to be. Not *that* complicated, Bill."

"But it is," says Director Moriarty. "For example, a man can love his wife. He can be devoted to her. But he can still acknowledge that he has certain...needs."

"So Betsy has a stroke and is confined to a wheelchair, and that gives you an excuse to *acknowledge* your *needs?* Which I assume means 'fuck one of my agents.'"

"I didn't say an excuse. I didn't say that. And I'll remind you to be cautious both in your judgments and in your tone."

"My *tone?* I don't work for you anymore, Bill. I came to help out on this investigation at *your* request. *You* asked *me.*"

Books draws back, letting his own words sink in.

"Okay, I get it now," he continues. "I always thought it was a little odd that you'd have me investigate the leak when you thought the prime suspect was Emmy. I took it as the ultimate compliment that you had so much faith in my integrity that you thought I'd even bust my own fiancée if I believed she was the leaker."

"That's true. It's completely—"

"Bullshit," Books snaps. "You wanted an outsider, an outsider you could trust to keep your secrets. You knew I'd have to investigate everyone. You knew that might end up including Elizabeth. And you knew that if I looked into her, I'd see that she seemed to have an awful lot of cash on hand. Which would certainly make her look suspicious. If someone was going to find that out, you wanted it to be someone who doesn't work at the Bureau. Someone you could trust to protect you. Someone who looked up to you as a mentor."

"You're . . . twisting this, Books."

"You could have told me this straight off, Bill. You could have said, 'Look, this is embarrassing, but I'm sleeping with Elizabeth, and I don't want my wife seeing the credit card bills for hotel rooms and dinners and whatever else—but I'm too much of an old-school guy to let *her* pay, so I'm giving her cash while she puts all the expenses on her credit cards.' Yeah, that would have been helpful information for me to have, Mr. Director."

"I owe you an apology for not telling you," says Moriarty. "You're exactly right about that. I hoped it would never come to you investigating Elizabeth. I was certain—*we* were certain—Emmy was the leaker. Are you telling me she's not?"

Books drops his head into his hands. Until about fifteen minutes ago, he was certain it was Elizabeth. He thought he was about to close the loop on the leak investigation, and maybe more. Instead, he's back to square one.

"But Agent Bookman, I do *not* owe you or anyone else an apology for what I do with my personal life. I love Betsy dearly and I've been very, very good to her. She wants for nothing. She never will. You have no idea what it's like to love someone who wants to love you back but can't."

With that, Books raises his head and looks over at his mentor. *Actually,* he thinks, *I do know what that's like.*

He opens the door and leaves the town car.

117

I STARE at the computer screen, at the vehicle registration of the one car whose license plate was captured at all three bombing sites: the bank in Seymour, Connecticut, accused of racial discrimination in lending; the fast-food restaurant in Pinellas Park, Florida, its parent company accused of animal cruelty; the city hall in Blount County, Alabama, that wouldn't marry same-sex couples.

A license plate that was scrubbed from the bulk data, deleted forever, so that when Rabbit organized and collated it, we'd never see it.

My phone buzzes. Books. I reach for the phone, but my hand is shaking so hard I don't think I can lift it. The buzzing stops. My phone beeps a minute later with a voice mail. Without lifting the phone, I push the button to listen to the message.

"Emmy, it's not Elizabeth Ashland. She's not the mole."

I know she isn't.

"She's having an affair with Director Moriarty. They've been meeting at the Payton Club. He's been paying her cash so she can put everything on her credit cards and he can hide the bills from Betsy."

My brain is telling me this is a *wow* moment, but I'm not wowed. I couldn't care less about Elizabeth Ashland right now. Though this must be what she meant when she was talking about her complicated love life on the airplane.

Books isn't done, but I get the point. I turn off the phone when Bonita Sexton comes rushing down the aisle. "Okay, what's up?" she says. "What happened?"

"Hey, Rabbit." I gesture to my computer. "Somebody hacked into the bulk data for the Citizen David investigation."

"*What?* Somebody messed with my data?"

I nod. "I re-created the file," I tell her. "From the original data."

"You did?" she says. "That's my job."

I throw up my hands. "Well, Rabbit, what can I say? I did it." My eyes are blurry with tears.

"Well, okay, then. Let me run it for a compatibility anal—"

"I did that too," I say. "See for yourself." I nod toward the computer screen. She turns and looks at the license registration I pulled up.

"No," she says.

I stand and leave my cubicle, not feeling my legs, moving as if I'm floating. I reach Rabbit's cubicle and pick up the framed photographs, joined together, of her boys, Mason and Jordan. I hear her come up behind me.

"Jordan, I assume—it was when you were in New Haven visiting him," I say. "Not that hard to drive over to Seymour and blow up that bank. Mason? In Tampa? Pinellas Park isn't too far away. Plant a bomb at the fast-food restaurant and make the chain pay for being cruel to the chickens that are in its sandwiches."

Rabbit doesn't say anything. I can hear her heavy breathing, nothing more.

"The city hall in Alabama? That one would have been harder. But by then," I say, turning to her, "you knew you were in charge of the data for the Citizen David investigation. You didn't need to be careful anymore. You could just scrub yourself out of the data."

Her eyes are cast down; her chest is heaving.

"What about Chicago?" I say. "Was that—"

"Chicago wasn't me, and you know it," she hisses. "I never killed a single person. I never would have. That's why it made me..." She shakes her head.

"That's why the Chicago bombing sickened you so much," I finish. "Because someone was taking *your* crusade and bastardizing it, bombing people you genuinely care about." I remember now how upset Rabbit was after Chicago, how personally she took it. I hadn't realized *how* personal it was to her.

Rabbit lets out a big sigh. She's relieved, probably, in a weird way. How this must have weighed on her.

"If you're waiting for an apology," she says, "you aren't going to get one. Everyone I hit had it coming. Banks that deny loans to black and brown people? Screw them. Restaurant chains that torture animals? You actually feel *bad* for them? This country is going to hell, and *somebody* has to stand up for the little guy."

"Did somebody have to leak information to Shaindy Eckstein at the *Post*?" I ask.

That question knocks some of the air out of her.

"You needed a buffer, right?" I go on. "If Citizen David is always one step ahead of our investigation, someone will eventually suspect it's an inside job. But leak to a reporter who tells the whole world, and the only thing people will suspect is that there's a leaker. Nobody will think that someone within our own Bureau is Citizen freakin' David himself. Or herself, apparently."

Bonita breaks eye contact, stares at something in the middle distance. No tears have fallen, I notice. Her face is a stone wall. I didn't realize how hardened she'd become. All the protest rallies she attended, all the volunteer work she did, weren't enough. Her kids were grown up and she'd had a fulfilling career. It was time for her, I guess, to take bolder steps against what she was seeing happen to her country. And to gather a national following in the process.

"Guess who the prime suspect for the leak is, Rabbit?" I point to my chest. "Me."

"I wouldn't have let that happen," she says softly.

"No?"

"No, Emmy." She fixes her eyes on mine. "If it came to it, I'd have said it was me."

"You wouldn't have told them everything, though. Just the leak part, right?"

She raises her hands. "I guess we'll never know now. Because now the question is, what are *you* going to tell them? Are you going to tell them everything?"

I look again at the photos of her two boys. I set down the frame.

"How many times did we talk?" she says. "How many times did we say to each other, 'David's one of the good guys'? You know what I was doing was right. When I hacked into that pharmaceutical company and exposed all their lies about that hepatitis drug—that they knew all along it would destroy people's kidneys but didn't say anything? That wasn't wrong. Or when I hacked into that bullshit Ivy League school that claims to care about diversity and exposed their hypocrisy?"

"The bombs were different," I say.

"Why? I just damaged property. I didn't kill anybody. Or even wound anybody. I called in bomb threats to scatter anyone who might be inside. And the explosions themselves—they just messed up the interiors of the buildings. I didn't knock down buildings, like Darwin did in Chicago. I just wanted to shake them up. And I did."

She's not wrong. We always noted how Citizen David took precautions to avoid human casualties. And it's true that we privately rooted for Citizen David even as we tried to catch him. Or I did, at least.

"I can't do this right now," I say. "There's something bigger at stake."

"Darwin," she says.

"Darwin. I need to stop him. And one thing I know for certain is that I need you to help me."

She nods.

"You want to catch this monster, right?" I ask.

"More than you do," she says.

Before now, I wouldn't have believed that. But although chasing Darwin has become my obsession, it's never been personal. For her, this is personal. I can harness that energy and determination. I need it right now.

Catch Darwin first. Deal with Rabbit later.

"See you tomorrow, bright and early," I say.

118

BOOKS PICKS me up at the Hoover Building after ten. He's still reeling from what he learned about Elizabeth Ashland and is full of commentary on the subject. It makes it easier for me to stay mum about what I just learned.

I haven't decided what I'm going to do about that information yet. Until I do, telling Books would only put him in a compromising position.

"So I guess we're back at square one on the leak investigation," he says.

"The leak investigation doesn't matter," I say too quickly, too harshly. "All that matters is Darwin."

If Books notices the tension in my voice, he doesn't say anything.

"Tomorrow morning," I say, "we're going to chase down the Chevy Impala registration list. If you're right that it's the model of car Petty was driving, and if he lives somewhere nearby—which he probably does—we'll be able to narrow it down pretty quickly. Now all I need is a photo of Petty to show the people at the rehab facility."

"I think I can help you with that."

"You got a photo of him on your phone?"

"Not exactly. My store has a security camera in the alley, remember?"

I forgot all about that. "Perfect. Petty came in through the back door today, right?"

"He did."

We drive to Alexandria and he slows the car as we approach the rear of the store. "The last time we came here," says Books, "I told you to be careful, that you never knew where Darwin might be. Remember how you pooh-poohed that?"

"I'm not pooh-poohing it now," I say. "No pooh-poohing. Negative on pooh-poohing."

We pull into the alley. The security camera looks down on us as we enter the store. Books draws his weapon just in case. It's dark inside, so Books flicks on the light immediately. Rear inventory room, empty. The remainder of the store, Books quickly confirms, also empty.

"Okay." He goes to work on the video equipment, pulling up yesterday's video, stopping where it showed Petty hobbling down the alley, his heavy bag over his shoulder. Books downloads the video onto a DVD and hands it to me.

"Keep it safe," he says. "With any luck, we'll know a lot more about Petty tomorrow. We may even find him. And hopefully Tom or Louise at the clinic can identify him and help us start building a case."

"Great."

"Now, one more thing," he says. He walks over to the corner of the inventory room where Petty slept. The bed is still neatly made. Next to it, two crates are stacked, and on top of them, there's a glass vase of fake flowers.

Books finds a stray plastic bag on one of the bookshelves and throws it over the vase. "Petty put this vase here," he says. "It used to be up front, but I moved it back into the storage room."

"I remember it."

"Petty must have seen it on the shelf and put it here." Books carefully lifts the vase, now securely in the plastic bag. "Fingerprints," he says, holding it up.

"Oh, that's perfect." We are keeping the fingerprint techies busy these days.

"Glass holds fingerprints pretty well. I'll run it over to Rich Rudney tomorrow morning," he says. "And maybe we'll have an ID on our mysterious Sergeant Petty."

119

I WALK into the office at seven sharp. Pully isn't in yet, but Rabbit is in front of her computer, looking different—rested, oddly enough, maybe because she feels unburdened now that I know her secret.

She sees me come in but says nothing. The look she gives me—a mix of scorn and defiance—fills me, more than anything else has, with a palpable sense of loss. We will never look at each other the same way again. We will never, in any way, be the same again.

She must know that I have no choice but to turn her in. She *must* know that.

She will probably go to prison for the rest of her life.

Pully rolls in not long afterward, his hair sticking out in all directions, looking about fifteen years old. How I envy him not knowing what I know about the third member of our team.

But there's no time for that now. By eight o'clock, we are humming like the old days, a three-headed crew of data analysts. Pully is looking at registrations on Chevy Impalas in Virginia on the assumption that Books correctly guessed the model of car Petty was driving.

Rabbit, meanwhile, is doing what she does best—compiling. This time, she's gathering and combining ALPR records extending out from the location where Petty jumped Books in Huntington, the assumption being that some police squad car or some mounted reader on a traffic-control device caught Petty's license plate.

Hopefully, we'll be able to cross-reference Virginia-registered Chevy Impalas with plates caught on ALPRs near the scene where Petty and Books tangled.

Books himself has a busy morning. After he gives Agent Rudney the glass vase that hopefully has Petty's fingerprints on it, he swears out a complaint for an arrest warrant against a man known to him only as Petty for the crime of assault of a federal officer with a dangerous weapon. So now, if and when we find him, we don't need to immediately stick murder or domestic terrorism charges on him; we can scoop him up for the assault alone.

By noon, Rabbit has compiled data within a five-mile radius of the spot where Petty jumped Books. If Petty sped away in his blue sedan—hopefully an Impala—which he must have done, we have his license plate in here somewhere.

"Run the ALPRs against the vehicle registrations," I say.

Rabbit does. We get two hits, two matches on the cross-reference. Two Chevy Impalas registered in Virginia crossed the path of some license-plate reader within five miles of the ambush spot yesterday.

She pulls up the registrations. The first one is to an African-American man who lives in Roanoke, on the other side of the state. "Gotta be a couple hundred miles in distance," says Pully. "And the wrong race. Petty's a white guy, I assume?"

Yes, he is.

The second registration is to Mary Ann Stoddard, age fifty-one, who lives in Huntington, Virginia.

Huntington. The town next to Alexandria. The town where Petty ambushed Books.

I grab my phone and dial Books. "We got it," I say.

120

BOOKS LAYS out a satellite view of a Google map before the other FBI agents he's assembled for the raid.

"The Meredith Court and Gardens," he says. "A twelve-story apartment building in downtown Huntington, just off Route One. Mary Ann Stoddard lives on the seventh floor, unit seven-nineteen. Officially, she lives alone." He looks around at the agents. "But obviously, we have reason to believe she's not alone at the moment."

"Seven-nineteen," says one of the agents. "Is that an interior unit?"

"Actually, that's the good news—no, it's not. It's a corner unit." Books spreads out an architectural layout of the apartments that Emmy found online. "Unit nineteen on each floor is on the southeast corner. That means . . ." He returns to the Google map, the satellite view of the building. "Right here, this side. So we can set up shooters on the roofs of these buildings right here."

"Do we know he's there?"

"We don't. I think it's fifty-fifty at best. He could definitely be in the wind. I may have spooked him yesterday."

"You mean yesterday, the day he kicked your ass?" That comment from an agent named Hendricks, whom Books has known for years. He's got a chaw of tobacco in his mouth and a smirk on his face. It's like Books never left, these guys and their bullshit.

"Yeah, Hendricks, that yesterday. I'm taking four agents with me to the seventh floor. The rest of you?" He holds up three fingers. "Three ways to exit that building. One is the front door. One is the rear door. The third is through the underground parking garage. We station two agents at each of them. I don't think he could make it to the underground parking, because we're going to kill the elevator service. So we should station agents there who are less experienced or just general pussies. Hendricks, you'd make sense."

Like he never left.

"No fooling around, boys," he says. "This man is wanted for blowing up that building in Chicago and killing two hundred innocents. We like him for over a dozen other murders around the country. He's capable of anything, so we have to be ready for anything. Okay?"

Nods all around the room, nervous energy and performance adrenaline so thick you can almost smell it.

"Let's go catch a bad guy," he says.

121

"BE CAREFUL," I say to Books over the phone.

"I will. I'm not alone this time. I'm working with pros. If you find anything on Petty, either through the fingerprint search or at the rehab facility, let me know right away, okay?"

"Of course. And you keep me updated."

"Will do."

I end the phone call before I say something mushy or touchy-feely to Books. It's not what he needs right now. He's in performance mode.

"I'm heading to the rehab facility," I say to Rabbit and Pully. "I'm going to show Tom Miller the video footage of Petty."

"Right," says Pully.

Rabbit glances at me but says nothing.

"That was good work, guys, getting that address so fast."

"Thanks," says Pully.

Rabbit looks away, remaining silent.

I check the clock. It's now two thirty. "It won't take me

long," I say. "I should be back no later than . . . four. See you guys then?"

"Of course you'll see us," says Pully. "Where the hell else would we go?"

But I wasn't really addressing that comment to Pully, and the third member of our team knows it. "Rabbit," I say, "I'll see you around four."

This time, I say it not as a question but a command. Rabbit clenches her jaw but doesn't respond. Pully senses something between us but isn't sure what, and he's not the type to ask. He probably chalks it up to some older-women thing.

"Four o'clock, Rabbit," I say, and I head out, not even bothering to wait for a response.

122

MICHELLE FONTAINE paces the hotel room, checking her watch, holding her cell phone, a phone whose number only a handful of people know. She calls her landline voice mail again, listening to the message for the third time.

"Michelle, it's Tom Miller. Hey, listen, I was sorry to hear that you're leaving. I hope you're doing okay. But the reason—I think Louise called yesterday and told you the FBI is investigating Lew? I think it's about the Chicago bombing, but they never actually said that. Has to be, right? How crazy is that? Anyway, one of the people at the FBI is coming to the clinic today at three o'clock. She's going to show us a photo array. They're looking for some guy they call Sergeant Petty. They must think he's a . . . I don't know, a coconspirator or something. We're right in the middle of some crime story! So, can you make it at three o'clock today? I hope so. Or if not—well, I hope you're doing okay, kiddo."

She puts down the phone. Checks the time again: 2:37 p.m. She grabs her keys and heads for the door.

123

I DRIVE my car to A New Day. The parking lot is nearly empty now, just after three o'clock on a Friday afternoon. No one is at the reception desk, and the door to the main hallway has been propped open. I walk in and call out, "Hello?"

"Oh, hi." Tom Miller comes out of an office. "Sorry, the physical-therapy clinic at this facility is basically closed now. Nobody schedules late-afternoon appointments on Fridays."

"I hope I didn't keep you here," I say.

"No, you're good. Being part of an FBI investigation is more exciting than anything else I had on my social calendar. Actually, I don't even *have* a social calendar."

"I know the feeling," I say. "So...should we get to the video footage?"

"Sure." He looks past me. "I called Michelle. I was hoping she might be here."

"You still haven't heard from her?"

He shakes his head. "Nope. I don't know her cell number. The clinic only has her landline. I left a voice mail there, hoping she'd pick it up."

"I suppose we could wait a bit," I say. It's only a few minutes past three.

We sit in the reception area. Tom's dressed pretty much as he was yesterday, which is how I suppose you'd expect a physical therapist to dress, in a T-shirt and sweats.

"So you like Michelle," I say.

"Michelle? Sure. She's a nice person. I didn't get to know her all that well."

"But you strike me as someone who gets to know people well."

He blushes. "Well, I try to get along. I knew Michelle only a couple of weeks. Some people open up more than others, I guess."

"Michelle didn't open up?"

"Oh…" He tilts his head. "She didn't seem very interested in talking about her past. Y'know, she'd change the subject or whatever. So I just minded my own business."

"Give me examples," I say. "I mean, we're just killing some time here."

He takes a breath. "Well, I asked her where she was from, and she said she was from the Midwest. I said, 'Yeah? Whereabouts?' And she didn't—she changed the subject."

"She didn't tell you where she was from?"

"No. Or, like, I remember asking her what brought her to Virginia? Y'know, I thought she'd say something like family or a boyfriend or school or something."

"What *did* she say?"

"She said she needed a change of scenery. And then she kinda started talking about something else. So I didn't push it." He raises a hand. "She's a great therapist, though, and, really, she's a very sweet lady."

I understand. I also understand that she's apparently not accepting Tom's invitation to join us. I look at the clock. It's now twenty past three. I want to get back soon. This wasn't supposed to take more than a few minutes. I show the video, people either recognize him or not, and we move on.

I'm anxious to hear from Books, but it will take him some time to reach the apartment building in Huntington, get everyone in strike formation, and then execute the search of Mary Ann Stoddard's apartment.

I ask Tom, "Have you had a chance to think about whether you might have seen Sergeant Petty?"

"Yeah, I mean—well, the video will be good to see. But I told you some of the people who'd listen to Lew in the court-yard weren't patients?"

"Right. You said others would come. Other veterans."

"Yeah. I mean, a guy who's bald and in his forties—I wouldn't say he was one of the regulars. But there was a guy who came around sometimes, and he might be the guy you're talking about. He was very serious. Like, this was all just guys sitting around talking politics, y'know? Lew was definitely do-ing most of the talking, but it was, like, banter. But this guy, he seemed like he was concentrating more, if that makes sense. Like it was super-serious to him. And he didn't really seem like he was part of the group, I guess you'd say. Like he was this outsider who'd come around and listen really closely and leave."

This could be helpful. I need to get this video footage in front of Tom.

"Is there a DVD player around here?" I ask. "Maybe we'd hear Michelle come in."

"Yeah, there's one here in Louise's office."

Tom leads me into one of the administrative offices, a spacious one, neatly arranged, the walls lined with photos of family and diplomas and certificates. In the corner is a television and a DVD player. "I've never used this, but how hard can it be?" he says.

I hand him the DVD of the surveillance footage, and he puts it in. The TV screen goes from black to...fuzz.

"Hang on." Tom tries buttons on the DVD player. He picks up one remote, points it, and pushes buttons. He changes channels. He changes the source. He puts down the remote and tries another one. "This will do it, I think." But no, it doesn't.

I sigh. "Is there another DVD player around?"

Tom thinks for a moment. "Maybe the assistant director's office." We try that. The door's locked, so Tom has to retrieve the master keys and open it. No TV inside, no DVD player.

Ultimately, he tries every administrative office, including Payroll and HR. No functioning DVD player, at least not one we can make work.

It's now three forty. We are way beyond the time I wanted to leave. I need to go. "Tom, wasn't there a DVD player in that conference room up on the second floor where I was talking yesterday?"

"Oh yeah, there is," he says. "And I've used that one. I can use that one. C'mon." We pass through the administrative offices and go back to reception.

Tom looks out the front door. "Still no Michelle," he says. "I just...don't know where she'd be."

124

BOOKS MEETS with the bomb squad and SWAT team a block from the location in downtown Huntington. The SWAT team is dispatched to the rooftops of the adjacent buildings. The bomb squad will keep its distance but stand ready to respond on Books's command.

The agents fan out around the Meredith Court and Gardens. Books enters the lobby with several agents. Two of them will secure the area and make sure the elevator service is cut after Books reaches the seventh floor. Two others will secure the underground parking garage. The rest will go with him.

They show the lobby clerk their badges and explain the situation. The man, young and wet behind the ears, nods his head in compliance and can barely speak. The assistant manager comes into the lobby. After more conversation, he hands Books a key that will open unit 719 and probably all the others too.

Books and four agents—one of them Hendricks—take the elevator up to the seventh floor. "We're here," Books says into the collar of his coat. "Bring the elevator down to the ground floor and kill it."

"Roger that," he hears through his earpiece.

The agents hold their weapons out but low as they jog along the tattered carpeting and past the gray walls toward the southeast corner, unit 719.

They spread out, two to a side, flanking the door. Books pushes the buzzer and waits. The agents have their weapons up now, stern expressions, masses of bundled energy.

Books pushes the buzzer again. "Mary Ann Stoddard!" he calls out. He pushes it again. "Mary Ann Stoddard! This is the FBI! Open up!"

Nothing.

Books nods at one of the agents, who takes the key, places it firmly in the lock, and turns it. The door opens but is caught by a chain.

The agents look at one another, catching the significance. You couldn't put the chain on the door from the outside.

Someone's inside that apartment.

"Mary Ann Stoddard!" Books calls out again, this time through a partially opened door.

He waits, trying to hear inside over the pounding of his pulse.

Finally he steps back and kicks the door, popping the chain. The agents swarm inside, weapons aimed at the various corners of vulnerability, sweeping the front room.

Nothing. A dingy open room with old furniture and a large window facing east. A kitchenette with coffee cups in the sink and the smell of something fried in the air.

Next to it, a closed door—must be the single bedroom.

"Mary Ann Stoddard!" Books calls out.

He hears something inside the room, glass breaking.

"South," Books says quietly into his collar, speaking to the SWAT sniper on the roof to the south of the building, "do you have a visual?"

"Negative. Blinds are pulled."

"East, a visual?"

"Negative, Books. Blinds are pulled on this side too."

His heart races. He reaches his hand out for the door. Nods to the other agents, who gather behind him. Turns the knob. It isn't locked.

He pushes the door open, rushes in, weapon up—

A woman in a hospital bed is struggling to sit up; a glass has shattered on the floor next to the nightstand. Her head is wrapped in a bandanna; her skin is pale, her eyes sunken. She looks frail, and her movements are shaky. The rest of the room's empty. The other agents confirm the bathroom is unoccupied.

"FBI, ma'am," says Books, "Mary Ann Stoddard?"

"Yes. I...heard you. I was...sleeping."

"Where is he, ma'am?"

She squints at him. "Are you Agent...Bookman? Books?"

"Yes, ma'am."

The woman's head falls back against the pillow.

"Agent Bookman," she says, "do you have any idea what you've done?"

125

TOM MILLER and I climb the stairs to the conference room on the second floor. We enter the room, which is the same as yesterday, with the nice table and AV equipment surrounded by drop cloths, roller pans, and paint cans, partially painted walls, and the pack of water bottles, minus one bottle I took yesterday. The heat here is just as oppressive as it was yesterday, the sunlight blazing through the windows.

"Okay, this shouldn't take long," says Tom. "*This* machine, I know how to use."

He pops in the DVD and waits for everything to boot up.

I pull out my phone. This is the one part of the building where I can get some reception.

My phone is lit up with voice-mail messages from Rabbit—one from twenty-eight minutes ago, one from twenty-one minutes ago, one from twelve minutes ago.

All while I was downstairs, unable to receive them.

The TV screen comes to life and starts playing the DVD,

showing the alley outside Books's store in grainy black-and-white.

I access my voice mail and lift the phone to my ear as the image of Sergeant Petty ambling down the alley with the duffel bag over his shoulder appears on the screen.

"Emmy, we just got the prints back," I hear Rabbit say, her voice higher-pitched than usual, urgent.

"My God, I've seen that guy," says Tom, pointing at the TV screen. Rabbit's voice, in my ear, keeps going, rapid-fire.

"...real name is Todd Crisman. He was in Special Forces, later recruited by the CIA. You know how these people talk, but I could read between the lines. He was an assassin. He did special-ops assassinations around the world."

A fire erupts in my chest and cascades down my arms and legs. My phone slips from my hand and falls to the drop cloth at my feet. I can't breathe. I try to draw in oxygen but can't.

No, please, no, not now—

The fire runs through me as the room starts to spin, everything at an angle, the pounding of my heart throbbing in my ears—

"Emmy, that's him, that's the—are you okay?"

I stagger back, grab the radiator for support as my legs threaten to give out.

"Hey, what's happening? Are you having a heart attack?"

"No. No," I whisper breathlessly, shaking my head furiously.

"A panic attack?"

He reaches for me, but with my free hand, I swat him away.

He draws back, startled, alarmed, his head cocked. He looks down at the phone at my feet and then back at me as I struggle for air, any tiny bit of oxygen.

Tom picks up the phone and pushes a button, putting the

voice mail on speakerphone, then starts the message again. We listen together to Bonita Sexton's urgent voice.

"Emmy, we just got the prints back. From your water bottle, I mean. It somehow ended up in Michelle's evidence bag. His name isn't Tom Miller. His real name is Todd Crisman. He was in Special Forces, later recruited by the CIA. You know how these people talk, but I could read between the lines. He was an assassin. He did special-ops assassinations around the world. His mother was a prostitute who would stay in homeless shelters and SROs. She was murdered, apparently, by two homeless men when Tom was twelve. He's our guy. It's Tom Miller. His psych profile says that he—"

Tom punches off my phone and holds it at his side. "Well, Emmy, I can't tell you how disappointed I am in myself." He looks over at the pack of bottles on the floor. "When you asked for a bottle of water yesterday? You tricked me there."

He takes a single step toward me.

"That must have been before you got so excited about this other guy, Petty, whoever the hell he is."

He walks right up to me as I struggle to stay upright, as I pray that oxygen will come, that I won't lose consciousness—

"But you still have no proof," he whispers to me, putting his hand on my cheek. "Whatever I did in the military doesn't make me a killer now. Any proof you come up with is proof that points to Lieutenant Wagner. Who has fled, by the way, which doesn't exactly make him look innocent."

"We…we…found his body," I say, black spots flashing before my eyes.

His expression changes, the confidence disappearing, but only for a moment. "No, you didn't," he says. "That's a lie."

"People…know I'm here," I say.

He grips my hair in his hand, jerks my head. "But then you

left here," he whispers, "and I have no idea where you went. Must be that this Petty character killed you. Or maybe Lieutenant Wagner. Oh, the list of suspects."

"Petty is...Petty..."

"Petty is what?" He jerks my head again. "Hmm? Petty is what, Emmy?"

"...in...cust—custody..."

"You already have Petty in custody?" Tom releases my hair, scrolls through the messages on my phone. "Well, Emmy, here's a text from your beloved Agent Bookman from nine minutes ago that says 'We missed him.' That must be Petty... *not* in custody. All these lies."

In one powerful movement, Tom grips my hair again and jerks me to the floor like a rag doll. My elbow hits something, a pan and a paint roller, and they're knocked to the floor along with me, making a loud commotion.

I land hard on my shoulder, turn over onto my back, and look up at my stranger danger.

He drops down on me, pinning my body. He holds my arms with his hands and leans into me, his eyes ablaze.

Need air...can't breathe...can't pass out...can't lose conscious—

"I need to know everything the FBI knows," he whispers. "You have ten seconds. If you don't tell me, I'll find that fiancé of yours and gut him like a fish. If you tell me, Books lives. Go. One, one thousand...two, one thousand...three, one thousand..."

"No...no..."

"Oh, you won't tell me." His hands grip my throat and his thumbs press down on my windpipe, everything shutting down, everything dimming—

Books. Books. I'm—

"It didn't have to be this way, Em—"

An explosion, then another following it instantly, glass shattering above us, raining shards of the window down on Tom and me. Tom releases me and bounces to his feet.

I suck in oxygen in exaggerated, raspy gulps. Then I turn and look toward the doorway.

I see Bonita Sexton, a gun in her hand, tears streaming down her face, the gun shaking so violently she can hardly maintain her grip.

126

"WHO ARE you?" Tom Miller asks. Then, quickly recovering: "Thank God someone's here. We need an ambulance."

I force myself up onto my elbows.

Rabbit takes another step into the room. "You kill...*homeless* people? *Sick* people? Why? How could anyone do that?"

"What? No. No, it's not me. Me? Are you kidding? Please—please just put the gun down and we can talk."

Rabbit shakes her head, her mouth in a snarl, fresh tears rolling down her face.

Using the window ledge for support, I get to my feet.

"You killed so many...innocent, harmless people," Rabbit says, her voice cracking.

"Rabbit," I say, finding my voice, my throat scorched.

She shakes her head and takes another step closer.

"Be careful with that thing," says Tom. "Do you even know how to use it?"

I have the same question. She's worked at the FBI for decades. She could've used the firing range in the Hoover

Building as much as she wanted. But did she? It's one thing to shoot at a large picture window, another to shoot at a dangerous man like Tom if he makes a move. Which he's going to do.

"Bonita," I say. "Don't kill him. Stay right where you are. Let me call it in."

"No," she whispers, the gun threatening to fall from her grip, the trembling of her arms increasing the more emotional she gets.

"Honey, you're not a killer," I say. "Don't become one."

Her eyes narrow; her jaw clenches. "Why not?" More tears, more sobbing. "What do I have to lose?"

Prison, she means. For the Citizen David bombings. She figures she's going to spend the rest of her life behind bars anyway.

"What's left for me now?" she whispers.

"I won't turn you in," I say. "I won't!"

Her eyes shut, but only for a moment, the gun moving in her hand. "Yes, you will."

"Bonita, is it?" Tom raises one hand, palm out. "Listen to me. I'm not coming any closer. I just—"

"Don't listen to him, Rabbit. Listen to me. *I won't turn you in.*"

Tom snaps his head toward me, then back to Bonita.

"Yes, she will," he says. "But you know who won't? Me, Bonita. I won't turn you in. I don't even know what you did."

"Shut up!" Rabbit snaps, spit spraying from her mouth.

"Think about it," he says. "Use that gun on Emmy and let me go. You blame the shooting on me. Everyone will believe that—"

"No, Rabbit, listen—"

I move toward her, but she steps back, turning the gun in my direction. "Both of you, stay where you are!"

Both of us.

"You," she spits at me. "You know I did the right thing. I never hurt anybody. I made *sure* I didn't hurt anybody. *You*," she snarls at Tom. "Taking what I did and bastardizing it. Killing hundreds of people who never hurt a soul in their lives."

I look at Tom, who has moved away from me. We are a triangle, each separated by about ten feet. Only one of us has a weapon, but the harder Rabbit trembles, the less in control she seems.

"You're a good person who shouldn't go to prison," says Tom.

"He's playing you, Rabbit—"

"And you can still try to catch me after I'm gone!" Tom shouts over me. "You can keep doing your good work! Don't let her ruin your life, Bonita!"

Rabbit's mouth opens, and she draws deep, ragged breaths. The weapon is still in her hands, but it's not held straight out, more of a sixty-degree angle from the floor. She looks at me. She looks at Tom.

In the distance, through the window shattered by Rabbit's bullet, we hear sirens. The cavalry is coming.

"Shoot me if you want," I say. "But keep Tom right where he is."

Rabbit takes a breath and gives me a look. "I'm not going to *shoot* you, Emmy—"

Tom is already in full sprint, rushing her—

"Rabbit!"

She raises her gun but he's too fast; he puts his hands on the weapon as he barrels into her, pinning her against the wall.

I rush forward too—

—an explosion of gunfire, once, twice—

—and, off balance, I ram my shoulder into Tom.

We both fall, and Rabbit crumples to the floor, two bloody gashes coloring her shirt, the gun still in her hands.

I reach for her. "Bonita! Rabbit!" I shout, staring into her vacant eyes.

I hear shuffling to my right as Tom gets to his feet.

I take the gun from Rabbit as Tom starts toward me. I fire once, twice, three times.

The third shot hits him, stopping his momentum, staining the right side of his shirt red. He staggers back a step, looks down at his chest, then at me.

I turn to Rabbit. Her head has lolled to the side; her eyes are open, her body still.

Tom reaches out for the wall, wincing, struggling to remain upright.

"Rabbit," I whisper in her ear, "I'm so sorry."

I stand up, gun still in my hand, my body no longer on fire. Now I feel cold.

I approach Tom Miller as the sirens grow louder, as I hear a commotion downstairs, men calling out, "FBI! FBI!"

One hand on the wound to his upper chest, hunched against the wall, Tom lets out a moan. He'll probably survive that wound. And what he said before was right. We'll have a very difficult time ever proving in a court of law that he killed a single person. He killed Rabbit, but now he has some kind of story to spin about her too, something about her going to prison. And if he was paying attention, he might even figure out what it was she did.

I raise the weapon. We lock eyes. We understand each other.

"If it had to be anybody," he says, "I'm glad it was you."

I nod and fire the gun.

127

BOOKS WALKS away from Emmy, who's still seated in the hallway outside the conference room, motionless, her eyes vacant. Eric Pullman, with his wild hair and big ears and tear-streaked face, is nearby. Books puts his hand on Pully's shoulder. "I'm so sorry," he says.

Pully doesn't respond; he's too choked up, a mess of emotion. "Oh," he says, pulling a file out of the bag. "Here's the background on Michelle Fontaine."

"Go sit with Emmy," he says. "You two need each other right now."

He glances at the file on Michelle Fontaine, compiled today after the fingerprint sample was confirmed. She'd been a volleyball star at New Mexico State and after graduation, she became a physical therapist focused on athlete rehabilitation. She moved in with a man after dating him for four months. The abuse, according to the petition for the restraining order she filed a year ago, escalated from slaps and punches to sexual assault and threats to her life. She left

New Mexico and moved to Seattle. He found her and almost killed her. After his arrest, she changed her name and moved across the country to Virginia, hoping that chapter of her life was closed forever.

Books finds Michelle downstairs. She pulled into the parking lot only ten minutes after he and the rest of the FBI agents did. Books spoke with her briefly two hours ago, and she's stuck around since.

Someone found her a chair. Her head is buried in her hands. He finds a chair of his own and pulls it up next to her.

"I seem to attract violence wherever I go," she says with a bitter chuckle.

"That's why you quit when Wagner got too...creepy."

"Scary. Whatever." She looks up at him. "I couldn't be around...anything like that. Then when I heard he was missing..."

"You thought he might come looking for you. That makes sense, Michelle. You didn't do anything wrong. Not one thing."

"I actually had a *crush* on Tom," she says, tears welling up again. "Can you believe that? What is it with me and predators?"

"He fooled a lot of people," says Books. "For a very long time, Michelle. It wasn't just you. Remember that, okay? It wasn't just you. Your only crime is being a good person."

One of the investigating agents comes down the stairs and nods to Books. "We don't need Emmy anymore," he says. "If you want to take her."

"The shooting was righteous," says Books.

"Hell yes, it was."

Good. Emmy was ready to blame herself up there when they first arrived. She kept saying, *I shot him*. Books was always quick to add, *After he charged you, and after he already killed Bonita.*

Emmy and Pully walk down the stairs, holding hands. She kisses him on the cheek, hugs him, whispers something to him that makes him cry, and walks over to Books.

"I'm going to stay with Pully," she says. "He needs me right now."

"Sure, of course, Em. But...*you* need *me*." There's a catch in his throat as he says those last words, part statement, part question.

She puts her hand on his cheek. "I do. But someone else needs you right now too."

Books nods.

"So go," she says. "I'll see you later."

128

BOOKS PARKS the car at the Meredith Court and Gardens in Huntington. He gives his name at the front desk. A moment later, he's buzzed in and takes the elevator to the seventh floor. He knocks on the door, softer than he did earlier today and with much less adrenaline.

The door opens. Sergeant Petty nods to him.

"Sergeant Petty."

"Agent Bookman. You, uh, wanna...come in?"

"Only if you want me to."

Petty backs up and lets Books in. The last time Books came through the door, he was ready to use his weapon, ready to order the SWAT team to open fire.

"How's Mary Ann doing?" he asks, nodding toward the bedroom.

Petty shrugs. "About the same. She was glad I came back."

"I'll bet she was. I am too, Sergeant. We were afraid you'd run away for good."

Afraid is an understatement; Mary Ann was terrified she'd

never see her younger brother again. She told Books that Petty suffered from posttraumatic stress disorder, something that didn't really surprise Books in the abstract, but he'd never thought about it, didn't know how that illness played itself out in Petty's life.

"How long has your sister . . . been like this?"

"Ah . . ." Petty scratches his head. "She started getting bad last winter. That's when I came here."

That's when Sergeant John Petty moved back here from California, where he'd been living since his discharge from the army, to be with his sister Mary Ann, who was dealing with a recurrence of her cancer.

"She's lucky to have you," says Books.

"Yeah, it works out okay."

It does, in fact. Her insurance, Mary Ann explained, covers caregivers Monday through Friday. Her brother comes every Friday afternoon and stays the weekend. It gives her care seven days a week, and it gives her brother a place to stay that's warm and comfortable.

"I know what you're thinking," says Petty. "If I got this place to stay, why don't I stay?"

"You have your reasons." Books raises a hand. "None of my business."

"I can't sit still. Mary Ann probably told you about that."

She did. *He can't stay in one place more than a handful of days* was how Mary Ann put it. *Can't put down roots. Even if he goes back and forth between the same places, he has to keep moving. Always moving.*

Books saw some of that in Petty, his inability to commit to working at the store on even a semipermanent basis.

And that's the easy part of his illness. The worst part is the paranoia.

It doesn't happen often, Mary Ann had said. *But when it happens, it's scary. He thinks he's back in the war being hunted. He thinks he's in danger. He has that part of the PTSD mostly under control, but stressors can trigger it.*

Stressors like an FBI agent looking at you suspiciously and then following you in his car.

"Sergeant, I'm sorry for what I put you through. Following you like I did."

He looks away, as he often does, nodding a bit, fidgeting with his hands. "Seems like I should apologize. For what I did to your face. Looks like it hurts."

Books laughs. "It does."

"Mary Ann told me why you did it. You thought I was...the serial killer."

"It was just...well, your schedule, leaving every weekend—"

"Homeless people are either lazy or crazy, right?"

"No, Sergeant, it's not that—"

"Yeah, it is. Yeah, it is." He glances at Books, a quick peek, before looking back at the floor. "It's okay. Everybody thinks that way. A homeless guy can't carry on an intelligent conversation. A homeless guy can't read *War and Peace.*"

There's no point in getting into a debate. Petty lives this life every day, sees the looks on people's faces as they pass him.

"You're welcome to stay at my store anytime, Sergeant. My house too, if you ever wanted."

Petty doesn't look at Books, but his eyes fill with tears.

Books puts a hand on his shoulder. "Sergeant. John. I'm your friend. I'm here if you ever need anything. A job. A place to stay. Something to eat. Anything."

He acknowledges the statement, a tear rolling down his face. "Mary Ann, she doesn't have long. I'll probably try to spend some more time with her. Y'know, try to sit still a little more. When it's over, I'll probably go back to California."

"Sure. Well, I'd like to be at the funeral, if you could let me know. Or maybe you could stop by the store to say hi sometime."

Petty peeks at him again, his eyes narrowed. "Is there still gonna *be* a store?"

"Is there—you mean—"

"I mean that I never seen you so happy as this last week, when you were back to being an agent." He shrugs. "None of my business, I guess."

"Well, that's...complicated."

"If you say so." Petty points a finger to his head. "I mean, if I didn't have all this going on inside? If I had a woman I loved and a job I loved, I'd grab both of 'em and never let go. It wouldn't be *complicated*," he says, shaking his head. "I just wouldn't let go."

129

"BONITA LIVED her life as a hero," I said, "and she died a hero." That's how I began my eulogy, before an overflowing crowd in the Baptist church in Alexandria. I spoke first, before her two boys, Mason and Jordan. They asked me to do it. They said she would have wanted it.

"Heroes are people who go out of their way to help others, who make sacrifices to help others, who reach beyond themselves to make the world a better place. I can't think of anyone who fits that description more than Bonita."

When it was over, we spilled outside into mild weather, a shiny blue sky and a gentle breeze. It felt unfair that the weather would be so beautiful on a day like this, but then, I figured, Rabbit probably would have smiled.

The funeral was this morning at nine. I told Books I wanted to head into work afterward. He tried to talk me out of it, but he knew he couldn't.

So I went home, changed out of my funeral attire, and drove to the Hoover Building. Which is where I am right now.

I have only two goals today, and then I'll go home and see what comes.

First: I delete all of the data files we initially received during the Citizen David investigation, all the data containing license plates caught on cameras and readers at all the bombing sites. Rabbit couldn't delete them. She didn't have that level of access. But I'm a supervisor; I do. And besides, Rabbit took all the bulk data and collated it into a workable format. That, we'll keep. Only Rabbit and I will ever know that there is a single license plate missing from that data.

I press Delete and watch all evidence of Rabbit's crimes disappear from our records. The Citizen David investigation will remain unsolved.

That's okay. Rabbit made it clear in her last Citizen David posts on social media that there would be no more bombings. David's already dying down as a story in our short-attention-span, all-news-all-the-time world. And the Bureau certainly has plenty of other things to work on. Sooner or later, Citizen David will be a distant memory, the answer to a trivia question.

I look around our little area, usually bustling, sarcastic zingers flying back and forth, nervous energy as we hunt for tiny gems buried within reams of data. It's quiet now, with Pully taking off the rest of the day after the funeral and Rabbit gone forever. I'm going to miss what we had.

I hope Pully will be okay. He's a rock star in terms of talent, but both Rabbit and I filled some kind of maternal role for him. Losing both of his coworkers at once will not be easy for him.

By Rabbit's cubicle, I pick up the photographs of Rabbit's two sons. They both have her eyes, her nose, and that overall air of defiance. They held up well today at the funeral, choking back tears and speaking of all the things she taught them, all the values she instilled in them.

"I still can't believe you're gone," I say to the air.

I put down the photos. It's time for the second item on my to-do list today—my meeting with Dwight Ross and Elizabeth Ashland.

I say hello to Dwight's secretary, Roberta, always with a wink and a smile, who should get a medal just for tolerating Dwight. Her grin slowly dissipates as she reads the expression on my face, but she doesn't say anything.

Dwight and Elizabeth greet me warmly enough inside the office. Why shouldn't they? They solved the Chicago bombing and nabbed a serial killer along the way. Dwight, of course, was front and center at the press conference, magnanimously calling it a "team effort."

"It was a nice ceremony today," says Elizabeth, still wearing her funeral black, immaculate as ever. She's also been decent to me since we caught Tom Miller. Then again, she was decent to me before we caught him. Most of the time, at least.

Does she know that I know about her affair with Director Moriarty? She doesn't give any indication that she does. But she wouldn't. It's not her style.

Dwight says, "So...you wanted to meet with us?"

"Yes, thanks." I draw a breath, thinking it through one last time.

"What's on your mind, Emmy?" Elizabeth asks.

It's more of a *who* than a *what*. Rabbit is on my mind. All the great work she did here in the office and beyond, all the causes she fought for. And how she should be remembered.

"I'm the leak," I say. "I'm the one who leaked information on Citizen David to Shaindy Eckstein at the *Washington Post*."

130

ELIZABETH ASHLAND draws back, eyes narrowed. I was her prime suspect all along. It can't be *that* much of a surprise to her. "*You* leaked the information to Shaindy Eckstein," she says.

"I did."

Dwight and Elizabeth look at each other.

She says, "You realize you've just confessed to a felony."

I nod but don't speak.

"You'll lose your job. Probably go to prison."

I am more than aware of that. I've thought about it for days now. But hearing it from her sparks a wave of heat through my chest.

"Have you..." Dwight shakes his head. "Have you talked to a lawyer about this?"

"No."

"Have you talked to Books?"

"He has nothing to do with this," I say, which is true. If I told Books about my intentions, he would have moved heaven and earth to stop me. He would've handcuffed me to my desk, slashed my tires, locked me in my apartment—anything to stop me.

"I don't understand why," says Elizabeth.

"Why did I do it?" I say. "It...doesn't really matter, does it?"

"No," she says. "I mean, why would you confess to something you didn't do?"

Huh? I look at her, then at Dwight.

"Bonita Sexton was the leak," says Dwight. "Shaindy Eckstein told us this morning. She was in here just a few hours ago."

"I..." Shaindy Eckstein gave up her source? Reporters don't do that.

"Apparently," says Elizabeth, "Bonita was concerned that you'd be implicated as the leaker. So they made a deal that if you were ever charged with that crime or anything ever happened to Bonita, Shaindy could disclose Bonita as her source." She shrugs. "And something happened to Bonita, obviously."

"Bonita signed an affidavit," says Dwight, handing me a piece of paper. It's a photocopy of a document bearing Rabbit's signature, dated two months ago. A sworn, notarized statement confessing that she was Shaindy Eckstein's source. But nothing else. Not confessing to the Citizen David bombings. Just enough to make sure I'd never take the fall as the leaker.

It's just like she told me when I confronted her. She wouldn't have let me go down for the leak. *If it came to it,* she'd said, *I'd have said it was me.*

Oh, Rabbit. My eyes cloud with tears.

"It's...noble of you to want to protect her memory," says Elizabeth. "You should know, we have no intention of making any of this public. She's gone now, killed in the line of duty, even if confronting a serial killer wasn't exactly in her job description."

"She saved my life," I say.

"Exactly. There's no point in tarnishing her reputation when we couldn't punish her even if we wanted to."

I drop my head with relief.

"I'm pretty sure I'll never understand you, Dockery," says Dwight. "Confessing to a felony you didn't commit? Willing to go to prison to protect a friend? But you're one hell of an analyst, and we never would have solved Chicago if it wasn't for you. Don't think we don't know that."

"Go get some rest," says Elizabeth. "You've earned it. And then come back to work."

131

BOOKS IS standing across the street by his car, waiting for me. His cell phone is pressed against his ear. The look on his face tells me he's talking to Elizabeth Ashland. By the time I cross the street, he's off the phone.

"Rabbit? *Rabbit* was the leak?" he says.

"Yeah," I say.

"Why would she do that?"

I shrug. I can't ever tell anyone, not even Books, that Rabbit was Citizen David. It would be unfair to ask him to keep that secret. "She was sympathetic to his cause, I guess."

"You can be sympathetic to someone's cause without leaking information to a reporter. There's gotta be more to it." Books shakes his head.

I touch his arm. "I wouldn't be here today if it weren't for her."

His expression softens. "I know that."

"So let it go. Whatever happened, happened. The why doesn't matter. Okay?"

He looks into my eyes. "If you say so, ma'am."

"Besides," I say, "we have another mystery on our hands, remember?"

A gentle smile finally appears. He turns and takes me in his arms. "The mystery of Emmy and Books," he says.

"Talk about unsolved," I say.

We look across the street at the Hoover Building as the wind kicks up. Then we jump into his car and drive off, unsure of our destination.

ABOUT THE AUTHORS

JAMES PATTERSON is the world's bestselling author and most trusted storyteller. He has created many enduring fictional characters and series, including Alex Cross, the Women's Murder Club, Michael Bennett, Maximum Ride, Middle School, and I Funny. Among his notable literary collaborations are *The President Is Missing,* with President Bill Clinton, and the Max Einstein series, produced in partnership with the Albert Einstein Estate. Patterson's writing career is characterized by a single mission: to prove that there is no such thing as a person who "doesn't like to read," only people who haven't found the right book. He's given over three million books to schoolkids and the military, donated more than seventy million dollars to support education, and endowed over five thousand college scholarships for teachers. The National Book Foundation recently presented Patterson with the Literarian Award for Outstanding Service to the American Literary Community, and he is also the recipient of an Edgar Award and six Emmy Awards. He lives in Florida with his family.

DAVID ELLIS is a justice of the Illinois Appellate Court and the author of nine novels, including *Line of Vision,* for which he won the Edgar Award, and *The Hidden Man,* which earned a 2009 *Los Angeles Times* Book Prize nomination.

JAMES
PATTERSON
RECOMMENDS

JAMES PATTERSON

THE BLACK BOOK

& DAVID ELLIS

THE BLACK BOOK

I have favorites among the novels I've written. *Kiss the Girls, Invisible, 1st to Die,* and *Honeymoon* are top of the list. With each, I had a good feeling when the writing was finished. I believe this book—*The Black Book*—is the best work I've done in twenty-five years.

Meet Billy Harney. The son of Chicago's chief of detectives, he was born to be a cop. There's nothing he wouldn't sacrifice for his job. Enter Amy Lentini, an assistant state's attorney hell-bent on making a name for herself—by proving Billy isn't the cop he claims to be.

A horrifying murder leads investigators to a brothel that caters to Chicago's most powerful citizens. There's plenty of evidence on the scene, but what matters most is what's missing: the madam's black book.

THIS BOOK
WILL MAKE YOUR
JAW DROP

INVISIBLE

THE WORLD'S #1 BESTSELLING WRITER

JAMES PATTERSON
& DAVID ELLIS

INVISIBLE

When I started writing *Invisible,* it seemed like every other TV network was telling the same kind of stories about police, robberies, and crime twists. So I wanted to tell a different kind of suspense story, one that would really make your jaw drop. In the novel, Emmy Dockery is a researcher for the FBI who believes she has stumbled on one of the deadliest serial killers in history. There's only one problem—he's invisible.

The mysterious killer leaves no trace. There are no weapons, no evidence, no motive. But when the killer strikes close to home, she must crack an impossible case before anyone else dies. Prepare to be blindsided, because the most terrifying threat is the one you don't see coming—the one that's invisible.

THE WORLD'S #1 BESTSELLING WRITER

NEVER NEVER

IN THE NEVER NEVER, NO ONE KNOWS IF YOU'RE DEAD OR ALIVE

JAMES PATTERSON

CANDICE FOX

NEVER NEVER

Alex Cross. Michael Bennett. Jack Morgan. They are among my greatest characters. Now I'm proud to present my newest detective—a tough woman who can hunt down any man in a hardscrabble continent half a world away. Meet Detective Harriet Blue of the Sydney Police Department.

Harry is her department's top sex crimes investigator. But she never thought she'd see her own brother arrested for the grisly murders of three beautiful young women. Shocked and in denial, Harry transfers to a makeshift town in a desolate area to avoid the media circus. Looking into a seemingly simple missing person's case, Harry is assigned a new "partner." But is he actually meant to be a watchdog?

Far from the world she knows and desperate to clear her brother's name, Harry has to mine the dark secrets of her strange new home for answers to a deepening mystery—before she vanishes in a place where no one would ever think to look for her.

For a complete list of books by

JAMES PATTERSON

VISIT
JamesPatterson.com

 Follow James Patterson on Facebook
@JamesPatterson

 Follow James Patterson on Twitter
@JP_Books

 Follow James Patterson on Instagram
@jamespattersonbooks